"I cannot promise that you will never regret marrying me, Annique. I have no idea what kind of husband I'll make."

Annique refused to let his reservations steal her happiness. Banded by the circling assurance of his arms, she gazed up into his handsome face and quipped, "After all the mistakes I've made in the last few weeks, I should think you might be the one with regrets."

"I waste no time with regrets," he murmured.

Then he kissed her, hard and deep.

A thrill of confusion _____ o the tips of Annique's _____ randy on his tongue, bu _____ she felt him pull free o _____

She ope _____ vay, mount his huge bla _____ unsettled stare in her directio _____ her farewell with, "Until tomorrow."

Tomorrow.

As she watched him ride away, Annique shivered, unsure whether her reaction was prompted by foreboding or the memory of his kiss.

After tomorrow they would have the rest of their lives for getting to know each other.

Or for regrets.

SHADOWS IN VELVET

Haywood Smith

St. Martin's Paperbacks

For Jim, who has given me more than twenty-seven years of happily-ever-after.

SHADOWS IN VELVET

Copyright © 1996 by Haywood Smith.

ISBN: 0-312-95873-0

Printed in the United States of America

St. Martin's Paperbacks edition / July 1996

10 9 8 7 6 5 4 3 2 1

Acknowledgments

Special thanks go to Betty Uzman, Ph.D., who by Divine Providence answered the phone at the University of Georgia History Department when I called looking for help researching this book. Then and many times thereafter, Betty generously shared her expertise in mid-seventeenth-century history, helping me make sense of fascinating, but complex, events.

Thanks, too, to Betty Cothran, Jan Dale, Carol Otten, Lillian Richie, and Ellen Taber for their critique and endless patience during the birth and rebirths of this book. I would also like to express my gratitude to Georgia Romance writers for their encouragement and invaluable instruction.

The gracious professionalism of my agent, Damaris Rowland, and editor, Jennifer Enderlin, have made the creative process a joy.

Most of all, thanks to my husband, Jim, and my sister, Susan Carlsson, for believing in me and not letting me quit.

❧ CHAPTER 1 ❧

Southern France—January 1652

$\mathcal{T}$his was her private sin, this daily ritual of self—a silent celebration of comfort, of warmth, of feeling. Father Jules would never hear her lips confess these stolen moments of mindless pleasure. What difference would one more secret make, anyway? There were so many already.

Was it so wicked simply to want to lie warm in her feather bed for a few extra minutes each day? Annique burrowed deeper into her mattress. It held her, caressed her like the arms of the mother she had dreamed of, but never known. She savored the sensation and stored its memory against the cold day ahead.

Then, inexorably, the faintest of rustlings stirred the convent to life. Her ears picked out the soft insistence of fabric upon fabric and the whisper of well-oiled hinges as careful hands delicately closed the heavy wooden doors of the cells, the other novices ever-mindful to preserve the peace of the sphere in which they all worked and prayed.

She must get up. The others were already on their way to chapel.

Drawing in a deep breath, Annique launched upright, swinging her feet free of the stone-and-stucco ledge that held her feather bed. The warm vapor of her breath clouded the air in front of her. She tiptoed in woolen-stockinged feet across the freezing floor to break the glaze of ice in her washbowl with her elbow. A splash of frigid water jolted her fully awake and left her skin tingling. She heard her own voice whisper the waking prayers of every day, *"Ave Maria, sacra mater Deum—"* By thus breaking the Grand Silence, she sinned even in prayer.

A thick auburn braid uncoiled down her back as she

exchanged her sleeping cap for the coarse wimple on the peg beside the washstand. Dressing was accomplished swiftly, her movements schooled by a thousand mornings' practice. She smoothed the feather bed, ignoring the silent indictment of its presence. None of the other novices or sisters had such a bed.

Annique's devotional stopped short with a most unsaintly oath when she opened the door of her cell. "Blessed Saint Peter and Saint Paul!"

The hallway was deserted, its walls bleached by the promise of dawn. She was late to morning Mass again! If Sister Jonah caught her, she'd have to scrub the chamber pots for certain.

She stepped out of her wooden shoes and scooped them up on the run. Annique burst into the colonnade of the cloister and sprinted fifty yards before coming to a halt alongside Sister Thomas at the rear of the silent procession of nuns and novices. With a graceful stoop Annique restored her shoes to her icy feet, then melted into grave anonymity.

Sister Thomas kept her head bowed and her hands folded behind her apron, but her whisper easily reached Annique's ears. "It seems our Little Bird isn't an early bird anymore. Take care, little one. Sister Jonah would love any excuse to punish you."

Annique did not lift her own head as they filed toward the chapel. "I know, Sister Thomas. I know. But lately, the Lord has not quickened me in the morning. I can hardly drag myself from my bed."

Disquiet shadowed the amusement in Sister Thomas's retort. "I might have known you'd blame it on God, Annique, and not your own lack of discipline." The plump older nun shook her head. "Now we'll both have to confess breaking the silence."

Annique stifled a grin. "I broke it before I left my room."

Sister Thomas lifted her face heavenward. "Why does that not surprise me?"

When they closed the chapel doors behind them, both of them were smiling.

After Mass, Annique was the first out of the chapel. Luckily, Sister Jonah made no mention of her tardiness.

Perhaps the mistress of novices had, at long last, decided to show her a little mercy.

Crossing the silent cloister, Annique was filled with a bittersweet appreciation of the timeless rhythm within these ancient walls. This convent was the only home she'd ever known. In earlier days she had felt as if she and all the sisters were floating along like leaves on the surface of a slow and gentle river. Day into day, week into week, year into year; life into death, death into life. Work, worship, praise, peace.

There had been a time when she had wanted nothing more than to be a part of this community of souls, but now such certainty seemed only a fragile memory. She quickened her pace toward the dairy. At least there was still comfort in study and in work.

A faint mist rose from the roof of the barn as the first rays of sun touched the frost on its clay tiles. Annique stepped inside and addressed the two cows she had cared for over the past seven years. "Good morning, ladies."

Old Blackie lifted her head for a good scratch on the forehead, and Mamoo stamped jealously in the next stall.

Annique scooped up her pail and milking stool. "Don't be impatient, Mamoo. You were first yesterday. In good time." She sat down and rested her temple against Blackie's warm flank. Soothed by the scent of hay and the rich, moist breath of the stable, she settled into the numbing rhythm of milking, losing herself in the peace of the moment, her mind slipping away into nothingness.

She was safe here. Blackie and Mamoo knew nothing of Grand Silences, of discipline, of denial, of mortifying the flesh. Unlike human beings, these gentle creatures asked little and never criticized, never punished; they only gave of their substance and their trusting gratitude in return for her simple care.

When her chores were completed, she released her charges into the crisp January morning, then delivered her pails of milk to the kitchen a full half hour before she was due for her lessons with Father Jules in the reverend mother's study.

Annique strolled back across the empty cloister. The sundial confirmed that she was, indeed, ahead of schedule. She considered using this extra time in prayer, but rejected the idea immediately. What she really wanted to do was go to Mother Bernard's study early. If no one was there, she just might be able to steal a few minutes alone with the ancient illuminated Bible that always lay open, tantalizing and forbidden, in the alcove.

Hastening into the hallway and up the stairs, her only prayer was that she would find the room deserted so she could read the Song of Songs by daylight, for a change, instead of huddled in secret by a midnight candle.

At the top of the stairs, she slipped off her wooden shoes and padded quietly to the study. Annique pulled the heavy door ajar and was greeted by the sound of angry voices from inside. She froze. Mother Bernard was actually shouting.

"Jules, I think you've gone mad! At least she's safe with us, here. She doesn't even know who she is. How could you possibly justify such a course of action? She'll never—"

Father Jules's voice interrupted, "Celeste . . ."

Celeste!

". . . it is done. What choice did I have? The marshal knows where she is, and *who* she is. We both know Harcourt is hand in glove with Cardinal Mazarin, just the way he was with Richelieu. If I hadn't acted quickly, who knows what might have happened? We could have received orders from the Mother House or the bishop, sending her to . . . who knows? Maybe to a leper colony, or worse, to nowhere. He could arrange for her to disappear in transit, and we'd never be able to find out what he'd done with her."

Annique heard the priest pacing back and forth as he spoke. "No, no. This alliance will be for the best. It's her only hope. I shall be careful for everything to be very public, very visible. I still have my contacts at Court. It wasn't difficult to get the regent's approval. The queen realizes this is merely a means to solidify the child's claim to what is rightfully hers."

Mother Bernard remained adamant. "Jules, you're sending the lamb to the lion. What makes you think she will be able to survive at Court? She hasn't been outside these walls since she was three. The child would be hard-pressed to cope as a simple merchant's wife, much less in the role you propose!"

Her tone became cold. "What's really going on here, *Father?*" The term was an epithet, not one of respect. "I thought you put such plots behind you when you married the Church. Were all those endless hours of talk about leaving the ambitions and the evils of the World behind, just that—talk? Is this some scheme to avenge yourself, your family? Is this the old Jules speaking? Or are you fulfilling your own ambitions through her? I won't have it!"

Father Jules's response was grim. "The ambition *we* must fear wears the scarlet robe of a cardinal. Mazarin is an evil, devious man. I put away the World when I married the Church. *He* means to use the sovereign power of the faith to bend the World to his own devices. For the life of me, I cannot see the hand of God in that man's power. He isn't even a priest!"

"Might I remind you," Mother Bernard scolded, "that you are speaking of a Prince of the Church? His Eminence has been placed in authority by the will of God. And if he is as evil as you say, how can you countenance sending the girl into his lap? No, she's better off here."

"Oh, for heaven's sake, Celeste! You know as well as I do that she can't stay *here* forever. We've spoken of it a dozen times in the last four years. Annique—"

Annique's entire body stiffened at the mention of her name. She knew she shouldn't have been eavesdropping, but now she was unable to move. The whole world was reduced to two voices.

"—isn't cut out for the convent. I think she's known it all along." His tone shifted, calmed. "The child has no vocation to the cloistered life."

The pacing stopped. Annique heard a chair groan in complaint under his weight. "I have prayed long and hard for guidance in this matter, even before I found out Harcourt knew of her whereabouts. For a while, I had considered arranging a match with one of the men in my parish. Someone kind and reliable. But now circumstances have closed that door. Perhaps Divine Providence is working in this, after all."

"You priests," Mother Bernard snapped. "How like you to rationalize your own decision as the will of God."

When Father Jules spoke again, his voice was fainter. "Annique is better equipped for life at Court than you think, and she can thank you for much of that. You have taught her discipline and denial. I know it's been like trying to bottle up a spring, but she has learned to be quiet and to conceal her true feelings. Such abilities could be her saving grace." This remark elicited a cynical snort from Mother Bernard.

"For my part," he continued, "I have tried to teach her to recognize the currents of intrigue and political poison within the Court. You've told me often enough that her education would more properly befit a man. Well, that education befits a duchess of France. History is a wise teacher, and Annique has learned hers well—well enough, I hope, to help her avoid a disaster like the one fifteen years ago. She's already paid dearly for my brother's lack of foresight."

What had he said? *His* brother? Annique must not have heard him correctly. She leaned closer, her ears straining.

"Marshal Harcourt thinks he's in control. Good. I shall take what he has proposed and turn it to her advantage." The priest chuckled. "The old man has no idea what he's getting for a daughter-in-law!"

A breath of wind shifted the door, creaking its hinges. Father Jules stopped talking abruptly, the sound of his voice replaced by approaching footsteps.

Annique twisted in panic, her hand still on the heavy door ring. Caught! She'd never make it to the stairs in time. She glanced about frantically for some shelter in the empty hallway, but she knew there was none. Could she convince them that she'd just arrived?

She swung her gaze back directly into Father Jules's angry, startled face. Too late! He saw everything. All the strength went out of her legs, and she sank kneeling to the floor.

Catching her under the arms, he called out, "Mother, look what we've done now! I think she's swooned. Help me get her to the bench." Supporting her on either side, they guided Annique to an upholstered bench in the study.

"I'll shut the door," Mother Bernard offered, "although it's of little use at this point." That done, she returned to glare down at Annique. "Well, Little Sister, it's obvious you've been eavesdropping. How much have you heard? The truth, now!"

Annique had no intention of telling her the real reason she'd come so early. She was in enough trouble already. Instead she stammered, "I . . . I finished my chores earlier than usual so I came to the study for my lessons."

"I didn't ask why you were here," the mother superior thundered. "I asked what you heard. Answer me!"

Annique lowered her eyes. "The door was open just a bit, and when I started to knock, I heard you speaking. You sounded so angry I was afraid to interrupt. Before I could decide what to do, I heard Father Jules say something about sending me away." Tears began to flow down her cheeks, but her face did not betray the tangled jumble of questions that churned in her mind. What was this talk of plots and disasters? Who was Harcourt, and what did he have to do with the regent's advisor, Mazarin? Why had Father Jules called Mother Bernard "Celeste"? The questions formed faster than she could sort them out.

She looked imploringly at the abbess. "Oh, Mother, are you going to send me away?"

"Stop that crying at once. It won't do any of us any good," Mother Bernard grumbled. "I always knew your curiosity would be your undoing, Annique." She turned to the priest in exasperation. "The child's heard just enough to frighten her. Ready or not, you'd better tell her the rest." She aimed a finger in his face. "I shall leave you to do what you must. Meanwhile, I'll be in the alcove, praying for forgiveness for myself—and for *you!*" She swished away to her prayer rail.

Annique was so taken aback by Mother Bernard's treatment of Father Jules that she stopped crying and hiccoughed.

His features shaped by a mixture of pain and compassion, Father Jules drew up a footstool and sat beside her. "I had hoped that there would be time for us to deal with these matters gently, but there is not. In His infinite wisdom, God has contrived for us to come to this moment in just this way. Now I shall do my best to explain things to you."

A skeptical frown tugged at Annique's mouth.

The priest cocked his head. "You know I promised your father to educate you, and I'm certain you're aware of the, ah, unusual subject matter of your studies." He paused. "Be honest, Annique. Haven't you ever wondered why we spent so much time on secular history and politics? And the other subjects. Didn't it occur to you that I might be preparing you for something besides the cloistered life?"

Dangerous, this truth he was speaking, but it fanned her

curiosity to a blaze, despite her sickening sense of foreboding. "Well, sometimes I wondered." She looked at the floor. "But then I saw how useful the science and medicine were in my work with the lay sisters at our hospital."

"What about the mathematical theory and the military strategy? How could those possibly be of use in the convent?" He put his finger gently under her chin and drew it up until he could see her face. "Did you really think that Plato or Aristotle or Pliny or Cicero or Caesar had any place in the parochial life?" His kind eyes burned into hers. "Truthfully, child, do you really believe you have a vocation to the contemplative life?"

She could not lie, even to herself, any longer. "No, Father . . . no." Annique covered her face with her hands and began to weep in earnest. She had known this day would come. Ever since God had visited the monthly penance of blood on her, she had grown more and more sinful, her body longing for the comforts of the flesh and her mind preoccupied with earthly, rather than spiritual, things.

Father Jules reached into his cassock and drew out a clean square of coarse linen. Roughly dabbing the tears from her cheeks, he spoke with confidence. "There, there. You mustn't be sad."

She tugged the kerchief from his grasp and loudly blew her nose.

He chuckled knowingly. "I've seen the dreams in your eyes when we studied about foreign places and the seats of power and earthly rule. I know you've imagined great adventures."

Annique blushed and peeked over the handkerchief.

"Soon you shall embark on a real adventure. You'll be presented to the king and the queen mother." He grinned when her eyes opened wide at the prospect. "Sister Jonah will begin instructing you tomorrow in the proper manners and protocol of the Court."

She straightened abruptly. Now *there* was a penance, indeed, for her secret sins. "Sister Jonah? Father, she's always punishing me. Must it be Sister Jonah?"

His smile disappeared. "You must trust me in this. But don't worry. You're such an able student, I'm sure you'll learn very quickly. Then, when you're ready—perhaps in a few months—I shall personally escort you to Paris." Father

Jules gripped her hand so tightly Annique wondered what other unpleasant surprises he had in store for her. She soon found out.

He blurted out, "Annique, after much prayerful consideration, I have arranged for you to marry. The man I've chosen is a kind young nobleman of the Court—an officer in the Queen's Guard." He hesitated, as if the next words stuck in his throat. "The Duke de Corbay. The match is a good one, worthy of your heritage."

Annique's mouth dropped open in shock just as she hiccoughed again. The resulting sound echoed loudly across the study, prompting a gruff response from Mother Bernard. "Wonderful! She'll do beautifully at Court with the likes of that!"

A flush of outrage rose to Annique's scalp. Married! To a man she'd never met, in a place she'd never seen! How could Father Jules *do* such a thing to her?

Before she could sputter a reply, Father Jules's face hardened. He addressed her formally and with awful finality, "On this earth, Annique, I am the only father you have. I've taken that responsibility seriously and done the best for you that I could. You have no choice in this matter. The queen has approved the marriage, and contracts have been signed, binding all parties by law. I know it will take some time to get used to the idea, but I hope you'll come to see the wisdom in my decision."

His tone softened. "I'm told that your fiancé is an honorable man, of good reputation and lineage. You shall want for nothing as his wife, and your children will have a noble inheritance. Try to think of these things as you prepare for your new life." He stood. "I'll look in on you and Sister Jonah tomorrow. As for today, you may go to your room and pray for a joyous and obedient spirit. You are dismissed."

Annique rose like a sleepwalker and started for the door. With every step, she felt her anger drain away, replaced by helpless frustration. She turned. "But, Father Jules, surely you can't—"

"You are dismissed."

Stung by the coldness of his rebuke, she pivoted and marched into the hall. But once the door was closed behind her, her steps faltered. She stumbled toward her room, unable to look about her. Soon she would be leaving this familiar landscape forever.

When she entered her cell, she fell prostrate on the cold tile floor and sobbed out her misery with a depth of anguish available only to a teen-aged girl. After what seemed like hours she fell asleep as she lay, exhausted. It was dusk when she awakened, stiff and cold. Annique felt like an old woman as she undressed and curled up in the welcome softness of her feather bed. There her body began to warm, but inside she had turned to ashes.

The bell for evensong tolled. Annique lay silent, no more tears left to shed as the sound of lilting voices from the chapel filled the convent.

An invisible cord had been severed, and for the first time in her life, she felt truly, finally, and terribly separated from the sisters. And she had spoken her fate upon herself! Annique found no comfort that in so doing, she was only facing the inevitable.

There in the dimness of twilight she finally retreated into her dreams, her hope as yet a shapeless, unformed thing hidden behind her hurt.

❊   CHAPTER 2   ❊

*M*any times Philippe had traveled the darkened alleys of Paris to the apartments of the Great Mademoiselle, but this time his pace was tempered by a certain edgy anticipation. Usually he found his way through the narrow maze of streets as swiftly as a cat, his face shaded into obscurity by the broad brim of an ordinary workman's hat and his sword hidden beneath a swirl of dark cape. But tonight, the closer he came to the Tuileries, the slower his tread.

His future, perhaps even his freedom, depended on how well he acted the part of the wounded lover this night. He only hoped he wouldn't choke on the words. Not that lies didn't come easily—like most aristocrats, he'd been nurtured on deception—but submission was as alien as indecision to him, so his performance must be a convincing one. Otherwise, the Great Mademoiselle would never let him go.

Philippe had known that bedding the princess was playing with fire, yet the prospect of wooing so powerful and shrewd a woman had given the seduction a razor-sharp edge. The chase had excited him almost as much as soldiering once had before years of killing fellow Frenchmen dulled his appetite for a military career.

His affair with the Great Mademoiselle had been exhilarating, but the time had come to end it. At Court, it was use or be used, and he had no intention of letting the Great Mademoiselle—or any woman—use him. Even as he contemplated his royal lover's wrath, a sardonic grin split the shadow of his face. The princess might not know it yet, but she had met her match. He'd outwitted armies with his keen sense of strategy; he would not fall prey to the princess, no matter how clever—or inviting—a trap she had laid for him.

By the time he reached the Palais Royal, the last faint glow of daylight had left the cloudy sky. With every step he took his resolve deepened. He'd learned long ago to allow others only the illusion of using him, and then only when it suited his purposes. Duty and survival had forced him to endure his father's manipulations, but he would not be the princess's pawn.

Not that she hadn't been a stimulating opponent. His royal lover had played the seduction well, allowing him to believe he was the victor of some rare and exotic prize when she—richest heiress in all of France, reared to be the wife of a king—had succumbed to his charms.

The thought elicited a wry chuckle as Philippe moved through the darkened streets. Victor, indeed! There had been no mistaking her look of exultation when she had rolled over after their first coupling and lifted the candle to survey his naked body. When his own eyes had answered with realization, then anger, she had become almost wild with desire, letting loose a guttural cry of conquest that had incited them both to frenzy. Theirs was no casual coupling born of boredom or lust. It was a battle of wit and will, and the stakes had gotten far too high.

He'd flirted with disaster long enough. If he didn't act boldly and quickly, the Great Mademoiselle would use their liaison to suck him into her rebel schemes. He knew it, just as surely as he now knew that the princess—not her father, Gaston d'Orléans—was the real force behind the Fronde.

Philippe was convinced that her vast fortune funded the
rebellion, but in all his weeks as her lover, he'd garnered
not a shred of incriminating evidence to protect himself
from her plots. If the Great Mademoiselle had her way,
she'd use him to help replace Queen Anne with Gaston as
regent. And then what?

The royal family was like a pack of wolves, endlessly
struggling for the biggest chunk of the kill. Even before
Louis XIII's death eight years ago, Gaston had plotted to
seize the throne from his brother. Why should the Great
Mademoiselle be any different from her father? She'd
grown up amid Gaston's constant plots, learning well the
lessons of sedition.

*Just like my own father, always plotting, manipulating, first
with Richelieu, and now with Cardinal Mazarin.* Philippe
shuddered and shook off the unwelcome thought. He
wasn't anything like his father. *The princess hates Gaston,
almost as much as I hate the marshal. We have that in common, at least.*

Still, he couldn't afford the slightest weakness when it
came to the Great Mademoiselle. By allowing Philippe
into her bed, she'd lured him to the heart of the rebellion.
Him, a captain of the Queen's Guard! The perverse irony
of that had stirred his blood almost as much as his lover's
regal status and voluptuous figure. Though he'd enjoyed
the dangerous affair, his instincts now warned him that the
princess intended to close her talons. It would be nothing
overt at first, probably just a casual question or a seemingly
innocent request. The nobility was littered with ruined rep-
utations, even "suicides," of those who had refused to play
along with the Great Mademoiselle.

He had to act. Passion meant nothing, infatuation meant
nothing. At Court, winning was all that mattered. Philippe
enjoyed the dangerous games of power and seduction and
played them well, earning himself—an impoverished second son—a coveted spot among the *crème de la crème* of
society that even his father might envy. Now that he'd
carved a place for himself in the world, he wasn't about to
let the princess take it from him.

She was in for a surprise. The Great Mademoiselle had
never tasted rejection from anyone as lowly as he.

The smell of the Seine set his senses on edge. He looked
up and saw a faint glow of reflected torchlight on the low-

ering clouds. Almost there. He crossed the rue de Rivoli to follow the lower walls of the Tuileries palace. At last, he reached the heavy wooden door set well back into the foundation. Philippe ducked into the alcove, his eyes scanning the deserted street. The cobblestones glistened darkly in the aftermath of a winter rainstorm. No sound crept from the waiting gloom, no motion tugged at the shadows. He extracted the heavy key from his pocket, turned it in the lock, and slipped inside.

On the floor of the narrow passageway a lantern flickered, its presence a signal that she would be waiting. Philippe locked the door behind him, tucked away the key, then scooped up the lantern and bent to make his way through the secret corridor, his broad shoulders scraping the stones on either side.

After navigating a dozen cramped hallways and half as many turns and twisting stairways, he paused at the panel that led to her chamber, took a deep breath, then pushed it open.

She was ready, as usual, elegantly posed on the pale gold satin sheets of her bed. Candles glowed softly throughout the room, and an intimate dinner for two was spread on a small table before the drawn draperies. Without warning a stab of ardor pulsed through him, as much in answer to the hungry intelligence of her eyes as to the sight of her languid body.

Though she looked far older than her four and twenty years, Philippe knew she did everything she could to disguise the fact. It was no accident that the room's subtle illumination lit her skin to alabaster and washed the toll of living from her face.

Propped upon one elbow, she reclined like the image of a Greek goddess. Philippe knew the scent of lilacs lingered in the wanton cascade of her blond hair. She could drive a man wild in bed using only her hair. His eyes followed delicate lace into the shadow between her full breasts, and he knew that there, too, was the scent of a hundred flowers.

His determination wavered. What difference would one more night make? The sight of her tempted him to abandon himself to the familiar geography of her voluptuous body. But just as the last vestiges of his resolve melted away, a smug smile flickered on her carefully moistened lips. Its effect was more bracing than a splash of icy water. The princess was beautiful, compelling, and intelligent, and she knew it, but her smugness was premature. He would not succumb to her charms.

"You're looking delicious, as always, Philippe. Come, sit beside me. Let's . . . talk a bit before we sup."

Talk, indeed.

Time for the performance to begin. He shrugged off his cape with a gesture of masculine simplicity that sparked a gleam of passion in her eye. Philippe tossed his hat into a chair, then began to remove his gloves, one finger at a time. The golden hilt of his sword gleamed in the candlelight. "Yes. We must talk, your royal highness." He made no move toward her.

Instantly she abandoned the carefully staged tableau and sat up, her nostrils flaring. "You know you may speak freely with me."

He sat down by the fire, his tall frame almost too large for the dainty settee. From across the room he could just make out a slight narrowing of her eyes. Philippe paused, savoring her uncertainty. His soldier's heart was hungry for this contest.

In all their months together, he had never once forgotten that his princess was as dangerous as she was desirable. She wore intrigue like a heady perfume, and every word that was said or not said had the weight of nations behind it. An intoxicating mixture in a mistress, but a chilling arsenal in an adversary. His blood surged now with the same elixir of danger that had drawn him to her in the first place.

"Well?" The princess watched the firelight lick at the aristocratic planes of her lover's face. Gold danced off the waves of his coal black hair and struck a spark of amber in his blue eyes. The young duke made an arresting picture. Beneath the velvet and lace of a gentleman was the hard, disciplined body of a fighting man, and she hungered now to have him in her bed. What was this about, this distance, this silence?

When he finally spoke, formality widened the space between them. "Your royal highness has been most gracious, most kind in granting me her . . . friendship. Even though that friendship has been known only to the two of us."

Was that it? she wondered. Wounded male pride at being her secret paramour? She had thought him above such pettishness.

The slightest hint of exasperation colored her voice as she reassured him. "Dearest, have I not explained that the reason for such secrecy is my concern for your own safety? As an officer of the Guard, you are sworn to uphold the regent. My sympathies with those who seek to depose her are well-known. I hardly think the queen and her devil, Mazarin, would take kindly to our friendship. I should imagine you would welcome my discretion."

Philippe's level response stilled her. "That's not what this is about, and you know it."

Interesting. He moved early to the offensive. The princess studied him. Was it money, then? She knew about Philippe's debts. This could be difficult, but certainly not insurmountable. She had the means to help him. The question was, how to do it without insulting him? The poorest young men often seemed to be the proudest. Still, it wouldn't be difficult to have one of her other "friends" drop Philippe a tidy sum at the gaming tables. But she was not prepared for what came next.

"Mademoiselle, I must ask your leave to withdraw from our relationship."

Her features froze.

He looked up, his eyes haunted. "From our first moment together, we have both known that our destinies lie far apart, that our friendship was fated to be a precious and momentary thing."

Her pulse throbbing heavily in her neck, she waited for the rest.

He rose and came close, bending upon one knee near enough to touch, but not touching. His voice was earnest, yet the words sounded rehearsed. "To know that your destiny will promise you into the arms of another man, to live with the certainty that the only hand worthy to take yours will be a sovereign hand—such knowledge is more bitter than I can bear. It has come to poison every moment we are together. I can endure it no longer."

Her outrage was checked by sheer surprise. Rejection, cloaked in humility? Philippe was anything but humble, and yet he seemed sincere. Though she herself employed the truth sparingly, the Great Mademoiselle convinced herself that she heard it ringing in his words and saw it, dark and painful, in his eyes. The gift of it bound them more tightly than passion ever had.

He took her hand. "If you have any pity, if I have meant anything to you, release me." His great, deep blue eyes burned into her own. "Let me go, to make whatever life I can without you." Philippe's words slowed. "I am to be married. My father arranged it, to a girl of eighteen, an orphan straight out of a convent in the south. She is a distant cousin."

The Great Mademoiselle willed herself to remain supple. Though his words stung her to the heart, her reply was almost casual. "You are of an age to marry, Philippe. What is that to us?"

"If you will release me, I might find some peace in what is to come. It is the most I can hope for, after loving you." When she made no comment, he went on. "There is a great dowry involved. The queen has approved the match. Duty and honor demand that I obey. Circumstances permit me no choice in the matter."

No choice, he said! Why, she had rejected *kings,* standing firm under pressure from her father, the throne, and the Church. She had paid dearly to direct her own destiny, and *he* was telling her *he* had no choice! A flame of bitter anger flickered through her, but the echo of his words snuffed it out. There was no defense against his confession. No amount of calculation or pretense could change the core of truth in what he had spoken. Their destinies did lie on different planes.

But Philippe's sudden unattainability merely elevated her desire for him, and his unexpected gentleness soothed her ruffled feelings. Quite a man, this one. She wanted him so badly that she almost listened to her baser instincts. Almost.

"So dramatic, Philippe." She gently withdrew her hand. "One of the things I've liked best about you was the fact that you confined your passions to the mattress. I'd hate to have you spoil things now with a torrent of sentimentality."

Philippe's skill and unpredictability as a lover had left her breathless more than once, but she had never imagined he would catch her off-guard beyond the bed curtains. No lover had ever dared to take the upper hand, and no one, man or woman, had ever caught her so unprepared. She couldn't help but admire the elegance of his audacity.

She walked to the mantel and stood, fully aware that the firelight shone through her gown, intimately revealing her form. She had never wanted anyone more than she wanted him now, but this was no time to let emotion cloud her judgment. She sifted her alternatives and reason, as always, won out. A concession now by no means meant defeat.

She strolled to the table and plucked a grape. "Imagine that. An orphan girl coming out of a convent to marry a duke. Why, the whole Court will be abuzz about such a thing. Everyone will want to see this creature. You'll be deluged with invitations."

Philippe shifted slightly and wondered what was going on behind the princess's pale blue eyes. Where once they had glowed with desire and indulgence, they were now as frigid as a winter sky. For the longest time, she did not blink. Had he convinced her?

Then she smiled. "Let's not make too much of this, Philippe. You are, after all, a most perceptive man. We have had fun, you and I, but I must confess, it was beginning to, shall we say, *wear* a bit." Returning to the fireside, she put her back to him. "I fear that lately I have not found your company as stimulating as I once did. Perhaps it would be best to end it now." Only a slight thickening of the last phrase betrayed the sting of his rejection.

So she had chosen to accept the lie—superficially, at least. Yet he'd noted the bitterness in her voice and the stubborn erectness of her posture. A moment of genuine remorse struck him. For the first time, he realized how very alone she would always be in the solitary cage wrought by her birth and her ambition.

Hiding his pity, he looked her boldly in the eye and murmured the lie she needed most of all: "I love you beyond all sense, beyond all station. I will cherish for the rest of my life the time we have had together. You have my love— more than that, my admiration—forever."

He left her as he had come, in secret.

Phillippe's step was lighter as he made his way back to his modest town house. Only time would tell the effect of tonight's confrontation. The Great Mademoiselle had never been one to give up without a fight or, at the very least, an elegant revenge. He did not delude himself into thinking he had heard the last of this.

Once inside the sanctuary of his study, he went straight for the brandy, then sat heavily and propped his feet on his desk. A mound of correspondence and accounts spilled across its surface. Bills. Debts. The heel of his boot dislodged a slip of parchment that drifted into his lap.

"For renovations to the manor house, Maison Corbay, Sèvres, by the carpenter Galoise in the hire of His Grace, the duke de Corbay—seventy-five francs."

His thoughts shifted to his recently acquired title: a secondhand duchy for a second son. He studied the ducal ring on the hand that held his goblet. Not unlike the young duke himself, the ring was a mere replica of the missing original. What a fool he had been to think that his father had actually wanted to help him by insisting he acquire the duchy of a long-dead second cousin. Philippe's usually indifferent father had been so adamant, so suddenly attentive, that Philippe had instantly suspected his motives. Still, the elevation in rank and the hope of income had convinced him to go along.

The whole matter was very odd. He'd wondered more than once why his father hadn't simply claimed the estate for himself. Philippe was fairly certain the marshal, as the dead duke's eldest male first cousin, had been closest surviving relative at the time of the late duke's death. But then again, the Corbay duchy was hardly a prize.

His older brother hadn't wanted to bother with it either. Philippe should have known that Henri would never have waived precedence if the estate had had any real value. What was the marshal up to? There had to be something in it—power or money—to attract his father's notice.

Yet there seemed little to be gained in the estate. Though not without a certain coarse charm, Maison Corbay and its neglected holdings had only further depleted Philippe's limited resources. He'd barely had time to put the place in order and supervise an inventory before the marshal had summoned him into his presence and shoved the betrothal contracts at him, declaring, "I've arranged for your marriage. The dowry will be substantial. There's a space for your signature just below the queen's. Sign it."

In that moment, Philippe had felt as trapped and angry

as he had been all those times his father had brutally beaten him as a child, then ordered him locked in the dovecote for days at a time. Was the marriage another of the marshal's punishments, another prison?

Yet Philippe had swallowed his resentment and signed—not only because of duty or honor or filial obedience or even financial expediency, but because of something his father knew nothing about. The truth was, Philippe wanted a son of his own, more than he wanted anything else in this cruel, uncertain world. The marriage would make that possible. And then there was always the dowry.

He took another swig of brandy and savored the mellow smokiness on his tongue. There would be no more rationing of good brandy after the wedding. Once he'd deposited his wife in the country, he'd return to take his rightful place at Court, no longer an invisible second son whose poverty limited his tactics to intrigue and seduction. He would return to the country only often enough to assure that there would be a son and heir.

Standing, he yawned loudly and stretched as the brandy's warmth spread through his body and lightened his head. The princess had a point. He *was* of an age to marry, and one wife was as good as another, as long as she was fertile. He just hoped this one wasn't poxed or stupid.

On second thought, he mused bitterly, it just might simplify things if she were both.

❧ CHAPTER 3 ❧

*P*acing her boudoir like a caged tigress, Louise, Duchess de Montpensier and Great Mademoiselle of France, flicked open the golden spines of her fan with a snap.

The nerve of Philippe! she fumed. Her attentions had elevated that insignificant creature beyond all reason, and now he repaid her with rejection. That's what she got for casting pearls before swine.

She dared not concede, even to herself, how much he'd come to mean to her—how the very thought of their love-making sent a shivering thrill through her; how he'd managed to hold his own with her, mind to mind and will to will, as no man ever had. Those admissions were far too dangerous. So she settled for anger. And the icy comfort of revenge.

Her fine young duke would rue the day he considered breaking it off with *her!*

As for the bumpkin bride, she'd make short work of her when the time came. It would be simple enough to see that their marriage bed was scattered with thorns enough to prick for a lifetime.

Slapping her fan shut, Louise hurled herself into a chair beside the table. She snatched a morsel off the plate, then spit it out. It was cold, ruined. The fan sailed across the room and into the flames. She watched, smiling, as its silken embroidery blackened and curled in the fire.

Perhaps this would work for the best, after all. Philippe had been far too distracting, causing her concentration to wander from the one thing that really mattered. A lapse, that was all he was. Louise reminded herself that paramours were mere diversions. She was far too clever to expect any real tenderness in the yearning looks and lovely lies offered by those she selected to share her bed. Such couplings could only briefly satisfy her hunger for excitement. And not even Philippe could fill the aching emptiness inside her. Only the man King Louis himself would one day become—he alone could banish the barren void made by the secret in her heart, the secret that had changed everything.

She paced afresh, her arms clasped tightly across her breasts in an unconscious gesture of self-protection. Guttering candles flickered in the wake of her passage. Then a calming resolution brought her to a standstill.

I will have you back, Philippe, you ungrateful wretch. Maybe not right away, but soon enough. And when I do, I'll make a game of hurting you. No one spurns me without punishment. No one.

A sudden chill drew her close to the fire. Curled on the edge of the same settee Philippe had occupied, she could still smell the faint scent of him. Louise stared into the flames and tried not to think of the truth in what he had said, but a cold trickle of loneliness bled through her defenses from the tiny wound his rejection had made.

For just a moment, she actually considered summoning her faithful nurse, Nourrie, from the next room.

Nourrie was always there, always sympathetic. Hers was

the only love Louise could really count on. Faithful Nourrie, with her constant whispered warnings: "You are special, above all others, destined to be the mother of kings. Only those who rule are your equals. The rest just want something from you. Never let down your guard." Louise could almost hear her in the hiss and crackle of the fire. "Trust no one; use them before they can use you." Drummed into her from earliest memory, the admonitions had hardened Louise, deprived her of the luxury of trust, the comfort of friendship, the hope of real love. That was the curse that came with privilege.

She sighed, dismissing the urge to feel Nourrie's thin arms around her as a momentary weakness. Sympathy was for lesser beings. One must be hard in order to rule, and rule she would one day. In September, King Louis XIV would celebrate his fourteenth birthday. The coronation would follow within months. By then she would be ready, her power consolidated.

Allowing herself a secret consolation, Louise rose and crossed to an enormous inlaid chest. After unlocking it and raising the lid, she reverently lifted a corner of the magnificent robe that lay folded inside. Louise brushed her cheek across the wide ermine border, then buried her face into the plush velvet lining. A dozen seamstresses had labored for three years to make this robe. Encrusted in jewels and pearls, it was thirty feet long and so heavy she would need twenty attendants to make the procession down the aisle of Notre Dame. Louise had designed it to do justice not only to herself, but to the crown that would be placed upon her head the day she wore it.

She pictured herself standing beside young King Louis at the altar of Notre Dame. She *would* marry him, and Bourbon blood would rule France, undiluted. With her at his side, young Louis could restore France to the greatness established by their grandfather, Henry IV. What did it matter that she was eleven years older than he? The difference in their ages could work to the boy-king's advantage; Louise possessed the experience to guide him, shape him into the great ruler their country so desperately needed.

She, and she alone, would be the perfect consort: lover, nurturer, advisor, and friend. Only then would the queen mother's Spanish talons be loosed from the heart of

France. Louise stared at the Bourbon crest embroidered on her coronation robe.

Soon.

Her plan was working. Even before the old king's death, the country had seethed with food riots and tax protests. When the widowed Queen Anne had become regent for her son, it had been a simple matter for Louise to stir the political kettle to a boil. Looking back over the past few years, she smiled at how the regent queen mother had unwittingly sown the seeds of her own destruction. No self-respecting Frenchman could tolerate the queen mother's naming her paramour Mazarin—an Italian by birth and a puppet of the Vatican—to run the country for her. That political blunder had spawned the Fronde, a noble rebellion Louise had been only too happy to subsidize.

She smiled, her failing spirits rallied. It had been expensive, raising her own regiments and underwriting her cousin Condé in the rebellion for almost four years, but the investment was beginning to pay off. Thanks to the immense fortune she'd inherited from her dead mother, Louise's coffers were far deeper than Queen Anne's. The royal treasury was almost empty, while Louise's wealth remained virtually intact. Day by day, Louise's power was growing, not just with the armies of the Fronde, but with the people of Paris and Orléans. Soon, if all went as planned, she would be a force to be reckoned with. Then she would go to the regent and offer to end the insurrection in exchange for marrying Louis. Queen Anne would have no choice but to accept. And then Louise, not that Spanish witch, would rule as queen.

She buried her face in the ermine border of the coronation robe. Queen Louise and King Louis. They even shared the same name. Perfect.

Not so perfect, whispered a nagging inner voice, but Louise ignored it. The problem of heirs could be dealt with later. After all, when they married the king would be only fourteen—old enough to consummate the union, but not old enough for anyone to expect children right away. There would be time to come up with something.

The sound of a knock on her door sent a sting of alarm to Louise's fingertips. Hurriedly, she dropped the robe back into the trunk and locked it away.

She turned and shouted, "What?" in a voice as strident as any fishwife's.

The door opened to reveal a cowering Duchess de Frontenac, her hair a mass of twisted rag curlers. "Your highness, there is a messenger."

"Who dares disturb me at this hour? I left strict instructions I was not to be wakened." If not for Philippe's defection, Louise would have been taking her pleasure and in no mood for an interruption. Pricked by the thought of Philippe, she glared at Frontenac, whose gaze darted to the table laid for two, then to the empty bed, then to the floor.

"Forgive me, but your highness said that if anyone ever came with a certain greeting, they were to be admitted at once, no matter what. This messenger greeted me so."

A practiced veil of obscurity settled over the princess's features. Suddenly Philippe was the farthest thing from her mind. Her instincts honed to the sharpness of a rapier at this unexpected development. Matters must be desperate for a messenger to come openly. Half the palace would know by now. But if the courier was from Condé, why hadn't he used the secret passageway? This smelled of a trap. Her plans, her future, her very life might depend upon how she dealt with this matter. She must regain her composure. "Bring me a fan."

When Frontenac obliged, the Great Mademoiselle sat on the side of the bed and fanned herself briskly until the telltale flush of agitation disappeared from her throat. "Send the messenger in. And see that no one listens at the door. That includes you!"

"Yes, your highness." Frontenac hastened away.

Louise watched a furtive young man in soiled silk enter, cross the room, and drop to one knee beside her bed, his face downcast. "Great Mademoiselle, I bring urgent news from a friend who loves our king."

The words were right, so far. "What sort of friend would send you to me at this hour? My friends are more considerate."

Without looking up the young man wavered, bracing himself with an unsteady hand upon the carpet. He completed the secret pass-phrase. "May God preserve those who love and protect France." His next words were just above a whisper. "I fear there is no time for games, your highness. You have been betrayed. As I approached the entrance to the secret passage, I was set upon, cast into the gutter for dead, and my key taken from me—"

When he swayed again, Louise noticed the dark stain that trailed down his arm into the thick pile of the rug. Behind him, small blotches marked his path across the carpet. Her whispered reply was tight with anger. "You fool, you've left a trail of blood to my very bedside! If you have a message for me, speak, while there's still breath enough to do so!"

The grime-streaked face that turned upward was hardly more than twenty. "The traitor must be someone close. The cardinal and his witch know your every move. One of your attendants, or perhaps one of your lovers—"

Her palm snapped across his cheek. "You impertinent lout! How dare you speak to me in such a fashion!"

Caught off-balance by the impact, the messenger teetered, then toppled slowly to the floor, a sardonic grin on his face despite the obvious effort of every word. "I deliver my message for love of him who sent me, not for any love of you. I'll not waste my dying breath protecting your feelings. Look closely, lady. Those favors you give so freely may have brought you treachery with your pleasure. Death might find you between the sheets. He's found me at your bedside."

The princess leapt from the bed like a fury, her hair flying wildly as she drew back a bare foot to take the smile from his face. But before the blow found its mark on his backside, she pulled back. The messenger's dark, wide-open eyes still reflected the firelight, but the life had gone out of them.

She poked him gently with her toe. "Fool boy." Louise crouched and pulled open his jacket. The front of his shirt was wrinkled, but unmarred. She rolled him over and found the back of his jacket soaked black from a single narrow tear, and a soggy stain beneath him. Strange, how small a wound it took to kill if the dagger met its mark.

Sinking to her knees, she closed her eyes and groaned. How many more foolish, impertinent young men would die before this was over?

Louise forced herself to her feet. There would be time for regrets later, but not now. Now she must act, and quickly. Looking down, she murmured softly, "Damn." She would never get the incriminating blood out of the rug. Now there was that to deal with, as well. If this was a trap, the cardinal's men or the queen's guards would come beating on her door any minute. She couldn't let them find the body, but it was too heavy for her to carry. She would need help to dispose of this inconvenient young man. A tug on the cord by her bed summoned Nourrie.

Grumbling accompanied the shuffling footsteps from the adjacent dressing room. "What is it now, your highness? I'm too old to be wakened in the middle of the night, unless Mademoiselle is ill."

"I'm not ill. Just come inside and do as I say." She pulled her old nursemaid into the room. "And whatever you do, don't cry out." She shoved the door shut, threw the bolt, and turned back to the bedside.

Seeing the body, Nourrie let out a gasp, followed by a rasping, "Blessed Virgin! I *knew* I wasn't strict enough with you when you were a child. Now look what you've done!"

Louise's eyes narrowed in indignation. She owed no one explanations, least of all a servant, but Nourrie could be stubborn. "I didn't kill him. Mazarin and the queen are behind this; I'm sure of it." She motioned Nourrie to the foot of the bed. "We must get rid of the body. Help me roll him up in the rug." While the frail old woman struggled to help her, the princess sorted through her options and hastily formulated a plan of action. She dared not summon the palace guards; that would be playing right into Mazarin's hands. But the body couldn't remain here. "I'll pull, you push. Let's get him to the secret panel."

That done, she returned to the bedside and opened the drawer of her nightstand to withdraw two slender daggers in jeweled sheaths. "The assassins have a key to the secret corridor, but there's no other place to hide the body. I'd rather risk an ambush in the passageway than face the cardinal's inquisitors about this." She handed Nourrie one of the daggers. "Don't hesitate to use this, but take care. The blade is poisoned; a single scratch can kill."

Nourrie's eyes widened, but she nodded obediently.

Every nerve on edge, Louise listened at the entrance to the secret corridor, then preceded Nourrie into the darkness. With a supernatural strength fueled by desperation, the two women tugged and shoved their ominous burden through the narrow passageway. At every bend and opening along the way, Louise braced herself for an attack, but her fears proved groundless. They reached the bottom of the spiral stairway without incident and shoved their unholy bundle into a dank alcove.

Panting from exertion, she cautiously approached the outer door and found it secure. Louise pulled Nourrie back toward the stairway. "Come. Let's see if the guards are waiting in my room." When they found the chamber empty, Louise allowed herself to believe that she might be able to avert disaster; but there were still a few loose ends to be tied up. She pulled coarse clothing and a servant's cloak from the depths of an ornate trunk. "Help me dress, Nourrie, then get dressed yourself. You must fetch a locksmith to change the lock to the passageway. While you're doing that, I'll get another rug from one of the empty guest rooms. Everything must look as it was."

"A locksmith, is it?" Making no move to obey, Nourrie eyed her skeptically. "I haven't forgotten the last time you sent me for a locksmith in the middle of the night. As I recall, the poor man never made it home."

Feigning innocence, Louise protested, "And how should I know anything about that?"

"How, indeed? All I ask is that I be able to stand by and listen in Glory when you answer for these plots of yours." There was a familiar singsong to the nursemaid's lament. "I don't know why you couldn't have married one of those kings or archdukes you were offered. By now you'd have a batch of little princes and princesses for me to tend. *That's* what nannies dream of, not dragging dead bodies into the night and fetching honest people out of their beds to change the locks—"

The words stung like wasps. Louise's heart constricted, but her tone was icy calm. "Take care, Nourrie. Such insinuations presume greatly upon the deep affection I bear you." She handed the clothing to her. "As for the other locksmith, can I help it that Paris has become such a dangerous place for those who have been of assistance to me? Why, even you might be at risk after tonight's business. Mazarin's henchmen are everywhere."

The veiled threat was effective. Nourrie's resistance evaporated. With shaking hands, she hastened to dress her mistress.

Satisfied, Louise softened. "You'll find a purse of gold coins on my dressing table. Tell our locksmith that if he values his safety, he'll take the money, change his name, and get out of Paris for good. No packing. No good-byes." She knew better than to leave wagging tongues, but there would be plenty of time to take care of that later. She mustered up a convincing smile. "Have I made myself clear?"

Nourrie gulped. "Very clear, your highness, and very generous."

"Good. Now hurry along. We must be finished before dawn." Louise twisted a carved flower on the bookcase, and an entire section of paneling noiselessly swung open. It closed behind her just as quietly, leaving her in dank, musty darkness.

An hour and a half later, she emerged from the same opening with a heavy rug slung over her shoulder. Dusty and exhausted, she spread the rug and replaced the tables and chairs, then surveyed the results. Close enough. If she didn't know better, she might not even notice, herself. Less than two hours after the unfortunate messenger had discharged first his duty then his life, the room looked as if nothing had happened. She was safe. No one in all of France would ever believe she'd dragged the body away, much less carried that heavy rug all by herself.

So tired she could hardly lift her arms, Louise washed the grime from her face and hands, stripped off and hid her coarse garments, then slid the dagger beneath her pillow and crawled into bed.

Only then did she allow herself to think about the messenger's warning. Someone close had betrayed her. Philippe? After what he'd done, Louise wouldn't put it past him. But if the traitor *wasn't* Philippe . . . it could be anyone, even Nourrie.

Louise would find out. Until she did, only a dagger would share her pillow.

❈ CHAPTER 4 ❈

*T*he sound of curtain rings echoed like clashing sabers in Philippe's ears. He groaned and pulled the pillow over his aching head to shut out the sunlight that stabbed through his eyelids.

Where in blazes was Jacques? He knew how to ease Philippe awake, unlike Suzanne, who was banging about his bedchamber louder than a runaway tinker's wagon on the cobblestones. Even his pillow wasn't enough to drown out the infernal racket she was making.

He bellowed, "For heaven's sake, woman, be quiet!"

The breath that bounced back from the starched linen over his face was so foul Philippe tugged the pillow off, despite the noise and light admitted in the process. Through a tentative slit of one eye, he saw Jacques creeping up behind his wife as she bent to retrieve her master's discarded breeches from the floor.

Suzanne deserved a scare for being so noisy. Philippe watched Jacques grab her backside, but his smugness disappeared when she let out a shriek that brought him bolt upright, his palms to his temples. "By all that's holy, have mercy!" A wave of nausea abruptly silenced him.

Suzanne gave Jacques a harmless swat. "You randy old coot, see what you've done! You've made me frighten his grace half to death."

Jacques settled a lustful grin on his wife. "It's your own dear fault, wavin' that lovely backside right at me. You know what the great chefs say: All the flavor's in the fat. I couldn't resist getting my hands on it."

Philippe panted softly in an effort to dispel the queasiness. Neither of his servants seemed properly impressed with how miserable he felt. But then again, they weren't proper servants in the first place. Until Philippe had ransomed Jacques out of prison four years ago, the man had been a farmer, not a servant.

The truth was, Philippe had no one to blame but himself for the sad lack of discipline in his meager household. When he came home from the garrison or the palace every day, the *last* thing he wanted to do was give more orders or whip the staff into shape.

Staff. The word hardly applied. There were only Jacques and Suzanne, and neither had the vaguest notion about proper protocol. Though the couple was never openly disrespectful, they treated him more like a pampered son than a master. After four years Philippe told himself it was far too late to remedy the situation, but he had secretly come to rely on their affection. The humble couple provided the only real warmth in his life.

At this moment, though, he simply wished they would leave him alone. Still queasy, Philippe lowered himself back onto the pillows. The change in position revived his headache with crushing intensity.

Suzanne moved closer and peered down at him before retrieving the empty chamber pot from beneath the bed. She settled it with a firm *thunk* beside him on the quilt. "Looks like you might be needing this, your grace. You're green as a summer sea." She aimed a wicked grin at her husband, whose concerned expression turned to alarm when she added, "I apologize for cryin' out, your grace. It was all Jacques' fault. I wouldn't blame you for sending him back to the gallows, and me to the poorhouse."

"Hush, woman!" Jacques tugged her toward the door. "You know the master won't send me back. His grace purchased my loyalty when he bought me out of prison, but he won my love when he brought you here to serve beside me. He knows he'll find no more trustworthy servants in all of France. Now be gone with you while I attend to him." He shoved her out the door.

A slight smile flickered across Philippe's mouth. "Very pretty speech, Jacques. If memory serves, I hear it every time you get into mischief." The sound of his own voice set his skull to pounding harder. "Now make your final farewell, for my head shall surely split in two any minute, and that will be the end of me."

As usual, the valet was undaunted. "Nay, your grace, nay. You say this every time, then you just go out and injure yourself with drink again when your heart is heavy. Allow me to compliment your grace, however. I believe it's been over seven months since you last put yourself in such a sorry state." He proffered a small tray bearing the customary fare for such occasions. "Now eat the bun and drink the brandy. Then I'll do my best to make your grace presentable for the obligations of this day."

Philippe waved away the tray and rose stiffly to his feet. The fine linen shirt he had worn the night before hung haphazardly in a mass of wrinkles to his bare thighs. After pulling the garment off over his head, he lurched toward the washstand to slake his thirst straight out of the pitcher. The morning light seemed to accentuate the well-healed battle scars that marked his bare torso.

Jacques handed over his dressing gown without com-

ment. Its lining, of the softest Turkish wool, felt good
against the chill of the room. Philippe eased into his chair
by the window. "Honestly, Jacques, the penance is twice
the prize. I think my eyes really are going to fall out this
time." He reached for the brandy and took a sip, then tore
off a small piece of the roll and began to chew it tenta-
tively. "I'm too ill for a real bath. Just wash my hands and
feet, then shave me."

Jacques obliged, then draped a linen towel across Philippe's chest and filled a porcelain bowl with steaming water from a kettle on the hearth. As he worked up a lather
with the shaving brush, he asked his master, "I was won-
derin' if perhaps your grace might have changed his opinion about growin' a beard—or perhaps at least a
moustache? Very dashing, that."

Philippe closed his eyes and savored the feel of the
warm lather on his neck. "No. I shall remain clean-shaven.
Stop trying to talk me out of it." He opened one bloodshot
eye to glare at his servant. "I suspect you're just trying to
reduce the work required by my daily shave."

"Nay, your grace. I just noticed that none of the other
fine gentlemen go about barefaced."

The eye closed. "Exactly." Though Philippe rarely gave
much thought to his features, he was not unaware of the
effect his bare face had in the sea of neatly trimmed chin
beards and moustaches at Court. That distinction, at least,
set him apart. Invariably when he was introduced to a lady,
her eyes would linger on the tiny fencing scar that creased
an otherwise unmarred jaw.

Perhaps that was why the princess had noticed him in
the first place. He did not mind in the slightest attracting
such feminine attention, though he was amused by the effect of his appearance on the opposite sex. Women loved
battle scars and the tales that went with them, and his personal collection—public and private—could impress the
most jaded in Paris.

Philippe had learned very quickly that impressing the
right women provided the easiest access to power at Court.
Until his liaison with the princess, his carefully planned
amorous campaigns had been unqualified successes. As a
career soldier, he found the strategy of assignation similar
to that of war, but he preferred the spoils of the gentler
combat.

Yet war was simpler. In battle a man won, was wounded, or lost. In the bedroom he could be all three at once, and the consequences of a misstep were far more perilous and lingering there than in the field. Women were such strange creatures, capable of demure delight one moment, indifference or relentless cruelty the next. He had long ago given up trying to understand them.

Philippe shuddered slightly at the memory of the impassive mask that had settled on the Great Mademoiselle the night before. Then he sighed and forced himself to relax under Jacques' ministrations. Why waste energy worrying about how the princess would react once she had time to consider what he'd done? What would be, would be.

Grateful that he had no duties scheduled for the day, he murmured, "No wig today, Jacques. Just the usual." At least he wouldn't have to squeeze his aching head into a wig or submit to being fluffed and curled. Jacques' vigorous attention to his tangled hair unleashed a fresh wave of pain with every tug of the comb, but Philippe endured in silence until his servant tied the gleaming black waves neatly at the base of his throbbing skull.

The valet proffered a pair of stockings. "Will these be all right, your grace? Suzanne has darned the holes."

Philippe hated the feel of patched stockings inside his boots, but he raised his left foot and motioned for Jacques to put them on. "They'll do." They'd have to. Every article of clothing he owned had been subtly patched or mended.

Checking his shave with a cursory glance into the hand mirror, he paid little attention to the classically proportioned face reflected back at him. "At least I'm not still gray around the gills." He laid the mirror facedown on the table, then stood to his feet and stretched. "I think I'm feeling better."

Jacques helped him out of his robe and into a clean shirt. "I'm glad your grace hasn't given himself over to a spell of melancholy. I feared—"

Philippe interrupted him with a wry smile. "No. Not this time." He tugged on a clean pair of woolen breeches. "After I'm dressed, you may go down and help Suzanne. I have work to do in my study, so I won't need my horse this morning."

The rest of the toilette was completed in silence, until Jacques fastened the last button on his master's jacket.

Then he squirmed and ventured, "Beg your pardon, your grace, but there's a small matter . . ."

Philippe knew that look. He smoothed the deep, lace-trimmed collar that spread from shoulder to shoulder. "Spit it out, Jacques. Is the money gone already? I just gave Suzanne ten francs for the marketing yesterday."

"It's not the money, your grace. Not exactly. It's the brandy. When I took the decanter from the study to the cellar to refill it this morning, I discovered that the cask was almost empty. After I strained out the dregs, there were but a few swallows left to put into the decanter."

Philippe's teeth ground together as he stepped onto the landing that overlooked the marbled foyer. "I'll see if I can bully some of my back pay out of the quartermaster. We can't run out of brandy. You're sure there's enough food for all of us?"

Obviously more embarrassed than his master by the all-too-familiar difficulties, Jacques hastened to reassure Philippe as he followed him down the hallway. "We're fine for a few days, your grace. Suzanne has a lovely joint of beef on the spit. That should do us all for a while."

A bitter smile cocked Philippe's lips to one side. He'd never gotten used to depending on the generosity of his wealthier acquaintances, but necessity dictated that he must. "I probably won't be eating at home much this week, in any event. I have received several invitations. This looks like a politic time to accept them." He paused in the doorway to his library. "Tell Suzanne that our financial problems won't last much longer. After the wedding she'll not have to beg credit from the baker or the butcher. There will be plenty of money for all of us, and help for the both of you."

Jacques grinned. "Aye, your grace. We'll be a grand household then, won't we?"

"I don't know how grand, but comfortable at least."

As the valet bowed and retreated toward the kitchen, Philippe stepped inside the small library that served as his study. *After the wedding.* The words resonated like a prayer through his aching head.

But the wedding was weeks away, weeks of keeping up appearances, of relying upon the hospitality of others. He hated being debtor to anyone, but he'd do almost anything to avoid having to go to his father for money. That was one humiliation to which he would never submit.

As he closed the library door behind him, Philippe wished he could shut out his worries as easily as he shut out the world. This was his sanctum, his retreat. All about him on the crowded shelves of the study were books of history and philosophy. Not even his father knew of his fondness for study and contemplation, for Philippe had learned as a very young boy that the marshal's expectations for his younger son lay in more vigorous pursuits.

He pulled the account books from the shelf and settled to the unpleasant task of putting his affairs in order. His hunger for organization demanded that he have every entry properly logged before the marriage. Once the dowry was safely deposited with his bankers, the interest would be enough to settle his debts and provide a decent living. Then he could safely tuck away his bride—pregnant, if all went well—at Maison Corbay, turn these blasted books over to an accountant, and get back to Court where he belonged, this time as a man of substance.

He opened the ledger and tried to focus on the columns of tiny, precise numerals, but his eyes refused to cooperate. As far as Philippe was concerned, accounting gave numbers a bad name, and today his headache left him even less inclined than usual for the distasteful chore.

I wish somebody would just shoot me! Then I wouldn't have to do these blasted books or marry that blasted orphan or live with this stone in my heart—

It wasn't easy allowing himself to be manipulated by his father, accepting without dispute the marriage that had been thrust upon him. But Philippe knew that in this one instance the path of least resistance was the wisest. His head still aching dully with every heartbeat, he stared unseeing across his desk. If by pretending to go along with the marshal, he would discover some means to be free, at last, of his father's schemes, it would all be worth it. He'd had enough of his father's plots and plans and secrets.

He sighed, then turned his thoughts away from the relentless, corrosive suspicions about his father.

Accounts. For now, he had to think about accounts.

As the hours of the morning passed, he gradually reduced the jumble on his desk to three neat piles. He was so absorbed in his work that he didn't hear Jacques' gentle tap on the door, and he looked up in surprise when his servant set the luncheon tray on the table by the window.

Jacques bowed and pulled out a chair. "Suzanne has prepared some broth and toast. Please eat something, your grace; you'll feel better if you do."

"I could use a break." Philippe stood. "I've almost made some sense of these numbers, though I can't be happy with what they tell me." He crossed the room and sat down. "The unfortunate truth of my finances isn't likely to change while I eat a little soup."

Jacques draped a napkin across his master's worn breeches. "That's the trouble with bein' able to read. Seems like accounts and letters and such always bring trouble and put folks in a right bad mood. If *I'm* to get bad news, I want it from somebody's lips—personal—so I can at least take a poke at 'em if I don't like what they're telling me. No, your grace, I'm right glad neither the wife nor I can read."

"I wish you'd reconsider letting me teach you." Philippe took a spoonful of broth, awakening his appetite and improving his disposition. Between sips, he mused, "I take great pleasure from my books. They ask so little, and they're always there when I need them, always the same as when I first discovered them." He scanned the volumes crowding the shelves of the cozy room. Books offered the wisdom, the experiences, the emotions of great men, with none of the danger. His truest friends were Cicero and Horace, Julius Caesar, Lao Tsu, and Moses. "Books never beg anything of me, and they can do me no harm; for that, I am most grateful."

A sad smile marked Jacques' response. "Sounds mighty lonely to me, your grace." He bowed and left Philippe to his "friends."

Philippe finished the broth and returned to his desk, determined to bring the accounts up to date before he treated himself to an afternoon ride. He was soon immersed once more and barely heard the sound of approaching hoofbeats in the courtyard below. Insistent rapping of the door knocker succeeded in getting his attention, though. He rose and crossed to the window in time to see a panting young messenger in Harcourt livery hand Jacques a letter.

Jacques was at the study door in moments, his face

flushed and his expression anxious. He proffered the sealed paper. "Message from your father, your grace. The lad awaits a reply. I hope it's not bad news."

As always, something deep inside Philippe shut tight at the mention of his father. He broke the seal and read:

> Philippe—
> Your fiancée will arrive here in a few weeks. My reports indicate that she is healthy. Taking into account your financial circumstances, I will of course be happy to bear the considerable expense of her maid and the cost of properly introducing her into society. In return, all I require of you is that you show up when and where you're supposed to for the necessary engagements before the wedding. I'll send a schedule as soon as your mother and I—

Anger scalded Philippe's cheeks. Hélène wasn't his mother; she was his stepmother. He barely knew the woman, and from what he'd seen, she was an insipid creature who lived to please his father's whims. Philippe scanned the precise script to find his place.

> —your mother and I make the arrangements. The first banns will be published this Sunday. I expect you there at Mass to sit with the family.
> The wedding shall be April 21 at the cathedral in Paris. I will notify you when your betrothed arrives here and we have settled the details of the ceremony.
> P.S. I am happy that you have finally learned the value of prudence in your social life. Since gossip about your escapades would hardly make a proper introduction to your future wife, I commend your recent discretion.

No salutation, no words of respect or endearment—even for etiquette's sake—and in place of a signature, a scolding disguised as a compliment. Philippe crushed the letter in his hand and spoke to Jacques through clenched teeth. "Tell the boy the reply is affirmative."

When he was alone once more in his study, he jerked the message open and reread it, becoming angrier with every word.

As usual, his father gave with one hand while slapping with the other.

Seething, Philippe made for the brandy. Halfway across the room he was stopped short by the memory of how wretched he'd felt upon waking.

No. Brandy wouldn't help anything.

A glance at the decanter reminded him that it couldn't help. The container was almost empty.

Out of brandy. Out of money. Out of credit. Philippe had no choice but to allow his father's charity until he could take advantage of the dowry. Then everything would change.

Then at last he'd be able to pay his own way. He could take his place on a more level playing field with the rich and powerful at Court. And in time, there would be a son. He was sure of it, as sure as if the depth of his wanting had already made it so.

Philippe scanned the shelves and chose a volume of Roman poetry, then settled into the familiar contours of his favorite chair. Soon he was thousands of years and a thousand miles away, rocked by the rhythm of Latin poetic meter and drowned in the passionate adventure of Dido and Aeneas.

Sunday would find him dutifully present with his father, elder brother, and stepmother in the chapel of Maison d'Harcourt—Philippe obedient to his family responsibilities, and they aloof and indifferent as ever. But for now, he was free with his beloved books. Free to be someone else, somewhere else, and all the endings known.

❧ CHAPTER 5 ❧

"*No*, no. *Gracefully*, like this. Not like a lumbering cow." Despite her rigid bearing, Sister Jonah swept into a curtsy as smoothly as a tall cedar bows to the wind.

Annique wondered how a woman of such advanced years—at least forty—could so easily accomplish what she, herself, couldn't seem to master despite weeks of intensive training. "I try, Sister, but it's these infernal shoes. They pinch, and the heels make the floor run downhill. I can barely walk, much less curtsy." She scowled. "And those silly dance steps, perched on one foot while wiggling the other. I tell you, it's hopeless."

Sister Jonah had presided over their sessions with a definite air of martyrdom from the very beginning, but today she seemed even more annoyed than usual. "Perhaps you should spend more time on mastering the art of grace than on excusing your clumsiness."

Annique flexed her toes in the tight slippers. "It isn't reasonable for supposedly civilized people to prefer such painful, impractical footwear over a sandal or a sabot."

A withering glance accompanied Sister Jonah's reply. "How perceptive of you, Annique. Why don't you just show up at Court in your sandals and persuade them of the error of their ways. I'm sure they'll be most grateful." She tapped Annique's foot with her stick. "The gentlemen are certain to enjoy the spectacle of your stockinged toes."

Goaded beyond prudence by her instructor's sarcasm, Annique spoke a question that had been nagging at her since their first lesson two months ago. "And just who are *you*, Sister, to instruct me on such matters?" To her surprise, she could have sworn her question sparked a flash of respect in the older woman's eyes.

Sister Jonah retorted, "Who *I* am is none of your concern."

A flush of controlled anger warmed Annique's neck beneath her cowl. "On the contrary; it's very much my concern. Whose manners am I learning? Those of a great lady, or those of a commoner? How can I know that what you've taught me will be proper for a duchess? And I shall be a duchess when I marry the duke, shall I not?"

An unexpected smile curled Sister Jonah's thin lips—her first in the two years since her transfer from the Mother House. She tucked her hands behind her apron and studied Annique through narrowed lids. "Very good, Annique. Spoken like a duchess, indeed. You seem to have mastered a certain sense of station with no help from me. Perhaps you were born with it. Blood will tell."

Annique's voice was bitter. "Really? I don't suppose you happen to know *whose* blood it is that flows through my veins."

"That is not for me to tell. Ask Mother Bernard." A sly expression erased Sister Jonah's haughtiness. "Or better yet, ask Father Jules."

Annique knew she had ventured onto dangerous ground, but she was determined not to let the matter drop. Sister Jonah always found some excuse to use the wooden rod in her hand, anyway. The truth was worth risking a rap on the knuckles. Eye to eye, Annique matched the older woman's arrogance. "I'm asking *you*. And I remind you of the consequences to your soul if you do not tell the truth."

"Truth? Ha! You really are naive, aren't you?" Sister Jonah actually laughed out loud, if one could call the bitter sound a laugh. She sobered, the predatory gleam returning to her eyes. "At any rate, I hardly think it appropriate for *you* to lecture *me* concerning the state of my soul."

Realizing Sister Jonah could not be intimidated, Annique felt her anger fade as quickly as it had come. Her shoulders drooped. "Please. Can you imagine what it's like, not knowing who I am? All these years, I have been afraid to ask for fear I *had* no name, even though Mother Bernard told me my parents died of fever." She tried to connect with some shred of humanity, no matter how small or deeply buried it might be. "Who am I, Sister? What harm could it do to tell me? You know I'll find out soon enough."

The nun was silent for what seemed a long time, her eyes darting to the study door, then back to the floor in front of her. When she finally responded, her tone was cold. "You are the legitimate daughter of a duke, his only issue." She prodded Annique with her stick. "But do not allow this to puff you up, Little Sister. Your status is by the grace of God and your parentage, not through any merit of your own. Your parents are dead. That is all I am at liberty to tell you. If you are impertinent enough to demand more, ask Mother Bernard." It was obvious she wouldn't offer more.

Annique stood impassive, wondering what it meant in the world beyond these walls to be the daughter of a duke. The *legitimate* daughter of a duke, Sister Jonah had said. That quieted one unspoken fear, at least. But what of her mother? Before she could speak the question, Sister Jonah's wooden rod glanced off her knuckles in an instant of white-hot pain. Annique bit her lips to keep from crying out.

"Pay attention! We've wasted too much time with talk.

Let's try your curtsy once more. Perhaps you'll get it right at last. We live in hope."

It took all Annique's training to hide her defiance as she rubbed the sting from her hand. Sister Jonah seemed to take some secret delight in shaming her. How much longer would she have to endure the woman's contempt? She glared spitefully at her instructor before lowering herself into the curtsy.

As she bowed, Annique's gaze swept down past the ornate silver crucifix swinging from Sister Jonah's belt. The cross was turned backward, revealing for the first time an inscription on its polished back: *"Ma Soeur, Mon Coeur. Louis XIII."*

Annique bent her head to conceal the curiosity that rushed through her. She knew she had read the inscription correctly. *My Sister, My Heart. Louis the Thirteenth.*

There was only one Louis XIII—the old king, dead for several years. Could this bitter, cruel woman actually be his sister?

Something inside Annique said no. The late king had three sisters, but their names were . . . what? For the last two months Father Jules and Sister Jonah had crammed so much protocol, politics, and manners into her brain Annique could hardly think. She closed her eyes and called up the image of the royal family chart. Ah, yes. Louis's sisters were Christine, Elizabeth, and . . . and Henrietta-Maria, now exiled queen of England.

None of the old king's blood sisters had entered a convent.

Who *was* Sister Jonah, really? Resolving to find out the truth once she reached Paris, Annique turned her eyes toward the floor and waited for the insufferable woman to finish criticizing her clumsiness.

She heard Sister Jonah's slender rod whistle through the air only a split second before it licked a path of stinging pain across her back. Annique snapped rigidly upright, tears springing to her eyes.

The nun ordered, "Stop daydreaming! I said we're done for today." She exhaled in exasperation. "As a matter of fact, we're done altogether. I told Mother Bernard this morning that you have progressed as far as you are able. There is only so much I can do, considering what I had to work with." Still holding the wooden rod, she crossed her hands at her waist. "Now run along to Mother Bernard's study. She wants to see you."

Shuddering inwardly from the savage blow, Annique blinked back the unwelcome tears. When she trusted herself to speak without shaking, she asked quietly, "Then our sessions are at an end?"

"Yes, I am happy to say." Sister Jonah opened the door and stood beside it.

At the sight of Sister Jonah standing there, her posture impeccable and the rod held in her hand like a scepter, something snapped inside Annique. Smiling coldly, she crossed the room to stand within inches of the older woman. "In that case, you won't be needing *this* any more." She snatched the rod and in one swift motion broke it across her thigh. Annique hurled the pieces to opposite corners of the room. "Good-bye, Sister Jonah. I pray our paths will not cross again in this life." With a grace born of pure satisfaction, she pivoted and glided toward Mother Bernard's study.

"Sit down, my child." Mother Bernard indicated the empty chair beside her desk.

As she obeyed, Annique shot an apprehensive glance at the study door. Though she had heard no angry footsteps behind her in the hallway, she knew Sister Jonah would waste no time in telling Mother Bernard of her rebellion.

Guilty though she might be, Annique wasn't sorry. As a matter of fact, she'd do it all again, just to feel the glorious sense of power that came from finally standing up to her tormentor. The memory of Sister Jonah's shocked, dismayed expression was worth any punishment Mother Bernard might mete out.

But penance for that particular crime would wait for another day. Sister Jonah didn't arrive, and Mother Bernard seemd preoccupied with something else entirely. Usually brisk and to the point, the abbess busied herself rearranging the contents of her writing box without making eye contact with Annique.

After several minutes passed, Annique took the initiative. "You wanted to see me about something, Mother?"

Mother Bernard closed her eyes and murmured an unintelligible prayer before replying. "Sister Jonah feels you are as ready as you will ever be to take your place in the world. Father Jules agrees." She paused, then announced bluntly, "You will be leaving tomorrow for Paris with Father Jules and Sister Thomas."

Annique tried to let the words sink in, but they didn't seem real. Tomorrow! After months of preparation, she was really leaving.

"First light, tomorrow." The abbess cleared her throat. "Though your wedding won't take place for several weeks—late April, I believe—it falls to me, as the only mother you have, to discuss certain matters with you, matters concerning your marriage." She shifted restlessly in her seat. "To begin with, once you leave these walls, you are never, under any circumstances, to permit yourself to be alone in the company of any man until after your wedding. There can be no exceptions to this."

Annique concealed her curiosity beneath a look of blank expectancy. "Not even Father Jules?"

"Not even Father Jules." Mother Bernard adjusted some papers that were already in perfect order. "As for after your wedding . . . there are certain, ah, physical acts which shall be your duty to, ah, perform as a good wife." Her cheeks became very red. She rose from her chair and strode to the window, muttering, "I don't know how Jules expects me to do this! I was only out of convent school for one Season before they sent me here. What do I know of such matters?"

The abbess turned and clasped her hands together. Her next words were slow and deliberate. "On your wedding night, your husband shall . . . shall, ah, perform . . . certain physical . . . acts upon your person, which shall be . . . to which you shall, ah, submit—yes, submit— yourself as a dutiful wife."

Annique was fascinated by Mother Bernard's floundering. She was usually so certain about everything.

The mother superior went on. "These acts are ordained for the purpose of procreation. You *do* know what procreation means?"

Chewing the inside of her cheek, Annique raised her eyebrows and studied the blotches on Mother Bernard's face. "Something to do with children?"

Mother Bernard heaved a sigh of relief. "Exactly. You have assisted in the dairy with the calving, and you have helped the lay sisters in our hospital when babies were born, so I know you are familiar with birth itself." She grew tentative again. "As for their conception . . . perhaps your science studies have touched upon the propagation of animal species?" Her expression was hopeful.

"I studied pollination, but I can't imagine what that would have to do with *people."* Annique watched the abbess's smile flatten.

"And you have observed nothing in nature to enlighten you further?"

Since the convent's animals were segregated by sex as strictly as the human inhabitants, Annique had no idea what Mother Bernard was getting at, but she was enjoying the spectacle. Wide-eyed, she shook her head. "No, Mother. I don't understand."

"No?" Mother Bernard tapped her forefingers together. "Well then, let me see. On your wedding night, he—your husband, that is—shall . . . I mean to say that *you* shall—" Frustrated, she searched the room with her eyes as if somehow, magically, her gaze would light upon something which would provide her with the words she needed. Ultimately, she drew in a great breath and looked squarely at Annique. She accented each word that came next, so there could be no question of having to repeat herself. "The truth is, you are to submit your body without question to your husband's disposal when you are in your bed together. There! That's all I can tell you!"

She reclaimed her usual confidence by firmly directing the conversation to safer ground. "Madame Flobert has finished the last of your trousseau. Your trunks are all packed and ready." She shepherded Annique to the door. "You may spend the rest of the day helping in the dairy. And be sure to wear your gloves! We can't have you ruining your hands at this late date, after all it took to get them looking better."

Annique allowed herself to be pushed into the hallway before she halted. "About my husband, Mother. You haven't explained exactly *what* it is that he'll do—"

Mother Bernard cut her off. *"Whatever.* It doesn't matter. All you need to know is that you are to do as he asks. It's as simple as that." She motioned Annique toward the cloister. "Run along, now. We'll all have plenty of time to say our good-byes after supper."

Annique stood her ground. Tomorrow, she would be

shipped off to a place she'd never seen to marry a man she'd never met and live a life for which she was ill-prepared. She would *not* be dismissed now like a bothersome child! She grabbed the edge of the door as Mother Bernard attempted to close it. "No. I will *not* 'run along.'"

Mother Bernard looked up in surprise. "You forget yourself, my child!"

"I forget myself?" Annique kept her features impassive. "How could I forget what I never knew, Mother?" She stepped back into the study and closed the door. "I don't even know my name. Can you imagine what that's like?"

A look of bleak recognition crossed Mother Bernard's features. "No."

"Will you tell me my name?"

The abbess retreated to the window and looked over the colorful beds of hyacinths and tulips in the cloister gardens below. "For both our sakes, I had hoped we'd be able to avoid this conversation." After a moment of strained silence, she pivoted to meet Annique's gaze. "Ask Father Jules."

Annique moved closer. She could see that Mother Bernard knew who she was. Why wouldn't she tell her? "I *have* asked Father Jules, hundreds of times, but he refuses to tell me anything." Tears of anguish sprang to her eyes, but she fought them back. "In the last two months, I have submitted to everything you and Father Jules have inflicted on me, including Sister Jonah. I have been obedient. I have been patient. I have agreed to leave the only home I've ever known to marry a man I've never even met. Will you not grant me this one thing in return?"

"Trust me, child. We have only your best interests at heart." Mother Bernard's voice became conciliatory. "Be patient a little longer. Father Jules has very good reasons for what he's done. One day you'll understand."

"What possible reason could there be for not telling me my name? I'll find out soon enough, when I reach Paris." Annique's hands closed into fists as she struggled to keep the desperation from her voice. "Sister Jonah said I am the legitimate daughter of a duke, but her words had the sound of a weapon. Was she just making up another lie, one that would raise my hopes, only to have them crushed by the truth?"

Mother Bernard's mouth set into a hard line. "I told Jules we shouldn't leave you alone with that woman."

"I suppose he had his reasons for doing *that,* too." Annique crossed to stand in front of Mother Bernard. "Father Jules has always taught that ignorance is tyranny, yet now you claim he's keeping the truth from me for my own protection. Well, I don't believe him. He's hiding something, some terrible secret that's been between us from the very beginning."

Compassion softened Mother Bernard's features. "Trust him, Annique, for just a little while longer. You know how much he loves you."

A sudden coldness smothered Annique's anger and frustration. She whispered, "Yes, I know how much he loves me." She had always sensed something special about the bond between her and Father Jules, but priests were supposed to love everyone the same. Perhaps the time had come at last to speak of things that had haunted her for years. "He loves me better than any of the others. Why is that?" She took a deep breath, then blurted out, "Does he love me best because he's my real father? Is that why no one will tell me my name? Because I don't have one?" She searched the older woman's shocked face. "Am I a priest's bastard? Is *that* the terrible secret you've all been keeping from me?"

Mother Bernard recoiled, her bosom heaving in indignation. "May God forgive you for even thinking such a thing, much less saying it!"

Annique was both relieved and disappointed at the conviction in Mother Bernard's reaction. "Then he's not my father?"

"No. As God is my witness, he is not!" She glowered at Annique. "You always did have an overactive imagination, but I never thought you capable of such wicked, unfounded suspicions. How dare you dishonor Father Jules with such a question! The man has shown you nothing but kindness and affection, and this is how you repay him. Shame on you, Annique! Shame!"

Cheeks throbbing, Annique murmured, "I meant no dishonor, Mother. I only wanted the truth." Truth. Though she now knew who she *wasn't,* she still didn't know who she was. "You will not tell me my name?"

The mother superior's face reddened. "I have sworn not

to! Would you have me endanger my soul simply to satisfy your curiosity? No, Annique, I will not tell you."

"Very well." Annique walked to the door and pulled it open. She scanned the chamber that had been her school-room for the past decade, then settled a look of indictment on Mother Bernard. "I only hope that one day *you* will understand how it feels to be denied something so inno-cent that you want so desperately."

As she closed the door behind her, she heard Mother Bernard's soft reply. "I already know how that feels, Little Sister. I have since the day I came here."

❊ CHAPTER 6 ❊

*E*leven grueling days and nights of travel later, Annique pushed herself from Sister Thomas's shoulder and rubbed her eyes. The only sound she heard, except for her travel-ing companion's incessant snoring, was the drizzle of rain on the coach roof.

Why had the coach stopped? They had taken on fresh horses only hours ago, and Father Jules had promised her then that the next time she got out of the coach, she would never have to return to its cramped confines.

Annique looked to the priest for an explanation, but found him staring out the window, a wistful expression on his face. Following his line of vision, she saw the silhouette of a great city above the treeline in the distance.

At last, after almost two weeks of the coach's relentless abuse, they had reached the capital. Annique leaned for-ward for a better look. Softened by the misty spring rain, Paris looked like a landscape from a dream.

Father Jules murmured to himself, "There you are, my *grande dame*. I thought never to see you again."

He spoke with such tenderness and regret it occurred to Annique that Father Jules had not always been old, nor always a priest. Wondering what memories Paris held for him, she felt her own eyes drawn back to the impressive expanse of turreted walls, church towers, and angular slate roofs.

The city was his past and her future. Annique should have been excited to see it at last, but she wasn't. She was too exhausted. In the last eleven days she had seen so much, tried to absorb so many new sights and sounds and smells that her mind had been overwhelmed, her sense of wonder dulled to mere endurance by some self-protective mechanism. All she could feel was relief that their destination was in sight.

Now that they were so near the end of their journey, she allowed herself the luxury of asking, "How much longer until we reach Maison d'Harcourt, Father?"

At first, the priest didn't seem to hear her, but after a moment, he turned and blinked like a man coming out of a trance. "I'm sorry, my dear. What did you say?"

"How much longer until we reach Maison d'Harcourt?"

"Only a few hours." There was that look again, but this time it was directed at her, and a deep sigh accompanied it. Annique recognized that sigh. She'd heard it often enough, usually before he sentenced her to a particularly stringent—but always well-justified—penance. Was he having second thoughts about what awaited them? She knew better than to ask. Ever since they'd left the convent, he had deferred all her questions with "after we reach Paris." Today she would have her answers at last. He'd promised.

Father Jules lifted his cane and rapped on the ceiling to get the coachman's attention. "Drive on!"

Two hours later, they rode through the gilded gates of Maison d'Harcourt.

The outside of Maison d'Harcourt was impressive enough, but when a satin-clad servant opened the tall double doors into the foyer, Annique followed Father Jules into a splendor that robbed her of everything but awe.

Gold and ivory and ebony and silk were everywhere. Above the gray wainscoting, gilded mirrors shared the walls with huge portraits of men and women in jewels and furs. Pale gray and pink marble formed an intricate pattern beneath woolen rugs so thick the soles of Annique's sandals disappeared when she stood on their muted softness. And flowers. Though the weather held no hint of spring, tulips and narcissus lifted colorful blossoms from ornate ceramic pots.

Removing his hat, Father Jules leaned close to Annique's shoulder and whispered good-naturedly, "Close your mouth, my dear. It's not advisable to appear *too* impressed. You're liable to swallow a gnat." For the first time in weeks, he sounded like his old playful self.

Annique's lips snapped shut. She was hardly comforted by his gentle teasing. Her grand surroundings brought home the enormity of what she was facing, and fear tingled down her neck. She spoke, her voice sounding at the same time lost and too loud in this magnificent place. "Oh, Father, how shall I ever manage?"

"Pretend you're Sister Jonah. That should do it."

He was right, of course. Closing her eyes, she took a deep, calming breath. When she opened them again, Annique had been transformed to a woman of gravity and consequence. She even felt taller, somehow.

"Well done, mademoiselle." Father Jules offered his arm, and together they preceded Sister Thomas into the center of the enormous foyer.

To their left, a servant opened a tall set of double doors. "His grace will receive Father and the sisters in the library."

Father Jules led her into the room beyond, where elaborately carved shelving housed thousands of leather-bound volumes. At the sight of such literary treasure, Annique lapsed into her unguarded self, her gaze roaming hungrily over the titles until a squeeze and a warning look from the priest restored her dignity.

Hugging her tapestry valise, Sister Thomas followed close behind. "By all the saints! Would you look at the books!" At Father Jules's flat-mouthed disapproval, the sister shrank in apology. "Sorry, Father. It just slipped out. I promise not to say another word."

He gestured toward two facing settees in the center of the room. "Please be seated, Sisters." When the servant left them alone, Father Jules cautioned softly, "Remember what I told you both last night. Say nothing unless you are asked a direct question." He turned to Annique. "Even then, temper your response. First impressions are most important."

Annique nodded, frowning. She had never seen him so edgy. "I'll be careful, Father." Trying to cloak herself once more in Sister Jonah's arrogance, she took three deep, leveling breaths. But when her gaze fell on the satin upholstery beneath her, she noted the contrast between the coarse weave of her habit and the smooth, subtle perfection of the silk cushion.

At the sound of Father Jules's measured pacing, she looked up. He seemed to be staying deliberately where the light was poorest, as if the shadows offered refuge. "Are you all right, Father? You seem so ill at ease."

His clipped response was hard as iron. "I said keep silent."

Annique put on a look of passive obedience, but she still managed to have the final word. "Yes, Father."

At long last, the doors opened and the butler announced, "His grace, the Duke d'Harcourt, marshal of France."

A statuesque elderly gentleman, clad in the most ridiculous attire Annique had ever beheld, swept to the center of the room. Her future father-in-law wore more lace and ribbons than anyone Annique had encountered in all their travels, including the gaudy women she'd seen in the teeming streets of Paris.

Keeping her expression bland, she stole a closer look at his costume. Over the marshal's gold-embroidered doublet stretched a satin sash secured with elaborate, ruffled rosettes at the hip. More rosettes encumbered his knees, his elbows, and the spur lashings of his boots. Ornate lace peeked through the slashed sleeves of his jacket, and the intricate lace scallops of his cuffs, collar, and boot-tops were more than seven inches deep!

Her eyes traveled back up to his powdered face and hair. His cheeks and lips were a strange shade of red, and his skin looked as if it had been plastered with flour. Stiff rolls of silver-gray curls rose to his crown, then cascaded down his back. A wig, obviously.

Though the tension in the room was thick enough to slice, Annique had to bite her lip to keep from laughing. It was hard to imagine danger from such a ludicrous character.

The marshal bowed briefly to Annique and Sister Thomas, then addressed a strangely distant Father Jules. "Good afternoon. You are the priest, then?"

Father Jules answered without coming forward. "I am Father Jules. Your grace, may I present Anne-Marie Celeste de Bourbon-Corbay."

Annique looked about for this Anne-Marie, then the significance of the priest's words sank in. He spoke of her.

At last she was whole; she had a name.

Anne-Marie Celeste de Bourbon-Corbay. A beautiful name.

Bourbon-Corbay . . . Philippe's name was Corbay. But then, Father Jules had said they were distant cousins.

Annique repeated her name in her mind. The sound of it finally sated the hunger that had eaten away at her happiness for so long. Now the dignity she wore became real, no longer an imitation of another woman's pride. She had a name.

Annique dropped gracefully into a curtsy, but her joy was snuffed out with the marshal's next words.

Raising his eyebrows, he glanced derisively at Sister Thomas and touched a lace handkerchief to his nose. "Oh, good. I feared it was the fat one."

Sister Thomas's head bowed in shame.

What sort of man would say such a careless, hurtful thing? Annique lifted her chin defiantly and glared at him in rebuke, but remembering Father Jules's instructions, she remained silent.

The marshal placed his finger under her jawline and looked her over as he would a farm animal, top to bottom. When he spied the woolen stockings protruding from her crude sandals, a small shudder of contempt rippled across his face.

Smoldering, Annique deliberately wiggled her toes.

A bored expression claimed the marshal's features. Peering critically at her face, he directed his comments to Father Jules as if Annique were a small child unworthy of conversation. "I regret the necessity for receiving you before you've had a chance to refresh yourselves, Father, but duties of State require that I depart for St. Germain momentarily, and I was most eager to meet this young lady." He withdrew his hand from her chin and turned to the priest. "My wife will receive Anne-Marie Celeste at dinner. Meals for you and the sister will be provided in your rooms. Now with my apologies, I beg your leave." With a flourish of his handkerchief and a cursory bow, he left.

Her stomach knotted in outrage, Annique was glad to see him go. She knelt beside Sister Thomas and looked into her reddened eyes. "Don't let that horrid man bother you, Sister. The duke d'Harcourt obviously suffers from too much money and not enough manners." Then she fired a look of indictment at the priest, only to find him staring malevolently after the marshal. She had not thought Father Jules capable of a look of such unadulterated hatred.

When he realized she was watching, he passed his hands over his face as if to wipe his features clean, then addressed her without emotion. "Do not be deceived by the marshal's manner, Annique. He misses nothing. Guard your expressions. The next few weeks here will be hard enough without making an enemy of your husband's father." He peered at her coldly. "And guard your tongue, even when you are alone. He hears everything within these walls." Father Jules motioned for them to rise. "Now let's all go up and get some rest."

Annique did as he asked, but even though she was exhausted, she wasn't certain how well she would rest. How could she, after meeting Marshal Harcourt? If the son was anything like the father, she was doomed.

Annique awoke to a few seconds of blind panic. *The light! It's so late. How could I have slept past the bell?* Aching muscles cried out as she stiffly propped herself up on her elbows and gazed past the bed curtains into the dusky elegance beyond.

Then her flash of confusion gave way to realization.

This is Maison d'Harcourt, not the convent. She blinked, her eyes scanning the bedroom that was bigger than the convent refectory. The windows were covered by heavy damask draperies in the same pattern as the soft green silk on the walls, but a few shards of strong sunlight escaped around the edges. The bed beside her still bore the impression of Sister Thomas's body.

"Sister Thomas?" The large room seemed to swallow up her voice. Only a few coals glowed in the silent fireplace. She cleared her throat and tried again, louder this time. "Sister Thomas? Are you there?"

A small door opened near the marble mantel, and a thin, waifish girl of not more than fifteen emerged carrying a silver tray. As she drew nearer, the tantalizing smell of freshly baked sweets made Annique's mouth water and her hollow stomach growl.

The maid set the tray on the bed. "Good day, mademoiselle. I hope you are well-rested."

Suddenly aware that she was bareheaded in front of a complete stranger, Annique clutched the covers to her chest with one hand and with the other, self-consciously smoothed the curls that had worked loose from her braid. "Who are you? And how did I get here?"

"Why, I'm Marie, your maid. Don't you remember? I helped you undress."

"Undress?" Realizing that she had on only her chemise, Annique flushed with embarrassment. "No, I don't remember." How was such a thing possible?

The maid nodded. "When we couldn't waken mademoiselle for dinner last night, the sister sent word to the priest, and then she helped me put you to bed for the night."

"Last night!" Annique straightened in disbelief. "What time is it now?"

"It's past four in the afternoon. Mademoiselle has slept the clock around."

Groaning, Annique sank back into the pillows. "So much for first impressions."

"Mademoiselle?"

"Never mind. Please find Sister Thomas. I must speak with her."

Marie took a step backward and murmured apprehensively. "The sister left at noon, with the priest."

Annique stared at her in bone-numbing denial. "But they can't have left, not without saying good-bye." For one wishful moment she hoped she was still asleep and this was just an unpleasant dream, but she knew all too well that it wasn't. Her voice trailed to a wounded whisper. "Father Jules gave me his word. He *promised* he'd tell me about . . . He promised."

"The priest left you a message." Marie reached over and retrieved a folded paper from beneath the napkin on the tray. She handed it to Annique. "I offered to wake you, but he wouldn't let me."

Annique read the inscription on the outside of the folded paper. Odd, how strange it felt to see her name—still so unfamiliar, as if she had stolen it from someone else—written in Father Jules's familiar hand. She turned the letter over, noting his imprint in the red wax seal. But closer inspection revealed the paper around the seal was faintly pink and frayed. Someone must have tampered with it. Realizing the priest had not exaggerated his warnings, she opened the message and read,

> My precious child,
>
> I know I promised to speak with you before I left, but pressing business demands that Sister Thomas and I leave immediately. You were sleeping so deeply that I did not have the heart to wake you. To be truthful, I did not have the heart to say good-bye, for you have always been dearer to me than any child has ever been to any man. I shall answer to God one day for loving you more than the rest of the precious sheep He has entrusted to my care, but I readily confess it. Please do not think too harshly of my weakness in not being able to say good-bye.
>
> Regarding your past, Anne-Marie Celeste de Bourbon-Corbay, know that you possess a heritage as proud as any in France. Your parents were of the highest conscience and lineage. They brought no shame to the noble names of Bourbon-Corbay. No matter what you might hear to the contrary, your parents left you an unsullied legacy of honor and sacrifice. I, above all men, can swear to it.
>
> Regarding your future, I pray you will put away any lingering questions and look for contentment in marriage. Lasting joy can be found in any circumstance if you are patient and obedient to God's will. Mother Bernard and I have done our best to equip you for what is to come. May God bless your union and guide your ways. And may poor old Father Jules still have a place in the corner of your heart.
>
> Write me when you can, always remembering the rules of correspondence.
>
> I remain your humble servant and father in Christ.

Annique sagged. Gone. He had left her, abandoned her among strangers without even saying good-bye. How could he have done such a thing?

She wanted to weep, to scream, to smash something, but she could not let herself. Not here. Not now. Instead, she forced the pain behind an inner door and closed it away, leaving only a dull, throbbing heartache in its place.

She glanced back at the letter . . . *remembering the rules of correspondence.*

His rules: Put nothing in writing that could bring harm to either of them. The tampered seal had been reminder enough. She was alone now and could trust no one.

An anxious Marie intruded upon her thoughts. "May I pour mademoiselle some chocolate?"

"No." Annique shook her head. The bitter disappointment she had just swallowed left little room for food. "Take it away. Please."

Marie removed the tray, returning with one of the dressing gowns from Annique's trousseau. "Begging your pardon, but mademoiselle is expected downstairs for dinner at seven-thirty. It's already rather late, but if I might begin mademoiselle's toilette . . ."

Annique sighed. Just as it had at the convent, life went on regardless of disappointments. She slipped her arms into the warm, velvet-lined sleeves. "Very well. After last night, I suppose it wouldn't do for me to be late." She rose, wrapping the robe shut. "But I have a confession to make, Marie. I've never dressed for dinner before. My clothes have only been worn for fittings. I shall have to rely on your experience entirely."

Marie bit the end of her finger and winced. "I'm afraid I don't *have* much experience, mademoiselle." She hastened to add, "I've helped when some of the ladies' maids were ill, or when there were extra guests—I'm very good with coiffures—but I've never been a real lady's maid before. I usually work in the scullery."

A perverse chuckle escaped Annique. For some strange reason, the irony of having a scullery maid as her attendant lightened her spirits. "Well, I've never been a real lady before." She offered Marie an encouraging smile. "We shall have to teach each other."

"Then you're not going to send me back to the kitchen?" Marie's reddened hands twisted her apron.

"Only for some water. I'd really like a bath, if there's time. I haven't yet washed off the last of the dust from my journey."

The maid glanced uncertainly toward the dressing room, then nodded. "If some of the laundresses are free to help me. I'll see to it right away, mademoiselle." She disappeared through the small door beside the mantel, leaving

Annique blessedly alone to find the chamber pot and answer the urgent needs of her body.

Twenty minutes later, after much thumping and bumping and splashing from beyond the dressing room door, a disheveled Marie emerged. She smoothed her soggy apron and gestured into the cozy chamber behind her. "Mademoiselle's bath is ready."

Annique crossed the threshold in amazement. She had expected a sponge bath. Instead, an enormous tin slipper tub draped in fine muslin stood before a crackling fire in the cozy dressing room. She stepped closer, inhaling the perfume of spice and exotic flowers in the vapor that rose from the tub's cloudy, aromatic contents.

"Blessed Saint Peter and Saint Paul." The oath escaped as easily and softly as a breath. Enchanted, Annique barely noticed when Marie untied the silken cord of her robe and drew it from her shoulders. But when the maid reached for the delicate ribbons that bound her chemise, Annique clutched the làcings to her breast. "That's quite all right, Marie. I can manage the rest. You may wait for me in the bedchamber."

Marie hesitated. "But who will wash mademoiselle's back?"

Annique could feel the crimson flush that spread from her torso to her arms and face. "Please leave me."

"As mademoiselle wishes." The serving girl exited, shaking her head as she pulled the door shut behind her.

Safely alone, Annique lowered her hand into the perfumed water. Every hair on her arm stood on end at the delicious sensation of warmth. Until now baths had been cold, hurried affairs, a price willingly paid for her strong sense of fastidiousness. This was another matter entirely.

Warmed by the fire, she untied the ribbon that bound her braid and shook her hair loose. Then, inch by inch, she lowered first one foot, then the other into the tub. The rest of her body seemed to cry out with exquisite hunger for the water's heated embrace. She knelt, and something deep inside her contracted as the displaced tide rose above the tops of her legs. Savoring every sensation, she eased her torso slowly beneath the surface. Her long hair floated at first, then gradually sank to fill the space around her with graceful clouds and eddies of auburn filament.

Her chemise ballooned above her chest, and suddenly

Annique resented its presence. Unlacing it underwater was not an easy task, but soon she was unencumbered in the water's seductive pleasure.

She closed her eyes and sank back until only her head remained in the relative coolness of the air, but all of her longed to be under the surface. Slipping lower, she listened as enfolding warmth crept past her ears to shut away the world. Annique held her breath and submerged, giving herself fully to the water. It was so quiet there, so safe, so all-encompassing. Her skin awakened to the delicate caress of her hair in the subtle currents.

Then suddenly there was pain as she felt herself jerked roughly by the hair atop her head into a calamity of sound and motion.

"Oh, mademoiselle! Are you drowned? I *knew* I shouldn't have left you alone!" Tears streamed down Marie's face.

Annique sputtered, "What are you *doing?* I wasn't *drowning!* Let me go!" When Marie released her grip, Annique splashed unceremoniously onto her rump, sending water everywhere.

The maid wailed, "I'm sorry, mademoiselle. I waited just outside, but it got so quiet in here. When you didn't answer my call, I opened the door and saw you drowned. I was only trying to save you." She twisted her apron into a wretched wad as she spoke.

Suddenly Annique realized she was naked. But before modesty could prevail, she looked from her maid's anguished face to the huge puddle surrounding the tub and burst out laughing.

A shocked Marie blinked, then joined her mistress in an explosion of eye-watering, tub-rattling hilarity.

❧ **CHAPTER 7** ❧

"Not that way, Balthus." Philippe reined his mount away from Maison d'Harcourt's secret river gate. "Tonight we're going to the *front* door."

After three years of clandestine visits only when his father and Hélène were away, Philippe felt as if he were approaching enemy territory instead of the main gates of his boyhood home.

As much of a home as it had been.

He'd fled at sixteen, swearing to return only on his own terms. He'd believed he could escape the loneliness, brutality, and relentless manipulation by leaving his father's house. But escape had been an illusion. Loneliness had gone with him; brutality merely wore other faces and answered to other names besides his father's. Eight years as a soldier and three more in the royal guard had taught Philippe that the world could be a cold place for a second son with little means.

Now he must suffer the worst humiliation of all, pulled by the purse strings back to Maison d'Harcourt at his father's bidding. Philippe's only comfort lay in the fact that after the wedding, *his* would be the hand that held the purse strings of his bride's substantial dowry.

It was probably no coincidence that this was Fool's Day. The marshal had always said Philippe would come to nothing on his own, and the marshal loved to be proven right. A bitter chuckle escaped Philippe as he prodded his mount to a brisker pace. "Come on, Balthus. We might as well get this prodigal business over with." As if Balthus could sense his master's disquiet, the horse danced skittishly on the cobblestones, settling into a trot alongside the piked fence that defined the marshal's Paris domain. Only the richest and most powerful could afford such spacious grounds within the city. The marshal was both.

The gatesman heard them coming and greeted Philippe with a wave of his hat as he opened the way. "Welcome home, your grace!"

The face was one Philippe remembered well. Memories of the gardener's friendship and patient attention warmed his response. "Good evening, Jean! I see you've graduated from the garden to the gatehouse."

"Aye, master. Quite a grand position for an old man like me."

"You've more than earned it." Philippe doffed his hat in a sweeping salute. "Good to see you, Jean." He rode beneath ancient elms whose budding branches laced like bony fingers overhead.

Inside the gates, everything appeared as it always had. Even in the fading light, Philippe could see the marshal's stamp of relentless precision on the towering hedges and the vast rectangle of manicured lawn.

The house loomed ahead, unchanged from Philippe's earliest memories, yet tonight it looked sinister. Perhaps because his father was waiting inside—and his bride-to-be.

Philippe wasn't certain *how* he felt about meeting her. Wary. Curious—even his most persistent inquiries had yielded nothing about the girl. She seemed to have sprung full-grown from nowhere. The mystery of her past provoked his interest along with his suspicions. Yet Philippe knew his jangled nerves had more to do with the marshal than with meeting the woman who would, God willing, be the mother of his sons.

The closer he got to the house, the slower his pace. Why was his pulse pounding like a blacksmith's hammer? After all, Maison d'Harcourt was merely a house—the same house in which he had grown up. And the marshal was merely a man, neither more clever nor more dangerous than others Philippe had bested.

Philippe halted at the sandstone stairway. He dismounted, handing the reins to a waiting groom. "See that my horse is well fed and curried and ready to leave within two hours." Balthus, at least, would have a pleasurable evening to look back upon, even if his master did not.

"Good evening, your grace." Bowing deeply, the butler admitted him. "Monsieur le maréchal and madame la duchesse are in the main salon. I shall announce your grace immediately."

The interior of the great house was warm and fragrant after the cool evening of this first day of April, but the crackling fire in the entry hall did Philippe little good.

He forced his hands to unclench and his features to settle into a mask of urbane indifference. He was no longer a defenseless schoolboy being summoned to his father's study for a scolding and a beating; he was a grown man, well-equipped to match wits with the old duke. More devious adversaries than the marshal had been taken in by Philippe's casual half-smile and the misleading indolence of his manner. Yet underneath his confidence, some small remnant from Philippe's childhood still saw the marshal as a mystical, larger-than-life villain who could read his very soul with a look.

Not tonight, Philippe resolved. Tonight he would turn

the tables on the old fox. Though he had obligated himself to this union with a stroke of the pen, Philippe was determined to make this match the key to his freedom.

Two footmen opened the tall double doors, and the butler announced, "His grace, the Duke de Corbay."

What Philippe saw at the far end of the grand salon raised a subtle flash of warning. Though the prospective bride was absent, Philippe's father and stepmother were not alone. Tensing, Philippe studied the four men and two women who watched him enter. Bad enough that his older brother and Henri's harpy of a wife were here—he'd expected that—but what in blazes were Broussel and Vendôme doing lounging against the mantel? Their distant connections to the family hardly qualified either man to be present for such an intimate, and awkward, occasion. What was the old man up to? Approaching his father, Philippe leveled a look of open question at him.

The marshal's smug expression provided answer enough. The fact that Philippe would have wished it otherwise was sufficient reason to invite the others.

Philippe responded with a bow so brief it bordered on insult, but his smile remained relaxed. "Father."

"Good evening, son. You're late, as usual." The marshal adjusted his lace cuff. "I should have thought curiosity, if nothing else, would spur you to promptness tonight. Henri and Patrice arrived five minutes early." He cast an indulgent smile toward his elder son.

Though Philippe detested tardiness as much as his father did, arriving late had always provided a foolproof way to irritate the old man. He kept his voice amiable. "Perhaps my bride and I have something in common. I see she is tardy as well."

Henri's flushed face crinkled with amusement. "Touché." He stepped forward and clasped Philippe's upper arms. "Still like to have the last word, eh, brother?"

Grinning, Philippe recoiled discreetly from the smell of alcohol on Henri's breath. "I see that *you're* in fine spirits tonight, Henri."

His brother whispered affably, "Bes' way to get through these little family get-togethers, I've discovered," then released him.

The marshal was not amused. He turned his attention to Philippe. "Your fiancée isn't late. She was told to come down at half-past. I thought we'd all enjoy a little time together before she arrived."

So the old man had planned to have him squirm for half an hour waiting for the girl.

The marshal sniffed. "Aren't you going to speak to your mother? Or do you plan to ignore her all evening?"

Mother? Philippe gave no outward sign of the tightening in his stomach. Though his own mother was but a distant memory, he hardly considered the marshal's second wife as her replacement. Hélène seemed harmless enough, but she was a year younger than Philippe himself. Putting on his most winsome manner, he kissed her hand and murmured, "Hélène, how lovely you are tonight. I do believe you look younger every time I see you."

Oblivious to the veiled sarcasm in his remark, she broke into a dimpled smile, but a brief glare from the marshal told Philippe the jab had met its intended target. Before he had a chance to enjoy his father's response, Patrice interrupted.

"*Dear* brother." Henri's wife extended an elegant hand—her narrow, pointed nails evoking, as always, the image of talons. "Where have you been keeping yourself lately? Henri and I have missed you. Have you given up parties and balls altogether?" Philippe's only response was a bemused shrug. She continued, "Or have your tastes turned exclusively to more *intimate* affairs?"

What had she heard? Philippe knew better than to underestimate Patrice, but he had no intention of letting her get the best of him. Ignoring her outstretched hand, he bowed with exaggerated deference. "Dear Patrice. Observant and thoughtful as ever."

At the sharp undertone in his voice, she flapped her fan briskly before her bosom. "Henri and I were so pleased to be included tonight. I wouldn't miss this for anything. And how fares our future bridegroom?"

His grin was calculated to disarm. "Busy, as usual."

She arched an eyebrow. "So I hear."

She couldn't possibly know about the princess. Patrice was just throwing out her nets, trying to snare him into confirming some vague suspicion. Well, he wouldn't oblige. Smiling lazily, he bowed and backed away. He could handle Patrice. But if his fiancée were as provincial and naive as he had been told, Patrice would make mincemeat out of the girl.

Moving a safe distance from Patrice's unwanted attentions, he stepped to the fireside. Military protocol, as well as etiquette, demanded that Broussel be greeted first, though Philippe was curt. "Hello, Captain."

Broussel's thick lips gave him a look of permanent petulance, an impression confirmed by his disagreeable nature. He bowed slightly to Philippe. "I understand congratulations are in order, cousin. When's the wedding?"

Philippe's features congealed. "I forget. Why don't you ask Father?"

Cocking his head back, Broussel focused beady eyes on his taller cousin. "My, my. Such eagerness from our bridegroom."

Philippe straightened, emphasizing the full six inches that distinguished their heights. "Speaking of fathers, how's yours? I know he was pleased to see you appointed to command the Bastille. Quite an honor for a man of your age and experience." It was an open secret that Broussel's father had used bribery and all his influence as a councilman to secure the position at the Bastille for his son.

Broussel's puzzled expression indicated that he suspected he had been insulted, but found no proof. Deciding to take the remark at face value, he nodded smugly. "It *is* a big responsibility. A great deal of paperwork, what with requisitions and reports." He leaned forward. "My predecessor was most disorganized. It took me months to find out where we stood, and even then the news wasn't good." He turned toward the group and raised his voice to override all other conversation. "Never enough supplies, never enough men. And never enough money. My men haven't been paid in five months." He jabbed an embroidered elbow into Philippe's ribs. "*You* know how that is, Philippe. I hear the Queen's Guard hasn't been paid in over a year!"

Philippe's lazy smile didn't register the slight.

Broussel winked. "But your lean days will soon be over, no?" He glanced around. "We're all dying to meet this mysterious fiancée of yours. Have you seen her yet? The marshal says she's quite . . ." He paused. ". . . strictly brought up."

Philippe put his arm around this waspish cousin's shoulders and winked back. "Straight from the convent. Pure as rainwater, I am told. An excellent credential for a wife, don't you think?" Everyone in the room knew Broussel's wife had slept with half the Court before her tarnished reputation forced her to settle for marrying him.

Broussel frowned, his neck flushing. "That should pose quite an adjustment for you, cousin. You've always seemed to prefer feminine companions of a more . . . *sophisticated* nature."

Easy as it was to bait this puffed-up bore, Philippe was in no mood to continue. Things were already complicated enough. He defused his cousin's anger with a flippant, "Ah well, life is change. My lean days *and* my bachelor days will soon be over."

Patrice reclined against the settee. "Philippe, a respectable married man? Imagine that. Of course, marriage is no reason to end *all* of one's . . . friendships."

Henri guffawed, then offered, "How true, my dear. I do believe *your* friendships with attentive gentlemen have tripled since our marriage."

To Philippe's surprise, the tone of Patrice's reply was indulgent—almost affectionate. "At least I restrict myself to those of my own class, husband. Your weakness for serving girls is legendary." Her folded fan delivered a playful swat to Henri's thigh. "But we are not children. We agreed before our wedding that as long as discretion is observed, our individual friendships would continue. I think we have *both* found that to be a most practical arrangement." She turned a salacious smile upon Philippe.

Oblivious to his wife's open flirtation with his own brother, Henri raised his glass in a toast. "Ha. Practical it is, my dear. Here's to friendship."

Discretion. Clandestine affairs. That was the nature of most marriages Philippe had seen since coming to Court. He could count on the fingers of one hand the couples who seemed to be happily wed. He held no such romantic illusions for his own marriage. His expectations were far more realistic; if his marriage brought financial stability and healthy heirs, that would be enough.

Philippe turned an ironic smile on Patrice. She would be livid if he were to produce the first Harcourt grandchild. Despite her many "friendships" during her ten-year marriage to his brother, Patrice had been unable to conceive. It was the one thing for which he truly pitied her.

His musings were interrupted by a firm hand on his shoulder. "Cousin! Have you decided not to speak to me, or have I turned invisible?"

"I was saving the best for last." Philippe gave Antonin a playful clout. Though he felt real affection for his adoring younger cousin, the boy's presence was unsettling. "When did you get back into town? I thought you were at Orléans with General Turenne."

Antonin's freckled face broke into a grin. "I *was* until yesterday. I had some leave time coming, so they sent the dispatches back with me. When I delivered your father's, he was kind enough to invite me to dinner."

"Well, it's good to see you." Philippe cast a brief side-long glance at his father. Before the evening was over, he would know why the marshal had included Broussel and Antonin. Meanwhile, he intended to take full advantage of their presence. He asked Antonin, "Tell me, what's the news of young Guitaut? The last time I saw him, he was having the time of his life with a beautiful gypsy girl. Does she still follow him around?"

Upstairs, Mademoiselle Anne-Marie Celeste de Bourbon-Corbay struggled to breathe within the unforgiving confines of her padded damask bodice while Marie tucked one last hairpin into her hair, twisted a final curl with a smoking iron, then announced, "There. All done."

Annique looked into the mirror, the corners of her mouth drawing downward. Feeling completely out of her element and frightened almost witless by the ordeal that lay ahead of her, she balked. "Marie, I told you from the very beginning I don't like my hair this way. I can't possibly go out there looking like this. It's too absurd." Parted in the middle, her hair was drawn tightly to either side, where clumps of sausage curls sprouted to cascade over her ears. To Annique the two frizzy earmuffs looked as much like a handful of sheepshorn as anything.

Marie squirted on more hair lacquer from the atomizer. "*All* the ladies wear their hair in such a fashion, mademoiselle. Well, almost like this. I was so nervous I forgot something important." She picked up a pair of silver scissors from the dressing table. "Across the brow there should be a fringe of short curls. May I cut them? Then mademoiselle's hair will be perfect."

A fringe of curls? Annique recoiled. It was bad enough

to be bareheaded, but she had no intention of allowing Marie to chop away at her hair. "No! Put those scissors down. I would have cut my hair when I took my vows, but I'm not about to cut it for something as silly as a fringe of curls." She reached up to tug loose the carefully arranged earmuffs, but Marie's cry stopped her.

"Please don't, mademoiselle. There won't be time for me to make it right!"

Annique tried to remain calm. "I've already told you, I wish to wear my hair simply drawn back, without all this *froufrou*. Now come and comb it out."

Marie's voice cracked. "But madame la duchesse will have me *beaten* if I allow mademoiselle to go downstairs with her hair improperly dressed. Please leave it, I beg of you."

At the terror in Marie's eyes, Annique's back tingled with the memory of Sister Jonah's rod. Peering at her reflection, she shook her head gently from side to side. Even though the curls looked ridiculous, they felt pleasant bobbing against her ears. She sighed in resignation. "Oh, very well." Annique pointed a buffed fingernail at Marie. "But if you're wrong, and I look silly the first time I meet my future husband, I shall beat you myself!"

They both knew the threat was as empty as Annique's stomach.

Bronzed silk damask rustled over the gold satin of her embroidered underskirt as Annique rose to leave. At the sight of herself in the enormous pier mirror, Annique watched her cheeks redden in embarrassment. She tugged upward on the wide lace collar that framed the skin exposed above her bosom. "Marie, I *know* the dressmaker didn't pull this neckline so low when she fitted this blouse."

Marie handed her a fan from the dressing table drawer. "Mademoiselle's skin is like alabaster. She should show it off." She reached up with a grin and pulled the collar lower than ever, then opened the hallway door. "Good luck, mademoiselle."

The butler was waiting outside to escort her to the main salon. After she navigated the treacherous marble stairway in her new shoes, Annique crossed the foyer, her breathing restricted now more by fear than by her tight bodice. Trying to remember everything Sister Jonah had taught her, she composed herself while two liveried servants opened the double doors.

Annique flinched visibly when the butler bellowed behind her, "Mademoiselle Bourbon-Corbay." She regained her aplomb only by sheer force of will.

At the far end of the salon, conversation dropped to a murmur in the knot of elegantly dressed people. The marshal stood up, as did a younger, portly man who fit Marie's description of the Viscount of Harcourt. Seven pairs of eyes followed Annique's progress as her feet, still unsteady in her stiff new slippers, picked a course through the clutter of furnishings. Annique fought the urge to look down, remembering Sister Jonah's harsh instructions about the importance of grace. She said a silent prayer that she wouldn't knock over a stool or small table.

Jewels flashed in the soft light as the duchess and viscountess fanned themselves slowly, their eyes raking her up and down. The looks Annique received from the three men at the mantel were no less critical. Any one of them could be her future husband, but her eyes were drawn immediately to the one farthest away. His tall, powerful build and clean-shaven chin set him apart from the rest, but his coloring was his most striking feature. The man's hair gleamed blue-black, a compelling contrast to skin as flawless as a swallow's egg. Only a pleasing ruddiness across his aristocratic cheekbones relieved his pale complexion.

As she came closer, Annique had to employ a conscious effort to keep from staring, openmouthed, at the breathtakingly handsome stranger.

He bowed slightly in acknowledgment, his movements fluid and elegant.

He made her think of some giant, gleaming bird of midnight, his skin as fine and fair as moonlight, his dark blue eyes as brilliant as stars. Next to him, all the other men in the room seemed somehow incomplete.

Regaining her senses, she scolded herself inwardly. Marie had said nothing about the Duke de Corbay's being handsome or clean-shaven when Annique had asked about him. It was foolish to think, even for a moment, that he would be the one. And there was little profit in longing after what she couldn't have. Yet she couldn't keep her eyes from him. Dear heaven, but he was pleasing to look upon.

Annique assessed the two men beside him. She hoped her betrothed was the amiable-looking blond, rather than the short fellow with a high forehead and a petulant expression.

Across the room, Philippe and the others watched the slender young woman in matronly clothing move unsteadily toward them. Philippe could almost feel his family's eyes darting from him to the girl and back again, but he kept his features impassive and his focus on the young woman his father had chosen for him.

Patrice giggled behind her fan. "Goodness, take a look at those clothes!" She smiled wickedly. "How charming, Philippe. Obviously she's not a slave to fashion."

He narrowed his eyes the better to see across the candlelit room. Yes, her clothes were unfashionable, the colors drab, but there was something arresting about the girl. At least she had escaped the prominent Bourbon nose that distinguished so many of their relatives. He watched as she passed under the first chandelier, its light briefly and ominously shadowing her eyes. Perhaps that accounted for the impression of intensity she seemed to radiate.

As she drew closer, Philippe could make out russet highlights in her dark hair. Where had he seen that coloring before? He resurrected the memory of a certain ancestral portrait. Perhaps they shared the same Stuart great-grandmother.

The girl took a few more measured, uncertain steps, and her wide-set eyes came into focus. Brown or blue? She was too far away to tell. Yet almost against his will, he felt his own gaze drawn into hers. The sense of intensity seemed almost palpable now.

Philippe noted and analyzed every detail of her appearance. Her entire pattern of movement communicated fear cloaked with a thin veneer of bravado, like a virgin sacrifice on her way to a pagan altar. Instinctively, part of him wanted to reach out in protective reassurance. She looked so young, so vulnerable. But he knew better than to be taken in by appearances. Her terror might be born of conspiracy.

Was she his father's creature? Philippe searched the marshal's eyes, then looked back to the girl. No sign of complicity passed between them. No knowing looks, nor any equally telling failure to make eye contact. Perhaps she might be what she seemed, an innocent orphan from the provinces.

If only things could be that simple. But things were never simple when the marshal was involved.

Philippe's next appraising look was that of any man for the woman who would share his bed. Her ivory skin was unblemished. Her face was unexceptional—her mouth a bit too wide, her lower lip a bit too full, her well-defined chin hardly delicate—but the effect was not unpleasant.

Not beautiful, but not bad.

Just then the girl's heel caught on the edge of a carpet, and she barely managed to regain her balance. Philippe felt his own cheeks flush with embarrassment.

Was she halt, or merely clumsy? Such awkwardness would be an insufferable liability at Court.

Patrice tittered behind her fan again, causing him to stiffen. Philippe knew all too well what it was like to be the object of his family's scorn. Now they insulted him further with their open contempt for his betrothed. Plain and provincial though his fiancée might be, Anne-Marie de Bourbon-Corbay was soon to be his wife, a duchess of the realm, and as such she merited deference and tact, not ridicule.

Did the girl have any inkling of the nest of vipers that passed for a family at Maison d'Harcourt? He wondered, but ignored the sympathetic impulse that came with the thought.

Why should he feel sorry for her? She might prove to be as brittle and vicious as Patrice, or as thoughtless and vapid as his stepmother, Hélène.

Yet something undefinable told him she was not. Something in those fathomless eyes.

Philippe's thoughts were interrupted by Broussel's loud whisper to Antonin. "She walks as if she's fortified herself for this auspicious occasion with drink. That's just the way you move, Antonin, when you've had a few too many." A quelling glare from Philippe erased Broussel's grin, but there was precious little repentance in the man's sullen silence.

Abashed, Antonin offered, "Lovely girl, Philippe. Such a modest appearance. Quite refreshing in this day and age."

Philippe turned back to see his fiancée pause stiffly in front of his father. The marshal's introduction was openly condescending in tone. "My dear Hélène, may I present Anne-Marie de Bourbon-Corbay, our future daughter-in-law. Anne-Marie, my wife, the Duchess of Harcourt."

The girl dropped a clumsy curtsy. After the marshal presented her to Henri and Patrice, she curtsied again a little less awkwardly. When she rose, Philippe saw that her brown eyes were huge and liquid.

He'd seen that same wide-eyed, frozen look on a doe beset by hounds. The comparison was fitting in more ways than one. His fiancée moved and looked like some frightened woods creature, completely out of her element in the salon's ornate artifice.

Yet despite her fear, she projected a compelling presence. Her darting scrutiny was anything but random. She seemed to be absorbing everything, evaluating the currents around her even as she trembled before the assembled company. Philippe's instincts told him she possessed a keen intelligence, but there was no hint of cunning or malice in those eyes. Unaccountably, he thought of his little half sister, Elise. Strange. They were so different; Elise was springtime, fair as a day in May, and this one was all russet and ivory.

Annique knew the women had been whispering about her behind their fans, and there was no mistaking the marshal's condescending tone when he introduced her, but she was determined to maintain the illusion, at least, of dignity. Her first curtsy had been a disaster, but the second had come more easily. She wondered if there would ever be a time when she could comport herself with as much ease and assurance as the duchess and viscountess.

She saw the marshal turn toward the three men at the fireplace, and her curiosity almost overrode her fear. At last, the introduction she had been waiting for.

The marshal said, "Philippe, may I present your bride-to-be. Anne-Marie, my second son, the Duke de Corbay."

Heaven smiled as the tall, raven-haired soldier with deep blue eyes and a firm, clean-shaven chin stepped forward.

CHAPTER 8

*P*hilippe watched the look of apprehension in his fiancée's expression melt into one of patent relief. Her smile transformed her face from plain to almost pretty. He took her hand and bowed. "I have awaited this moment with great anticipation."

"As have I, your grace." The voice that answered made him think of autumn, its tone deep and full, its accent surprisingly cultured.

An almost imperceptible tremor accompanied the dry touch of her skin. The girl was obviously terrified. Philippe's answering stab of sympathy was tempered by consternation. Such open vulnerability would make her easy prey in the salons of Paris and at Court. Telling himself that he was only doing it to prevent his fiancée from embarrassing him further, he briefly tightened his fingers around hers in a subtle gesture of encouragement.

She seemed to understand. Her hand stilled, but in response to his penetrating stare, all expression disappeared from her eyes. The protective mechanism was one he knew well; he used it often himself. For the first time since he'd seen her, Philippe felt his interest sharpen. Finding out what hid behind that mask of modesty would provide a challenging diversion. He deliberately held her hand far longer than etiquette permitted.

Perhaps this courtship would be less of an ordeal than he had anticipated. He could swear that a subtle current coursed from her fingertips into his own.

The salon doors swung open. "Dinner is served."

At the butler's words the tremor returned, threatening to shake her hand from Philippe's grasp. He tightened his grip and guided her slowly across the room. She was so young. And if her table manners were as rustic as the rest of her, Patrice would slice the girl up and serve her as the main course.

Philippe had no intention of being made a laughing-stock. He murmured into Anne-Marie's ear, "Come, mademoiselle. I don't care what seating arrangement my stepmother has planned; we shall sit together. I refuse to be deprived of your company at dinner."

Annique heard his murmured invitation with immeasurable gratitude. She could face the ordeal ahead with some sense of courage now that she knew he wasn't going to abandon her at dinner.

As they entered the great hall, she was confronted with a forest of silver, porcelain, and delicate glassware on the long table. She halted abruptly, fear chasing away all she had learned in endless hours of manners training with Sister Jonah. But just when blind panic threatened to overtake her, she felt a slight pressure from the large, shapely hand that held her elbow. She looked into Philippe's riveting blue eyes and took strength from the determination she saw there.

The handsome young duke's voice was kind. "If anything tonight is not to your liking, mademoiselle, you have but to tell me, and I shall make it right."

There was a subtle stir among the footmen when he guided her to the seat of honor beside the marshal.

The marshal lowered himself ceremoniously into the ornate chair at the head of the table. He muttered dryly, "You've completely disrupted the seating arrangement, Philippe. We had planned to give Anne-Marie and Hélène a chance to chat tonight."

"I'm certain you and I can keep her adequately entertained, Father." Philippe's raised eyebrow corresponded to the half-smile that twisted his mouth. "After all, Anne-Marie is our guest of honor; we can't relegate her to the far end of the table." Ignoring the astonished footman who held his chair, Philippe deposited himself firmly beside her.

Though the marshal made no further protest, Annique noted a dangerous glitter in the look of reproach he shot his son. So *that* was how things stood. The two men obviously mistrusted—perhaps even detested—each other. Annique found the prospect promising, since she'd already developed a healthy dislike for the marshal herself. She and Philippe had that in common, if nothing else.

The stone inside her chest seemed to shrink a bit. Perhaps the son was *not* like the father, after all.

Then a fresh tide of humiliation overtook her. Though nothing in the handsome young duke's manner had betrayed his embarrassment, she was certain her rustic appearance and clumsy manners had disappointed him.

Hands clenched in her lap, she vowed not to give him further cause for shame—not tonight, at least. She looked aside to find him gazing at her as if she were the only woman in the room.

A tide of warmth spread from her bosom to the roots of her hairline. Flustered, she tried to divert his attention. "I understand that you enjoy hunting, your grace." Sister Jonah had said all men liked to talk of such things.

"Please call me Philippe."

"And I am Anni— . . . Anne-Marie."

With a sardonic smile, he responded, "Hunting's a thing better done than talked about." His gaze continued to devour her. "Do you enjoy hunting, Anne-Marie?"

Her name—still new to her—sounded like someone else's on his lips. And he'd asked about hunting. Would he be disappointed to discover she could hardly sit a horse? She dared not cover her ineptness with a convenient lie. So she told the truth. "I've never been hunting." Annique fought to keep the emotion from her voice. "I know almost nothing of your world, Philippe." His name felt alien on her own lips. "The convent where I grew up is a cloistered order. There was no hunting, only hard work and prayer and solitude." Self-consciously, she rubbed together the hands that were once roughened by toil.

His amusement changed to somber intensity. "Hard work and prayer—the noblest pursuits of all. Some people live a lifetime without learning either." Then his mood shifted, his sincerity replaced by a cynical grin that showed white, even teeth. "As for solitude, that's another matter." The smile didn't reach his eyes. "Being locked in a dovecote for days on end might provide a boy with solitude, but I'd call it torture."

Though his gaze never left her, Annique had the distinct impression the remark wasn't directed at her.

Philippe continued, "But then again, solitude can be most gratifying. When I was eight, I decided I'd had enough of nursemaids and tutors, so I ran away to the ruined west wing, taking only my favorite books, a flagon of wine, and a kerchief full of cheese and bread. I built a secret fortress there. No one found me for three whole days. That solitude was heaven."

Annique blinked. Books! He'd taken his books. Not only was her future husband elegant and handsome, but he liked books. And he didn't care to talk of hunting. A most exceptional man, if what Sister Jonah had told her about men had been right.

While Philippe elaborated on the anecdote, Annique tried not to stare openly at his brilliant, dark-blue eyes. They were the color of a December sky just past twilight, and it took all her self-control not to tumble past thick black lashes into their depths.

The man was perfect. At least, he seemed to be.

Then an inner whisper intruded like a sliver of blackness into the golden glow that surrounded her. She could almost hear Father Jules's voice. *Take care! Appearances mean nothing. How do you know what is in his heart?* The echo of that warning forced her to look at the young duke afresh. For just a moment, she saw the accomplished courtier whose polished exterior was as smooth and impenetrable as onyx.

"Is something wrong, Anne-Marie? You've suddenly gone pale." His concern seemed genuine.

Keeping her voice low, she used a half-truth to cover her lapse. "It's nothing. I'm just feeling a little nervous about dinner. This is my first evening in company."

Humor traced the deep creases of a thousand smiles at the corners of his eyes. He leaned close, his breath against her ear sending a tingle clear to the pit of her stomach. "Don't worry. Just watch me, and you won't go wrong."

His hair smelled of herbs and woodsmoke.

Despite a lifetime of protecting herself from disappointment, despite all of Father Jules's warnings, despite everything, Annique let go of objectivity to bask in the warmth of being wooed. Deep inside, a lonely, abandoned little girl reached out to the faint, shimmering hope that someone, at last, might want her.

Eight courses later, Philippe smiled at the wonder on Anne-Marie's face when she tasted the wine served with the fruit and cheese.

She whispered, "This one tastes like liquid sunshine."

He marveled at the accuracy of her statement. "I couldn't have put it better myself. Obviously you have a most discriminating palate."

All through dinner, her childlike appreciation for each morsel had made him see and taste the delicacies as if he, too, were experiencing them for the first time. Her innocence was most convincing, but he knew better than to accept it as truth. For the moment, he entertained only the possibility that she was as she appeared to be.

He lifted his wineglass. "I'm glad you like this vintage. You barely tasted the others."

"I'm not accustomed to so much wine." She drank more deeply of the golden liquid.

Philippe congratulated himself. It had taken some effort, but at last he had succeeded in putting his fiancée at ease, and the results were most gratifying. The fear in her big brown eyes had given way to a tentative trust. And the arrogance in his father's face had been replaced by irritation.

Good. Philippe wanted his father to think he was pleased with his bride-to-be. But no sooner had he begun to relax a bit, than the marshal fixed him with a challenging glare and loudly cleared his throat.

"Ahem. Antonin has most interesting news of the troubles at Orléans last week. I understand our Great Mademoiselle made quite a mess of things. What was it she did, Antonin? Swam the moat and single-handedly opened the gates for her troops? That's what the street ditties say."

Foreboding raised the hairs on the back of Philippe's neck. Had his father invited Antonin just to set up this conversation? Did the marshal know . . . ? But he *couldn't* know about the affair! It took every ounce of control for Philippe to maintain his cloak of *ennui*. He aimed a lazy smile at his father. "Really?"

Antonin always had been a talkative sort, given a few drinks and a little encouragement. Right now he seemed more than happy to be the center of attention. "She didn't swim the moat, but the truth is almost as preposterous." He paused for effect. "We all know her highness considers Orléans her own *personal* city. When she found out our regiments were headed in that general direction, she begged her father to intervene, but of course he wouldn't. Personally, I think Cardinal Retz has Monsieur Gaston so frightened he dares not stir from his own house."

The marshal's expression darkened, but Antonin kept talking. "Though General Turenne had no intention of taking the city, her highness appointed herself savior of Orléans. Frankly, were it not for her actions, I doubt we'd have marched within five miles of the place." His comment stirred a chorus of murmurs around the table. When they subsided, Antonin continued. "Our troops had scarcely entered the province when the Great Mademoiselle arrived at the gates of Orléans in her velvet riding habit. Her troops were right behind."

Philippe wasn't surprised to see that Patrice, Henri, Hélène, and Georges sat enthralled by Antonin's animated account. Such gossip was the very currency of Paris social life, and the city had talked of nothing else in the past week. But Anne-Marie's attention pivoted from Philippe to his father. Why wasn't she listening like the others?

The marshal never took his eyes off his second son.

Philippe should have known better than to let himself be lulled into a false sense of security. What trap had his father laid, and what was the girl's part in it?

Antonin's voice cut through his thoughts. "The princess met with the governor of Orléans and demanded entry into the city. I'm told the poor fellow gave her a box of sweets and begged her to withdraw, play sick, anything—just go away until our armies had gotten past. But she insisted he allow her and her men inside the walls to 'defend' the city."

The marshal snorted, his eyes leaving Philippe at last. "Pure mischief! The queen should have married off our hotheaded princess years ago!"

Antonin chuckled. "The story gets better. Despite the Great Mademoiselle's request, the gates were sealed. Furious, our princess rode up to the locked city gates and commanded the garrison to open up. They say she made quite an imposing figure. The citizens lined the walls and cheered her on with great waving of handkerchiefs, but the gates remained shut." He shook his head. "After consoling herself with the governor's candies for a few hours, she got back on her horse and rode along the walls, only two of her ladies and a single guard in attendance. All the while, she shouted accusations about Mazarin and praises for the king. What a sight that must have been!"

He took a deep draught of wine, then went on dramatically. "The people on the battlements cheered her and His Majesty, and denounced Mazarin. Their cries made her more determined than ever. She whipped the mob to a frenzy. Fearful of the citizenry, the garrison opened the outer gate. But when her highness found the inner gate still sealed tight, she was forced to retreat. Frustrated, our

Great Mademoiselle went back across the bridge and paced along the edge of the river on foot, her ladies complaining all the time that their slippers were ruined by the mud and their feet hurt."

This elicited a derisive chortle from Henri and Georges Broussel.

Antonin became even more expansive. "There they were, trekking about in the mud, when two fishermen who had been watching from the river rowed over and offered to take her highness across to the quay and show her a way into the city." He tapped his head knowingly. "Clever woman, our princess. Taking only a footman with her, she paid the fishermen a purse of gold and treated them like the noblest knights of the realm. All this in front of the populace. No wonder the common people love her. What a show."

Patrice leaned back in exasperation, her words dripping venom. "She always *was* good at putting on a show. But that's all it is, you know. She's not so clever, really. And the woman doesn't know the meaning of propriety."

As if Patrice *did!* Philippe bestowed a sarcastic smile on his sister-in-law.

Antonin leaned back into his chair. "I dare not comment on her highness's propriety, but—much as I hate to admit it—I can't help admiring the lady's courage."

The marshal scowled. "Courage? Hardly. *Foolishness* would be a more accurate assessment. Or stupidity."

Antonin shrugged. "Maybe. But if that is so, then our princess is the luckiest woman alive, for things always seem to go her way."

The cleverness of the retort caught Philippe by surprise. Perhaps Antonin was neither as innocent nor as thick as he appeared.

With that, general discussion erupted, the marshal taking Antonin to task while Patrice and Henri discussed the princess' shortcomings.

Philippe's intimate knowledge of the Great Mademoiselle lent a special irony to what he was hearing. The princess, vain? Yes. Hotheaded? Undeniably. Courageous? Absolutely. Stupid? No. He was acutely aware that the Great Mademoiselle's every move—at Orléans and elsewhere—had been chosen for its effect. What he *didn't* know was whether her wit was the result of instinct or calculation.

And he didn't know what was behind this conversation.

Anne-Marie had gone deadly still.

Hélène shifted uncomfortably. "Gentlemen, I caution you to remember we are discussing a lady of great influence, linked to us by blood. Let us not be unkind."

Simple, bovine Hélène. Philippe had long suspected that the marshal had chosen her as companion for his final years precisely because of her guileless lack of perception.

Patrice's fan snapped shut. "You haven't finished your story, Antonin. What happened next?"

"The Great Mademoiselle scrambled in a most undignified fashion up the ladder to the quay, only to find that the only way through the wall was a rough hole in the river gate."

The two women exchanged surprised glances. The image Antonin conjured up hardly matched the princess's notoriously elevated opinion of her personal dignity. Hélène leaned forward, her eyes wide. "She actually climbed the ladder in front of everyone, showed her legs to the whole regiment?"

Antonin nodded. "After she got to her feet on the dock, she joked with the onlookers about the comedy of her situation. Then she pulled off her bonnet and stuck her head through the hole in the gate. The soldiers on the other side tugged her through, to the accompaniment of a drum tattoo and much merrymaking. Once she was inside, the people set her upon a chair, paraded her through the streets, showered her with flowers, and opened the gates to her troops."

Georges was unconvinced. "Who can believe such a preposterous thing? We've all heard rumors, but *this* account is fantastic."

A less affable man would have called him out for such a remark, but Antonin ignored the insult. "I was present when the governor related the incident to General Turenne. And all of Orléans swears to it!"

Then the other shoe dropped. The marshal blinked lazily before asking, "Why don't we ask Philippe what *he* thinks of the story. He, of all people, should know whether it's accurate."

No one else at the table seemed to know what the marshal was talking about. Philippe yawned behind his napkin, then responded indifferently. "I haven't been near Orléans for years. I get my news of the campaigns from gossip and street ditties just like the rest of you do."

The marshal's eyes darkened. "I understood you to have a more . . . *intimate* source."

Blast! Somehow his father had found out about the affair. Philippe kept his expression blank. The marshal couldn't possibly have proof of the liaison; Philippe had ended it weeks ago, and he knew the princess would never talk. She'd die before admitting she'd been rejected. "Sorry to disappoint you, Father, but I have no idea what you mean."

He turned his attention to Anne-Marie, whose brows were drawn together in confusion. Perhaps she didn't know. "Come, my dear Anne-Marie. Suddenly there seems to be a draft in here. Allow me to escort you to the salon."

This breach of etiquette succeeded in silencing even the marshal. After a helpless glance around the table, Anne-Marie nodded toward their host and hostess as she rose. "Please excuse us, your graces. Dinner was most enjoyable." She turned to Antonin. "And the discussion was most informative." She took Philippe's proffered arm and accompanied him out of the room. The moment they crossed the threshold, an angry buzz of conversation erupted behind them.

Annique waited until they were safely out of earshot to ask, "Are all dinner parties like this one?"

As he had all evening, Philippe seemed pleasantly surprised at her directness. "Only in this house. I hope our suppers will be more peaceful affairs."

She glanced back into the great hall. "Perhaps they will be, as long as it's just the two of us."

His surprise escaped in a delighted, "Ha!"

Annique avoided the open curiosity in his eyes. Instead, she turned to gather one more vivid impression of the tumult in the other room.

So this was her new family. Hardly what she had hoped for as a child or dreamed of during the long, dangerous journey from the south.

If secrets could be seen, the air of Maison d'Harcourt would be black with them.

She pivoted to look her future husband full in the face. She could sense that Philippe had secrets of his own.

But then again, so did she.

❊ CHAPTER 9 ❊

*A*nnique limped into her bedchamber. "Marie! Where are you?" She flopped onto a footstool. "Saints! These wretched shoes are pinching like demons."

"Here I am, mademoiselle." Marie hurried from the dressing room. "Is something the matter? I didn't expect you back from dinner so early."

Annique tugged off her slippers and rubbed her aching toes to bring back the circulation. "The evening *did* seem to end rather abruptly, but by then my feet hurt so much I didn't really mind." She paused and leveled a mildly accusing look at her maid. "Why didn't you *tell* me the Duke of Corbay was such a beautiful man?"

"Sorry, mademoiselle," Marie hastened to apologize, but her mischievous smile said she was anything but sorry. "How could I know mademoiselle would find his grace handsome? After all, he doesn't look like the other gentlemen."

"No, he doesn't look like the other gentlemen." Annique's insides shivered deliciously at the indelible impression of Philippe's handsome, clean-shaven face and his remarkable coloring.

Yet there was darkness in the depths of those brilliant blue eyes. And despite his offhand manner, Philippe's cynicism was as sharp as the exquisitely wrought golden dagger he wore.

He was beautiful . . . and dangerous.

She shivered again, this time from a provocative mixture of excitement and dread. "His grace is different, and I'm glad. *I'm* different, too—not like all those other elegant ladies." She offered Marie an ironic smile. "I felt so clumsy, so unsure of myself." She knew the ladies had laughed at her behind their fans, but Philippe had treated her like a queen despite her lapses.

Though she had enjoyed his attentiveness, Annique was glad that the evening was over. Had she not been so tightly trussed, she would have let out a deep sigh of relief. As it was, she struggled to her feet, suddenly feeling trapped. "Whew! This bodice is about to squeeze the life from me. Get me out of it before I faint."

She sucked in and stood very straight to make it easier for Marie to unfasten the hooks and laces, but her thoughts reverted to Philippe. "I'm glad the duke doesn't have a beard. He looks just the way I always imagined Marc Antony would have."

"Marc Antony?"

The moment the words were out, Annique realized she had said too much. "Never mind. Please hurry, Marie. I'm seeing sparkles." After the last bodice hook surrendered, she tore the hated garment from her, almost ripping the deep cuff off her sleeve in the process. "I vow, I'll never get used to such a brutal contraption. It isn't sensible to wear such clothing."

Marie's fingers moved nimbly to undo the skirt fastenings that still imprisoned her mistress. *"Fashion* and *sensible* are two words that don't go together, mademoiselle."

Annique struggled with the buttons of her sheer blouse. "After dinner the viscountess pretended to compliment my dress, but it was easy enough to see that my clothes are all wrong. Then the Duchess of Harcourt told me her dressmakers would be arriving tomorrow to fit me for a *proper* wardrobe. I was so embarrassed. But monsieur le duc took my hand and told me that the color of my gown set off my beautiful hair." The memory of his compliment trickled through her like warm honey.

Annique's underskirt crumpled stiffly to the floor. She stepped across the fabric, oblivious to the imprints of her stockinged feet on the silk. Her mind was on other things. She crossed to the mirror and stood before it. Her fingers touched the cluster of curls at her ear. "My fiancé, Philippe, Duke of Corbay, said my hair was beautiful."

The next morning Annique awoke to a gentle tugging on her long braid. She opened her eyes to see two plump little hands stroking the thick plait that trailed across her pillow.

A rosy-cheeked little girl with golden curls peeked over the side of the bed. After inspecting Annique's hair more closely, she declared, "It doesn't look so very red to me."

Annique reached out to touch the child's halo of blond curls. "And who are you?"

A dimple punctuated the little girl's cheek. "My name is Elise, but *Maman* calls me Lili." She propped her chin on the coverlet. "What does your *maman* call you?"

So this was Philippe's half sister. Annique felt as if a bluebird had lighted on the edge of her bed. She spoke softly, so as not to frighten her charming little visitor away. "I haven't got a mother. She died when I was very small."

"Poor mam'selle." The child's blue eyes became large and liquid. "Philippe's *maman* died when he was small, too." She brightened. "But now he has mine instead." Elise paused, then added emphatically, "When you marry Philippe, you can have my *maman,* too. I'm sure she won't mind, even if she *did* say you walked funny and your hair was too red."

After last night, the words came as no surprise, but they still had the power to sting. In spite of that, Annique couldn't help smiling at the prospect of calling the young duchess *"maman."* "I don't think your mother would like it if I called her *maman."* Not that it wouldn't serve her right, after the woman's backhanded compliments and bewildered condescension at dinner. "But thank you very much for offering to share her."

Annique pulled herself to a sitting position and patted the mattress. "Come sit with me, Elise." She had never been so close to a clean, healthy child. The ones at the convent hospital had always been sick or dirty, or both. Elise smelled of soap and roses. With a great rustling of skirts and petticoats, the toddler scrambled onto the bed and curled up beside Annique as if they were sisters, indeed.

Annique asked, "How old are you?"

Elise carefully tucked her index finger behind her thumb and extended three plump digits toward Annique. "I have this many years, but soon I shall get another finger. Very soon, and Philippe has promised to bring me a present."

"You like Philippe, don't you?"

"Yes. He comes to see me often when *Maman* and Papa are away. Nanny likes Philippe, too, 'cause he's a real gen'lman." She plucked at her stockings and rocked back and forth. "Philippe says he's my very truly brother, and I'm his special princess and very best sister." The dimple appeared again as the little girl unselfconsciously stroked smooth the intricate tatting across the front of Annique's nightgown. Then a cloud crossed her fair face. "When you marry Philippe, will you be his best sister, instead of me?"

Annique gave Elise's small hand a reassuring kiss. "Don't worry. You may be his best sister and special princess forever and ever. I shall only be his wife."

Elise considered for a moment, then broke into a smile. "That's what *maman* said to Papa, that you would only be Philippe's wife, but I was afraid you'd be his best sister, too."

Only his wife . . . The words settled like a stone in Annique's heart. Last night had shaken her illusions about finally becoming a part of a real family, but the innocent words of this child killed what little hope remained. *Only his wife.* The duchess was probably complaining to the marshal even now about Annique's shortcomings.

Elise cradled Annique's cheeks in her soft little hands and offered, "Don't be sad, mam'selle. You can be his best sister sometimes. I won't mind."

Surprising both of them, tears sprang to Annique's eyes. She hugged Elise and fought to control the emotions that had surged to the surface. "Thank you, precious." She smiled and wiped her eyes. "But I should like it even better if I could be your friend."

Elise frowned and knitted her brows. "I don't think so."

"Why not?"

Chubby fingers toyed with the blue ribbon that laced Annique's gown. "I don't know your name. Nanny says friends must be presented. I presented my name, but you didn't present yours back."

"Silly me." Annique stroked a blond curl from the child's high forehead. "I forgot to introduce myself. My name is Annique—" She corrected herself, savoring the sound of her own voice saying her name. "I mean, Anne-Marie Celeste de Bourbon-Corbay. You may call me Anne."

The child nodded gravely and murmured a stilted, "Enchanted." Then she wiggled free of Annique's arms and slid off the feather bed. "I like Annique better."

"Very well. That can be our secret friendship name, but only when there are no other grown-ups around. The rest of the time you must call me Anne. Agreed?"

"Yes, mam'selle Annique." Elise skipped toward the hallway. "Good-bye, friend."

"Visit me again soon."

Annique waved as the tall door closed. Alone once more, she absently stroked her braid and sighed. *Such a sweet child.* The little girl couldn't possibly have been aware of the cruelties she had unwittingly repeated.

A reassuring thought eased Annique's feelings. Elise had been the innocent bearer of Philippe's words, as well—words that revealed a tender side to the man who was to be her husband and, God willing, father of her children.

Annique glanced down at the dark auburn plait that trailed over her shoulder. So the mistress of Maison d'Harcourt thought her future daughter-in-law was clumsy and her hair was too red. Annique didn't care. Elise's special prince and best brother had said Annique's hair was beautiful, and that was all that mattered.

Two and a half weeks later, Annique could scarcely believe how quickly the time had passed. Seventeen hectic mornings had been filled with fittings, riding lessons, or dance lessons. Afternoons were spent in endless social calls with Hélène or Patrice. And every night was taken up with receptions, balls, and late suppers that lasted until dawn.

No wonder she felt exhausted. She'd barely had time to change her clothes between engagements. Now only two days more remained before her wedding.

Tonight's ball would be the last, except for the final celebration tomorrow night at Maison d'Harcourt, and then—after one blessed day's respite—the ceremony.

Annique held onto Philippe's arm as they followed Hélène up the sweeping stairway toward the grand ballroom of Hôtel de Bouillon. She stifled a yawn, then whispered, "I'm so sorry, Philippe. I had no idea I'd fall sound asleep after Hélène and I returned from our calls. It's my fault we're late." She sighed. "From the day I arrived, it seems I've done nothing but say the wrong things and make mistakes. No wonder I wasn't brought to Paris sooner."

As usual, Philippe was ready with a smooth but superficial response. "Don't be so hard on yourself, Anne-Marie.

From the moment we met, I've found your company both interesting and amusing."

The right words seemed to come so easily to this man who would soon be her husband, but lately Annique had come to wonder if he ever *meant* what he said. She wished she had a better feel for the real man beneath Philippe's seamless manners. For seventeen days he had been patient, attentive, amusing, and unfailingly kind. Why wasn't that enough? Why did it matter so much to her that he was still a stranger?

Perhaps she was foolish to want more. After the ceremony there would be a lifetime to get to know each other.

The strain of the social whirl could be heard in Hélène's voice. "Do hurry, children. Thank heaven the queen and his majesty are still in St. Germain. It would be unforgivable to have kept her majesty waiting. Bad enough that you're the honored guests and last to arrive."

"I'm going as fast as I dare, Hélène." Annique knew all too well why her shoes were called slippers, and marble stairways still merited slow, careful progress. The last thing she needed tonight was to slip and end up flat on her face. Their tardiness was embarrassing enough. "I'll explain to the Duchess of Bouillon why we're late."

Hélène stopped on the top stair and clasped her fan in exasperation. "You shall do no such thing. Just smile and act as if nothing were amiss." She rolled her eyes toward Philippe and murmured, "Will she *never* understand how one deals with such matters?"

A lazy smile curled Philippe's chiseled lips. "Don't worry, Hélène. Most of your crowd is still at St. Germain with his majesty and the queen. They'll never know we were late. As for those people waiting in the ballroom, I'll wager that the majority of them are Frondeurs, and I know you don't care what they think."

"Philippe, you are too wicked for words." Flat-mouthed, Hélène motioned them to her side for the presentation. "Don't you dare bring up that wretched rebellion tonight."

He winked slyly. "Of course not. It wouldn't be polite. And since manners seem to be the only thing holding France together at the moment, far be it from me to tip the balance by speaking the truth." He stood between the two women and offered an arm to each. "Come, ladies. Time for another night on the *real* battlefield—the ballrooms of Paris."

As usual, the reference flew over Hélène's head, but not over Annique's. A formidable wit was not the least of Philippe's attributes.

Hélène didn't see things that way. "Philippe, you are such a rascal."

Annique smiled. *He is a rascal! And I'm glad.*

As they entered the ballroom, Hélène gasped and whispered, "Would you look! The receiving line has already dispersed. I vow, I don't know how I'll hold my head up after this." Her fan fluttered up and down as rapidly as a dragonfly's wing.

Philippe kept smiling and murmured under his breath, "Calm down, Hélène, and for heaven's sake, stop that flapping."

The herald rapped his staff on the floor and announced, "The Duchess of Harcourt, the Duke of Corbay, Mademoiselle Bourbon-Corbay."

With Hélène on one arm and Annique on the other, Philippe directed the two women toward their hosts. The enormous chamber before them resounded with music and the lilting cadence of genteel laughter and conversation.

Annique clutched his arm, a now-familiar rush of excitement coursing through her. No matter how weary or frightened she might be, no matter how out of place she might feel, the sight of such a grand assembly stirred her to her very soul. In contrast to the stark simplicity of the convent, the opulence of the Court seemed like stepping into heaven itself. Beneath frescoed ceilings framed in gilded plaster, a thousand crystal prisms reflected the light of hundreds of candles. On the intricate parquet, scores of dancers bowed and shifted like exquisite flowers gently buffeted by a spring breeze. The air was redolent with a hundred exotic perfumes. Hovering over it all was the heady scent of power and intrigue.

Everything was beautiful, yet nothing was as it seemed. Meticulous inanity masked ravenous ambition, and a glittering shell of gaiety covered the throbbing heartbeat of a civilization in the throes of change. For all its grandeur and ceremony, the Court was really just a huge family of constantly plotting, incessantly arguing cousins. The stakes—whether personal or political—were high, and the drama was played out for anyone who had the patience and the keenness to watch. Annique had both.

Now as Philippe guided her toward their hosts, she smiled and nodded, reserving her true attention for the ebb and whorl of conversation that flowed about her. Who spoke to whom. Who avoided whom. A look, a word, the lack of a word: Annique missed nothing.

She couldn't help wondering if behind the other guests' carefree smiles and easy manners, they were watching as closely as she. The thought sent a provocative tingle through her.

Philippe's voice reached her ear. "It seems odd to me that a shy girl like you should come alive the way you do at such functions. Your eyes begin to sparkle the moment we walk in. If I didn't know better, I'd swear you liked these stuffy, boring affairs."

Stuffy? How could such splendor be considered stuffy? Philippe had said it himself: This was the real battlefield of France. Annique *did* come alive here, fed by the undercurrent of desperate energy just below the surface.

An enigmatic smile teased her lips. If her future husband had even an inkling of what went through her mind, he'd send her straight back to the convent, marriage contract or no.

Annique's smile stiffened as they approached the Duchess of Bouillon. Judging from the look of icy politeness on her face, their hostess had indeed taken offense at their lateness, but in true Court fashion, she said nothing about it. Her greeting wasn't cold; it simply wasn't warm. "Ah, Hélène, there you are." The duchess squeezed Hélène's hand, then dropped it. "And dear Philippe. How handsome you look tonight." She turned to bestow a bored, but faintly indulgent nod on Annique. "And here is our blushing bride-to-be. Charming." She shooed Philippe in Annique's direction. "I think everyone else is already here, and I know they're all eager to say hello. Why don't you two stroll around a bit while Hélène and I chat?"

Her ears burning from the veiled reference to their lateness, Annique took Philippe's arm and gratefully escaped. After what seemed like hours of greetings and small talk, Philippe turned to her, a look of genuine relief on his face. "There. We've said hello to everyone, from the most powerful prince to the lowliest viscountess and marquis. At last we are free to dance." He offered his arm. "Shall we?"

"I'd like that." She followed him onto the gleaming parquet. Sometime during the past three weeks, she had actually come to enjoy the intricate steps and pantomimes of the dance. Nimbler but numb, her feet no longer occupied all her concentration.

Philippe circled with measured pace to the music. "Having a good time?"

Trying not to lose count, she answered, without meaning to, in the same cadence as the stately beat of the melody. "Yes. Now that I'm more accustomed to my new shoes, I'm not even afraid to dance. I haven't bumped into anyone in quite a while."

He sobered. "You've mastered many things since we met. I suspect that there is far more to Mademoiselle Anne-Marie than she would have us all think."

Her step faltered slightly, but she didn't lose her place. Annique's gaze met his squarely. "And what if there *were* more to me than I have shown? How would that make you feel?"

Danger flashed in his deep blue eyes, despite the challenging smile that lifted one corner of his mouth. "If that were true, then I'd keep my feelings to myself."

The music stopped.

Philippe guided her toward the far side of the room. "Let's get a breath of air. It's bound to be cooler over by the terrace." A gentle stirring of April breeze met them at the open doorway, but he stopped short of the threshold.

Annique sank gratefully onto an upholstered bench. She scanned the crowd. "Has there been a recent development in the rebellion?"

"Not that I know of." Philippe frowned, his eyes narrowing. "Why do you ask?"

She could see her question piqued his interest. Annique made a mental note to add unpredictability to the list of things that captured her future husband's curiosity. If she played her cards right, perhaps that spark of interest would grow into a friendship.

She paused deliberately, her eyes sweeping the room. "I detect a certain tension tonight—almost a brittleness, like something about to shatter."

He arched an eyebrow, looking at her long and hard

before responding. "Yes. I can sense it, too. But I've heard nothing new about the Fronde."

Just then the herald rapped his staff on the floor and announced, "Her royal highness, the Great Mademoiselle."

A collective intake of breath was followed by dead silence.

Annique, like everyone else in the room, was stunned by the unexpected appearance. The heroine of the Fronde, here? The princess hadn't been seen in public since her escapade at Orléans! Her presence elevated what would have been a routine social event to the highlight of Annique's prenuptial celebrations.

As if on cue the guests stepped back, clearing a wide pathway to the arched opening where the herald stood. Annique rose, her gaze, along with two hundred others, riveted to the doorway. And then the Great Mademoiselle was there, her face framed by a shining riot of golden blond hair. The princess's slightest movement released a glimmering explosion of light from the diamonds gracing her fingers, wrists, necklace, and coronet. Gold embroidery encrusted the red satin of her gown, and across her milky bosom cascaded rubies the size of ripe cherries framed in diamonds.

The Great Mademoiselle. Princess of the blood royal. The wealthiest, most highborn Frenchwoman in the realm. The woman behind the legend was no disappointment. Everything about her was larger than life. Her lush figure swelled above the low bodice of her gown, and her strong profile testified to the Bourbon heritage that had governed the throne for centuries.

Her very presence held the entire assembly captive. Shoulders back, chin high, she stood like a goddess, a creature more than human and supremely conscious of her power. Then at the last possible moment, she broke the spell and began a measured progress into the waiting, breathless crowd.

Abruptly, conversation resumed, its tight buzz moving through the assembly like a swarm of bees through an orchard.

Even Annique's active imagination had never conjured up such a regal presence. Excitement resonating in her whisper, she reached out and touched Philippe's arm.

"She's coming this way, Philippe. I can't believe I might actually meet her."

"Um."

The single syllable was thick with import, pulling Annique's attention from the princess to Philippe's face. All the life had drained away. His pleasant expression congealed. She whispered, "Philippe, are you ill?"

He gazed at the princess. "I'm fine."

Annique remembered Antonin's tale of the Great Mademoiselle and the tension his story had inspired. That night she had been too nervous to understand the significance behind the marshal's insinuations and Philippe's abrupt departure from the table, but now she had an inkling that all was not well between Philippe and the princess. One look at him told her something was about to happen, and it wasn't something good.

Philippe bowed stiffly. "Allow me to fetch you some punch." He stalked away toward the refreshments.

Was he trying to avoid the Great Mademoiselle? Annique watched him smile and nod to those around him as he downed several servings of sparkling wine. She'd never seen him drink so much so quickly. When he returned with her punch, he failed to look her in the eye for the first time since he'd met her. He thrust the cup into her hand, saying, "I suggest you drink this slowly. It's quite potent."

She took a sip, then leaned into his field of vision. "Perhaps we should leave."

His head snapped around. "Why do you say that?"

Speaking quietly so no one could overhear, she took a chance on honesty. "I may be naive, but I'm not stupid. Obviously the Duchess de Montpensier's presence disturbs you. Avoidance can be a most effective tactic when dealing with relationships."

A rakish grin splashed the tension from his expression. "Anne-Marie, how you continue to surprise me." His eyes searched the sea of faces beyond her shoulder. "I'm inclined to agree. In this case, avoidance would work to both our advantages. Perhaps we could slip out one of the side entrances. But I don't want to compromise your reputation. Wait here while I collect Hélène."

Too late, he turned to find the Great Mademoiselle and Hélène standing right behind him.

Annique rose and executed a deep curtsy.

In the blink of an eye, Philippe became once more the smooth courtier. "Your royal highness, may I present my fiancée, Anne-Marie de Bourbon-Corbay. Anne-Marie, the Great Mademoiselle."

Annique straightened before the royal personage. At little more than five feet tall, the princess was half a head shorter than she, yet the difference in their heights wasn't what Annique noticed most. It was the Great Mademoiselle's pale blue eyes—not their color, but their unmistakably territorial gleam.

Suddenly in Annique's mind the jumble of unexplained remarks and odd reactions about the Great Mademoiselle sorted themselves into place like pieces of a puzzle. The picture that materialized was devastating.

The princess and Philippe!

She felt as if she had slammed headlong into a granite wall. Breathing took a conscious effort. In. Out. Mustn't let her feelings show. In. Out. Face calm, eyes level.

What a naive fool she had been to hope that one day she might win Philippe's friendship, even his affection. She had never once considered that his heart might already have been claimed, and by a magnificent vision such as this! How could she possibly compete with the bravest, most popular woman in Paris?

The Great Mademoiselle spoke. "What a charming girl, Philippe." Under a thick dusting of golden lashes, her cold eyes narrowed. "I always enjoy meeting a cousin. But then, it's a frequent pleasure. We seem to have so many."

Annique's self-pity evaporated. She bristled in response, her direct gaze challenging the princess's. "I am honored to meet the heroine of Orléans. Your highness's courage is legend."

Flattery had little effect. The Great Mademoiselle's smile was anything but warm. *"Noblesse oblige."* She glanced at Philippe. "You say her name is Anne-Marie? How droll. We have those two names in common. I wonder what else we share."

Dark spots of red appeared on Philippe's high cheekbones.

Puzzled, Hélène interjected, "I beg your pardon, your highness?"

Annique felt her own cheeks grow warm. There was no mistaking the possessive way the Great Mademoiselle looked at Philippe. Abruptly, dismay gave way to smoldering fury. The princess could choose from the most eligible suitors in Europe! Why would she set her cap for a man who was already promised?

Suddenly Annique became aware of the deep creases beside the princess's mouth and the heavy coating of powder on the woman's skin. A closer look revealed that the glow on her rounded cheeks came from a paint pot, not from nature. Royal princess though she might be, the Great Mademoiselle was well past the bloom of youth and took great pains to hide the fact. The woman was years older than Annique and looked it!

Impulsively seizing that one advantage, Annique leveled a stinging reference to the princess's advanced years. "I am privileged to share two of your highness's Christian names. Perhaps my mother named me in your honor."

The Great Mademoiselle's features congealed, and Annique wished immediately that she could call the words back. She had just declared war on the wealthiest, most powerful woman in France.

Philippe shot Annique a look of shocked amusement and coughed.

After a pregnant pause, the Great Mademoiselle turned grimly to Hélène. "I understand Philippe is to be married day after tomorrow. I don't recall receiving my invitation to the wedding."

A strangled squeak escaped Hélène's lips, followed by, "They were sent weeks ago, your highness. Perhaps yours was mislaid at the palace." Philippe's eyes widened slightly as she went on. "I'll send a messenger with another tomorrow."

Annique inhaled sharply. The Great Mademoiselle, gloating at her wedding to Philippe, making a mockery of the solemn sacrament? A wave of outrage threatened to rip away her veneer of calmness. She had to bite the inside of her cheek to retain her self-control.

Hélène's prodding brought her back to the conversation. "Her highness has extended a most generous invitation, Anne-Marie. Have you no response?"

A rush of heat crept up Annique's neck. She lied without thinking. "I'm sorry. The music was so loud I couldn't hear."

"I said that there is an opening in my retinue." The princess's pale blue eyes glittered with amusement. "I wish for you to attend me at Court after your honeymoon."

His voice oddly tight, Philippe said, "Your highness is too kind, but I have no idea when we'll return. I have planned a lengthy voyage after the wedding."

The princess closed her fan and gave Annique's shoulder a less-than-gentle tap. "I shall hold the position open. Any time will suit. But the moment you're back in Paris, dear Anne-Marie, I shall expect you at my apartments in the Tuileries. See that she doesn't forget, Philippe."

A malicious smile tugged at her lips. "As to a wedding gift . . . I'd like to give Anne-Marie something special." She shot a pointed look at Philippe. "Something *memorable*. I'll have it sent over tomorrow. Be sure our bride-to-be opens it immediately." She glided away without a backward glance.

The moment the Great Mademoiselle was out of earshot, Philippe turned to Annique with a sardonic grin. "Though I cannot say what you've just done is prudent, allow me to compliment your courage."

Hélène collapsed on the bench behind them, her fan pumping. "And I invited her to the wedding!" She looked up. "Of course, she left me little choice. What else could I do?"

Though Annique's hands had gone cold, inside she was boiling. Princess or no princess, how dare that imperious creature humiliate her so? She opened her own fan and employed it briskly.

Hélène's lower lip trembled. "The marshal will be furious when he hears I've invited the princess of the rebels to the wedding. Oh, why couldn't she have stayed in Orléans?"

Philippe patted Hélène's shoulder in consolation. "Our Great Mademoiselle is famous for turning up where she's not welcome. I doubt she had an invitation, tonight." He offered Annique a rueful grin. "She probably would have attended the wedding, anyway, just to steal the attention from Anne-Marie for putting her down so elegantly."

Annique noticed their little drama had become the center of attention. Everyone was staring. Only then did she realize the grave consequences of her actions.

As if he had read her thoughts, Philippe asked quietly,

"My dear Anne-Marie, do you have any idea what you've just done?"

She retorted, "A better question might be, do *you* have any idea what's just been done to *me?*" Though she sounded confident, she didn't feel it. How could she have spoken so rashly? She must have been mad to forget Sister Jonah's cautions and everything Father Jules had taught her!

In only two sentences, Annique had dug her social grave with her own tongue.

She took a shaky step toward the bench. "Move over please, Hélène. I'm feeling weak in the knees."

❈ CHAPTER 10 ❈

*P*en poised, the Great Mademoiselle stared at the blank card before her and carefully weighed the words she must write. She glanced at the open box lying on the settee. "Be sure it's not wrinkled, Nourrie. I don't want her to suspect."

The nursemaid smoothed a careful fold. "The gown's not wrinkled, your highness. And I've sponged off the spots. It hardly looks worn at all."

"Just so it's wearable for tonight." Louise turned her attention back to the enclosure card and wrote, "Please accept this gift, along with my felicitations for your coming marriage. This gown is unique, especially appropriate for Philippe's bride. I would consider your wearing it to the ball tonight a personal favor." She signed it with a flourish: "Anne-Marie Louise Therese, Duchess of Montpensier."

That should do it. Philippe's fiancée would comply, even though—from everything Louise had heard—the girl probably wouldn't realize the distinctive gown was secondhand, one the princess had worn on a particularly memorable evening only a few months ago.

But Philippe would recognize the dress, as would most of the Court, providing a most amusing retribution for the bumpkin's sly reference to Louise's age.

The feathered tip of Louise's quill tickled a smile from her lips. She couldn't wait to see the look on Philippe's face when his plain, scrawny bride-to-be appeared in front

of everyone in the same dress his royal lover had worn the
first night they'd consummated their liaison. The same
dress Philippe had removed, ribbon by ribbon and hook by
hook, from her willing, voluptuous body.

"Mademoiselle, look what's been delivered!" The highly
polished, flat wooden box was almost too long for Marie to
carry. She laid it on the bed.

Brushing away the last crumbs of the lunch she'd eaten
in her room, Annique crossed to the bed and ran her fingers over the box's glassy finish. "Who's it from?"

Marie shrugged. "The messenger didn't say. And he
wasn't wearing livery."

"Maybe there's a card inside." With Marie peering over
her shoulder, Annique raised the lid. Both women gasped
aloud at what lay inside.

Marie uttered, "Would you look at that!"

Nestled in the box's moire satin lining was the most
beautiful dress Annique had ever seen. The gown's translu-
cent collar rose a full twelve inches in the back to provide a
delicate shell that would frame the wearer's face. As if a
giant butterfly had neatly nibbled six perfect, even bites
around the collar's edge, six arcs met in seven graceful
points, a huge teardrop-shaped freshwater pearl dangling
from each point. The effect was magical.

Annique reached out to touch the dress, but drew back.
"Bring me a basin and a towel, Marie. I want to wash my
hands." That done, she reverently lifted the dress halfway
out of the box.

"Oh, mademoiselle. It's fit for a queen," Marie murmured.

The gown was unusual, constructed in one piece; no un-
derblouse was needed. Its tapered leg-of-mutton sleeves
were sewn in, as were the collar and softly gathered skirt.
Seed pearls and tiny crystals covered the supple white
faille, reflecting a hint of soft peach one moment and sil-
very gray the next. The luminous effect reminded Annique
of the rare dusting of snow that had surprised the convent
only twice in her lifetime.

Marie stood on tiptoe in her excitement. "Is there a card
to tell who it's from?"

Annique retrieved the enclosure card and read it. The

elegantly penned words turned her awe to foreboding. "It's from the Great Mademoiselle."

"The Great Mademoiselle?" Marie's mouth dropped open.

Rereading the card, Annique said, "Yes. I met her last night." She drew the gown from its resting place as if she expected a scorpion to fall from its folds. "Her highness wants me to wear this tonight."

There was no scorpion, only the strong scent of the princess's distinctive perfume. Annique wondered wryly if the Great Mademoiselle had marked the dress with her unmistakable scent as a not-so-subtle reminder of the gift's source. Despite the gown's donor and its unusual design, Annique was captivated by the exquisite creation. Then she held the dress up against her.

Marie put a hand to her lips. "Oh, dear. It's too short. And too wide."

The waistline stopped short at Annique's ribs, and the bodice's cut was generous even for her own substantial bosom. And though the skirt now hung like a slender, fluted column to the floor, the addition of petticoats would leave Annique looking as if she were expecting a flood—or wearing a shorter sister's castoff.

"Dear Heaven, Marie, what shall I do? The princess's note 'requests' that I wear the gown tonight as a personal favor. I dare not refuse; that would be an unthinkable affront. But the dress is too short by inches. If I wear any petticoats, everyone will be able to see halfway up my calves!" She grasped at a slender thread of hope. "Perhaps it's a new style, meant to be worn without petticoats."

Marie's mouth puckered into a skeptical frown. "No petticoats? I've never heard of such a thing."

"You're right. All the ladies wear petticoats." Annique held the dress up against her again. Her reflection in the mirror merely confirmed what she already knew. "We have to do something. Hélène would faint dead away if I showed up with my ankles hanging out. And Philippe!" She flushed with shame remembering her clumsiness and many mistakes over the past three weeks. Philippe had never criticized her, but she'd seen the subtle stiffening of his posture with every *faux pas*. The last thing she wanted was to embarrass him further.

There was little hope of lengthening the delicate, pearl-studded hemline in time for the ball. Of course, she could simply ignore the Great Mademoiselle's edict and wear her own dress.

Annique quickly rejected the notion. She dared not risk such a direct insult to the princess's generosity.

Perhaps she could feign illness and skip the party altogether. But before that thought was fully formed, she realized that nothing short of death would be an acceptable excuse to Hélène, after all the trouble and expense of the ball.

A single choice remained. She'd have to wear the dress and make the best of it. Annique inspected the gown's construction. "With a few tucks to the bodice, and perhaps a sash, I think it might be quite becoming. Different, but becoming."

She laid the dress back into the box and handed it to Marie. "We'll have to hurry, but there may be enough time for alterations. Take this with you to the dressmaker's shop so she can match the color for some extra fabric and ribbon. Tell her it's an emergency. Use the coach."

Marie paled. "But what if she's not there? What if she's busy? What if she says no?"

Annique urged her maid through the dressing room toward the back stairs. "She'll be there. She *must*. Have her bring all her seamstresses. If she says she's busy, promise her a bonus. Anything. Just bring her back with you." Annique could worry about how to pay her later. "*Threaten* her, if you have to."

Marie nodded. "I'll do my best, mademoiselle."

"I know you will. Now *hurry.*" Annique waited till Marie disappeared down the narrow stairway, then dropped to her knees and began some of the most fervent prayers of her life. The only trouble was, she wasn't too sure how the Lord would feel about coercing seamstresses.

The dressmaker arrived at two, bringing three seamstresses, a bolt of pale pink satin that complemented the gown's fabric, and some matching ribbon. But when Annique donned the gown, the tailoress blanched, then asked if it had come from the Great Mademoiselle. Annique was too anxious about getting started to wonder at the woman's question. She simply responded, "Yes, and I *must* wear it this evening. I have no choice, so we'd better begin right away."

Clearly flustered, the dressmaker hesitated, then stammered, "But, surely mademoiselle realizes . . . That is, the dress, it's . . ."

Annique glanced at the clock and cut her off. "Please, madame. I know the gown looks terrible on me; that's why I sent for you. But the clock is ticking. May we not begin?"

The woman shot a sidelong glance to her seamstresses, shrugged, and set to work without further comment.

At eight o'clock Annique nibbled a piece of dry toast in an effort to settle her stomach while Marie arranged the folds of her gown, but the butterflies inside her wouldn't go away.

After four hours of frantic pinning, cutting, and stitching, the dress had been rendered a decent fit at last, but by then Annique's nerves were as frayed as the hidden seams inside her bodice.

She took a deep, calming breath and thanked Divine Providence that there hadn't been time to replace all the bodice's stays and padding. At least she would be able to breathe easily, for a change.

Marie smiled with satisfaction as she smoothed the skirt's last fold into place. "I think it looks very elegant, mademoiselle. All the other ladies will be jealous."

If only Annique could agree with Marie's assessment, but her knowledge of fashion was woefully limited. She looked at her reflection in the mirror. The gown was barely recognizable as the ill-fitting creation she had held up only a few hours ago. Yet despite its unusual construction, she felt almost regal wearing it.

The dressmaker had cleverly avoided the impossible task of lengthening the beaded hemline. Instead, she'd detached the skirt from the bodice, added the necessary inches of length as an inset waistband, then reattached the skirt. The pale pink satin insert accented Annique's height and slender waist. As for the too-short sleeves, they now properly covered her wrists, thanks to banded cuffs made from the bodice's excess width.

Annique took another small bite of toast and noted with satisfaction that her hemline, buoyed by a respectable number of petticoats, now hovered discreetly just above the carpet.

A knock at the door was followed by the butler's muffled voice. "His grace, the Duke of Corbay, awaits mademoiselle in the foyer. His grace asked me to inform mademoiselle that her highness the Grand Duchess of Montpensier has already arrived."

The toast slipped from Annique's fingers. So the Great Mademoiselle had come, uninvited, half an hour before any of the other guests were expected to arrive. Annique could only guess why, and her throat went dry at the prospect of finding out. To quell her fear, she closed her eyes and wrapped herself in an imaginary robe of dignity. When she had regained her composure, she said calmly, "Marie, have him tell the duke I will be right down."

One last look into the mirror bolstered her courage. With her hair swept softly into an artful cascade of curls from the crown, Annique's oval face took on a longer, more classic proportion. Freshwater pearl earrings, borrowed from Hélène, accented finely shaped ears that were usually concealed by Annique's hair.

Even her agitation seemed to work in her favor, brushing her cheeks with color and adding sparkle to her dark eyes.

Marie returned to her side and grinned into the mirror. "Mademoiselle looks like a princess in a fairy tale."

Annique made a face. "Anything but a princess. Please."

Downstairs, Philippe fought to conceal his tension from the Great Mademoiselle.

Of all nights for him to come early instead of late. He'd arrived from his town house to find the princess already there—uninvited, unfashionably punctual, and doubtless up to no good.

Even as he smiled politely, Philippe inwardly chided his own naivete. Until last night, he'd dared to hope she might forget about him. He might have known she'd wait until just before the wedding to move in for the kill.

This was going to be a long evening.

He kept his tone deferential. "I've sent word to my father and Hélène that you've arrived, your highness, but I'm afraid you'll have to settle for my company until they come down."

The princess glanced expectantly to the landing above them. "And Anne-Marie?"

"I sent word to her, as well." Philippe offered his arm. "We can wait in the salon."

His royal interloper refused to budge. "I prefer to wait here."

A thread of warning coursed through Philippe. The Great Mademoiselle never stood about waiting for lesser personages. "As you wish." He braced himself for the unexpected.

But nothing could have prepared him for the woman who descended the stairs. He followed the princess's perplexed gaze upward to see a breathtaking creature clad in a fluid gown of glittering white. He had never seen such a vision. She looked like a goddess, Venus descended from Olympus. Yet she wasn't Venus.

She was Anne-Marie.

But it couldn't be. Anne-Marie was almost plain.

By all that was holy, it *was* she! But what was different? The dress, of course, but there was more. Her hair. That was it. Yes. No. Something else, something almost indefinable. There was a certain regal glow about her he had never seen before.

Anne-Marie stepped closer and executed a graceful curtsy before the princess. "Good evening, your highness." She motioned to the exquisite gown she was wearing. "Your highness's gift is far too generous. I hardly know how to thank you." She turned to Philippe. "Don't you think my gown is lovely, Philippe? Her highness sent it as a wedding gift and asked me to wear it tonight."

Rarely at a loss for words, Philippe was almost speechless. And he couldn't help wondering why the princess had chosen such a gift. Looking Anne-Marie over again, he murmured, "The effect is quite amazing."

A dull flush heightened the princess's color, but her voice was controlled. "Why, Anne-Marie, whatever have you done with that dress? I hardly recognize it."

His fiancée's smile faded almost imperceptibly. "I regret, your highness, that necessity required a few alterations. I trust you approve."

Philippe came to himself enough to sense the charged atmosphere between the two women. What was going on here? But with one more long look at his willowy, elegant bride-to-be, the question evaporated from his mind, replaced by a more basic preoccupation.

The princess spoke again, her lips barely moving. "Come now, Philippe. Surely you recognize the significance of such a *memorable* costume."

His gaze swept from Annique's hem to her face, lingering on her eyes. "A most unique gift, your highness. I've never seen anything like it."

Annique felt herself blush, uncertain whether he liked the dress or not. He hadn't *said* he did, but he seemed to be looking at her as if for the first time, and the hunger in his eyes was something new.

The truth was, Philippe barely noticed the dress itself; he was too preoccupied with its wearer. The sight of Anne-Marie, so changed, stirred an unexpected surge of desire and confusion.

Marriage was one thing . . . from the beginning, he'd expected to work out an acceptable, perhaps even comfortable, relationship with his wife—even after the Great Mademoiselle had complicated matters by inviting Anne-Marie to Court as her attendant. He'd planned to lead his life and his wife, hers, once the children were born.

But Anne-Marie's transformation put their union in an entirely different light. He'd never considered being yoked to a woman who could affect him so. The prospect was most disturbing.

She was stunning tonight. He wanted her, as would every other red-blooded man who saw her.

He'd never felt jealousy before. Nor had his lust been captured so unaware. And he dared not let anyone know—particularly Anne-Marie.

Determined to maintain his composure, he offered an arm to each of the women. "Come, ladies. Allow me to escort you into the ballroom."

The Great Mademoiselle stepped out of his reach and addressed Anne-Marie. "You'll attract quite a bit of attention tonight. But then again, that's what you had in mind when you altered my gift, wasn't it?"

Anne-Marie's face reflected only composure. "Decency was what I had in mind, your highness. Only decency."

That night Annique discovered what it was like to be the object of both feminine envy and masculine admiration.

Without exception, the ladies reacted to her attire with surprise or thinly disguised derision. But the sting of feminine criticism was softened by masculine attention. From the callowest young bachelor to the most grizzled old nobleman, the gentlemen fairly drooled at the sight of her. But Philippe remained curiously aloof, an enigmatic half-smile on his face as he watched her dance and talk with dozens of admirers. He didn't seem to be upset by their attentions. On the contrary, Annique would have sworn there was a proprietary gleam in his eye whenever he looked her way—but she couldn't help wondering why, after all these weeks at her side, he now kept his distance.

Perhaps it had something to do with the Great Mademoiselle. The ball had barely come to life when she'd flounced out, a herd of gossiping courtiers trailing in her wake.

But Annique didn't care what the princess—or the princess's friends—thought. Tonight she was the belle of the ball, and in two days she would be the Duchess of Corbay, wife of the handsomest man in Paris.

The dress was magic, making her beautiful and desirable in men's eyes for the first time. The sensation was more than gratifying. She felt powerful—powerful enough to ignore the whispered asides and critical looks of the women present. And she felt free. No longer did she worry about making a false step or an error in protocol. She danced, she laughed, she accepted punch from the swarm of attentive gentlemen who surrounded her, and for the first time since she'd come to Paris, she actually enjoyed herself.

The warm night flew by, swept on the music of violins. By the time the last guest had been bid farewell and the marshal had retired, dawn lightened the eastern sky. A weary Hélène trudged up the grand stairway. "Tell Philippe good night, Anne-Marie. Or good morning. Tomorrow is your wedding day. You must try to get a few hours sleep before we begin the final preparations." She yawned loudly as she moved out of sight on the landing above.

Philippe reached out to Annique. "Come. Walk me outside."

"Very well." Suddenly shy, she laid her hand lightly atop his. They strolled into the courtyard, where they were unchaperoned except for the sleepy groom holding Philippe's huge black stallion.

Philippe's step was heavy. "This has been a long night."

Annique smiled, breathing in the warm, dew-laden April air. "Not for me. It's been the most wonderful night of my life. I'm wide-awake."

He shot her an odd look. "I can see. There are still stars in your eyes." Then he drew her abruptly into his arms, almost as if he were doing so against his will.

His expression hardened. The hunger was back.

That, and the intimacy of his embrace, set Annique's heart racing. Was it the magic worked by the dress, or did he really find her desirable?

Afraid to know the answer, she searched his face, noticing for the first time the bluish circles beneath his eyes and the haggard creases that cut through the faint stubble on his cheeks. "Poor Philippe. I hadn't realized how hard the last few weeks have been on *you,* staying up with me almost every night, then putting in a full day at the garrison. You must be exhausted."

A welcome softness eased his features. "I am a little tired." He stifled a yawn. "Pardon me. If I nod off when we kneel at the altar tomorrow, just give me a poke. I don't know if the ceremony would be binding if I were to fall asleep in the middle."

"Don't worry. I'll make sure you stay awake." Annique looked away, her voice lightening to a whisper. "I want the ceremony to be binding."

He stiffened almost imperceptibly at her little confession. Then he changed the subject. "After the wedding, we can both get some well-earned rest. I planned our honeymoon with that in mind."

"Honeymoon?"

"I know it's unusual, but as I mentioned earlier, I have arranged for an ocean voyage. We'll sail to the Mediterranean, then along the coast to Savoy, perhaps even Rome."

"That will be lovely." Without thinking, Annique rested her head against his shoulder. "Ever since I was a little girl, I've dreamed of the sea and wanted to taste the salt water on my tongue." He felt so good, so strong to lean against, his arms hedging away all her doubts and shortcomings. She closed her eyes and murmured, "Is the ocean really as vast and beautiful as everyone says?"

Philippe's hand moved down her back. "Bigger and more beautiful than words can describe."

She tipped her face and grinned up at him. "I can't think of a more perfect wedding gift."

He looked down at her with a disturbing intensity. "I'm glad you approve."

Annique searched his dark blue eyes for some clue as to what he was really thinking. "Ours has been such a brief courtship. We've been together almost every day for the past three weeks, yet I feel I know little more about you than I did the night we met."

He offered a sardonic smile. "I'm of the opinion that courtships are deliberately structured to *prevent* intimacy of acquaintance, rather than promote it. Perhaps to protect the marriage contract."

He kept his heart so closely guarded. Philippe's true nature was as elusive as shadows in black velvet. Annique asked, "And do you think that's the case with us—that familiarity would drive us apart?"

His expression darkened. "I cannot promise that you will never regret marrying me, Annique. I have no idea what kind of husband I'll make."

Annique refused to let his reservations steal her happiness. Banded by the circling assurance of his arms, she gazed up into his handsome face and quipped, "After all the mistakes I've made in the last few weeks, I should think you might be the one with regrets."

"I waste no time with regrets," he murmured.

Then he kissed her, hard and deep.

A thrill of confusion and delight shot to the tips of Annique's toes. She tasted fire mixed with brandy on his tongue, but before she had time to respond, she felt him pull free of her embrace.

She opened her eyes to see him stride away, mount his huge black stallion, then level an unsettled stare in her direction. He bid her farewell with, "Until tomorrow."

Tomorrow.

As she watched him ride away, Annique shivered, unsure whether her reaction was prompted by foreboding or the memory of his kiss.

After tomorrow they would have the rest of their lives for getting to know each other.

Or for regrets.

CHAPTER 11

*M*ademoiselle . . .

Annique stirred at the gentle sound, a pleasant sense of sluggishness telling her she had slept more than just a few hours. She opened her eyes. Above her, a stripe of brilliant sunshine slashed across the pale green plaster, revealing that morning was well past. She yawned and let her gaze drop lazily until it stopped abruptly on the motionless figure standing at the foot of her bed.

"Marie!" She sat up. "You gave me quite a start. How long have you been there?"

Robe in hand, Marie moved to the side of the bed. "I'm sorry, mademoiselle. I didn't want to wake you, but another package has been delivered, and I thought you'd want to know."

Annique's eyes narrowed. "It's not from the princess, is it?"

"No. It's from the convent."

"Thank goodness!" Annique flopped back onto the pillows in relief. "Her highness's first gift was enough to last me a lifetime." Buoyed by a mixture of relief and anticipation, she rolled out of the bed and slipped her arms into the waiting robe. "Let's see what Mother Bernard and the sisters have sent me. Where is it?"

Marie disappeared into the dressing room, then returned laboriously pushing a small wooden chest across the polished floor. When she reached the edge of the rug, she straightened. "It's not very large, but I can't lift it alone. Should I send for a footman?"

"That won't be necessary. The two of us can manage, I'm sure." Annique walked over and crouched beside the intricately carved box. Deeply etched flowers and vines covered a surface unbroken by lock or handles. She tried to lift one corner, but met with surprising resistance. "Goodness. Feels like it's full of rocks."

She motioned to Marie. "Help me lift it onto the bed." Together, they transferred it to the coverlet. Annique inspected it closely, discovering an almost invisible seam between the lid and the body of the box. "What an odd little trunk. It looks quite old." Along one side, the spines of three inset brass hinges peeked from the seam. "The lid has hinges, but I can't find a lock."

After trying unsuccessfully to open it, she tipped the box backward to inspect the bottom. No keyhole or hardware there, either. "There was no key?"

"No, mademoiselle, but—oh, dear." Coloring, Marie thrust her hand into the pocket of her apron. "I almost forgot." She retrieved a folded letter and gave it to Annique. "The priest who brought the box told me to put this letter into your hands, and yours alone."

"A priest?" The handwriting on the note was Father Jules's. Annique's heart contracted. "Is he still here? Did you recognize him?"

Marie shook her head. "He's gone. I never saw him before. He was short and bald. Almost scared the life out of me. I was bringing fresh water into your dressing room, and there he was. He gave me the box and the note, then left by the back stair."

So it wasn't Father Jules. At least the letter was from him. Annique nodded. "You may leave me now. I'll ring when I'm ready for my breakfast."

Marie bobbed a curtsy. "Yes, mademoiselle."

Annique waited until the door closed to break the seal and read:

March 31, 1652
My dearest child,

I have just left you sleeping peacefully at Maison d'Harcourt. I begin by asking your forgiveness, once again, for leaving you as I did.

She hadn't forgiven him, not fully. A sense of betrayal and a dozen unanswered questions still dogged her whenever she thought of him. But she couldn't hate him, either, and she missed him terribly. Annique read on.

As to the gift that accompanies this letter, it traveled with us from the convent. I am entrusting it into the care of an old friend, to be delivered on your wedding day.

Many years ago I promised your father that if anything happened to him, I would watch over you and preserve what he left you. This box and its contents are your father's only belongings that came with you to the convent. Though a few books and a battered old coffer might appear to be of little worth, promise me that you will look upon these things as a treasure and keep this coffer always with you, for this is all that remains of a once-noble heritage. Like so many things in life, this humble gift is more than it seems. Think of it as a mighty legacy of the mind from your father to his only child. If you are diligent, you will derive great reward from studying the coffer's contents.

On this special day, I pray God's richest blessings upon you. How I wish I could be the one to perform the sacrament, but God in His wisdom has ordained otherwise. Yet I will be there in spirit, as will all the sisters.

Though you may still question what I have done, do not let bitterness take root in your heart. No one knows better than I how quickly unforgiveness can injure the soul. Don't let it poison yours. Try to think of me with kindness.

Your humble servant and loving Father in Christ,
Jules

Annique folded the letter and sat for a long time staring into the distance and seeing only Father Jules's face. She had hoped for some answers, but found only more questions.

She reread the final paragraph, then sighed. Perhaps he was right. Today she would begin a new life. What better time to leave past disappointments behind?

But this part of the past she would take with her, and gladly. Her father's books.

She sat on the side of the bed, her fingers exploring the ornate surface of the coffer's front. "There must be some way to get inside." After poking and prodding for several minutes, she felt something shift slightly in response to her touch. She looked closer at the carved flower beneath her fingers and pressed again. When that didn't work, she tried twisting. The ancient wood moved, and the flower's center sank by a hair's width. Annique pressed the center further inward, and the box lid sprang open with a click.

Reverently, she looked inside. The burnished leather spines of a dozen matched volumes gleamed back at her, their titles etched in gold. Several smaller volumes of Latin and French poetry filled the remaining spaces. A bolt of excitement shot through her. "Dear heaven. The collected works of Prince Machiavelli, even his discourse on Livy's history of Rome." She couldn't have been more surprised or delighted if the coffer had been filled with jewels.

Annique had read numerous references to these heretical humanist works, but hadn't found them in the convent's library. Nor had she expected to.

A knock at the door intruded into her thoughts, prompting her to shut the lid on her secret treasure. "Who is it?"

Marie's voice filtered across the room. "I'm sorry to disturb you, miss, but the duchess insisted I bring you your breakfast right away. She wanted the kitchen staff to begin preparing for the wedding feast."

Hélène had been in a beastly humor ever since last night's incident with the Great Mademoiselle. "That's fine, Marie. You may enter." Annique twisted the latch and slipped Father Jules's letter inside the coffer, then closed it again.

Marie's voice overrode the clatter of the breakfast tray. "I see mademoiselle got it open. What's inside?"

Annique hesitated. The books were hers, a treasure indeed, but hardly appropriate reading for a lady, particularly a lady-in-waiting for the Great Mademoiselle.

And what would Philippe think? If word got out that she owned such controversial works, they might both be brought before the Inquisitor for heresy. At the very least, the collection could be taken from her. Annique had no intention of giving them up. She told Marie just enough of the truth to satisfy her curiosity. "Just some books that belonged to my father."

Obviously disappointed, Marie set the tray on the table. "Oh. No wonder it was so heavy."

Annique beckoned Marie closer. Choosing her words carefully, she dropped her voice to a whisper. "These books are all I have left of my family. Because of that, they are very precious to me. Very private." She smiled conspiratorially. "I need your help to keep them safe. Will you do that for me, Marie, and see that they're with us wherever we go?" She paused. "It can be our secret, just between the two of us."

Marie straightened importantly. "I may chatter, mademoiselle, but I know how to keep a secret. And I know just the place for the box." She opened one of the large trunks they'd been packing for the honeymoon. "If mademoiselle will help me, we can hide it in here." After they had lowered the coffer into the trunk and covered it with clothing, Marie dusted her hands together. "There. Safe and sound and none the wiser."

Annique stared at the packing case, a vague, unsettling thought rattling through her mind. There was something about the letter, something she'd missed. As soon as she was able, she would read it over again.

Marie turned to draw aside the heavy draperies and throw open the windows to a cloudless April sky. The smell of the Seine blew in on a warm spring breeze. "Look, mademoiselle! The sun's shining. That means good fortune for your marriage."

Her marriage. In her excitement about the books, Annique had almost forgotten. She glanced at the trunk, then to the faultless blue sky. "I hope so, Marie. I hope so."

From that moment on, Annique was swept up into a frantic flurry of preparations and last-minute details. Everything seemed to happen so fast—packing and dressing, with countless flustered interruptions by Hélène. Time seemed to accelerate into a blur of motion, images, sensation, and sound.

Annique hardly remembered the carriage ride to Notre Dame and had only a fleeting impression of taking the marshal's arm and walking down an endless aisle through crowds of glittering courtiers. But one image was clear: Philippe, waiting for her at the altar rail, his black velvet uniform accenting his narrow hips and broad shoulders, his thick hair curling abundantly against his collar, his golden spurs and sword gleaming.

One look at him, and everything else had disappeared. Suddenly there were no curious onlookers, no jostling guests. She'd no longer felt the marshal's measured pace beside her. Annique hadn't even noticed the Great Mademoiselle seated in her ornate gilded chair in the royal enclosure.

There was only Philippe, and the words that bound them together in body and spirit for eternity.

And then the ceremony was over, and after a brief carriage ride back to Maison d'Harcourt, the newlyweds were swept up into the festivities. The wedding feast was a rowdy celebration comprised of food, flowers, politely rib-ald toasts, and laughter. But with every toast, every sly wink, Annique felt herself growing more apprehensive.

Why was she so nervous? Philippe had given her no cause to fear him, and yet as the time approached for her to retire to the wedding chamber, she grew more and more uneasy.

At ten o'clock, Hélène rose from the table. "Come, la-dies. Let us withdraw and leave the gentlemen to their brandy." With much animated conversation, the women escorted Annique to the door of the bridal chamber. When the door closed behind them, she was alone with Marie.

Neither of them spoke while Marie removed Annique's pearl-studded wedding gown. After carefully depositing the dress in a trunk, Marie proffered a nightgown of the finest cotton lawn trimmed with a deep lace ruffle at the wide neckline and cuffs. "I ironed this gown three times. There's not a wrinkle in it." She reached for Annique's chemise.

Annique recoiled. "What are you doing?"

"Sorry, mademoiselle." Marie blushed. "I mean, *ma-dame*—I mean, your grace—the gown's not meant to be worn over a chemise."

Annique felt the seed of fear growing larger. "Oh." To-night's bawdy conversations had been enough to convince her that Marie was probably right. "Very well."

Marie laid the gown on the bed, then turned her back in deference to Annique's modesty. "Let me know when you're ready for me to help with the ribbons."

Annique pulled the thin gown over her head before shrugging off her chemise underneath. She'd gotten used to being naked in the dressing room for her baths, but couldn't bring herself to stand exposed in this huge room, even if Marie wasn't looking. After stepping out of the undergarment, she threaded her arms into the nightgown's sleeves, then sat at the dressing table. "You can look now."

Without being asked, Marie adjusted the wide neckline lower to expose her mistress's shoulders. "The gown's meant to be worn this way, to show off your grace's lovely skin."

Annique tugged the ruffle back up over her shoulders. "I can't wear it that way. If I sneezed, it would fall right off."

Her servant grinned. "That's the idea."

"Marie!" Embarrassment flooded through Annique at what she saw reflected in the mirror. The nightgown's thin fabric left little to the imagination. She might as well be naked. "Lay my robe across the foot of the bed. I don't want to catch cold."

A puzzled expression clouded her maid's face. "Your grace, I don't mean to pry, but has anyone spoken to madame about . . ." Even plainspoken Marie seemed to have trouble finding the right words. ". . . about tonight, what's to happen when monsieur le duc . . . joins madame here?"

To cover her uneasiness, Annique began pulling the pins from her hair. "First Mother Bernard, then Sister Thomas, and now you. Why does everyone seem so concerned about what's to happen tonight? Mother Bernard already explained everything."

Marie didn't seem convinced. "I beg your grace's pardon. It's just . . ." Her words trailed off at a baleful glare from Annique. "Never mind. I didn't mean to pry." She turned her attention to extracting the rest of the hairpins, then brushing out her mistress's hair. When the last curl had been stroked into the shining cascade across Annique's back, Marie laid the silver brush down.

Annique didn't mean to sound cross, but she did. "You've forgotten to braid my hair for sleeping."

Her maid's worried frown returned. "Forgive me, but it isn't proper for a bride to receive her new husband with her hair bound."

How was it that even her maid seemed to know more about this momentous occasion than she did herself? Annique tried unsuccessfully to keep the anxiety from her reply. "Very well. But it'll probably take all morning to comb the tangles out."

A smug smile spread across Marie's lips. "I'll take care of the tangles, madame." She crossed the room and drew back the covers. "The sheets were washed in rosewater. I saw to it myself. The bed hangings were beaten and aired yesterday, and rehung with new silk cords to hold them back. I wanted everything to be perfect."

Annique climbed self-consciously into the high double bed and propped herself against the artfully arranged collection of pillows. When the maid smoothed the fold of the sheet across her lap, Annique caught hold of Marie's hand.

"I'm sorry I've been so cross. I'm just nervous about to-night. I really do appreciate everything you've done." She brightened. "I'll be all right in the morning. And just think. Tomorrow we'll all leave for the coast, and I shall see the ocean at last."

Marie's rough skin tightened against her mistress's fingers. She winked broadly. "If *I* had tonight to look forward to, your grace, I wouldn't waste one second thinking about tomorrow!" With that, she left Annique alone to await the consummation of her marriage.

❀ **CHAPTER 12** ❀

*P*hilippe's compatriots seemed determined to get him so drunk he'd have to crawl to his wedding bed. Henri wrapped an arm across his younger brother's shoulders and shook him. "Why, Philippe, your flagon's empty! Here. Let me fill it for you." More wine ended up on the table than in the goblet.

Philippe took one sip, then waited until no one was looking to pour the rest back into the pitcher. He knew better than to interfere with the male rituals of this occasion. Careful not to offend, he gave no sign to the boisterous acquaintances around him that he found their crude jests unamusing, their lewd instructions unpalatable, and their presumptions of familiarity most repulsive of all.

Philippe had known it would be so. Among the ribald, disheveled crowd who bore him up the stairs and deposited him at the door of the bridal chamber, not a man could truly be called friend.

Standing amidst them in the hallway, he deliberately swayed as he tucked his shirttail into his black velvet breeches. Someone from the crush hurled his jacket into his chest, causing Philippe to stumble into the arms of his laughing older brother.

"Let me help you with that." Henri draped the heavy jacket across Philippe's shoulders, then wiggled a lecherous eyebrow. "Perhaps you need assistance beyond the door as well, brother. I'll most happily offer my services."

Philippe suppressed a flash of anger. This was no time for confrontation. He restricted himself to a far-from-gentle clout on Henri's back with the words, "I think I can manage alone. Thank you just the same, brother."

Henri grunted from the blow, but he was so drunk he accepted it with a grin.

Philippe raised his hand for silence. "Gentlemen . . ." The tumult of voices quieted to a rumble. "Thank you for the escort. Now with your leave, I shall advance to conquer the objective." His broad gesture toward the door was accompanied by someone's off-key imitation of the cavalry's call to charge. Philippe laughed with the rest, then his manner stilled, and his voice rang with authority. "You may leave me now."

After a heartbeat's pause, Jacques announced from the rear of the pack, "Brandy and entertainment are provided in the library. If the gentlemen will kindly follow me . . ." The diversion worked as planned. The revelers retreated, leaving Philippe alone in the hallway. Suddenly he felt cold sober.

In twenty-eight years of living—ten of them soldiering—he had readily met and overcome many challenges of war and assignation. Strange that now the hastening of his pulse was not from desire, but from apprehension.

He refused to admit that the vows made before God and man in the great cathedral might have affected him. No, it must be the novelty of the situation that put him off his guard. He'd never made love to a virgin before.

He composed himself, then stepped into the shadowy chamber and closed the door.

His eyes swept past the crackling fire and softly illuminated furnishings to the high canopy bed. There the crimson hangings framed a dim cameo. His bride sat enthroned against a bank of delicately embroidered pillows, the cascade of her auburn hair like blood on snow, the wide neck of her sheer white gown exposing skin that shone like alabaster in the soft glow of the single candle on the nightstand. Her posture was rigid, her chin held high as any queen's. A familiar stirring pulsed within his loins.

Entranced, Philippe moved to the foot of the bed. Then he stopped. He knew all too well the look in those dark eyes. Many times, the tip of his saber poised upon the neck of an enemy for the *coup de gras*, he had seen that look. Only a thin veneer of defiance covered the terror that stared back at him.

A note of incredulity escaped into his quiet words. "Madame, I had expected a warmer greeting to my marriage bed. Why do you fear me?"

The directness of his question seemed to take her by surprise. All regal illusion evaporated, and the girl that remained looked far younger and more vulnerable than he had ever seen her. A slight quiver colored her voice. "I have been instructed, your grace, of my marital . . . obligations. My body is at your disposal. I ask only that you do me no lasting harm." Her hands clenched white above the counterpane at her waist, and her already pale skin faded alarmingly.

Philippe planted a shining boot upon the low bench that hugged the footboard. He leaned forward, his forearm resting on his thigh. His bride lay before him more like an unwilling virgin sacrifice to a ravaging pagan demon than a woman about to be initiated into the pleasures of the flesh. His eyes narrowed. "This instruction about your 'marital obligations' . . . just what have you been told?"

She stared at the coverlet. "That as your wife, I am to place my body at your disposal."

"And have you any idea precisely what that involves?" He welcomed the glint of interest that peeked through her martyred expression.

Her gaze locked with his in challenge. "Not really. Mother Bernard did not speak in specifics, but I have heard enough talk among the women to surmise you will probably want me naked. Shall I remove my gown, or would you prefer to do it?" She sounded as if she were preparing for an amputation instead of a consummation.

Philippe turned and stepped toward the hearth to conceal the mixture of surprise and amusement in his face. He should have known she would be innocent, but somehow he had never considered the depth of her naivete.

Paris was the center of the civilized world, a society where the rarest material treasures were commonplace, yet true innocence was a fruit Philippe had never tasted in all his years at Court. His finger absently traced the outline of his lips as he savored the prospect.

Where would be the pleasure, the challenge, in taking her like a sacrificial offering? A moment of release for him, of pain for her, and innocence lost. Far too wasteful an approach.

It would be easy enough to tear the thin garment from her body and take what was his, but Philippe wanted more. He had seen the subtle sparks of fire that smoldered behind those great, fathomless auburn eyes. He wanted to strip away the layers of calculation and concealment she hid behind. In exchange for her innocence he would lead her, touch by touch, into a world of sensation her sheltered mind had never dreamed of—a world where flesh and spirit fused in glorious communion that liberated both.

Philippe crossed to sit in a chair by the hearth. His blood coursed heavily as he scowled, unseeing, into the flames while he formulated the exquisite finesse required of such a challenge. First he must seduce her mind. After that, her body.

But there was the problem of guilt. Who could know what poison those frustrated celibates at the convent had poured into her about "sins of the flesh"?

Then an intriguing idea occurred to him. Of course. He could fight fire with fire.

His bride leaned forward, her mahogany brows drawn together, a curtain of shimmering hair slipping past her shoulder. "I'm sorry, your grace. Have I displeased you?" There was an element of sincerity in the apology.

An unguarded smile escaped Philippe, but his response was well-considered. "On the contrary. You please me greatly. But I'd much rather you addressed me as Philippe. After all, we are married."

She settled back. "Philippe." His name never seemed to come easily from her lips.

He spoke again. "What about you? Is Anne-Marie your preference, or do you have a pet name—something they called you in the convent, perhaps?"

A flash of suspicion escaped before she replied, "You are my husband. You may address me as you wish." The note of defiance in the last brought a certain irony to the statement.

Again, he smiled. Defiance was born of anger, and anger signaled passion. Awakening that passion would be a worthy objective for this night. Forearms braced across his thighs, he leaned forward, every muscle tensed in anticipation. As he had hoped, she mirrored him by leaning slightly away from the pillows. With the movement, her eyes disappeared into shadow, giving her an almost spectral appearance. Philippe recoiled inwardly at the sudden transformation from angelic woman-child to pale apparition, but then her head shifted to one side, the shadow disappearing.

Far away in the distant rooms of the house, the music and laughter grew faint, then silenced. The crackling of the fire was the only sound in the chamber now.

"Have you studied the Scriptures, Anne-Marie?"

She tensed visibly at the question.

Interesting. Philippe was careful to keep his tone gentle. "Mother Bernard taught you that this night brings obligation, but tell me, what do you know of the Holy Writ concerning the fleshly pleasure of our union?"

Twin blossoms of color stained her cheeks. "I know that fleshly pleasure is sinful."

In the pause that followed, he could clearly read the memory of punishment and shame upon her face. Then she hid her thoughts behind that damnable nun's mask of composure. He saw her grip on the coverlet tighten.

"Mother Bernard told me my physical duties in marriage were for the purpose of procreation alone. I am ready to submit."

So some frustrated celibate *had* polluted her mind. Philippe could barely conceal his contempt for such a travesty. He rose slowly, deliberately, and took two steps toward the bed. Anne-Marie's eyes widened with each step. Then he paused for effect, turned, and crossed to the bookcase to extract a heavy leather-bound volume. After settling back into the chair beside the fire, he opened the ancient Bible. "You'll have to bear with me. My Latin is not as good as my Greek, so this translation might leave something to be desired."

Curiosity was plain in her response. "Translation?"

"Of the Scripture. The kindest thing I can say about Mother Bernard is that her teachings about the sinfulness of pleasure were inaccurate—at least, when it comes to the physical pleasures between man and wife." He was rewarded by a gleam of curiosity in her face. "I'll give your Mother Bernard the benefit of the doubt and surmise that she spoke from ignorance. At any rate, she has misled you. I mean to see that remedied. Physical pleasure in marriage is a gift from God." He lifted the book slightly. "You don't happen to read Latin, do you?"

Her candor instantly disappeared. "Why would you ask such a thing?"

Philippe reassured her with a smile. "I would prefer you to read the words for yourself. Never mind. I'll translate." He turned the thick, heavy pages until he found the passage he was looking for. "These words are from Saint Paul's letter to the Church in Ephesus: 'Wives, unto your own husbands submit yourselves as unto the Lord, for the husband is head of the wife, as also Christ is head of the assembly of believers, and he is Savior of the body. But even as the assembly of believers is subject to Christ, so also wives to their own husbands in everything.'" He looked up from the book to see her arms crossed at her bosom and a skeptical arch to one eyebrow.

Though the tone was benign, her response was not at all what he expected. "Such words hardly come as a surprise from a *man* of God such as Saint Paul." She muttered, "I'm certain husbands all over Christendom find that passage particularly comforting."

Philippe nearly laughed aloud, but caught himself. Deliberately speaking so softly she had to strain to hear him, he asked, "Are you prepared to submit to me as your husband in all things, Anne-Marie?"

"I have vowed it."

Now was the time for that wicked grin that always worked so well with women. "Every wife at Court has promised to obey her husband, yet we both know how little *that* vow means in this day and time."

Her voice was soft. "My word is all I have to give. The vow is sacred to me, as I hope are the ones made by my husband before God."

Admiration tinged his response. "Well said." He stilled. "If you will only trust and obey this night, I promise to bring you no harm. Before God, I swear that my only motive is to bring you joy. Do you believe me?"

She shook her head and whispered. "I don't know. I wish I could."

Philippe shifted his attention to the book spread before him. "Perhaps it will help if I read to you the legacy of passion that God has given man and woman in marriage." He turned to the Old Testament, and the resonance of his voice filled the space between them. "I read from Solomon's Song of Songs: 'How fair you are, my love. Your

eyes are like those of a dove; your hair dark and wavy as
fleece from the goats of Mount Gilead. Your teeth are
white as shorn lambs . . . Your neck is like the tower of
David. Your two breasts are like two fawns, twins of a ga-
zelle, that feed among the lilies.' "

He paused, his eyes shifting to the swell of her bosom,
then he read on. " 'Until the day breaks and the shadows
flee away, I will get me to the mountain of myrrh and the
hill of frankincense.' " Briefly, his eyes roamed lower, focusing beneath her clenched hands. She shifted self-consciously, as if his gaze burned through the coverlet.

" 'Your lips, oh my bride, drop honey as the honeycomb.
Honey and milk are under your tongue.' " He focused just
above the strong curve of her chin, then he closed the book
and rose, the words from memory now as measured steps
brought him to stand beside her.

" 'A garden enclosed and barred is my sister, my bride; a
spring shut up, a fountain sealed.' " Slowly, he pulled the
edge of the coverlet toward the foot of the bed, exposing
the smooth white sheets and smoother ivory skin against
the lace of her gown. He did not stop until the tips of her
toes appeared. Then he sat beside her, the words coming
effortlessly, no longer mere poetry memorized by a romantic young man, but alive now, defined by this circumstance
in a way he had never anticipated.

Her breathing quickened, her eyes dilated. His voice caressed her, mesmerized her with the majestic cadence and
sensuality of the metaphor. She did not move away.

As he spoke, Philippe peered through the delicate gown
to the curve and rise of the slender body beneath, the
dusky, inviting crevices between her breasts and loins. But
still he kept himself aloof, letting the ancient words ask for
him. " 'Open to me, my sister, my love, my dove, my spotless one . . . for I am wet with the heavy night dew.' "

He leaned closer, breathing in the smell of roses from
the hollow of her neck. She shuddered involuntarily when
his lips grazed the soft skin below her ear. Suddenly the
room grew warm, the heat of his body working through the
linen of his shirt.

He stroked down the slender columns of her arms, his
hands freeing her shoulders from the fragile fabric as the
wide neckline dropped lower, catching on her breasts.

" 'Your rounded limbs are like jeweled chains, the work of a master hand.' "

He bent and lightly kissed the fabric that concealed the gentle mound just below her navel. " 'Your body is like a round goblet, in which no mixed wine is wanting; your abdomen is like a heap of wheat set about with lilies.' " At the touch of his lips, she gasped softly and closed her eyes as if to hide from him, but he willed her to open them again, and she did.

" 'Your neck is like the tower of ivory, your eyes as the pools of Heshbron . . . How fair and how pleasant you are, oh love, for delights.' " The tiny hairs on her arm stood erect at his touch, and desire traced a delicate texture on the creamy skin above the dark points that had tensed behind the lace at her bosom.

He paused to survey her rigid bearing and widened eyes. Word by word, desire was gaining over fear. He gently tightened his grip on her upper arms. " 'Let your breasts be as clusters of the grapevine.' " His thumb traced the outer curve of her breast, and she responded with a quick intake of breath. The sound of her awakening sent a frisson of triumphant passion through his own body.

Philippe's face moved to within inches of hers. He inhaled the clean, fruity scent of her breath. His lips brushed hers as delicately as a breeze rustles a still pond. " 'Your kisses are like the best wine . . .' "

Now there was no reservation, no sacrifice in her eyes as she searched his. Direct and unshielded, her nameless hunger reached across the charged atmosphere between them. Only then did he draw her to him to seek her lips in earnest. Her arms instantly answered his embrace, and he felt himself drawn into a vortex of feeling, his plan and purpose forgotten in the wave of sensation that rose from her and threatened to engulf him.

When he came up for air, her whispered words shot through him like a bolt of lightning. " 'I am my beloved's, and his desire is toward me. Let us go out early to the vineyards and see whether the vines have budded, whether the grape blossoms have opened and the pomegranates are in bloom. There will I give you my love.' " Eyes half-lidded with desire, she lay back, her voice husky. "I always thought that Solomon spoke of something besides gardens, but only now do I know what he meant."

Philippe blinked in surprise, grateful for the diversion to slow his runaway responses. Why had she concealed her education from him? What other secrets lay hidden beneath that chaste exterior? Her hand was hot and dry when he took it into his own. "So you *do* read Latin."

Fear clouded the hunger in her eyes. "I . . . yes, but— that is, I . . ."

He laid a finger across her lips. "It pleases me that you possess an educated mind. I find that . . . most stimulating. But tonight I wish to educate another part of you, one just as important." At the sound of his voice, the fear retreated from her eyes. "Tonight I will teach you to feel, to taste, to smell, what love can be between a man and a woman."

He could see that a battle waged within her, but the convent's poison was losing. There was nothing childlike about the woman who lay before him. Innocence had been eclipsed by appetite. Her open desire threatened to propel him into a precipitous consummation. Suddenly constricted by his clothing, he rose to his knees above her, his hands ripping his shirt as he pulled it open.

She scrambled backward into the pillows.

Blast! He had moved too quickly. She must be drawn, one delicate degree at a time, into trust.

Philippe became aware of the chafing confinement of fabric against the evidence of his own arousal. Under the circumstances, he was certain his nakedness would leave her with but one lasting impression. It was a distraction he preferred to avoid. Slowly unbuttoning his cuffs, he smiled gently. "Perhaps we should strike a bargain."

"What sort of bargain?" She settled somewhat, but remained wary.

The shirt slid from his hard, muscled shoulders, exposing his chest. "If you agree to trust me, I will swear upon my soul to stop whenever you ask me to, no matter what I may be doing."

Her gown was draped seductively low, the rise of her breasts the only thing that kept it from slipping off her. Philippe only hoped he could keep his part of the bargain. He watched as her gaze played across his bare chest, then met his own.

Her knees straightened, and she lay back. "Very well. I agree."

He slid from the bed and crossed to the table where wine and sweet pastries were laid out. The amber liquid inside the decanter was redolent of fruit, but he knew it to be potent. He poured each of them a cupful and returned to the bed. "Here. This will relax you." When she took a deep draught, he stayed her hand. "Slowly. Too fast will dull your senses."

Eyes watering from the bite of the strong spirit, she nodded.

Philippe sat back, measuring her every glance, watching as the tense creases between her brow faded and her mouth softened. She was really quite lovely, her dark hair reflecting the golden glint of the firelight, her darker eyes roaming his upper torso. No other man had ever seen the perfection that lay before him, and no other man ever would. His body stirred. The campaign was going according to plan, and he knew better than to rush her. The longer the wait, the sweeter the prize.

Annique's lips burned, then numbed as she sipped the potent liquid and tried to sort out the warring emotions within her. She had prepared herself for the unexpected, but her husband had still managed to surprise her. Never had she dreamed he would summon up her hidden desires with words—words of Scripture, the very words she had secretly committed to memory at the convent by the guttering light of a midnight candle. Those same hypnotic, compelling words had once spoken to her of ecstatic spiritual commitment, but had come to stir a darker side of herself as she had grown older.

How easily his deep, seductive voice had stripped away her self-control and called forth the shapeless appetites that had plagued her these past seven years. His voice made it so easy to believe that Mother Bernard had lied to her in saying pleasure between a man and a woman was evil, not good.

Mother Bernard and Father Jules had lied about so many other things. Why not that, too? It would be so effortless to let herself go, to trust Philippe, to believe what her body urged her to believe, to accept what her rational mind told her she could.

After all, her duty lay in such obedience. If her husband commanded her to sin, the stain would be upon his soul, not hers.

She searched Philippe's face for any sign of subterfuge, but there was none. Open desire darkened his piercing eyes and flushed his creamy skin, yet he waited. How easily those coiled muscles could overpower her, and yet he wooed her, offered to teach her joy in exchange for her innocence. It seemed a worthy bargain.

The throbbing of her heart moved lower still. She turned the goblet up and drank the last of its nectar, then set it aside.

"Come." Philippe took her hand and drew her from the bed, leading her slowly to the hearth. "Warm yourself. I wish to see you by the firelight."

She did as he asked. At the hearth, the heat from the huge logs in the grate pierced the thin fabric of her gown and spread across her buttocks. She closed her eyes and turned to bask in the sensation.

Philippe moved closer and whispered. "Good. Feel the warmth. Let it caress you. Concentrate on the sensation." He was so near she could smell the clean, herbal scent of his skin and feel the moist stirring of his breath as he spoke. "Now focus on the hunger of the part of you that is denied the warmth. There can be pleasure in wanting, as well."

He was right. In cool shadow, the front of her body tingled in anticipation, and she turned to face the fire, its glow piercing red through her lids as the heat penetrated her gown, releasing the scent of starch and rosewater. After a moment of savor, she turned again.

She could sense Philippe moving a step back, but his voice rolled into her ears. "Now open your eyes and look at me." She obeyed, her pulse quickening at the amber glow that washed across his arms, the sinews of his neck. Fine, jet hairs shaped into the hollows beneath his arms and lay smooth across his forearms. Her eyes shifted lower, and she saw for the first time the faint ebony trail that led downward to the waist of his velvet breeches.

"Touch me." The command was quietly spoken, but could not be denied.

As if it had a will of its own, her hand extended toward him to caress the sheen and shadow of his chest. Then her hand slid sideways, the nub of his erect nipple tracing across the crease of her palm.

His thick, black lashes fluttered in response.

Her fingers slid down the taut ladder of his ribs, and back up again to his shoulder, descending at last past the rock-hard swell of his bicep to the sleek furriness of his forearm.

An inner heat rivaled that of the fire behind her, threatening to overwhelm her. Annique could feel her skin flush. If this was sin, then sin she would.

"Close your eyes." He reached out and turned her until they faced each other, the flame glow flickering at their sides. "Feel the warmth, beloved. Wear it like a cloak. I wish to feast on the sight of your skin clothed only in the firelight." Philippe's hands loosened the ribbon that bound the neckline of her gown, and the fabric fell silently to the floor.

A soft moan escaped him, and she sensed him drawing away. Her eyes flew open, only to find his blue gaze devouring her.

She knew he meant it when he breathed, "You're perfect. Perfect." The declaration enveloped her, wrapped her in dignity, banished shame.

Something moist broke loose deep within her.

His hand reached out for hers and he led her to the bed as a king would take his consort to her throne. Her heart thundered, moving ever lower, lower, within her. She did not know what would come next. She knew only that she wanted, and there was pleasure even in that, as Philippe had said.

Strong arms scooped her up and laid her in the center of the bed. Philippe stepped back. Even in the dim light, she could see the pulse throbbing rhythmically in his neck. His eyes sparkled, and his cheeks were flushed.

Then he reached up and jerked free the braided cords that held back the thick damask bed curtains. One by one, he closed the heavy curtains until she lay in absolute darkness. Confused, Annique listened, but heard no sound. Then the curtains parted and Philippe entered with a single candle set in a gilded saucer. As he closed the curtains behind him, Annique's eyes were drawn to the scarlet cords that dangled from his other hand. Then she noticed that his feet were bare, and a diffuse covering of softly curling black hair enveloped the muscular calves below his breeches.

Annique's skin tingled at the scent of him and the heat of his body so near, yet not near enough.

He lifted the candle over her, his knees spread wide in the deep feather bed, his eyes once more roaming hungrily across her naked body. Then he placed the candle saucer on her belly. The cold touch of the metal caused her to gasp. He shifted toward the top of the bed, careful not to jar her. "Don't move, beloved. The candle might tip over." He threaded one end of the cord around the bedpost and deftly secured it with a knot. "Give me your hand." There was no threat in his eyes, no malice that she could see.

Still, she recoiled. "Why?"

"Your hands already know how to feel. They will only distract you. I'll untie you the moment you ask. Trust me. You will not be sorry, I promise."

Annique had little trust to give, and so she prayed that he meant her no harm. The glossy surface of the cords glowed crimson in the candlelight. Philippe's words seemed to make sense of something that appeared anything but rational. If he intended to abuse her, he could have easily done so without her consent. But why tie her hands, if not for the reason he gave? Fear, curiosity, excitement, and warning struggled within her.

His next words were resolute. "Do you want me to stop? I shall. Just say the word. I'll even leave you, if you wish."

"No." The word escaped before she could think. At this moment, she was certain of only one thing—she did not want him to leave her. Offering up her hand, she stared into the twin images of candle flame reflected in his eyes. "I shall trust you. But if that trust is betrayed, it will never again be granted."

"So be it." He looped the braided silk expertly around her wrist and secured it snugly, but not uncomfortably, with an intricate knot. More than a foot of surplus silken rope snaked across the pillows between her outstretched palm and the bedpost.

Philippe lifted the candle from her abdomen, then raised his knee and planted it gingerly on the other side, the velvet crotch of his breeches just brushing her thighs as he straddled her. She became aware of another smell—sharper, more pungent than the others that emanated from him, a smell that made her think of summer.

He shifted to her left side and replaced the candle. In moments, her left hand was tied, as well.

Then he raised the flame and murmured, "Listen now only to me. Pay no heed to those jealous, lying inner voices that tell you pleasure is wicked. You shall bear no guilt for this night. Our pleasure is a gift from a perfect Creator. Man and woman, we were made for this. Let go, Anne-Marie. Learn what it is to feel." With that, he blew the candle out.

The darkness was so close, so complete, that Annique felt as if she had been shut up in her own coffin. The faint sulphuric odor of the snuffed candle only served to intensify the moment of fleeting panic that seized her. Her arms strained reflexively to the limit of her bindings, but Philippe had moved beyond her grasp. The bed creaked beneath him, and she heard the rustle of fabric.

Philippe's quiet voice pierced the gloom. "Fix your mind upon my voice. Feel the warmth of the feather bed, the smoothness of the sheets beneath your skin. Listen to what your body tells you when I touch you." The heat of him moved lower, then strong fingers kneaded the arches of her feet, caressed her toes. Slowly, slowly, the fingers worked upward, lifting each leg and working the tightness from her calves, one at a time. The patient massage stopped just above her knees.

Still, she could see nothing. He moved again, this time the smooth skin of his torso burning into her side. The primitive, masculine smell became stronger, a smell that should have been unpleasant, but was compelling, instead.

"Now I want to taste you, beloved." His lips moved across her belly, then higher. At the base of her full breasts, he seemed to drink the scent of her, and she felt herself losing control. The soft caress of his unbound hair brushed on either side of his face, tracing a path of exquisite torture before and behind the moist, demanding pressure of his mouth.

She reached out instinctively to bury her fingers in the wavy, finely textured locks, but the cords held her back.

He paused. "Do you wish me to stop?"

"No. No." The words were ragged, faintly desperate. Her heart throbbed deep within her abdomen now, where something mystical and unknown opened and closed at his touch. She felt as if she were melting from the inside out, liquefying completely.

He circled her breasts, tasting everywhere but the two places that most wanted his touch. And then his lips closed where she had wished. His teeth gently grasped; his tongue flicked back and forth, back and forth, and she thought she would die.

He claimed her mouth, the gentle pressure of his lips quickly becoming insistent, his tongue parting and tasting her as she tasted him. Her hips shifted slowly in answer to the urgency of his kiss.

Without warning, he pulled away until his panting breaths slowed, and he renewed his odyssey of exploration. He touched her with his palms, his fingertips, his tongue. Her skin came alive, and she cried out at his delicate torture, but she begged him not to stop. His body shifted over her, then away, the occasional brush of something exquisitely smooth and hot contacting her skin, then gone again. With every sensation, the nameless hunger grew stronger until she was lost in it, oblivious to everything else.

Time suspended. There was only feeling, the sound of their breathing, the mingled smell of their bodies, and the pulsing rhythm of desire that coursed through her.

She heard her own voice gasp, "Please, Philippe, I can endure no more. If this is all there is, I shall die of wanting."

His fingers threaded into her hair as his body covered hers. "No, this is not all there is. There is union, but it comes with pain. Just this first time, there will be pain."

"I don't care."

His legs spread hers, and something smooth and warm invaded a place she had thought reserved for baser functions. But now that place had become the center of her being, a terrible void that cried out to be filled.

And when it was, she felt no pain, only an explosion of consummation that set off a cascade of sparkling phantoms in the darkness. All her life she had felt like two people trapped inside one body, her soul constantly at war with her flesh. Now in this single act of glorious fusion, she became one not only with her husband, but with herself.

A primal shout of affirmation escaped her.

Deeper and deeper, the void was pierced. She didn't even remember Philippe's releasing the knots at her wrists, but suddenly she was free and she pulled him to her, her nails digging into his back. Every breath was a cry now, raw and shuddering, until his own wrenching exclamation of release joined hers.

And then she was sobbing, still bound to him by flesh.

He rolled onto his side, his strong arms drawing her close. She felt his lips brush her temple. "Shh. Why do you weep? Have I hurt you?"

"Hurt me?" From the depths of her being she answered, "No, my husband. I have just been born."

Philippe was glad for the darkness, then, for it concealed his worried frown. He'd heard the hope of happiness in her unguarded confession, and shuddered inwardly.

If happiness was what she wanted from this marriage, she asked too much.

❧ CHAPTER 13 ❧

Still naked, Annique stretched catlike in the enveloping warmth of the feather bed. *Wonderful* was too pale a word for the way she felt. Complete. That was it. At long last, she felt filled up—whole.

Her hand reached out for the smoothness of Philippe's skin but found only cool sheets where he had been. She sat up, abruptly abandoning the dark, comforting netherworld at the edge of sleep.

Annique pulled aside the bed curtains. From the fireplace the frail light of dying embers lit the empty space beside her. "Philippe?" Shivering at the room's chill, she clambered to retrieve her robe and put it on. "Philippe? Where are you?"

The chamber was empty. Annique crossed the cold floor to the hearth, where she stirred the embers with a poker, then tossed on a small log. Where could Philippe have gone? She extended her hands toward the fire, her apprehension growing as fast as the yellow flames that licked across the wood. Why would Philippe have left her, especially after what had just passed between them?

Then she heard the distant sound of muffled voices from the hallway. She moved to the bedroom door and quietly turned the handle. The corridor beyond was deserted and dark, except for a pale glow and indistinct voices filtering from the foyer below.

Philippe? Grateful for the warmth of her heavy robe, she hurried to the landing, her bare feet soundless in the hallway. She peered over the railing, only to cover her mouth and retreat into shadow at what she saw. Below, a disheveled Philippe stood illuminated by the lantern of a waiting messenger whose livery proclaimed all too clearly who had sent him. He wore the red, black, and white uniform of the Great Mademoiselle's household.

Annique inched forward far enough to see but not be seen. Philippe's black velvet breeches appeared hastily buttoned, and the wrinkled shirt he had torn from his body in the heat of passion now hung haphazardly on his broad shoulders. Though his expression remained impassive as he read a message by the light of the lantern, she saw a shadow ripple across his jaw.

Crushing the paper in his fist, Philippe murmured to the messenger, then nervously scanned the darkened foyer.

Annique pulled back to avoid detection. Acutely aware of her nakedness under her robe, she drew the heavy fabric tighter around her, her thoughts churning in outrage. Would Philippe dare to leave her on their wedding night at another woman's bidding? She edged back to the railing just in time to see her bridegroom follow the messenger into the vestibule and close the door, leaving her alone in darkness.

He had left her. Annique stared into the gloom, her mind filled with a hissing, malicious chorus of innuendo from the past month. The knowing looks, the telling silences. The princess's sly double meanings. Until tonight, Annique's concept of infidelity had been limited by girlish innocence, her suspicions vague and formless. But now she knew what passed between a man and woman. Philippe had taught her.

Brutal as the blade of the executioner's axe, the truth fell upon her, cleanly and terribly cutting off her newfound happiness.

Philippe and the Great Mademoiselle had been lovers.

Would he share the princess's bed on this night, of all nights, with the scent of Annique's innocence still clinging to his flesh?

The thought left her feeling soiled to the depths of her soul.

She gripped the banister for support, shuddering at the memory of her wanton response to his practiced seduction. She had believed him, taken in completely. How could she have been so naive as to think herself blessed above all women, the unique object of her husband's desire?

Annique remembered the words little Elise had repeated. *Only his wife.* Why did it hurt so much to face that truth?

She could not admit that she had begun to care for him and hope that he might care for her. Instead, she wondered if their consummation had merely been one more seduction among many for Philippe. Worse yet, had it been a husbandly duty dispatched solely to secure the mockery of their marriage?

Annique didn't know what to think, what to believe. All she was certain of was the doubt, humiliation, and betrayal she felt as she returned to her solitary bed.

In the vestibule just beyond the foyer, Philippe raised the hood of a servant's cloak to conceal his face. The Great Mademoiselle's summons could hardly have come at a less convenient time, though he couldn't help wondering if she'd planned it that way. Still, the princess might, indeed, be caught up in a dire crisis of State that required his help, as her note claimed. Either way, he knew her well enough to know she would not be put off.

The truth was, Philippe was grateful for an excuse to leave his marriage bed. Things had gotten too intense for comfort, far too quickly. Anne-Marie had shaken him, awakened feelings he did not want to face.

He fastened the cloak.

This wouldn't be the first time he had gone from one woman's bed to another's, but before, it had always been *his* idea. Yet the princess's appeal for help might very well be genuine.

He pulled another servant's cloak from the peg and thrust it at the messenger, whispering, "Put this on. Too many people have seen you already. And shut that light."

The emissary obeyed without comment, then led the way with swift assurance across the grounds to an unmarked coach waiting beyond the "secret" river gate. Philippe motioned the messenger into the coach ahead of him, then followed. At the sound of the compartment door slamming, the horses sprang forward, the momentum thrusting Philippe into a dark corner of the seat. He raised his voice above the clatter. "How did you know about the river gate?"

The hooded messenger opposite him replied, "I received very specific instructions."

"From whom?"

"I make no secret whom I serve."

Philippe leaned forward. "How did you get inside my father's house?"

"I was expected." A note of smugness marked the envoy's response. "Her highness has friends everywhere." He paused. "You needn't worry, your grace. Your father knows nothing of my coming."

Philippe knew better than to believe that. Though the princess's agents had obviously infiltrated Maison d'Harcourt, the marshal had his own spies. Philippe's father probably knew already of his son's departure *and* his destination, but Philippe couldn't waste time worrying about that now. He needed all his wits about him to deal with the Great Mademoiselle and the "urgent matter of State" that had prompted her reckless summons.

"Urgent matter of State," indeed. More likely, an urgent matter of pride. Or desire.

Philippe stared out the coach's small window into the night. What if she meant to seduce him? Until tonight, he'd have obliged her without compunction to protect himself, even finding pleasure in necessity. But now, for some reason, the prospect filled his mind with a flood of unbidden comparisons. In light of what he'd just experienced with Anne-Marie, his joinings with the princess seemed calculated and almost mechanical.

Philippe shifted uncomfortably. Troubling, what this wedding night had done to his perceptions. Could it be that Anne-Marie had somehow gotten past his defenses? Philippe recoiled from the idea, deciding that an assignation might be just what he needed to prove she hadn't.

He tried to concentrate on the Great Mademoiselle, to plan for what might await him in her chamber, but a fresh tug of lust conjured Anne-Marie's face, instead. How could he think of the woman who had summoned him, when the lingering messages of his body drew him, again and again, to the one he'd left behind? Images of Anne-Marie flickered across his consciousness like the moonlight that flashed through the trees as the coach trundled into the night.

He knew there were secrets in the depths of those dark eyes of hers, and her physical awakening had scalded him with its intensity.

His blood stirred as he relived that epiphany. Breath by breath, touch by touch, he had fanned the fragile flame of her desire, only to find himself launched astride the pulsing force of a volcano. Then it had no longer been he who was in control, but she who had taken him soaring to an explosion of passion beyond any he had ever experienced.

A frown twisted his lips in the darkness. Quite a surprise, his little bride. Philippe shifted, his loins aching at the memory of her wild response. She had reached him in a way no other woman had, and that bothered him. It made him vulnerable, and he could not afford to be vulnerable, not with anyone. A mindless coupling with the princess just might prove cathartic, breaking the ties of passion that threatened to bind him too tightly to his wife.

The coach slowed. Philippe looked through the window to see they had halted at the Tuileries' main entrance. He retreated into the dark corner and whispered harshly, "I can't disembark here! I might as well march up to the front door at noon."

"I am merely following her highness's orders."

Philippe's voice firmed with menace. "Tell the driver to go to the side gate. And make sure no one's lurking about, or I won't get out." His hand settled beside the dagger tucked into his boot. "Do it. I'd rather not begin this visit by killing you. Her highness is probably cross enough, already."

The messenger complied. Minutes later, Philippe burst into the Great Mademoiselle's boudoir from the secret passageway, only to find her standing calmly by the window, her blond hair unbound and her robe open. He threw back the hood of his cloak. "Your note said 'a matter of life and death.' I expected to find you stabbed or poisoned or worse."

The princess moved smoothly past him to close the secret panel. Philippe tensed at the sound of a bolt blocking his only avenue of clandestine escape. He turned. "Why have you sent for me so openly? Half of Paris knows I'm here by now."

She took her time returning to stretch across the satin sheets of her bed before she responded, "Calm down. I knew exactly what I was doing."

As he had guessed, there was no real crisis. He recognized the smell of her desire, and she was redolent with it. All he had to do was take her.

The trouble was, for some inexplicable reason, Philippe didn't want to. Surely, it couldn't be because of Anne-Marie. Or could it?

He hesitated, angered at the possibility that his marriage had interfered already in such a delicate, volatile matter.

Philippe knew that the princess wanted him to take her, and do it roughly. Yet the sight of her, poised and cunning, turned his stomach. He just resented being trapped, that was all. But as he stood before the princess, he realized something had changed. She no longer had the power to arouse him.

Again, the image of Anne-Marie flashed through his mind. He dismissed the intrusion and focused on the matter at hand. He refused to be trapped against his will, especially by a captor as dangerous as the princess.

He inched backward toward the secret panel. Maybe he could find the hidden lock. "Perhaps your highness will tell me, then, what urgent matter merits summoning me from my wedding bed."

The Great Mademoiselle smoothed the fluid silk of her peignoir across her thigh. "It *is* a matter of utmost importance, Philippe." She turned a look of raw lust in his direction. "You see, I wanted you here in this bed, not in that one."

So she expected him to service her like a stallion at stud. Well, Philippe had other ideas. He might still be able to escape if he moved quickly enough. Behind his back, his fingers fumbled with the carvings that had always opened the secret panel. Until now.

"I wouldn't do that if I were you."

Though every instinct told him to break down the panel and get away, something in the princess's voice compelled him not to.

The Great Mademoiselle rose and approached him, her

steps languid. "As you said, your arrival has not gone unnoticed. But I doubt anyone would tell your little wife." She pressed her body to his, her hands sliding down his upper arms. The smell of her hair lingered in his nostrils. She kissed the bare patch of his chest exposed by his ruined shirt. "Of course, *I* wouldn't tell her. Not unless you hurt my feelings."

Philippe's voice resonated with controlled fury. "You call yourself a woman of honor. Where is the honor in this?"

Her finger traced down the vein throbbing in his neck. "I want nothing that I haven't already had." Her tone became petulant. "I was lonely tonight, and you were always such an amusing companion." Laying her head to his chest, she shifted suggestively.

Rigid, Philippe stared above her tousled golden curls. He forced his voice to smooth. "As much as I value your friendship, your highness, I cannot be your lover. That was over weeks ago. We both know it."

Her nails dug through the soft fabric of his sleeves. "It's not over until *I* say it's over. And I say that you shall come to my bed—unless, of course, you wish for me to call on your wife and tell her where you've been tonight. And other nights."

Philippe knew the princess would take great pleasure from destroying his marriage before it began. He had seen the sparks that invariably passed between her and Anne-Marie.

Now he realized that punishing him, alone, would not satisfy the Great Mademoiselle. Sooner or later, she would take her revenge on Anne-Marie. The affair would not remain a secret.

In that case, he had little to lose. "Tell my wife whatever you wish. After all, what can she do? We're married now. It's of no concern to me what you say."

Her head still pressed against his chest, the princess grew still. "Your heart is pounding like a galloping horse, Philippe. I'd like to think it's because of me." Her hand slid to his groin. Her voice sharpened. "No? Then perhaps your heart betrays you. It tells me you care very much what your dowdy little wife thinks." Her tone softened to a purr. "Of course, she isn't the only one who'd be interested in our little liaison. I imagine Commander Guitaut would be *fascinated* to learn that his most trusted officer has on seventeen occasions secretly visited the woman whose money finances the Fronde."

Philippe felt her claws closing around him like a cage. He should have known better than to come here!

Reaching the limit of his self-control, he grabbed the hair at the base of her skull and jerked downward until her face tilted into view. His mouth only inches from hers, Philippe's own breath bounced back hot off her skin as he snarled, "You're beneath contempt! I'd rather wring your neck than sleep with you now!"

An unearthly light flickered in her eyes. "Go ahead and try to strangle me. You wouldn't be the first man to take his hatred out on me in bed, and you won't be the last. Come on, Philippe. Stab me to death with *this!*" Her hand clutched his crotch. "I'm ready. Show me how much you hate me." Her voice was shrill with excitement.

Philippe shoved her from him. "By all that's holy, you're not a woman. You're a demon!" He made for the anteroom door. "I'm leaving. I'll take my chances with Guitaut. He, at least, knows the meaning of honor." He paused, his eyes narrowing. "Anyway, I think you're bluffing. You have no proof I've been here before tonight."

She hurled herself into his path. "No!" Hair straggling across her face, her mouth distorted with rage, she ripped open the neck of her gown, exposing her breast. Before he could stop her, she clawed four bright scratches across the tender skin.

Had she gone insane? Philippe seized her wrists before she could damage herself further. She struggled against his grip with surprising strength. A triumphant gleam in her eye, she took advantage of his nearness to grind a brutal, demanding kiss against his mouth. Then she bit his lip, hard.

Tasting blood, Philippe shoved her as far away as he could while still holding her wrists. "Stop it! Are you mad?"

His blood reddened her lips and smeared her milk-white chin. Her mouth shaped into the coldest, most chilling smile he had ever seen. "If you walk out that door before I say you may, I will summon the guards and have you charged with attempted rape."

Philippe's heart skipped a beat. "What?" As if by reflex, he released her and stepped backward.

Instantly calm, she inspected the reddened skin at her wrists. "There's more than enough evidence to support such a charge. These marks should bruise up nicely." She lifted her gown, exposing—along with her fair white nakedness—a red mark the size of his palm where he had shoved her. Then she let the fabric drop and casually strolled to pour herself a goblet of brandy.

Philippe's shock ebbed into nausea. She had him.

"Make yourself comfortable. At this point it's immaterial whether we go to bed or not. What matters to me is that you remain here until I release you."

His throat choked by a silent howl of protest, Philippe turned and gripped the mantel with such force his knuckles turned white. What choice had she left him? He croaked out, "You say you will release me. When?"

"When it pleases me." She downed the remainder of the brandy, then patted his cheek in a sadistic mockery of affection. "Don't worry. You'll be back with your bride before dawn." She smiled, her face as sunny as a girl's. "Come to think of it, watching you squirm for the next few hours appeals to me even more than the idea of forcing you to satisfy me in bed." Her eyes narrowed. "I shall enjoy that immensely, but not nearly as much as I'll enjoy having you banished from Court. You can thank your insufferable little wife for that!"

Philippe stiffened. Surely, she couldn't be serious!

The princess placed her empty glass on the mantel in front of him. "Now get me some more brandy, Philippe, and be quick about it."

An hour before dawn, Annique paced in front of the fire, her voice an angry whisper. "Where have you been? And don't try to lie! I woke up alone and went to the landing just in time to see you leaving with the Great Mademoiselle's messenger." She locked her arms across her chest and straightened to every inch of her five-foot-five-inch height.

Then her rigid posture sagged. *No. That will never work.* Philippe was far too proud a man to be backed into a corner. Direct confrontation would only provoke him. And what if he had a reasonable explanation? Though she dared not admit it, she secretly hoped he could explain his leaving.

She sank onto the sofa once again. Fueled by alternating fury and despair, she had rehearsed for what seemed like hours for the moment Philippe would return.

If he returned.

Annique huddled in the warmth of her robe, stricken. What if Philippe had gone to his lover? What if he remained there, the two of them flaunting their infidelity for all the world to see? The shame of such a thing was more than she could imagine.

She sprang back to her feet, her mouth compressed into an angry line. If he abandoned her for his paramour, she would leave him. Annulments were not unheard of. She'd apply for one, then return to the convent.

Her angry whisper once again broke the silence. "Philippe, I know where you went last night and what you did. Have you no shame? I've decided to leave you." The words sounded strident, even to her outraged ear. And how would he respond?

Against her will, imagination conjured up his dancing blue eyes and flashing grin. He would probably counter with something like, "What? Would you condemn me without giving me a chance to explain? There is a perfectly acceptable reason for what happened."

If only there were.

She paced back to the fire. Of course she must offer him a chance to explain. Maybe things weren't as damning as they seemed.

A log hissed inside the grate, echoing an inner whisper of cynicism. What explanation could there possibly be, other than the obvious? The entire Court had probably known about the affair all along! Everyone but Annique.

She placed two more logs on the grate before returning to the sofa to wait. Another hour passed, and she caught herself nodding. Exhaustion slowed the momentum of her anger to a crawl. Annique yawned loudly and unfolded her stiff, weary limbs. What was the use of being cold and uncomfortable? She might as well wait in bed.

She pulled back the quilt and in so doing uncovered the scarlet stain that testified to her loss of innocence. Annique jerked the rumpled sheets over it and crawled into the other side. There, knees drawn to her chest, she let the tears come.

Stepping into the silent bedchamber as he eased the door shut behind him, Philippe braced himself for the worst until he saw Anne-Marie's sleeping form in the tousled bed. The way things had been going, he'd expected to find his bride waiting up, ready to pounce with a handful of unanswerable questions.

He gingerly peeled off his perspiration-stained garments, then tiptoed beyond the bed and tossed the clothes into the corner. Tomorrow he would order Jacques to burn them. Hardly daring to breathe lest he rouse his wife, Philippe slid under the covers. Anne-Marie lay still, her breathing deep and even. Grateful that he'd managed to settle beside her without being caught, he relaxed.

First, sleep. Then he and Anne-Marie and the servants would leave for the coast. Once they were safely on board the ship, he would decide what to do. At sea there would be ample time to plan, and ample distance between him and the princess. Perhaps her threat would prove to be an idle one. If not, he'd have to pull every string imaginable to have himself reinstated at Court.

He might even have to ask for his father's help.

That prospect was almost as sickening as the idea of rotting away in the country, cut off from everything that mattered.

But for the time being, he must act as if nothing were amiss. And even though Anne-Marie was responsible for his disaster, the presence of her naked body so near him awakened a dull throb of lust. He reached out for the resilient smoothness of her bare skin, but by the time his fingers touched the heavy fabric of her robe, he had lapsed into exhausted slumber.

Annique huddled in silence next to him, struggling to keep her eyes closed and her breathing even. So he *had* come back. Part of her was relieved, even glad, but the greater part of her tightened into a huge, sickening knot. Despite a strong urge to confront him, she continued to feign sleep.

What if he confessed, confirming her suspicions? How could she live with that? Or what if he refused to answer, chiding her for questioning him?

Annique had never been so miserable in her life. She tried to move, but her limbs were like lead. She tried to speak, but no sound came. If he had betrayed her, that would twist everything, make a lie of all she'd felt and all he'd told her last night.

Perhaps Mother Bernard had been right. The sins of the flesh were seductive, and Annique had given in so easily, sealing her way to hell in this very bed.

Aching with fear and embarrassment at the thought of his naked body beside her, Annique tried to ignore the slack pressure of his hand against her hip. What if he tightened his grip and drew her to him, wanting to use her as he had before? Her breath caught in her throat. If he did, she would die of shame.

She lay still as death until she heard the soft rasping of his snore. She offered up a prayer of thanks to blessed Saint Anne and the Virgin. He had fallen asleep. Slowly, slowly, she turned her head to see him lying on his back, his mouth parted slightly, releasing the odor of strong spirits with each rumbling breath. Yet even with blue-black stubble shadowing his face, her husband looked as handsome as an angel.

Then she noticed his swollen lower lip. Her focus sharpened. Three small, evenly spaced red arcs marked his skin. Teeth marks, and not hers! Her faithless husband had been branded in his infidelity.

Annique shuddered. According to the Holy Writ, Satan was an angel, perfect and comely to behold. Perhaps Philippe *was* an angel—a fallen one, whose ease and beauty hid a treacherous heart.

The smell of hot chocolate permeated Annique's consciousness as the sound of Philippe's voice roused her from a sodden sleep.

"Time to wake up, Anne-Marie. Our ship sails with the tide in four days, so we must be off soon. Le Havre is a hundred miles away."

Their ship. Her lids strangely heavy, Annique started to smile before she remembered that something was wrong. When she did open her eyes, a freshly shaved and groomed Philippe waited beside the bed, their breakfast tray in his hands. A carnal gleam sparked his eye.

He placed the tray between them, then sat on the edge

of the bed. "Good morning, Madame Corbay. You slept so late, I was beginning to wonder if last night was too much for you."

Last night had been too much for her, but not in the way he meant. Suddenly conscious of the skin exposed by the disheveled robe she'd slept in, Annique clutched it closed and sat up.

Philippe fingered her collar. "Were you cold last night?" He leaned over and tucked a stray tendril behind her shoulder. "You should have asked me to stoke the fire."

Avoiding his eyes, Annique pulled away from his touch. Now was the time to confront him, but in spite of all her rehearsal, she still couldn't say the words. She could only stare with silent accusation at his swollen lip.

His puzzled expression shifted to one of suspicion, then a brief flash of recognition. Philippe raised his hand to conceal the marks, the gesture confirming his guilt.

So he *had* betrayed her. Annique's outrage grew stronger with every heartbeat.

Philippe spoke as he would to a frightened child. "What's the matter? Why do you look at me so?"

"I think you know the answer to that question."

"I wouldn't ask if I already knew. I'm not a man who enjoys such games."

"And what games were you playing last night after you left me? Rough ones, it would seem. You bear the marks, and I didn't put them there."

His only response was to close his eyes.

Annique bridled. Did he expect her to act as if nothing had happened? Her hands gripped the embroidered sheets. "After we . . . *after,* I woke to the sound of voices and found myself alone. When I went to find you, I saw you leave with a messenger in the Great Mademoiselle's livery. I waited hours for your return."

"Blast." So he *had* been caught! Philippe rose and paced to the window. If Anne-Marie hadn't baited the princess, none of this would have happened. Yet there his wife sat, indignantly demanding that he explain himself. He hadn't even done anything wrong!

It took all his self-control to remain outwardly calm.

Under the circumstances, he supposed she deserved some sort of explanation, but he bitterly resented having to give one. And he resented even more the way her wounded expression twisted his heart. Why did he care? Why *should* he care? He had not betrayed her.

But he knew enough about women to realize that he needed to smooth things over. They had to get out of Paris, and do it quickly, before the Great Mademoiselle could further complicate his life. He took a deep breath, then crossed to sit beside Anne-Marie on the bed.

Annique watched a mask of detached calm slide across his features. He said, "I am a soldier, and these are treacherous times. Sometimes a crisis requires immediate action, regardless of the circumstances of my personal life. I left last night on a matter of State." His voice was conciliatory. "I know it's hard to understand, but as the wife of a soldier, there will be times when you must trust me without question. This is one of those times." He took her hand. "Only the gravest of matters could have taken me from you last night. You must believe me." He stared intensely into her eyes. "There was no dishonor in my leaving. I swear it."

As always, the words were smooth, the manner flawless, but this time Annique had no intention of playing the silent victim. She wanted so much to believe him, yet—"You leave our wedding bed at the summons of another woman, one with whom you have obviously been personally involved, and stay out all night, coming home with her teeth marks on your lip, then ask me to believe that you were on a mission of *State?*" She threw back the covers, overturning the breakfast tray and its contents as she jumped to her feet. "Put yourself in my place, Philippe. How can I believe such a story? I may be naive, but I'm not stupid."

Philippe rose, his tone deadly. "Who has been talking to you? What have you heard?"

She tightened the sash of her robe. "No one has talked to me. I didn't need to hear anything. I could see the looks the princess gave you, the way you broke into a sweat whenever her name was mentioned." *And I can tell when someone's lying to me, like you are now. I've had a lifetime of lies to learn from.* An agonized whisper escaped her. "Was it amusing, Philippe, going straight from my arms to hers?"

Philippe's face darkened dangerously. "You should know me better than that."

"But I don't know you, Philippe; I don't know you at all. What else could I think, after seeing you leave that way?"

Experiencing the pain afresh, she fled to the hearth, wanting to put as much distance as possible between them, but he followed. Annique murmured bitterly, "Even after the princess tried to humiliate me with that ill-fitting dress, I still thought there was hope, believed that after our marriage whatever had happened between you would be in the past." Angry tears streaked her cheeks.

Philippe stepped closer, his fingers gripping her upper arms. "Anne-Marie, I can't have you thinking that I'm going to another woman every time my duty calls me away." The subtle undercurrent of frustration in his words made them more a command than a supplication.

Annique tried to pull free, but his grip was insistent. Still angry, yet wanting him to convince her of his innocence, she blurted out, "But why did you go to *her*? From our *wedding bed*? And how did you get those marks?"

"Again, I tell you this has nothing to do with us." Philippe looked into his wife's great, hurt brown eyes and felt a sharp pang of remorse, then asked himself again how she had managed to make him feel guilty when for once he was blameless, despite his motives. Somehow, her suspicions had the power to injure him. That fact was more unsettling than all the rest.

Before, it had always been so easy to lie. The women in his life had expected, even preferred, a reassuring falsehood rather than an uncomfortable truth. But Anne-Marie was different.

Why wouldn't she take him at his word? He *couldn't* tell her the truth, not without exposing the whole sordid, humiliating story, and he had no intention of doing that.

He cursed inwardly. He might as well have spent the night in the princess's bed. Anne-Marie seemed determined to believe he had.

Why did women always have to make things so complicated? Well, he was through crawling! Three hours as the princess's prisoner had given him a bellyful of feminine manipulation. His pride still raw from the Great Mademoiselle's abuse, he bridled. "I see no purpose in discussing this matter further." His words took on an edge of steel. "You vowed yesterday to honor me as your husband. Your accusations do neither. As your husband, I advise you to trust me and accept my explanation. Nothing can be served by prolonging this unpleasantness."

Annique swiveled to face him. "Unpleasantness?" All the anger that had taken root in the cold, lonely hours of the night rose up within her. Her low retort shook with it. "How dare you trivialize this with such a word?"

His fist met the table with a crash. "I'm *not* trivializing it!" Philippe rose. "By thunder, haven't you heard a word I've said?" He pointed to the tumbled disarray of the sheets and added grimly, "An empty bed is often the lot of a soldier's wife. Last night was the first time, but it won't be the last."

Too unhappy to speak, Annique remained silent as her husband stomped toward the door. When his hand touched the knob he paused. "This is no way to start our marriage." He turned back, his tone softening. "In but a few days' time, we'll be on a sailing ship, a hundred miles away from the princess and her damned rebellion. Can't we put this behind us and start over?" He coaxed, "I know how much you've looked forward to this trip. Our honeymoon voyage can be a new beginning."

Annique's teeth dug into the inside of her cheek at the thought of being trapped with him—perhaps for months— on a ship.

Philippe offered a conciliatory smile. "Come now, Anne-Marie. What can I do to make that sad, injured expression go away? Surely there must be something."

If only they *could* start over. If only there was something he could do to make things better . . . Then a single, ringing thought resonated through Annique's consciousness. She stilled. "Yes. There is something you can do."

He bowed with mock seriousness before her. "I'll stop at nothing to restore myself to your good graces, fair lady. Your word is my command."

"Take me home." The moment the words were spoken, she felt the healing in them. She could never compete with the princess here in Paris, but as mistress of her own house in the country, there would be a place for her. She could make a life for herself, away from the Great Mademoiselle's interference and all the petty humiliations of the Court. Annique had that left, at least. "Please, Philippe. I don't want to go on a voyage. Take me home."

He frowned. "To my town house? But Jacques and Suzanne have already closed everything up and packed for the voyage. And you seemed so pleased about seeing the ocean—"

"Not the town house. I want to go home to Maison Corbay."

Philippe's face betrayed his surprise. "What did you say?"

Annique didn't know why she drew such peace from the thought of going to a place she'd never seen, but her words became a prayer. "Take me home to Maison Corbay, Philippe. Please."

❊ CHAPTER 14 ❊

*P*hilippe stared unseeing at passing shops and houses as his open carriage approached the city gate. He should never have gone back to bed at dawn. The scant hour of sleep had left him more haggard than when he'd finally been released from the princess's torment. His eyes burned, his muscles ached, and a headache hammered inside his skull. Yet that was the least of his regrets.

Unaccustomed though he was to second-guessing himself, he noted bitterly that during the last twenty-four hours he'd made more mistakes and accumulated more regrets than he had in twenty-eight years of living.

His tongue traced the tender wounds inside his lower lip. Why in blazes had he allowed himself to be sucked into the princess's trap? That lapse caused him to reconsider the wisdom of agreeing to Anne-Marie's ragged, whispered plea to take her "home" to Maison Corbay.

The idea had seemed reasonable at the time. He would be out of the princess's sight, and hopefully out of mind, but still close enough to find out whether she meant to make good on her threat to have him banished from Court. Over the past few years he had been on intimate terms with several of the queen's attendants, ladies who held no affection for the Great Mademoiselle. They would gladly warn him if the princess petitioned to have him cast out of society. Yes, he'd be in a much better position to protect himself from Sèvres.

As long as the princess didn't find out where he was.

At this rate, she'd know in twenty minutes. The weather

was so warm and fair that he'd allowed Anne-Marie to talk him into taking the open carriage. Now any Parisian who cared to look could see them traveling south toward Sèvres instead of westward for the relative safety of the open sea. He scowled, ignoring the soft westerly breeze that replaced the city's usual stench with the perfume of blooming flowers from the surrounding countryside. Philippe turned to make sure Suzanne was following close behind with the baggage cart. Satisfied that she was, he settled back to glare across the carriage at his bride.

If only she hadn't wakened to find him gone . . . But she had, and she had known, in that cursed way of women, that his explanation held something back. So the lamb had been condemned as a goat.

Weary beyond sleeping, Philippe shifted his gaze to Marie, perched eagerly beside her mistress. His temper rose. His wife had insisted Marie ride with her—almost as if she needed a buffer, a protector from Philippe himself. The maid belonged in the baggage wagon with Suzanne, not sitting beside her mistress like a chaperone.

Philippe tugged the broad brim of his hat lower against the morning sun and closed his eyes.

War was simple compared to dealing with these blasted women.

A pox on his wife, and on her maid. And on the princess. A pox on the entire sex.

Until the carriage took the fork marked "Sèvres," Annique feared Philippe might reconsider his promise and insist they turn north to Le Havre and the waiting ship. For almost ten miles, she had alternated between fear that he would change his mind, and anger as she rehashed this morning's bitter confrontation. But now she felt nothing. Even the dull echo of last night's pain had left her. She was beyond hurting now. Reality had been a brutal teacher, but she'd not soon forget its lesson—that romance and fidelity in marriage were mere illusions, ideas that had no place in the real world. She could almost hear the sound of doors closing within her and the sigh of dying dreams.

Yet there was a certain liberation in cynicism. Being the Duchess of Corbay would have its compensations. For all his faithlessness, Philippe was not a cruel man. And he certainly knew how to give pleasure in bed.

Her heart turned over as she recalled his touch upon her naked body.

How could the memory stir such strong desire, yet—at the same time—such shame? Such pleasure, and yet such anger? Forever changed by the experience, Annique still wasn't certain what she had changed *into*.

One thing was sure: The next time she shared her bed with Philippe, it would be on *her* terms. The resolution hardened within her, blocking out some of the lingering sense of betrayal that clung to her.

When the clutter of the suburbs gave way to freshly tilled fields, Annique settled back and let herself think of what lay ahead. All her life she had longed for a place where she truly belonged. Her marriage to Philippe had given her that, at least. He might be a master of the estate, but she would be mistress of Maison Corbay. No matter what awaited her there, the manor house would be a home. She would see to it. Annique could take comfort in that, at least.

As they approached Sèvres, she studied her husband from the corner of her eye. Though he stared idly at the passing scenery, Philippe's arms and legs remained tightly crossed, his posture rigid.

He was probably still angry with her for refusing to believe him about last night. And he might well be more vexed than he'd let on about canceling their voyage. Odd, that he had insisted the servants not be informed of the change in plans until the carriage was well beyond the city walls. Even then, no word was dispatched to the ship's captain. Instead, Jacques had been sent ahead to Maison Corbay on Balthus to warn the staff of their imminent arrival.

The staff. Not just Philippe's couple and Marie, but The Staff. As the carriage rolled through the sleepy town of Sèvres, the new mistress of Maison Corbay daydreamed about putting her house in order, a dozen servants under her direction.

Just beyond the village, she spoke. "Philippe, I . . . I just wanted to thank you for canceling the voyage. I know the fare must have gone forfeit. It was probably a lot of money, but I'll try to make it up to you."

His reply was curt. "Think nothing of it."

The dangerous cast to his eyes stopped her from pursuing the matter further.

Down a broad country lane their progress slowed, then halted at a rusted wrought-iron gate. Annique peered through the neglected ironwork, and a tingle of foreboding caused her to straighten. The gatekeeper's cottage beyond lay in overgrown ruins.

It had occurred to her that Philippe's home might not be as grand as Maison d'Harcourt, but she'd never considered that it might be derelict.

A startling suspicion formed in her mind. Was Philippe poor? But Father Jules had assured her she would lack for nothing as Duchess de Corbay . . .

Not that Annique minded being poor; she'd known little else. But she minded very much being married to a man embittered by his lack of wealth. Could that be behind Philippe's estrangement from his rich, powerful father?

The driver left his perch to push the creaking gate inward, opening the way to a rutted passage that wound through tangled undergrowth beneath a canopy of ancient chestnuts. After the gate was dragged shut behind them, the little caravan moved on, the deep shade and unearthly quiet of the woods only adding to Annique's misgivings. She held on for dear life as the carriage jolted and swayed for what seemed like a mile before the woods gave way to a huge meadow full of wildflowers. In the middle of that meadow—its once-stately setting now a colorful riot of benign neglect—stood Maison Corbay. The rambling, three-story brick structure was a little worse for its venerable years, perhaps, but not derelict.

Annique's apprehension, along with the dregs of last night's anger, drained away, replaced by an overwhelming sense of completion. She stood straight up in the carriage. "Oh, Philippe! It's beautiful!"

Her gaze darted from the pointed roof of the cylindrical entry tower to the balconied windows, to the carved stone embellishments, to the crumbling chimneys. When the carriage hit a pothole, she bounced unceremoniously back into her seat. Steadying herself against Marie, she motioned to the two projecting wings of the house. "See how it seems to reach out in welcome. Like a real home, not some great, forbidding box."

There was nothing grand or elegant about Maison

Corbay; compared to the great houses of Paris, it wasn't even very large. Once painted white, its sun-warmed bricks now wore a mottled face brightened by window boxes and graceful urns brimming with narcissus, tulips, and pansies. Several slate shingles were missing from the turreted entry tower, and Annique could see blue sky through the broken upper windows of the westernmost wing, but somehow the old house had managed to retain a sense of serene immutability. Perhaps that was why she instantly and irrevocably loved it. "I can hardly wait to see inside."

Philippe's brows lifted in mild surprise. "I thought you might be disappointed."

"Disappointed?" Annique shook her head. "No. I love it."

As the carriage halted before the stone stairs, Philippe regarded her oddly, as if searching for some hint of sarcasm. When he saw none, his voice softened. "Maison Corbay is far from perfect, but I'm rather fond of the place, myself."

Jacques stepped into the courtyard to greet them. "Welcome home, your graces." Acting as footman, he opened the carriage door and folded down the step while addressing his master. "Madame Pleuris almost had a fit when I told her your graces were comin' right behind me. She sent her son to the village for food, then started snatchin' covers off the furniture. You can't see a thing inside for the dust she's stirred up."

Philippe followed Annique from the carriage. "What about Paoul?"

Jacques grinned. "Shufflin' and complainin', same as ever. I can't imagine why you keep him on, your grace. He's useless."

Though Philippe's response was modulated, a subtle hardening of inflection gave Annique a glimpse of Captain Corbay of the Queen's Guard. "I told you before, Jacques. For ten years, Paoul kept this place from ruin with no money and little help. He's earned a rest. I'll hear no more complaints about him."

Obviously, Philippe esteemed loyalty in those who served him. Annique found it ironic that her husband didn't apply the same standard of fidelity to himself or his marriage. Then she dismissed the stinging thought. Nothing good would be served by lingering on suspicions of betrayal. She refused to bring evil thoughts with her into her new home.

Annique was halfway to the front door before she realized Philippe hadn't followed. She turned to find him busy directing the unloading of the baggage cart.

Was he avoiding her? She could hardly blame him, after the argument they'd had this morning. Yet as she stood now in this peaceful, secluded place, last night's disappointment and this morning's conflict seemed very far behind them.

Eager to go inside, she lifted her hand to call out to him, but thought better of such an undignified outburst. She motioned, instead, for the valet. "Jacques, it would be bad luck to enter my new home alone. Please inform his grace that I await his presence."

"Aye, your grace."

After the servant delivered her message, Philippe looked briefly her way, then focused on the toe of his boot, digging at a weed in the graveled driveway. When he made no move to come to her, Annique straightened. Surely he wouldn't risk inviting ill fortune by refusing to accompany her across the threshold for the first time!

Her marriage had had a bad enough beginning. She could enter her new home alone, but why tempt fate? She would make the first move. Her hand extended toward him in mute supplication.

The gesture was all he needed. Annique's superstitious fear vanished when he strode up the wide stone steps and across the courtyard to her side. His palm was warm against her fingers. "Madame. Shall we go in?"

"Together, your grace. As it should be." How she wished things were as they should be.

Though Philippe smiled, his eyes remained wary. "Of course. Together."

Jacques opened the heavy wooden door, and Annique stepped into the turreted vestibule. To her left, a narrow stairway began its upward spiral along the curving white daub walls. Two quaint arched doorways peeked from the landings above, and high overhead the carved beams supporting the cone-shaped roof showed faint remnants of red and blue decorative painting.

Beyond the small, circular entry, an enormous foyer stretched to the back of the house. Without a word An-

nique crossed into the vast hall. Dust motes drifted like
stars in shafts of brilliant sunlight. Her eyes followed the
light upward to large stained glass windows whose ancient
crest designs recorded the history of the Corbay lineage.
Reflected fragments of colored light warmed the carved
chestnut paneling, its rich golden patina the evidence of
decades—perhaps centuries—of care and polish.

Annique hardly noticed the water stains on the walls and
ceilings. Instead, she marveled at the huge, ornate stone
mantels and inlaid wood floors. She paid little heed to the
frayed edges of the tapestries hanging between the high
windows. Rather, she wondered how many generations of
children had made up their own stories about the brave
knights and fair ladies who marched in subtle hues across
the ancient weavings.

Philippe stood just inside the doorway watching her, his
face impassive.

Then from the rear of the hall, a shuffling figure grumbled toward them, his spine bent downward with age.

Philippe stepped to her side and whispered, "That's
Paoul, my predecessor's manservant. He's harmless,
really."

The reference to Philippe's predecessor reminded Annique of Maison Corbay's tragic history. Father Jules had
seemed so sad when he'd told her about the carriage crash
that had killed the previous duke and his family. She shivered and crossed herself, grateful that their violent deaths
had happened far away. She couldn't help but wonder if
Paoul had grieved at the news of his master's death. If his
subsequent faithfulness was any indication, she imagined
the loss had been a bitter one.

The old man was almost upon them before he spent the
energy to look up. When he did, his eyebrows shot almost
to his hairline, and his mouth fell open in astonishment.
"Why, it's the duchess, herself!"

Taken aback by his unexpected intensity, Annique tried
to remain properly dignified. "Hello, Paoul. The duke tells
me you have given many years of faithful service here."

The old man buckled. Thinking that he was collapsing,
Annique reached out as he sank to his knees before her,
his rheumy gaze lifted to hers.

Wonder pulsed in his voice. "It *is* you. Welcome home,
your grace." A gnarled hand grasped hers. He bent his

head and murmured brokenly, "So many years this house has been empty. Praise be to God, you've come home at last."

Philippe answered his wife's questioning look with a shrug, then gently helped the old servant to his feet. "Come along now, Paoul. Why don't you see if you can help Madame Pleuris with supper?"

Beaming, the old man rose with surprising ease. "Aye, master. I'll have that contrary wench back to work in the kitchens before you can say 'rabbit's in the cabbage patch'!"

Annique waited until he disappeared to ask, "What was *that* all about?"

Philippe shook his head. "Who knows? He certainly took to you, though." Grinning, he added, "Paoul's old. Perhaps his wits were muddled by the excitement, though I've never known him to act confused before."

She was surprised how happy it made her to see Philippe smile. The grin transformed him, chasing away any questions raised by the old man's remarks. She offered a wry smile of her own. "So Paoul's old and confused, eh? And that explains why he took to me."

Philippe's cheeks reddened slightly. "I didn't mean that. I just meant . . ." He eased. "You know perfectly well what I meant. You're just having a little fun at my expense, aren't you?"

"We could both use a little fun, I suspect." She curtsied briefly. "Come, husband. Show me our home."

Philippe's tour was a brief one. Only a few of Maison Corbay's rooms remained habitable. By the time he escorted Annique into the spacious, rear-facing east bedroom on the second floor, she had realized that a great deal of work would be needed to restore the place to its former dignity.

She was up to the task. For the first time since she had left the convent, she felt a real sense of purpose.

Philippe opened a double door on the bedroom's inside wall and gestured. "Your dressing room connects with mine, with my quarters beyond, facing the front of the house. I thought you'd prefer this bedchamber. It's brighter and looks out over what used to be the garden."

Her very own room. She could be happy here.

Annique smiled, but her sense of well-being faded

slightly when she looked to the dressing room door. It bore no lock. There was no sign of a lock on the door that led to Philippe's dressing room, either. After an awkward glance toward the high canopy bed, she said, "I like this room very much." She refrained from telling him she'd like it better with a bolt on her side of the door. But that could be remedied soon enough.

Annique stepped across the pattern of faded flowers woven into the rug; she opened the glassed doors that led to a sunny balcony. Looking southward at the tumble of growth behind the house, she clasped her forearms in an unconscious gesture of contemplation. "I'm glad we came. It seems so peaceful here. I feel very safe, so far away from . . . all the complications of the Court."

"I wish it *were* safe here, but it's not." Philippe looked toward the distant spires of Sèvres. "Even in the villages, there have been food riots and demands for reform. The rebellion is all around us. We can't escape it by hiding in the country." Regret heavy in his voice, he turned his gaze westward toward the unseen Atlantic. "Maybe we should have sailed away, after all."

"I'm glad we didn't." How could she explain the sense of absolute security she felt within these walls, when she didn't understand it herself? "We *are* safe here, Philippe. Nothing bad will happen to either one of us at Maison Corbay."

Philippe placed a boot on the low railing and leaned forward, his forearm propped casually upon his thigh as he stretched the road-weariness from his legs. Then he smiled. "If it's made you happy, then I'm glad we came. But we can't stay here forever. God willing, I will be returning to my duties in Paris, and to Court."

At the mention of Court, Annique stilled. "Will I have to go with you?"

A tiny frown tucked the corners of his mouth. "Let's not think of that now. It's weeks away."

Was he disappointed or glad she wanted to remain behind? Annique couldn't tell. "You want to go back, don't you?"

"I must return to my post in the Guard. It's my duty." He squinted against the sunlight, his eyes still on the horizon. "As a soldier, I go where I'm ordered, when I'm ordered. I don't think about it."

What prompted the bitterness in his voice? Philippe's distant, closed expression reminded Annique how little she really knew about her husband. Curious, she asked, "Did you choose to be a soldier, or was it chosen for you?"

He faced her, one black brow lifted, and something akin to amusement playing about his lips. "Are you always so blunt when you ask personal questions?"

Her answering gaze did not waver. "We are husband and wife, Philippe. Is it unreasonable for me to want to know more about you?"

A subtle easing of his features replaced the cynicism in his smile with candor. "You're not easily put off, are you?"

Two could play at this game. She parried, "You still haven't answered my question." Then she waited in resolute silence, remembering Father Jules's admonition that after a difficult question is posed, whoever speaks first loses.

"As second son of a great house, I had no trade. Since soldiering was the only respectable job I could get, I took it. If that's choosing, then I chose." His manner was cavalier, but the tilt of his chin was defensive.

Moments of silence passed before she asked lightly, "Do you like soldiering?"

Again, bitterness hardened the lines of his face. "A soldier never asks himself that question."

Annique had thought of Philippe as companion, courtier, and member of the Harcourt family, but she'd never fully considered his life as a soldier. Childishly, she had thought of his life only inasmuch as it related directly to *her*. Chastened to realize how selfish her perspective had been, she frowned, her voice soft. "The last few years must have been very difficult for you, what with all your time between the Spanish campaigns being taken up with the Fronde."

At the mention of the endless fighting, Philippe crossed his arms at his chest. Bone-deep weariness radiated from his words. "This is only my second leave in the last six years."

Annique had always considered the rebellion and the war with Spain distant and unreal—games of politics and power played by anonymous characters. But now the haunted look in her husband's eyes brought the conflict home. "Father Jules told me you served with great valor in four campaigns against the Spanish before you transferred to the Queen's Guard."

At the mention of the Guard, Philippe's face grew even more shielded, but he made no comment. Obviously, she had crossed onto dangerous ground.

His reticence only piqued her interest. She prodded, "The Fronde has divided many great houses. How was it you chose to serve the regent?"

Philippe blinked at the sheer audacity of her question, then smiled. Brittle humor marked his reply. "As I said before, if a man with but one option has a choice, then I chose. But we've talked enough of me. Let's talk of you. What do you think of our garden?"

She knew better than to push further. Annique turned her attention to the grounds below them. "This must have been beautiful, once."

Through the trees to the left, she could just make out a bit of roof that must be the stables. Southward, at the far boundary of the clearing, a slow stream spread into a pond. Her eyes swept across the huge open field, and in a matter of moments she picked out an orderly pattern of dark green untrimmed boxwood. Then she saw the roses, their rampant branches arching over weed and wildflower. At the very center of the field, the weathered curls of a marble cherub peeked above the tall grass.

Her practical nature asserted itself. She ventured, "With a little help, it might be restored. Are there any gardeners on the staff?"

Philippe's eyes narrowed. "Besides Jacques, Suzanne, and Marie, *the staff,* as you call it, consists of Paoul, Madame Pleuris, and her son, Pierre."

"Obviously, that's not enough servants for a house this size. No wonder things look so neglected," she said matter-of-factly, then saw that her comment had somehow invoked a defensive arch to his brow.

Were all men so sensitive about the status of their households?

Ignoring his pettishness, she let herself be caught up in a vision of what might be. "A little hard work will go a long way here, Philippe. I'd like to put things right."

Philippe considered. Supervising such a large project could keep her busy—and out of his hair—for quite a while. Now that there was plenty of money for repairs, he could think of no reason to deny her request. "I suppose that would be all right."

She asked, "Do we have enough money to fix everything?"

Philippe's mouth flattened. "Yes. There's money enough for repairs and for servants. Even for gardeners, if you wish."

"I'm not an extravagant person, but anyone can see that there's much to be done."

Lips drawn, he rumbled, "I've always intended to fix the place up."

Annique could barely conceal her excitement. "May I start right away?"

His small, questioning scowl gave way to resignation. "Very well. I don't see why not. But I can't imagine why you'd want to spend your honeymoon that way."

Annique was so pleased she forgot to act dignified and aloof. "Oh, thank you. You won't be disappointed, I promise." She was glad the old house needed her. Now her new life offered not only purpose, but also the promise of re-creating Maison Corbay with her own personal stamp.

If anyone had told her this morning that she could feel this happy so soon after feeling so miserable, she would have scorned him for a fool.

As it was, she swept past her husband, her mind whirling with plans as she bubbled, "Just wait. This place will be beautiful, you'll see. And while I supervise the renovations, you can get some rest. Read. Hunt. I'll take care of everything. In only a few weeks' time, Maison Corbay will be a real home."

❀ CHAPTER 15 ❀

*T*wo weeks later, Philippe stalked across Maison Corbay's library, threw open the door, and bellowed, "Jacques! Get in here!" His shout was barely audible above the construction racket and the maids chattering as they cleaned the great chandelier that had been lowered to within a foot of the foyer floor.

"What does it take to get a little attention from my own valet?" he said to no one in particular. Jacques was probably still supervising the restoration of the garden, commandeered more than a week ago by Anne-Marie "for only a few days." A few days, indeed.

Philippe stormed back into the library. By thunder, a man should be able to get a little service in his own household. And find peace in more than one room! Northern light poured through the tall, unadorned windows into his sole remaining sanctuary. He felt a grudging stab of gratitude that this room had been renovated first. The carved cascades of fruit embellishing the walnut woodwork had been polished to a rich dark brown, and the shelves were crowded now with carefully dusted books—many of them discovered on his wife's forays into the attics and cellars. Reading those new additions to his collection had kept him occupied for his first few days at Maison Corbay.

Until the carpenters had come. And the roofers. Since then, there hadn't been a moment's peace from sunrise to sunset.

He couldn't even escape to ride or hunt or fish now, not without Jacques. After what had happened that last night at the Tuileries, Philippe knew it would be foolish to venture out into the countryside alone, and Jacques was the only servant he trusted to accompany him. So for the past eight days he'd been forced to hole up in his library, unable to read for more than a few minutes at a time without some loud distraction.

He chafed at the inactivity. It left him with too much time to think—about the nagging doubts raised by the destructive jealousies of the royalist command, and the haunting memories of fellow Frenchmen he'd killed in this cursed rebellion. For more than a year, he'd kept too busy to face those disturbing realities. Now there was no denying them.

And then there was the matter of his marriage. Anne-Marie had not only jeopardized his position at Court, she'd turned his life upside-down!

He paced now to the empty fireplace and glowered at the freshly scrubbed stone. When he'd given his wife permission to renovate the place, he'd thought the project would keep her occupied and out of his way. Instead, she'd destroyed all peace and decorum at Maison Corbay.

Granted, the food was considerably better. Madame Pleuris had willingly surrendered her kitchen duties to two capable chefs. Though the cuisine was unpretentious, Philippe now presided nightly over a table befitting the lord of the manor. And the staff was functioning far more efficiently these days. But those improvements hardly offset the turmoil his wife had unleashed on his once-sedate home.

What was her blasted hurry, anyway? Anne-Marie drove herself and the workers beyond all reason. Save Sunday, she rose every morning before dawn and worked straight through every day like a woman possessed. By suppertime she was so exhausted she could barely stay awake. With the exception of dinner and a few random meetings as she went about her work each day, Anne-Marie had managed to avoid being alone with him since they'd arrived. And when they were together at dinner, she took great care to center their discussions on the inevitable minor crises of renovation, then pleaded fatigue and retreated to her bedchamber alone.

This was hardly the honeymoon Philippe had envisioned. He knew she would eventually grow weary of channeling all her passions into the renovation, but he was tired of waiting. An all-too-familiar stirring shuddered in his loins. How many more nights must he retire to an empty bed?

Ironic, that he had been naive enough to believe his honeymoon would guarantee him regular, easy access to sexual satisfaction. He hadn't been this long without a woman since he'd left his father's house at seventeen!

Philippe picked up a book and tried to resume reading, but his current state made concentrating difficult. He told himself that his anger stemmed from forced inactivity and the constant interruptions. He refused to admit that Anne-Marie's continued coolness had any effect on him.

He paced to the library window, only to be greeted by the grinning face of a painter on the other side of the glass. Irritated beyond all reason by the sight, Philippe barked, "Work somewhere else while I'm in here!"

The painter pretended not to hear. He nodded cheerfully and kept right on working.

Blast! Anne-Marie had probably promised the fool a bonus for finishing early. She'd become entirely too involved with the workmen. Such familiarity was not appropriate for a woman of her stature. He'd mentioned the matter to her several times, but to no avail.

Philippe muttered under his breath all the way back to his polished, repaired desk. Spread out before him were receipts and bills from dozens of local suppliers, tailors, craftsmen, and Paris merchants. He scanned the invoices for rugs, furniture, bedding, fabrics, household equipment, wrought-iron, stable goods, oats, tack, seed, shrubs—not to mention the lumber, stone, mortar, and shingles. If she kept spending at this rate, they'd run through a year's interest on her dowry in just a few months! Philippe was determined not to borrow again. He'd had enough of creditors.

"I've created a monster." Throwing up his hands in resignation, he leaned back in the heavy Jacobean chair.

A cursory knock at the door preceded Jacques' entrance. "You summoned me, your grace?" Grimy and harried, the valet stepped gingerly to avoid dirtying the floor.

"Yes, I summoned you! What's going on back in the kitchen? I rang four times, and no one came."

Jacques' forehead shrank into a press of wrinkles. "I believe her grace has had all the bells disconnected, sir, for repairs."

"Well, *this* bell was working fine. Tell them to reconnect it."

The valet squirmed. "Straightaway, your grace. Was that all, your grace?"

"No, that is not all. Where is the duchess? I wish to speak with her."

"I believe her grace is in the west wing."

"What's she doing there?"

Jacques murmured reluctantly, "Dealing with the furniture vendors from Paris."

Philippe stopped shuffling through the bills. "Dealing? What do you mean, dealing?"

Jacques looked with longing at the door, obviously preferring the hot, dirty work of the garden to his present predicament. "Dealing, your grace." He tucked his chin to his chest, his eyes cutting upward. "Haggling."

"What?" This was the last straw. Philippe nodded tersely. "You may go back to your work, Jacques. I'll take care of this." He strode past his servant and out of the library. The mistress of Maison Corbay had no business haggling with merchants like a common shopkeeper!

Philippe crossed the foyer to the west wing. Beyond the ballroom's freshly sanded doors, a forest of scaffolding blocked his path. "Blast. A man can't even get through his own home!"

Twelve feet above him, the chief plasterer stopped work and bowed. "We regret the inconvenience, your grace."

When Philippe looked up, a tiny dollop of plaster hit his forehead. One of the faces peering down from the scaffolding retreated in shock. He swiped off the plaster and demanded, "Where is the duchess?"

The plasterer gestured toward the terrace. "I believe she's outside, your grace."

Fuming, Philippe worked his way through the maze of poles and platforms. When he finally reached the doors of the rear-facing terrace, he looked through the glass panes to see his wife rooting among the bolts in the cloth vendor's wagon, her petticoats and stockinged ankles exposed to the amused and appreciative glances of two bewigged merchants.

Embarrassment heated Philippe's temper past the boiling point. Hadn't she heard a word he'd said in the past two weeks? The woman was hopeless. She had no sense of station!

One powerful thrust of his hands sent the terrace doors flying, shattering the glass.

The merchants scurried backward as Philippe bounded down the steps and snatched his surprised wife out of the wagon.

"Philippe! What's the matter?"

He set her firmly to her feet without responding. Instead, he addressed the white-faced vendors with deadly calm. "How dare you embarrass the duchess by refusing to properly display your wares? Get off my property this minute. And if either one of you opens his mouth about this demeaning incident, you'll die for it. Do I make myself clear?"

Nodding frantically, the taller of the two shoved his companion into the front of the wagon, then leapt beside him and cracked his whip over the horses. The conveyance clattered wildly around the side of the house.

Annique put her hands to her hips. Had Philippe lost his

mind? "What in heaven was that about? I'd just picked out the nicest fabric for your library draperies—a perfect match for the rug. Now I'll have to send for another cloth merchant from Paris. That could take days and days."

Philippe let out a strangled oath. "That's not the point! But obviously, you have no grasp of the problem." She watched him struggle to regain his composure. When he spoke again, his voice was edged with irritation. "It's my library, and you've tinkered with it enough. I don't want any draperies."

Obviously, he didn't understand the practicalities of the situation. Annique explained, "There must be draperies. Without them, the room will be cold as a tomb in winter."

Several of the gardeners weeding nearby slowed their progress, all ears.

Philippe whispered through gritted teeth, "Madame, you are as relentless as gravity and twice as stubborn. I'll not stand here and argue with you in front of the servants." He grabbed her arm and practically dragged her along the graveled path to the pond pavilion. "Come with me. We'll settle this in private."

Annique almost lost her footing twice. By the time Philippe shoved her inside the columned pavilion, she'd had enough of being manhandled. "Let me *go*. How dare you embarrass me so, treating me like a disobedient child!"

"Me? Embarrass you?" Visibly struggling to restrain his temper, he countered, "How dare *you* embarrass *me,* acting like the commonest peasant, climbing into that wagon, your ankles and petticoats exposed for all the world to see!" Philippe leveled an accusing finger at her face. "I have overlooked a great deal since I met you, madame, but I refuse to allow you to sully the dignity of my household. I am your husband, not your governess. I've warned you repeatedly about becoming too involved in the work of the servants and hirelings. If you cannot conduct yourself properly, I'll be forced to . . . to . . . fire the lot of them and put an end to the matter. Do I make myself clear?"

Annique grew very still. His pointing finger was close enough to bite, but she resisted the urge to do so. Instead, she said quietly, "Regarding my involvement with the merchants, I was only being frugal. Every single one of them has tried to charge us double, simply because this is a manor house. It would be poor stewardship, indeed, to let them get away with such mischief."

Philippe's eyes narrowed, his jaw flexing dangerously. "Once again, I remind you, madame, of your rank and position in this household. You should *hire* someone competent to deal with the merchants and workmen. It's not dignified to deal with such people directly!"

Knowing that her husband considered himself to be a man of reason, Annique forced her anger aside and appealed to logic. "You know very well, sir, that I've tried to find someone to oversee the work. And you also know there's not a soul available for miles who can even add, much less keep up with a renovation this complicated. Until we can locate a proper overseer, necessity dictates that I take care of things. It's as simple as that."

Philippe flushed. *Curse the woman's condescending tone, and her obstinacy!*

She stood rigid before him, the look of a martyr in her raised eyebrows and the resolute set of her lips. "If you think my behavior so distasteful, sir, might I suggest you return to Paris. I'm certain you'll find no such unpleasant distractions there." The shadow of past betrayal flashed across her features, adding acid to the next. "And I have no doubt you'll find more *obliging* company, as well—a companion perfectly suited to your *bachelor* accommodations."

Philippe's teeth locked shut. How long did she intend to play the wronged, virtuous woman, hanging onto her fantasy of betrayal, punishing him by withholding her presence and her affection?

Indignation ripped away the last shred of his patience. He closed the distance between them. "Madame, can you swim?"

"I beg your pardon?"

"Can you swim?"

Eyes wide with confusion, she shook her head. "No. I—"

Before she could finish, his muscled arm circled her waist and abruptly hauled her off her feet. Philippe bore her across the pavilion as easily as he might carry a sheaf of wheat. "No matter. The pond's only three feet deep." With that, he heaved her over the wooden railing and into the water.

Annique surfaced, gasping and sputtering. "Why, you

blackguard! I told you I couldn't swim! Do you mean to drown me?" She jerked a water lily from the hair plastered across half her face.

Her grinning husband leaned against a weathered column. "I *thought* that might put a crack in your saintly veneer!" He crossed his arms at his chest. "Ah, my dear! If only you could see the sight you make!"

A futile stab of her fist failed to quell the billowing silk that rose with the mud she'd stirred up. "You cad! I don't care if you *are* my husband, you have no right to—" Annique's rebuke was cut short by the impact of something wet, slimy, and definitely alive on her bosom. She let out an ear-piercing shriek.

Philippe straightened in alarm until he saw the source of her distress was a small frog. He dissolved into helpless guffaws.

At the sound of his mockery, something snapped inside Annique. Her voice lowered with menace. "Why, you arrogant, insufferable . . ." She tried to move toward him, but the muck held her shoes in a sucking, unrelenting grip. Her predicament only made Philippe laugh harder.

Furious, she jerked one foot free with such force that the momentum sent her facefirst into the muddy water. Instinctively, Annique held her breath. Struggling to free her other foot from the muck, she felt her skirts slide forward over her head, enveloping her in yards of waterlogged fabric. Her eyes stung as they flew open to see a blurred confusion of mud and fabric and clinging, snakelike pond growth. She tried to right herself, only to be dragged down by the heavy folds of her skirts.

Several angry, thrashing seconds passed before she realized she couldn't break clear to the surface. Suddenly she wasn't sure which way was up. The harder she tried to fight free, the more tangled she became. Panicked, Annique sucked in a deadly breath of water. The paroxysms of coughing that followed only drew in more.

That very moment, something exploded into the pond beside her, and two strong arms scooped her into the sunlight. But enough of the pond came out with her to keep her from taking in the air she so desperately needed. Still flailing and coughing, she expelled a mouthful of muddy water right into Philippe's ashen face. He spun her around, his arms circling her torso. Once, twice, the iron embrace tightened and loosened, trying to force the water from her lungs, but still she couldn't breathe.

Philippe held her hard against him and struggled for the shore, his voice tight. "Don't worry. You'll be all right. Cough it out, Anne-Marie!"

Darkness crept into the periphery of her vision. Annique clawed desperately at his arms, her feet kicking with all her might as she fought for air.

He seemed oblivious to the bleeding scratches she made. "Dear God, Anne-Marie, I never meant to hurt you." Once they reached dry ground, he shoved her, facedown, onto the tall grass. "Stop fighting me! Lie still, so I can help you!"

But some primal force wouldn't let her give up. She kept struggling, even as she felt his hands spread across the base of her rib cage. He pressed down with a rough, jarring rhythm until she gagged and heaved up the remaining water from her lungs, followed immediately by the contents of her stomach. After that, she went limp, her chest finally filling with blessed air.

"Anne-Marie? Speak to me. Are you all right?"

All right? He dared ask her that, after almost drowning her! One more deep breath was all Annique needed before retaliating with the fury of a cornered badger. She rolled over and pushed into a sitting position, her fingers digging into the soft earth and pulling loose great clods of dirt and grass. "You faithless, overblown, stingy, pompous, spoiled, disreputable, selfish, heretical *boor!*"

He ducked the first clod of grass she hurled at him, but the second hit him square in the face, the dirt exploding against his wet skin and freckling his already muddy clothes with black blobs. Wiping the worst of it from his eyes, he spat grit from his mouth and grinned. "I always suspected there was a temper under that little nun's act. But your convent education's left you sadly lacking in vocabulary for occasions such as this. Remind me to teach you a few terms I picked up in the barracks."

"Why, you . . ." He was making a joke of this! Annique's lips curled as she rolled forward, determined to wipe the smile from his face. Despite the encumbrance of her soaked skirts, she launched herself at Philippe's knees with such quickness that he toppled like a felled tree.

Before he could recover, she clambered up his legs to let

her fists complete the job the clods of earth had started. Her every emphasis was punctuated with a heartfelt, though rarely effective blow. "How *dare* you *laugh* at *me*, you *lout?* Your little *jest* almost killed me! I could bear it *better* if you'd *really* meant to *murder* me, but I'll be *damned* if I'll give up my *life* for some *spasm* of male *pique*, some thoughtless *prank!*"

Philippe easily deflected all but the last of her angry blows, but when her knuckles made stinging contact just below his eye, he yelped and tossed her onto her backside as easily as if he were ridding his lap of a pesky kitten. "Enough!" His muddy fingers gingerly pressed the point of contact. "Curses, woman, you've blacked my eye!"

Annique massaged her knuckles. "More's the pity. I meant to black them both." Far from done, she struggled to her feet. Palms upward, she motioned him closer. "Come, sir! Let's see what sport you make of me on dry ground! I'm not afraid of you!"

For a few hammering heartbeats, they regarded each other, he in consternation, she in open aggression. Then Philippe felt his tension break. A chuckle bubbled in his throat.

He saw Anne-Marie's fingers tighten back into fists. "What, you scoundrel? Would you add ridicule to the indignities you've heaped on your own wife?"

Trying vainly to conceal his amusement, he shook his head. "No, lady, but look at us! What do you see?"

His wife's hostile expression shifted to one of dismay as she registered the state of her appearance. She plucked at the sodden folds of her skirt. "Saints! Look at me." She pointed at him. "And look at you!"

He did, and they both burst out laughing.

Bracing her palms against the ruined silk that clung to her thighs, Anne-Marie wheezed, "Your big toe's poking through your stocking, and there's pond weed a foot long tangled in your hair."

Philippe reached for the back of his neck, pulling loose both the pond weed and the black ribbon that had bound his hair. He waved the limp ribbon in her direction. "A fine duchess you are, with mud up to your gizzard and water lilies in your bodice."

"And a fine duke, you, with dirt on your face and a black eye, compliments of your duchess."

"Then we're well suited to each other." Still laughing, Philippe shook his head, spraying the air with fine droplets like a dog drying himself after a rain.

Annique watched the dark curls settle around his face, and an unexpected stab of desire caused her smile to fade.

He stepped closer, bowed, then scooped her into his arms. "Come. We must get you out of these wet things before you take a chill."

She felt a rush of answering heat at the warmth of his body against hers as he carried her through the tall grass. Unbidden, her mind conjured up a vision of the two of them lying on a carpet of matted river grass while Philippe removed her wet clothing, piece by piece. Annique relaxed against him and closed her eyes, imagining how it would feel to slowly peel the wet shirt from his muscled shoulders.

The sound of a startled gasp a few feet ahead shattered her fantasy. She opened her eyes to see that they had reached the main garden, where an astonished groundsman, rake in hand, stood beside the path. Philippe ignored him, but Annique felt a hot tide of humiliation set her muddy face aprickle. A quelling glance sent the gardener hastily into the hedges without a word.

Annique shifted uneasily in Philippe's arms. "And you dragged me to the pavilion because you were worried about being embarrassed in front of the servants. I can just imagine what they'll say now."

Testing his injured eye with a wink, he made no move to put her down. "This will keep the geese honking for weeks."

With each stride of his long legs, she grew more conscious of the smooth flexing of his muscles, the sinewed hardness of his body against hers, and the unmistakable smell of moss and masculinity. Her skin burned where the wet fabric of her dress pressed against his own damp clothes, the heat of her body rebounding from his until she was certain he, too, must be conscious of its searing pressure.

Yet Philippe seemed oblivious, carrying her across the terrace, up the stairs, and through the foyer as if nothing were amiss, despite the titters and shocked expressions of the workmen and servants they passed.

She felt the steady beating of his heart accelerate only

slightly when he started up the grand stairway toward their rooms. Her own heart hastened as she fought the urge to curl contentedly into his embrace.

Memories of their wedding night flashed into her consciousness, heightening the growing tension she felt in her nether regions. She shifted slightly, wondering how much longer she could maintain her self-control, but knowing she must. "You needn't make such a spectacle of us by carrying me. I'm perfectly capable of walking."

She could feel him tense. "Kind of you to offer to walk, madame. Particularly since we're almost at your door." At the top of the stairs, Philippe turned around and issued a general command to the covey of whispering maids in the foyer below. "Baths! Now!"

His toe left a muddy mark as he shoved open the door to her bedchamber. "Madame." He lowered her gently to the carpet. A wicked glimmer accompanied his half-smile. "If you will excuse me, I'll submit myself to Jacques for a thorough scrubbing." In response to her petulant frown, his own smile hardened. He strolled to the door that connected her dressing room with his. "You could use a good scrubbing, yourself."

One glance into a nearby mirror sent a fresh bolt of embarrassment through her. Stung by the condescending tone in his remark, Annique retorted, "I was perfectly presentable until you tried to drown me!"

She stepped forward to shove him from her room, but her feet bogged down in the soggy folds of her collapsed hemline. Dangerously close to losing her temper and her balance, she gathered up the ruined fabric and stomped toward him, determined to evict him and his infuriating grin from her chamber. "If you will leave me in privacy, sir, I will have my bath. I find myself feeling *soiled* from this afternoon's events in more ways than one."

Smiling as if she'd just complimented him, he opened the door before firing a parting shot. "I trust your bath will be more to your liking than your dip in the pond." He managed to close it a split second before her muddy shoe hit the exact spot where his face had been.

Ordinarily, Annique luxuriated in her bath as long as possible, sometimes sending Marie to the kitchen several times for more hot water. But today her soak offered no soothing, magical escape. She slipped below the surface only long enough to rinse the last vestiges of scented soap from her hair, but even that brief submersion brought back an overwhelming sense of terror from her near-drowning. She bolted upright, slopping gallons of water from the tub.

Philippe's voice rose above the sound of her ragged breathing. "Are you all right?"

Blinking the water from her eyes, she turned to find him frozen halfway between the tub and the open door to his suite.

In a gesture as old as womankind, Annique covered her breast with one hand and the dark triangle beneath the water with the other. "How long have you been here? Where's Marie?"

He stepped closer. The smell of brandy was strong from the blown-glass goblet in his hand, and stronger still from his breath. "I sent Marie to the kitchen with word that we'd be dining *en chambre* tonight. She won't be back until I call her."

Philippe hid his remorse by taking another swig of brandy. By all that was holy, he hadn't intended any harm when he'd tossed her into the pond. Regardless of his intentions, he'd been unable to erase the indelible imprint of her panic from his mind, even with three stout measures of brandy.

He wasn't certain what had prompted him to send the maid away and stand watching his wife in her bath, but when Anne-Marie had burst, gasping, from beneath the soapy water, the terror in her dark eyes had cut straight through him. She had every right to be angry with him.

His expression carefully oblique, he pushed the back of a chair against the side of the tub, then straddled its seat. "I'm sorry about what happened, Anne-Marie. I trust a hot bath has prevented your taking a chill." Apologies didn't come easily to Philippe. In the only gesture of supplication he could allow himself, he reached out, the fingers of his left hand dipping into the water and closing on a swirl of auburn hair. His gaze slipped past the sheen on her shoulders to the tantalizing outline of her nakedness in the cloudy water. By heaven, but the sight of her made him hungry to take what was his.

She pulled away slightly, her shoulders pebbling. "Until this afternoon, a hot bath was one of the few things that

afforded me pleasure in life. Your childish prank has
robbed me of that small enjoyment. Even rinsing my hair, I
relived what happened in the pond."

Her words sent a renewed flicker of regret through him,
but something more powerful remained after it was gone.
"Then let me make amends for robbing you of that small
pleasure." He traced a wet, wending path down the slender
arm that did little to hide her breasts. Philippe coaxed,
"Perhaps I can give you a greater pleasure. Don't think of
this afternoon. Think, instead, of the joy we found in each
other's arms. It's ours whenever we want, Anne-Marie."

Despite her indignation, Annique felt herself drawn into
the seductive laziness of his voice. When his hand slid beneath the water, grazing the side of her breast, a shudder
of desire quaked through her.

"We've been too long apart." He slid his palm down her
ribs.

Naked and vulnerable before him, Annique felt her
body betraying her and was powerless to stop. This wasn't
how it was supposed to be. She had vowed that the next
time they came together, *she* would be in control.

Philippe withdrew his hand. His tone was smooth as
mulled wine. "We're alone. The servants have orders not
to disturb us until I bid them."

So they were alone until *he* ordered it otherwise. Annique sank lower into the perfumed water, aware of how
little her arms and hands could cover. "I think I'll forgo
supper. I've little appetite after what happened this afternoon."

His nostrils flared slightly. "Actually, I'm not very hungry either . . . for food, that is." He scooped up a palmful
of warm water and drizzled it onto her shoulder.

Unable to hide the answering hunger in her own eyes,
she looked away. "The water is growing cool. I'd like to get
out. Please ring for Marie."

He stood, one powerful hand swinging the chair back
into place. "No need to bother Marie. Anyway, the bells
are disconnected, remember? Here . . ." He set down his
brandy and unfolded an enormous sheet of damask from
the linen chest. "I'll help you." Philippe's gaze seemed to
penetrate the cloudy water as if it were crystal clear, exposing her completely.

Annique ignored the surge of modesty that sent her

pulse throbbing in her neck. Trapped, but determined not to give him the upper hand, she rose with a dignity she did not feel and plucked the towel from his hands. Wrapping her torso in the thick, white damask, she stepped out of the tub. "I can manage alone now, thank you. If you'll grant me some privacy, I wish to retire."

There was something disconcerting in the offhand tone of his reply. "An excellent idea, retiring early. But not alone." He stepped closer.

Annique drew the towel tighter around her, only to see, as did he, patches of dampness darken the gentle protrusions of her breasts, lower abdomen, and hips. An unearthly light brightened his eyes at the sight.

Wife or not, Annique refused to be cornered. Trailing the end of the towel like a train, she sidestepped abruptly and sprinted for her chamber, the sound of his widespaced footsteps right behind her.

She made it halfway across the room before his fingers closed on her upper arm, leaving her little choice but to turn and confront him. "I've asked you politely to leave, Philippe. How can I make it plainer?"

"I understood you, but I have no wish to leave." He took hold of her other arm, bracketing her. Though he held her lightly, there was no mistaking the resolution in his eyes. "And you have no right to send me away."

Annique bridled. "This is my room, sir. No gentleman would remain where he's not wanted."

His fingers tightened almost imperceptibly. "And no *lady* would deny her husband his marital prerogative."

She stared contemptuously at the hands that gripped her. "You would force me, then?"

He released her. "It needn't come to that. No matter what demure facade you might effect, Anne-Marie, we both know you're a passionate woman. You enjoyed our lovemaking as much as I."

They both knew he spoke the truth, just as she knew she had to get rid of him before her body betrayed her completely. Annique could never resist him if he touched her the way he had that first time. Desperation hardened her reply. "I ask you once again, sir, to leave me." She strode resolutely toward the hallway door, but the towel remained behind. Stripped naked by her momentum, Annique took three steps, then spun around to see the damask stretched across the floor, Philippe's boot firmly anchoring the hem.

Miming surprise, he lifted his toe from the fabric. "Oops."

She froze, her flight arrested as much by indecision as embarrassment.

Philippe took advantage of the pause to move in. He stopped within inches to tower over her without touching. His indigo gaze radiated a compelling urgency, boring straight through the pretense of bravery she raised against him. He leaned close, his lips to her ear. "You're just as perfect as I remembered."

The need in his low whisper set her blood humming like a harp string. Annique closed her eyes and tried to steel herself for the inevitable response to his touch. She sensed the heat of his face close to hers, smelled the moist scent of his breath. She felt his lips graze her eyelids, ruffling her lashes.

The cool air of the room warmed perceptibly.

Annique remained immobile, dreading yet yearning for the touch of his hands on her body. But only his lips touched her, as softly as before, his mouth finding the curve of her neck just below her ear.

A shudder rippled through her.

His lips moved lower to warm her shoulder with his whispered words. "That's right. Let it happen. Let me please you, Anne-Marie."

No urgent body pressed to hers, no coarse embrace, no demanding, manipulating fingers. Only the tantalizing softness of his mouth, gliding now to skin that had never seen the sunlight. She heard the faint rustle of his clothing as his body shifted lower.

His hair brushed past the side of her breast, sending another shiver to the core of her abdomen. His lips traced down her rib cage, then parted so his teeth could close gently on the smooth flesh at her waist. The subtle pressure sent shock waves through her. Annique grasped his shoulders to steady herself.

At her touch a low moan escaped him. She looked down and saw that he knelt on one knee before her, his hands gripping his thighs, his cheeks flushed, his eyes closed. Helpless to stem the rising hunger that had bloomed in her most intimate recesses, Annique cursed her weakness even as her fingers threaded into his hair and drew him to her.

His hands slid up the backs of her legs in response. The skin of his palms felt as hot as that of a man in the last stages of the fever.

Annique surprised herself by demanding bluntly, "Take off your clothes."

The unexpected command seemed to incite him almost past the limit of his carefully bridled self-control. Philippe rose, his gaze locked to hers. Without wavering, he tugged off his boots and stockings, then fumbled with the tiny buttons concealed beneath the placket of his shirt.

Annique watched him with a strange feeling of exhilaration. Philippe had done as she asked, his compliance planting the seed of a novel idea in her mind. A subtle sense of power heightened the desire that grew within her at the sight of his muscled chest as he stripped off his shirt and began unbuttoning his breeches, his gaze now boldly locked to hers.

True, she had no right to deny her body to her husband. But nothing compelled her to remain passive, her pleasure dictated by his timetable, his plan of seduction.

Why not *her* timetable, *her* schedule of desire?

When he bent to remove his breeches, she spoke again, the thick harshness changing her voice to that of a stranger. "No. Let me take them off."

This time, his surprise showed. Unconsciously licking his lower lip, Philippe nodded his assent.

She slipped her thumbs into either side of the opened waist and slowly lowered his breeches. The garment crumpled to the floor, freeing the evidence of his arousal and releasing the same sharp, wild, male scent she remembered from her wedding night.

Annique stepped back, her gaze following the trail of smooth, coal-black hair from his waist down to his manhood. Fascinated, she openly stared.

Her boldness was more than Philippe could bear. He groaned and drew her naked body against his. "What sort of creature are you, keeping yourself from me for weeks, running away when I try to hold you, then brazenly devouring me with your eyes? By heaven, I swear you've bewitched me, driven me mad with desire." His hands cupped her buttocks and lifted her hard against him.

Annique locked her legs around his waist before he could satisfy his lust. "No. Not here. On the bed." Her plan, her place, her timetable.

Still tingling from the moist heat where the seat of her desire had contacted his bare skin, she untwined her legs and paced to the far side of the bed. She smoothed her hand across the covers. "Lie here."

Impatience glittered darkly in his eyes, but he did as she directed, then grasped her wrist and pulled her onto the bed with him. "Come."

With surprising agility, she straddled him. Philippe responded with a sharp intake of breath. He let go of her wrist. Her motions mimicking his from their wedding night, she leaned forward and jerked loose the silken cords that bound the bed curtains to the headboard. These were not as stout as the ones at Maison d'Harcourt, but they'd suffice.

Philippe's pupils dilated as she settled herself tighter against his abdomen. He murmured thickly, "And what do you intend to do with those cords?"

"Only what you did to me. That's fair, isn't it?"

Suspicion momentarily diluted the lust glowing deep in his eyes. "Though I find your sudden initiative most stimulating, I can't help wondering what you're up to."

Her thighs tightened against his waist. "You said yourself that we could take pleasure from each other whenever we wanted. I've decided that I want to." She wiggled her hips, convincing even herself of the truth in what she had said.

Philippe gasped again. "As you wish." The cords appeared far too fragile to offer more than a token binding, anyway.

"Very good," she purred. "Now close your eyes."

When he obliged, Annique doubled the cords and twisted them before looping them through openings in either side of the massive headboard. Her tone became seductive. "These aren't as long as the ones you used, Philippe. You'll have to stretch your arms." Years of experience in the convent stables enabled her to secure his wrists swiftly with intricate knots. She gave the final binding a firm tug. "There."

Philippe's eyes flew open. "Wait! That's a little tight." When he saw that she had doubled the silken ropes, trussing him firmly to the headboard, he raised his head. "Loosen them. I can barely move."

"Not yet." She slid downward on his torso until his maleness, smooth and hot, nestled upright between her buttocks.

"Ah." The ropes momentarily forgotten, he writhed with pleasure beneath her.

Annique's hunger deepened, yet she gloried in her yearning, taking pleasure from prolonging it. She reached up and gathered her hair, twisting it into a thick, damp coil. Leaning forward, she trailed the cool, wet tips across his chest, sending a shiver through him. Her answering contraction kissed the smooth, flat skin of his abdomen, awakening fully her other self, that hidden creature who had burst forth on their wedding night. That secret self who grew stronger now with every heartbeat, imbued with a tantalizing sense of power by the reversal of roles.

She bent down to nuzzle the shining black silk scattered across Philippe's chest. Her teeth closed gently first on one nipple, then the other. A tiny groan escaped him when her tongue flicked back and forth on the erect nub of flesh. He tasted faintly of copper and salt.

He shifted beneath her, seeking entry, but she evaded him, whispering, "Not yet." And the hunger within her grew.

Still astride him, she bent over again, this time exploring with her tongue, tasting him, testing where a smooth, wet touch would send a ripple of delight through him. His lips, compressed in passionate frustration, were tempting, but she did not kiss his mouth.

She could feel the tension building within him, until— his eyes half-lidded and cloudy with lust—he jerked at the bindings and growled, "Untie me. I've had enough of this game."

Her own voice hardened. "But I haven't." She leaned down and nibbled his earlobe, her breasts brushing his chest. She whispered, "Don't you enjoy being at my mercy? You expected me to enjoy being at yours."

"I didn't tie you this tightly, and I released your bonds the moment you asked me to."

She sat up, a sultry smile on her lips. "And I shall release you, but only when *I'm* ready."

He fought the cords in earnest now, a dangerous flush in

his face. "Untie me, now." The headboard shook, yet the ropes refused to give. He glared at her, the veins of his arms raised starkly against his straining muscles.

Annique's intention had been only to give him a dose of his own medicine. She'd expected him to break free long before this, never dreaming the bindings would hold against a man of his strength. Now, aroused even further by the knowledge that he could not break loose, she shifted forward until his member settled against his abdomen. Still denying him entry, she straddled his manhood, the moist heat of her own desire enfolding him in a delicious prelude to consummation. She rocked gently from side to side, the rolling pressure releasing an explosion of ecstasy.

Philippe's head pitched back, his struggle to free himself abruptly halted.

Annique's body wept with longing now, mingling with the sheen of exertion and desire that covered his. The hunger within threatened to devour her. She could wait no longer. She slid forward, then back, hesitating for one exquisite interval at the moment of entry, then impaling herself with all the pent-up force of her hidden resentment.

She rode him, slowly at first, then faster—every thrust a stroke of revenge for his betrayal, his control, his secretiveness, and the power he had to turn her own body against her.

His fingers convulsively gripped the silken cords. Philippe grimaced, rage blending with passion as his hips rose to meet hers.

Annique arched her back and rode him harder, each lunge detonating a burst of pure erotic intensity. She didn't stop, even when a wrenching, guttural cry of release escaped him. Anger and pleasure drove her on, the disparate forces surging together until the boundaries of emotion melted, and she collapsed, sobbing, against his chest.

When her tears finally subsided to soft shudders, he spoke. "Untie me."

Though his tone was subdued, Annique recognized an order when she heard one. No comfort. Just a command.

Still joined to him, she raised up, the mantle of her hair falling like a shawl over her shoulders. She searched for some sign of tenderness in his eyes, but found only anger. Annique rolled off him and headed for the dressing room.

"Where are you going? Untie me, I say!"

She wanted a bath now more than she had after coming in from the pond. The tin slipper tub was just as she had left it. Good. Cold water would suffice to wash the smell of him from her.

Behind her, Philippe planted his feet in the feather bed and pushed closer to the headboard in a vain effort to gain more leverage against his bonds. The whole room shook with his efforts. "Come back here!"

Annique looked back, wondering numbly what he would do to her if she set him free. Philippe's face was almost purple with fury, his features twisted by rage. She dared not cut him loose now.

She was tired. So tired.

First she'd bathe. Then she'd put on her warmest gown and robe. Maybe by that time he would have calmed down.

The last dry shudder of her tears catching in her throat, she closed the door between them.

❈ CHAPTER 16 ❈

*A*nnique stirred from the disjointed dreams of a restless sleep. Her bed seemed to have hardened in the night, and a dank, neglected smell assailed her nostrils.

When she stretched, her right arm bumped against the dingy paneling that surrounded the narrow cot on three sides. Blinking in the dimness, she focused on the bed curtain that separated her from the room beyond.

This isn't my room or my bed. Where am I?

A nagging sense of unease quickened her hand as she pulled back the bed curtain. The dressing room lay beyond. A thin strip of pale daylight bled under the bedroom door, illuminating her slipper tub and the dark stain of moisture on the floor around it.

Instant alarm brought her bolt upright. She'd fallen asleep on Marie's cot. Trying to clear her thoughts, Annique swung her feet to the floor and stared blankly at the narrow bar of daylight from her bedroom.

Her bedroom . . . *Saints in glory!* In a flash, she remembered everything.

Philippe. Dear heaven, she'd left him tied all night! Annique's stomach lurched as if she'd just been tossed off a cliff.

She crept, trembling, to the door and leaned an ear against it to listen. She heard no snores, no struggle, no heavy breathing from the room beyond. Was he still there? Annique sagged. She'd really done it now.

Then an inner voice sent a fresh stab of fear through her. "What if he's *not* there? What if he's gone?" He had left her the first time they'd made love, and after last night . . . Annique closed her eyes and shuddered at the memory of the answering exultation in Philippe's face when their passion had slipped past all restraint. What look would she find in his eyes now? Almost too ashamed and frightened to look, she eased the door ajar and peered through the crack.

Still bound, Philippe raised his head and stared straight back at her, his eyes dark hollows of anger in a gaunt mask of exhaustion. Even from across the room, she could see that his outstretched wrists were chafed raw around the silken cords. His silent gaze compelled her to look back into his eyes. Annique had never seen such cold fury.

Her heart hammering in her chest, she slammed the door and leaned against it. He'd probably wring her neck if she cut him loose herself. And who could blame him, after being left tied like a brute beast all night?

Annique decided it would be far safer to have someone else free Philippe—someone he trusted. Jacques. He wouldn't harm Jacques.

With shaking hands she opened the armoire and dressed, then hurried down the back stair, her hair unbound and her clothes half-buttoned. Suzanne and the entire kitchen staff stopped in midtask at the explosive entrance of their disheveled mistress. Annique gasped, "Where's Jacques?"

Suzanne lifted a batter-laden spoon toward the vegetable garden. "He's just gone out to pull a few onions, your grace."

Heedless of the servants' dismayed expressions, Annique broke into a run. By the time she reached the tidy enclosure behind the stables, she was so winded she could barely speak. "Jacques!"

He straightened, a fat bunch of shallots in his hand. One

look at her disarray and his color drained. "What's happened, my lady?"

Halting beside him, she covered her face and wailed, "Oh, Jacques, I've done a terrible thing. Terrible!"

Though Jacques' expression was grim, his voice remained gentle. "Take deep breaths, your grace. Slowly. Then tell me straight-out."

She shook her head, unable to look him in the eye. How could she tell him? "My poor husband! I'm so ashamed."

Jacques tucked his chin in alarm. "What? Have you killed him?"

Her head snapped up. "Of course not! What do you take me for?" Annique applied a most undignified swipe of her sleeve to the end of her nose.

"Forgive me, your grace. The way you were acting, I feared . . ." He nodded hopefully. "His grace is all right, then?"

"My husband is unharmed. At least, I *think* he's all right. A bit stiff, perhaps, but . . ." No matter how she framed it, the truth sounded too twisted to be spoken. But Jacques would see for himself soon enough. A scalding blush swept to her hairline. She straightened with the prim resolution of a queen readying herself for the headsman. "I inadvertently left his grace tied to my bed all night. He's there yet, with bloody murder in his eye."

Gripping the bundle of shallots so tightly that a cloud of onion-scent surrounded them, Jacques wheezed, "Holy Mother!"

"I dared not release him, myself, but I don't think he'll harm *you*, Jacques." Annique urged him toward the house. "You must go free him at once."

Jacques took one step in that direction, then stopped, a worried scowl on his face. "I've never known the master to be a brutal man, but his temper is a thing to be reckoned with. If he's as angry as you say, perhaps it would be best for your grace to stay out of his way. For a while, at least."

"Of course, you're right, but where can I go? He's bound to find me if I stay in the house, and I can barely sit a horse. I'd never be able to outride him."

"There must be somewhere . . ." Jacques snapped his fingers. "I know! The old mill, by the brook on the westernmost boundary of the property." He nodded toward the chestnut wood at the far side of the formal garden. "See

that lilac bush at the edge of the wood?" His voice lowered
to make sure no prying ears could hear. "There's a path
right behind the bush. Follow it until you come to the
stream. Cross over, then head upstream about a mile to
the mill. I found shelter there once when a storm caught
me out huntin'. There's a storeroom almost undamaged in
the far corner of the ruins."

Annique bit her lip, considering what might happen if
Philippe should find her there, alone in such a remote spot
without even the servants to protect her.

Sensing her fear, Jacques reassured her, "The place will
be safe; his grace knows nothin' about it. And don't worry;
I'll give your grace a good head start. I won't even go back
into the house till you're well out of sight."

Flight seemed the most sensible course. "Thank you for
helping me. I'll not forget it." Lifting her skirts, she made
for the woods as fast as her legs would carry her.

Jacques called after her, "Once the master's cooled
down, I'll come fetch you." He finished with a dry mutter.
"Assumin' he doesn't kill me first."

Annique raced along the narrow forest path for half a
mile before pain in her side forced her to stop. Panting,
she bent double. She should have paced herself. Once her
labored breathing and thundering pulse quieted, she listened for the sound of pursuit above the rushing brook.
But no crackling twigs echoed in the cool shade. No rustling leaves noised above the steady hum of insects. No
hoofbeats scattered the birds that sang from the treetops.

Though she might have escaped Philippe's wrath for
now, Annique knew she would have to return to face her
husband sometime. What then? Telling herself there would
be time to think about that once she reached the mill, she
cradled her ribs and pushed on.

Soon she emerged from an evergreen thicket to find herself in a shady fern grove beside the ruins of an abandoned
mill. Roofless, the stone walls rose from an outcropping of
enormous, moss-covered boulders that dominated the secluded clearing. Under different circumstances, she'd have
found the setting enchanting. As it was, she hurried to peer
into the vine-covered interior of the ruins. No sign of shelter, there.

A gust of wind rustled through the ancient trees overhead, stirring a nervous dance of sunshine and shadow across the hushed space. Anxious to be out of sight, Annique sought shelter behind a rhododendron growing against the far corner of the mill. There she discovered a low doorway leading into a tiny whitewashed chamber.

She ducked inside and crouched beneath the collapsed boards that formed a ramshackle roof. Annique inhaled the stale smell of lime and humus, freshened by a resinous note from the thick covering of dried hemlock needles that carpeted the dirt floor. For all its neglect, the hideaway was dry and sheltered from the May wind. After checking to make sure she wouldn't be sharing her hideaway with any wild creatures, she settled into a corner, tucked her feet beneath her skirts, and waited.

Desperate to calm her mind, Annique closed her eyes and turned her thoughts inward, seeking the still, quiet comfort of prayerful communion. Adoration. Confession. Thanksgiving. Supplication. For so many years at the convent the pattern had been her access to inner sanctuary. But today, she couldn't get past the dark, shameful images conjured by her own confession. Every time she tried to take control of her fragmented thoughts, some small sound from the forest snatched her back into the world.

Had she lost the way to the place of peace completely?

Annique knew the answer to that question before it was fully formed. Last night she'd given herself over to pride, self, lust, and revenge, swept beyond the limits of reason into the terrifying, exhilarating void of chaos. Now she was without excuse, aching with guilt.

She'd tied Philippe in a vain effort to control him and in so doing, gain some sense of power over her own life, her own body. But in the end, she was the one who'd lost control. Little wonder that now she could not find her way back to the place of peace. Perhaps she and Philippe deserved each other. Their appetites would lead them both straight to perdition.

Despite the warmth outside, Annique shivered. She couldn't bring herself to *consider* what Father Jules—or God, for that matter—would have to say about tying up one's husband and "forgetting" to set him free.

By late afternoon, her anguish dulled by hours of penance, Annique shifted restlessly. Her stomach growled, her legs cramped, and her shoulders ached. She stood with effort and cautiously crept out of her now-cold hiding place. Venturing into the clearing, she stopped in a patch of warm, amber sunlight that slanted between the trees from the west. Stretching, she worked the stiffness from her bones.

Then she heard the sound of footsteps. Annique froze, the hairs rising on the back of her neck. The crunch of dry leaves grew louder—too erratic for someone who knew their way, and too close-spaced for a man of Jacques' stature.

As quietly as she could, she hastened back to the storeroom. She'd been there for a hundred heartbeats when she heard the sound of Marie's plaintive voice close by.

"Your grace! Where are you? Your grace!"

Annique breathed a silent prayer of gratitude before answering, "Here, Marie." She emerged to find her maid standing in the middle of the fern grove.

Marie wrung her hands, forgetting to curtsy. "Thanks be to heaven and blessed St. Jude! I was afraid something might have happened to your grace."

"Where's Jacques? He said he'd come for me."

Wide-eyed, Marie shook her head. "He's gone back to Paris with monsieur le duc."

As the words sank in, relief and pain struck Annique with equal force. "Oh."

She was safe, but her bridegroom of only two weeks had left her. Why did she feel so terrible about that? In the heat of yesterday's argument, she, herself, had challenged him to return to Paris.

Annique kept her voice flat. "Did monsieur le duc say when he'd be back?"

Marie blushed. "He said he'd had enough of Maison Corbay and all of your grace's . . . well, he said your grace could have the place to herself from now on."

Annique sank numbly onto a nearby boulder. Abandoned.

Again, a tiny voice inside her added.

Saints, she'd made a mess of things. An overwhelming sense of failure engulfed her.

Marie's chuckle cut her maudlin thoughts short. "His grace certainly was angry this morning." She winked at her mistress. "Fit to be tied."

Annique grimaced. "What happened when Jacques . . . released him?"

"We had quite a bit of excitement. The master tore through the house wearing only his breeches, kicking open doors and shouting your name." Marie shook her head. "I'm sorry to say he broke that lovely urn your grace found in the attic."

"Never mind the urn. What happened then?"

"His grace sent all the house servants searching from the top floor to the cellars, and the grooms and gardeners to search the grounds." Obviously delighted to be the purveyor of such juicy gossip, Marie sat down beside Annique and leaned forward. "I don't mind telling you, your grace, I was frightened to death someone would find you, particularly me. But I wouldn't have turned you over, even if I *had* found you. His grace was so angry."

So Philippe had, indeed, been beyond himself. "Thank you for wanting to protect me, Marie, but I was safe. Jacques saw to that."

Marie offered a consoling smile. "Jacques and Suzanne love your grace almost as much as I do."

"What did my husband do when he couldn't find me?"

"He ordered Jacques to pack, then he stormed into his library and slammed the door." Marie's voice dropped conspiratorially. "Jacques took his time gathering monsieur le duc's belongings. I think he hoped the master would change his mind. It was after lunch before the baggage was loaded and the small coach brought around." She shook her head. "By that time, Jacques had to summon a footman to help his grace to the coach."

Annique's heart skipped a beat. Had Philippe suffered lasting damage from what she'd done? "My husband wasn't ill or injured, was he?"

Marie giggled. "Oh, no, your grace. Just in his cups."

Annique cared more than she was willing to admit that he was all right. Perhaps God had answered her prayers after all, but Philippe's departure didn't really solve anything. It only delayed confronting what had happened. "I've really done it this time."

Annique stood, her voice bleak. "Let's go back. Suddenly I'm feeling very cold and very tired." For now, all she let herself think about was a hot meal and a comfortable, solitary bed.

"Don't despair, your grace." Marie offered a steadying hold on her arm. "Everything works to the good. Maison Corbay is once again a great house, thanks to madame's efforts. Your grace will be happy in the country."

Marie had spoken the only consolation in the wreckage Annique had made of her life. Maison Corbay was well on its way to being the home she had dreamed of. And now with Philippe gone, she could complete her work in peace. "Maybe you're right, Marie. I think I shall enjoy having Maison Corbay to myself."

❦ CHAPTER 17 ❦

Seated by the window of her study, the Great Mademoiselle recognized the familiar sound of her secretary's footsteps behind her.

Préfontaine crossed to bow beside her. "You sent for me, your highness?"

Without taking her eyes from the gardens below, she motioned him to his desk. "Yes. Take a letter to his grace, the Duke of Corbay. He's at St. Germain with the Guard." She waited while Préfontaine gathered his quills and papers.

Blast the queen for being so stubborn about Corbay, she thought.

As soon as she had learned Philippe was still in France, Louise had discreetly employed her most powerful contacts to have the rogue reassigned as far from Paris as possible. Two weeks later, the queen still flatly refused the transfer, insisting that every guardsman was needed to protect her and her son.

The explanation made sense, yet Louise knew from experience that reasons given were rarely the *real* reasons. She couldn't help wondering if Mazarin had discovered she was behind the transfer. Louise hoped not. She couldn't bear thinking how much Mazarin and the queen would have enjoyed denying her.

"I'm ready, your highness."

"Very well." Louise turned and began dictating, "The usual greetings and salutations. It has come to my attention that your bride resides unprotected in the countryside while you bravely defend our queen and his majesty at St. Germain. Please allow me to extend, once again, the hospitality and security of my household to your dear wife. As I promised, I have held a position in my retinue open for her. I trust you will both agree that she should return to Paris as soon as possible, in light of the dangers of the current conflict."

Louise savored the thought of his reaction. She knew Philippe wanted his wife as far from Court—and her—as possible. That alone was reason enough to insist otherwise. Not to mention the prospect of humbling the presumptuous little wench. "Where was I?"

"The dangers of this current conflict . . ."

"I shall expect to receive Anne-Marie within the fortnight. If you are concerned about the perils of her journey from Sèvres to the palace, allow me to offer an armed escort from my regiment to assure her safety." Philippe would understand the threat implicit in that "offer."

She nodded to Préfontaine. "That's all. The usual closings. See that he gets it today." A warm current of satisfaction curled through Louise's chest. This just might prove to be better than sending Philippe away from Court, after all.

Annique had spent the two weeks since Philippe's departure winnowing the staff down to the bare minimum needed to keep the old house from sliding back into disrepair. When she was done, twenty hardworking souls had joined Marie, Madame Pleuris, and Paoul as permanent members of the household.

Every day Maison Corbay was astir from dawn to long past sunset. Yet despite the fact that there always seemed to be someone waiting for her to make a decision or mediate a squabble, Annique enjoyed a sense of solitude more satisfying than she'd ever felt, even at the convent. With her husband away, the entire staff readily obeyed her wishes. She answered only to her own conscience, free to choose when she rose, what she wore, what she ate and when, how she passed her time, and where she went. *She* controlled her life.

She even wrote bank drafts for wages and supplies, and to her relief, Philippe—or more properly, his bankers—honored them. For the first time, she wielded power, exercising her authority with caution, even awe, but she quickly came to like it. The benevolent control she had over Maison Corbay felt good, like a golden sword in the hand of the downtrodden. It brought security. It made her strong. And it took her one irretrievable step farther from the life of quiet obedience she had lived for so many years at the convent.

The staff and tenants—at first surprised by her concern about their personal lives and baffled by her willingness to admit her mistakes—soon warmed to her no-nonsense, practical approach in overseeing the manor. But though she was making progress, there were lapses. Annique regularly forgot herself, impulsively setting to work alongside a tired or sluggish servant. And despite Madame Pleuris' halfhearted protests, she refused to stay out of the kitchen, since only the prospect of a surprise visit by the mistress kept either chef from bullying the poor housekeeper.

By June sixteenth, almost all of the repairs to the house had been completed, allowing Annique to settle into a pleasant routine. As it had been in the convent, reading was her greatest pleasure. Every day she rose unprompted at dawn, ate a light breakfast, then took one of her father's books to a secluded spot on the grounds to read for a few hours before returning to the house to face her responsibilities.

This particular morning, though, a queasy stomach had cut short her reading and now distracted her attention from Madame Pleuris' daily report. Her digestion had been unsettled several other mornings this week. Odd that her stomach had waited until life calmed down to trouble her.

The housekeeper droned on. ". . . so all the rooms have been cleaned but the ones on the third floor of the east wing—the governess's suite and the nursery."

Unusually warm despite the open windows, Annique opened her fan and moved it slowly back and forth. "I meant to do that yesterday, but getting the plasterers finished and out of the house took up the entire afternoon."

The housekeeper straightened importantly. "As your grace instructed, we haven't touched a thing in those unopened rooms. Not until your grace has looked them over."

"Very good." Annique couldn't explain her compulsion to see the sealed-off rooms before they were cleaned and rearranged. A faint sense of looking for some elusive, missing element always accompanied her whenever she entered one of the abandoned chambers. Yet so far she'd found nothing more exciting than the usual dust, decay, and rat droppings left by thirteen years of neglect.

"I'll attend to the matter as soon as I've finished going through the paintings in the attic." She'd been looking forward to plundering the cache of oils for almost a week. The other chore could wait. "Anything else?"

"I believe that's all for today."

"Very well. You may go. Oh, and please tell the chef to prepare only simple dishes with no rich sauces for the next few days." At Madame Pleuris' frown, she added, "I know the chef is temperamental, but you mustn't be intimidated. Remember, until Suzanne returns he answers to you, and you have my complete confidence. I'll be happy to remind him of that, if necessary." Still fanning herself, she rose. "If there's no one else waiting, I'll go through those paintings in the attic now, before it gets any hotter."

Madame Pleuris shot an uncomfortable glance toward the foyer. "I'm afraid there is someone waiting. A messenger from Paris."

Annique closed her fan abruptly. "Another one?"

"Yes, mistress."

Philippe was stubborn as a mule! This was the third messenger in as many days. "Send him in." She sat back down and watched Madame Pleuris admit the emissary, leaving the door properly ajar as she exited.

This one was a soldier, not a mere page. He marched forward, stopping at the desk with a parade-perfect stomp of his burnished boots. The face was familiar. She'd met this young lieutenant—one of Philippe's junior officers—at the wedding reception. A hurried mental replay yielded his name. "Lieutenant Vercours. To what do I owe the honor of your presence?"

Obviously pleased that she'd remembered him, he bowed again. "It is I who am honored, your grace." Then he sobered, nervously adjusting his cape. "I bring a message from my captain, monsieur le duc."

She nodded and extended her hand to receive it. "Very well."

He remained at attention and stared over her head. "It's a verbal message, your grace."

Annique hesitated. She knew full well that the footman was listening just beyond the half-open door. "In that case, perhaps we should take a stroll in the garden." She rose.

A glint of admiration sparked the soldier's eye. He followed her through the foyer and into the hot sunlight of the rear terrace.

Annique led him down the stairs and onto the raked gravel pathway toward the center of the restored formal garden. She didn't stop until they reached the fountain, where a steady cascade of water from the marble cherub's pitcher would mask the sound of their voices from curious ears.

She sat on the wide lip of the fountain. "What orders has my husband sent *today?* The message must be important, to be delivered by a man of your rank."

The lieutenant cleared his throat and settled to an uneasy parade rest. "His grace, Captain Corbay, respectfully commands madame la duchesse to return with me to Paris without delay. I am instructed to escort your grace to the Tuileries, where your grace is expected by the Duchesse de Montpensier."

"What!" Annique sprang to her feet. Philippe's first two messages had been bad enough—their blunt wording stripped of even common courtesy, peremptorily ordering her to leave the security and peace of her home—but this was beyond comprehension, delivering her into the hands of his paramour!

She paced, fuming. Someone must have told him how well she was doing without him. He was punishing her, getting even! Clearly, he meant to humble her. He'd sent an armed soldier to drag her back and deposit her into the Great Mademoiselle's claws!

She turned on the messenger, her tone icy. "Obviously, my husband has little esteem for my intelligence, my comfort, *or* my dignity. Not to mention my safety. Now that Condé's troops have laid siege to the city, Paris is probably the most dangerous place in all of France. I wrote my husband to that effect yesterday, *and* the day before."

Vercours' already stiff bearing tightened perceptibly. "The rebels will never breach the walls of Paris. And no one would dare harm a member of her highness's household. But here in this unprotected house, your grace is at grave risk. I saw evidence of a fresh rebel encampment not two miles from here. For the sake of safety as well as duty, your grace must allow me to escort her to the Tuileries."

Annique would sooner run naked through the streets of Sèvres than submit to this outrageous order. Her voice smoothed, as pleasant as if she were delivering a dinner invitation. "This is my response. Listen well, sir, for I don't intend to repeat it. Under no circumstance will I return to Paris. Nor will I receive any more messages from my husband. If he has anything further to say to me, any more demands, he can tell me himself."

The soldier's features hardened. "I humbly beg your pardon, your grace, but I cannot return without you. My orders are clear."

She straightened. "Is her majesty, the regent, aware that her officers are being used as emissaries in the domestic matters of her guardsmen?"

"Your grace! Surely you can see that I am only following orders—"

She didn't let him finish. "And surely *you* can see that those orders are completely inappropriate. This is my home, sir, not some military fortress. And this matter is personal, not political. What passes between a husband and wife is of no consequence to the State. I bid you good day." She spun on her heel and marched toward the house.

"But your grace . . ."

When he caught up with her, she aimed a haughty glare at him. "I might ask what, sir, you are doing *here,* when a mutinous army is camped against the very foundations of the capital? I intend to write her majesty immediately to inform her of such blatant misdirection of the queen's resources."

He blanched, then stepped directly into her path. "Write if you must, but my orders are to bring you back, and bring you back I shall."

Avoiding him with a most undignified side step, she raced for the foyer. With the lieutenant hot on her heels she cried out, "Paoul! Henri! Thomas! Etienne! Quickly, I need you!" At the sound of her alarm, servants appeared from everywhere. Paoul preceded the chef through the kitchen door.

She pointed to the officer. "Paoul, this man claims to be a messenger from my husband, but he bears no letter from the duke, nor any seal to confirm his identity. For all I

know, he might be an imposter sent to kidnap me. Please
see that he's bound and taken back to Paris. The gardeners
and the groomsmen can assist you, if needed."

Vercours' eyebrows rose, his face reddening. "Your
grace! You know perfectly well who I am!" He addressed
the footmen who had gathered around her. "I serve your
master, the Duke of Corbay. Her grace knows this. She
knows *me*. She called me by name!"

Annique drew herself up majestically. "And I say, sir,
that I've never seen you before this morning."

Eyes narrowing, he muttered, "Very amusing, but it
won't do any good. I have my orders." He took a step
toward her, but the four burly footmen immediately
formed a barrier between the interloper and their mistress.
Taking advantage of their presence, Annique made for the
stairs.

Just then the gardeners arrived with a clatter of wooden
shoes. Armed with pitchforks, they were soon joined by a
contingent of threatening maids, mops and battering sticks
in hand.

Paoul's voice rang out behind the soldier. "Not another
step, sir."

Already halfway up the stairs, Annique leaned over the
wide banister to witness an improbable scene. Paoul
pressed a hastily retrieved medieval lance into the messenger's back. Raising his hands in surrender, the officer
glared up at her while two of the footmen relieved him of
his sword and pistol. That done, they tied him with his own
sash.

Paoul gave the hapless lieutenant a gentle poke with the
tip of the lance. "This one won't be givin' your grace any
more trouble. We'll have him on his way in no time."

"Treat him gently." The concern in Annique's voice was
real. She meant the man no harm. "Who knows? He might
be from my husband, after all."

"Madame la duchesse! I implore you," the soldier protested. "Tell them. I *was* sent by the captain!" When she
failed to respond, he twisted against his bindings. "Surely
you won't send me back to Paris in this condition. What
will everyone *think?*"

Annique replied with conviction. "Perhaps they will
think twice about trying to take the Duchess of Corbay
from her home against her will."

That should teach Philippe to treat her like an errant child!

Later that morning Annique worked out her frustrations by rooting through the jumble of paintings she had discovered in the far corner of the attic in the east wing. As she'd suspected, most of the canvases were damaged beyond repair. But after two stifling, dusty hours, she'd salvaged a respectable collection of portraits and landscapes. Enough to restore a sense of depth and history to the walls of Maison Corbay.

Marie swiped a grimy path across her forehead with her dusting cloth. "Isn't your grace ready for luncheon? Or some cool punch? It's so hot up here, I fear madame will faint."

Annique nodded absently. "We're almost done. Just two more. That last frame looks to be in perfect shape, but I can't see the painting for the one in front of it." She wiggled past the heap of discarded canvases, her back brushing against the rafters. "I think the one in front is a landscape."

Marie worked her way to the opposite side and cleaned a swath across the canvas with her cloth, revealing a detailed pastoral scene propped on edge. "Seems sound, your grace. Shall I dust the rest of it before I move it?"

"No. Just help me put it with the other good ones." Annique was so absorbed with moving the fragile old landscape that she didn't notice the painting they'd uncovered until she and Marie turned around.

Both women inhaled a breath of hot, dusty air.

"What a beautiful lady," Marie murmured.

Staring back at them was the life-sized image of an elegant woman, the rich depth of her dark hair and eyes as luminous and unmarred as the day she had been painted.

A tingle of *déjà vu* passed through Annique. The portrait was impressive, executed with consummate artistry and skill, but the beautiful subject was even more compelling. Her warm, brown eyes seemed to glow with life. Her creamy skin had the depth of alabaster.

"Shall we move it over with the others, your grace?" Marie's voice betrayed her impatience to escape the attic's heat.

Still staring at the image, Annique heard herself murmur, "No. It's far too large and heavy. Tell Paoul to have it brought into the great hall. This will be magnificent on the stairway."

"Will your grace have lunch now?"

"What? Yes." But a contradictory inner signal tugged Annique's attention away from the portrait. "I mean, no. I promised Madame Pleuris I'd check over those rooms just beneath us." At the look of disappointment on Marie's hot, dusty face, Annique offered, "I can check the rooms alone. Why don't you run along to the kitchen? I'll probably be waiting in my chamber by the time my lunch is ready."

"Thank you, your grace. But you must come down with me. It's too hot to stay up here alone, and your grace has been looking a little pale lately."

Annique moved away from the portrait's spell. "For some reason I don't seem to tolerate the heat very well this summer." She shooed Marie ahead of her. "I'm right behind you." They stepped from the attic stair and into the relative coolness of the deserted third-floor hallway. "I think I'd just like a little toast for lunch, and perhaps some cold soup." She paused beside the unopened rooms. "It won't take but a moment to look over these rooms. Then I'll meet you in my bedchamber. Run along, now."

"Yes, your grace." Marie hurried away.

Annique opened the first door. The small, sparsely furnished chamber beyond looked as if someone had left in a hurry. Drawers stood open. The dust-covered feather bed lay heaped upon itself as if someone had looked under it, and a cascade of dusty feathers trailed from a jagged slit in the ticking. More feathers lay under years of dust and cobweb.

"What a mess." Careful not to stir a storm of feathers with her skirt, she stepped gingerly toward a door in the side wall. The knob refused to turn under her hand.

Locked.

Annique exited into the hall and stepped to the entrance of the adjacent room. The handle moved smoothly at her touch, easily admitting her to the spacious, sunny chamber beyond. The nursery.

Instantly, the impression of what she saw was seared into her consciousness with the white-hot force of a branding iron. Annique heard a roaring in her ears. Her throat constricted as if something had sucked all the air out of the room.

A small bed stood against the far wall, its diminutive headboard painted with roses and cherubs and gilded ribbons. Strewn across the shelves that lined one wall were a dozen dolls, some of them with their heads torn off and cast carelessly aside, some half-stripped of their clothing. A child's wagon with iron wheels and gilded spokes carried only dust in its gilded interior. The broken pieces of miniature porcelain plates and cups lay scattered on the top of a tiny table, two small chairs overturned beside it.

Annique swayed. The room seemed to race away from her, perspective distorted by a blast of nameless dread. She staggered backward.

Run! Get away!

But her feet refused to obey. Why couldn't she move?

Inside her something splintered, releasing a shapeless, wordless terror. The floor seemed to heave as her surroundings spun. Annique dropped to her knees.

Must get out!

She forced herself to crawl backward into the hall, her hand pulling the door closed behind her. Once the mechanism clicked shut, she rolled against the wall and drew up her knees, hugging them tightly as she gasped for air. Tiny sparkles danced before her eyes, and her panting filled the empty hallway. Whatever sinister force she had encountered remained behind in the nursery.

A spirit. That must be it. The room was possessed. She had sensed such danger, such pain. Why hadn't anyone warned her the place was haunted?

"They *what!*" Philippe sprang to his feet, almost overturning the map-covered table in his tent. He could scarcely believe it—his brightest young officer, bested by a mere woman and a pack of servants! "And just what do you have to say for yourself?"

Red-faced, Lieutenant Vercours muttered sullenly, "They took me by surprise, sir, relieved me of my weapons." His hand moved unconsciously to the hilt of his sword. "The two footmen gave me back my sword and pistol when they untied me at the outskirts of Paris. I would've arrested them, but they set my horse agallop and escaped in their own carriage. It took me some time to recover my mount, and the rest of the night to get back here." Obviously humiliated, the junior officer leaned forward. "Request permission to return with a small escort and arrest those insolent louts who tied me up, sir."

"Forget them! They were only following orders." Philippe's flush of anger drained to a deadly calm. "No. *My wife's* the one who's responsible for this fiasco."

The lieutenant straightened. "Request permission to return with a *large* escort to deliver madame le duchesse to the Tuileries as ordered, sir."

Philippe snorted. "You might need a few cannons for that assignment." He'd married the most stubborn, vexatious woman in the kingdom. Things were complicated enough, and now *this* nonsense. Philippe only hoped the princess hadn't heard about it yet. He refused to be further humiliated by having the Great Mademoiselle's armed guards "escort" his wife to the palace.

He rose and paced to the open tent flap. Outside, the pastures surrounding St. Germain were dotted with canvas tents and artillery instead of cattle. Early morning sun transformed sparkling dew to tiny wisps of vapor on the tent tops.

Philippe's fingers kneaded his eyelids to ease the ache of another long night poring over the tactical maps of Paris and its suburbs. Guitaut had canceled his leave the minute word got out that Philippe was back in Paris. He'd reported straight to St. Germain over a week ago and hadn't gotten more than a few hours' sleep a night since.

Blast. Why in blazes wouldn't his wife do as he ordered? The woman had taken orders all her life at the convent. She'd picked a fine time to disobey!

And timing was everything, as Philippe was all too aware.

He'd had his chance to escape all this, and given it up. If only they'd sailed away, as he had planned. There was going to be a bloodbath soon, one he wanted no part of. Now he was trapped at the very heart of a conflict that threatened to destroy fully a third of France's noble families.

Why hadn't he taken that ship?

Because his wife had asked him not to.

Thoughts of Anne-Marie brought with them, as always, a disturbing conflict to his emotions. That night when she'd tied him, Philippe had gone along, surprised and titillated by the dangerous glitter in her eyes, the unfamiliar thickness in her voice. And even when she'd refused to release him, he'd been aroused by the heat of her anger, captivated by her reckless passion. Bound though he was, he'd watched her ride him beyond the limits of reason. He'd seen the fear in her eyes when the game had turned, drawing her beyond control. That culmination of rage and ardor had been one of the most erotic experiences he'd ever known. But then she'd left him.

He remembered the blankness in her eyes when she'd pulled herself aright afterward and stared straight through him. Philippe still had no idea what had caused her abrupt coldness. The woman was an enigma. In all his experiences with women and with war, he had never encountered a more baffling, unpredictable creature. And now she had the nerve to defy him publicly!

He returned to his desk and scribbled a brief note, saying, "General Turenne has offered me a few days' leave as consolation for recalling me so abruptly. I'd planned to head for the coast, but now I've changed my mind." He folded the message and tossed it to his lieutenant. "Order my horse brought round, then deliver this to headquarters. I'm off to Maison Corbay." He reached for his sword and pistol. "And the next time I give you an assignment, you'd bloody well better complete it, or you'll spend the rest of your career commanding the latrine detail."

Philippe strode past a surprised footman into the foyer of Maison Corbay.

"Welcome home, master."

The master was in no mood to note either the structure's improved exterior or the quiet elegance of the interior. A low growl escaped him. "Where is she?"

"Where is who, your grace?"

"The duchess. Who else?" Still hot and grimy from the ride from St. Germain, Philippe slapped his riding gloves impatiently against his palm. "Well?"

The servant shot a nervous glance toward the garden. "I'm sorry, master, but I don't know. Her grace often takes a walk alone at this time of day. But she's always back in time for supper."

Philippe stilled. "You let her go out unattended? Don't

you know that's dangerous? There are rebel troops in the area."

"We had no choice, your grace. Her grace ordered us not to follow. Says she wants a little privacy."

Philippe tugged loose the top button of his jacket. "This isn't a proper household! It's a lunatic asylum!" He tossed his scabbard and sword to the settee, followed by his pistol. "Have you all lost your minds, letting your mistress roam about unattended when there's a civil war raging all about us? Anything could happen." Unbuttoning his jacket the rest of the way, he pinned the footman with an ominous glare. "Someone might even try to *kidnap* her."

The man obviously understood Philippe's sarcastic reference to Lieutenant Vercours' unfortunate visit. All the color ran from his face. "Please, master, we've only done as madame la duchesse ordered us to. Surely your grace understands."

"I'll deal with that later." Philippe shouted toward the kitchen, "Paoul!"

The summons failed to produce the old man but yielded, instead, two more footmen. After exchanging looks of fearful surprise, they stood at attention.

Philippe tugged off his heavy jacket, exposing the perspiration-soaked shirt beneath. Pulling the limp fabric away from his flushed skin, he addressed the nearest footman. "Go fetch Paoul. I'll await him in the library." As the servant bolted for the kitchen, he turned to the next man. "You. Go tell Marie to pack her mistress's belongings immediately. And she'd better be quick about it. When I'm ready to leave, we'll leave—baggage or no baggage." He tossed his jacket to the third footman. "Have this brushed and sponged. Then bring me a clean shirt and some water to wash with. And some food." With that, he made straight for the library and slammed the door behind him. He had barely settled into his chair when Paoul entered.

"You sent for me, your grace?"

Only years of practice in concealing his anger enabled Philippe to remain superficially calm. "Where is she?"

"Her grace takes a walk every day at this—"

"I've heard all that. Do you know where she is, or don't you? And what's she doing that she wants no one watching." Not that he suspected her of assignation. She wasn't the type.

Paoul paled at the implication, then rushed to her defense. "She only goes walking or reading, your grace, I swear it. I knew you wouldn't want the mistress roaming about alone, so I had her followed. On my life, she only goes walking or reading. Alone."

Philippe frowned, stung by Paoul's protective response. The ungrateful old fool seemed more loyal to *her* than to Philippe, the master who had indulged and praised Paoul for the past two years. He bristled. "Am I, or am I not, still master in this house?"

Reminded of his obligation, the old man muttered, "Aye, your grace. It's just that the mistress works so hard, and all she asks is a little privacy to walk or read. But I always make sure someone follows to watch over her. Someone trustworthy." Shifting uncomfortably from one foot to the other, he ventured, "None of us here would ever let any harm come to madame la duchesse."

Philippe's lips whitened. "You still haven't answered my question. Where is she?"

Paoul met his master's challenging glare with a look of dignified resignation. "The last time I saw her, her grace was heading for the old mill. It's her favorite spot. I shall direct you to her."

Minutes later, Philippe crept up behind the sleeping stableboy who was supposed to be watching over his mistress.

Safe, indeed! What sort of protection was a sleeping guard?

He covered the husky lad's mouth with one hand while shaking him awake with the other. For a few seconds the boy put up a respectable struggle, but the moment he recognized his master, he grew still, his eyes wide.

Philippe motioned him to silence, then released him. He whispered, "Return to the stable at once and make sure my horse is ready."

The boy nodded, then scrambled away.

Hemlock branches brushed at Philippe's clothing as he stepped to the edge of the evergreen thicket. He paused behind the last concealing branch and scanned the shady clearing and ruined mill beyond. No movement stirred the peaceful setting.

Then he saw her.

Anne-Marie sat nestled on a low ledge of smooth, moss-crusted rock. Her simple gown spread softly from her raised knees, the green color of the fabric the same subtle hue as the lichen around her feet. Even in the shade, the creamy skin above her bodice provided a glowing contrast to the dark, burnished braid that trailed over her shoulder.

He'd forgotten how lovely she could be. She looked like a mythical princess of the wood sprites, ensconced upon her rustic throne. Philippe's gaze rose to her face, where he saw an expression of exquisite vulnerability and longing as she pored over the pages of the slim volume in her hands. Feeling an unaccustomed tug of sympathy, he brought himself up short.

He stepped forward. "Madame, I would have a word with you."

Anne-Marie nearly jumped out of her skin. The little book clattered to the ledge. As she scooped it up, Philippe noticed a small hole in the cover. She slid off the ledge and stood, the volume pressed protectively to her chest. "What do you want, Philippe?"

Determined not to let her escape again, he strolled close enough to smell the faint scent of lilacs that clung to her skin, her clothes, her hair. "I thought the wording of my messages was sufficiently direct." He propped one fist to his hip. "As was the message you sent me by way of Vercours. So here I am." Exhaling slowly, he looked down at the determined set of her head. "Nice fellow, Vercours. I sent him because he needed a break from camp. He hasn't had a leave in over a year."

Anne-Marie shifted subtly at his nearness, but did not give ground. Her words were tense. "I trust Lieutenant Vercours suffered no lasting ill effects at the hands of my footmen."

"*Your* footmen?" Philippe suppressed a flash of anger. A humorless smile shaping his lips, he repeated the phrase as an indictment. "*Your* footmen. Quite." He moved so close that she couldn't turn her head without brushing against him. Still, she wouldn't yield. He continued, "Lieutenant Vercours escaped with only minor injury to his career, though there was considerable damage to his pride." Philippe's tone hardened. "But then, you're an expert at that, aren't you?"

"I owe you an apology for embarrassing that poor man." Pinned between his looming presence and the rock ledge, she tried to step aside, but he smoothly mirrored her movements, hemming her in. Anne-Marie's voice faltered. "And I owe you an apology for what happened the night before you left." Her great, dark eyes lifted to face him. "I meant you no harm that night, Philippe. The game got away with me, and by the time I realized it, I was afraid to let you go. I must ask your forgiveness for not untying you."

He straightened, the memory of his humiliation crusting his heart in stone. His chilly tone made a lie of the words, "Consider the matter forgotten. I have more urgent concerns these days." He came to the point. "I can waste no more time or energy seeing that you safely reach Paris and *stay* there. The rebellion is about to explode. God only knows what will happen when it does. You cannot remain here unprotected."

Anne-Marie's eyes narrowed. "Perhaps you can explain to me precisely how I would be safer inside a besieged city, under the 'protection' of the very woman whose legions threaten to bring destruction upon the entire capital."

Blast the woman! He tried to keep the impatience from his voice. "The Great Mademoiselle has offered you the protection of her household at the palace, as well as a position in her retinue. I know you don't want to be with the princess any more than I want you there, but neither of us has any choice. If you aren't at the palace by tomorrow, she will send an armed guard to fetch you."

Suddenly the heat and the fatigue of the past few weeks crowded in on him. He went on wearily, "I have no time for this, Anne-Marie. The rebellion is reaching a crisis, and I've been working twenty hours a day to see that France survives. At least at the palace, you'll be safe. That I can guarantee."

Anne-Marie made no move to leave.

Philippe straightened. In the past few weeks he'd devoted many precious hours arranging for her safety. He'd spent a fortune in bribes and payoffs to protect their assets from possible seizure should the rebels win the day. But instead of trusting him, his wife defied him at every turn. "I am under no obligation to explain myself in this matter, madame. Might I remind you, however, that you are under *every* obligation to do as I say!"

Anne-Marie's hands formed into fists at her sides. "I know I embarrassed you by leaving you tied up, Philippe, but nothing I've done justifies the kind of humiliation you propose for me. I don't care if she is a princess. I will not be handed over to that woman."

"You *shall* do as I wish. And it is my wish for you to accept the Duchess of Montpensier's kind offer of hospitality."

Before she could react, he bent forward and folded her neatly over his shoulder. His left arm tightened across the back of her thighs, locking her to him in an iron embrace.

"How dare you! Put me down!" She struggled against him, her braid flailing.

Philippe grabbed hold of the thick plait and pulled it under his arm, tethering her head against his back in the process.

"Ouch! You're pulling my hair! Let me go!" Anne-Marie pounded his hip with one hand while groping frantically for the hilt of his sword with the other. But the taut braid kept her safely away from both his sword and his pistol.

Philippe grinned. Handy thing, that braid. For once, he was glad she'd gone out improperly coiffed. He shifted her roughly into a more comfortable position on his shoulder.

Her fists flailed away at his back. "You brute! You bully! Let me go!" She kicked fiercely, but her soft leather shoes did little damage against the thick fabric covering his thighs.

He headed down the narrow path, his words punctuated by the rhythm of exertion. "You're only hurting yourself by pulling against me. If you relax, this will be a lot more comfortable for both of us."

He could hear the thickening in her voice as the blood rushed to her head. "Why, you ill-bred, arrogant son of a goat! I'll snatch loose every hair on my head if that's what it takes to get away from you!" She struggled harder than ever, but against his size and strength her efforts were useless.

He plowed through the overlapping branches of two rhododendrons, their leaves snapping back in his wake.

"Ouch! Philippe, be careful! That branch almost put my eye out!"

Her weight dragged at his shoulder, straining the muscles of his neck, but he consoled himself with the evidence that she was more uncomfortable than he.

"Oof! Put me down! Philippe, I can't breathe. You're jouncing the life out of me."

After the way she'd defied him, he took grim satisfaction from her discomfort. Heedless of the perils of the narrow path, he kept up a brisk pace. Only twice did he stop briefly to rest, but his grip never relented a fraction. Though Anne-Marie had given up struggling by the time they reached the edge of the forest, Philippe knew she was merely conserving her strength for the moment he released her.

That would be simple enough to deal with. Still holding onto her braid, he broke off a stout lilac branch as they passed.

Betraying fear behind a show of bravado, her voice bobbed up and down with the steady shock of each stride. "Why did you do that? What's that branch for, Philippe? Answer me! Do you mean to beat me?" The last resonated with indignation. She tried to shove free, but after almost a mile of jouncing head-down through the woods, even a single arm was strong enough to hold her.

Philippe said nothing. The rhythmic swish and thud of his boots across the meadow gave way to the crunch of gravel as they reached the driveway. Sweat trickled from his hairline. Almost there, thank goodness. His wife grew a stone's weight heavier with his every labored pace. As they rounded the corner to the front of the house, his step lightened somewhat at the sight of the waiting carriage, loaded and ready, an anxious Marie perched beside the driver. Balthus whinnied, his reins held by a nervous groom.

Using the last of his wind, Philippe shouted, "Open the carriage door. Driver, whip your team to a gallop the instant the duchess lands in the carriage! And don't stop until I tell you to. If she escapes, it'll be your head!"

Marie gripped the seat as the driver suppressed a smile and readied his whip. "Aye, yer grace. Full gallop, it is!"

Anne-Marie resumed her struggles in earnest, bleating, "No! Don't you dare! Stop this, Philippe!"

Philippe bounded onto the step and heaved his protesting wife into the seat with such force that she hadn't righted herself before he'd slammed the door, delivered a whack of the lilac branch to the rump of the carriage horse, and shouted, "Go!" He launched himself clear of the departing vehicle, his boots landing solidly on the driveway.

Angry and disheveled, Anne-Marie reared aright and fired a furious glare over the back of the seat before the lurching carriage knocked her askew again.

Philippe mounted Balthus with a single, graceful sweep. As he urged the beast forward, he considered discarding the slender lilac branch still in his hand, but thought better of it.

Paris was three hours away. Who could say? Anne-Marie might earn a beating yet.

❦ CHAPTER 18 ❦

*A*nnique ignored her husband the entire way back to Paris, right up to the moment they arrived on the doorstep of the Tuileries. There he reined Balthus to a halt beside the carriage and ordered, "Get out."

At his order, Marie obediently gathered her bundle and started to rise, then froze halfway between sitting and standing when her mistress resolutely refused to budge.

"Sit down, Marie." Oblivious to the footmen waiting to help her from the carriage, Annique leaned forward. "Driver, take us to the town house."

The driver quailed visibly at her counterorder, but there was little question where his loyalties lay; the carriage remained still.

Philippe repeated quietly, "I said get out. Both of you."

When she didn't move, Annique felt the limp, withered lilac leaves caress her jaw. She could hear the smugness in her husband's voice.

"Your stubborn disobedience didn't accomplish much back at Maison Corbay, did it, Anne-Marie? If you refuse me again, I won't hesitate to pick you up bodily and deposit you in the princess's salon on your backside. Her highness would *love* that." He paused to let his words sink in. "Which way shall it be? The choice is yours."

Curse the blackguard! If he dumped her in the Great Mademoiselle's parlor like a sack of turnips, she'd become the laughingstock of Paris. Frustration and rage boiled up afresh inside her, but she quickly realized her options were limited. She rose and addressed her husband through gritted teeth. "You leave me little choice. My hands are tied."

Philippe's brows drew together briefly at her choice of words, giving Annique a flicker of satisfaction. She exited the carriage with a dignity she did not feel, gliding majestically toward the open doorway without a backward look. As her foot struck the threshold, Philippe's mocking voice echoed against the stones. "Have you no fond words of farewell as your husband goes off to battle, madame?"

She spun around. He presented a maddeningly handsome picture astride his mount, so dashing in his uniform, a rakish smile lighting his features, but she wasn't fooled. Mere comeliness could not erase the fact that he had betrayed her and now delivered her into the hands of her rival. If a benediction was what he wanted, she'd be happy to grant him one. "I hope you get exactly what you deserve!"

He clutched his plumed hat to his chest in mock agony. "As harsh as that? I was hoping for mercy, instead." He reined Balthus up onto his hind legs. "For myself, I pray that God will keep both you and Paris safe. Adieu." With that, the horse catapulted forward, carrying a smiling Philippe back to his regiment—and perhaps his death.

Twenty minutes later, Annique was escorted into the Great Mademoiselle's sitting room. As she had feared, there was quite an audience for her humiliation.

The princess looked her up and down, then wagged her riding gloves in Annique's direction. "Everyone . . . this is Corbay. Corbay, I trust you've met my friends."

Annique recognized the Duchess of Châtillon, the Duchess of Frontenac, and the Great Mademoiselle's aged chaperone, Madame Fiésque, but the two men were unfamiliar. She correctly surmised that the fussy older man standing a discreet distance behind the princess was Monsieur Préfontaine—personal secretary and confidant. But the thin, rather unattractive young man at the princess's side was unfamiliar. Annique nodded to him. "I do not have the honor of being acquainted with the gentlemen."

The Great Mademoiselle dismissed her secretary with a wave of her hand. "But everyone knows Préfontaine. I couldn't function without him." Then she turned an indulgent smile on the younger of the two men. "The Marquis de Flamarin and I have been inseparable since Orléans."

Flamarin looked toward his royal patroness before responding to Annique's presence. Only when she nodded did he grant Annique a cursory glance and a brief bow. "Enchanted."

So that's how it is, Annique thought. Watching Flamarin fawn over the princess like a lovesick suitor, Annique realized Philippe was probably just one of many among the Great Mademoiselle's conquests.

The princess wasted no time making Annique's role in her entourage clear. "I'm sure we'll get along famously, dear. After all, we have so *much* in common."

The only thing they had in common was Philippe.

Obviously amused at the reference, the Duchess of Châtillon cut her eyes slyly in Annique's direction.

Annique wondered in horror if everyone else in the room knew what was behind the princess's remark. She felt a telltale blush creep up her neck. So she was to be Court Fool, bearing the brunt of the Great Mademoiselle's wit. Well, perhaps there'd be less sport for the cat if the rat refused to run.

She curtsied deeply. "Your highness is most generous to extend me her protection during this . . ." She caught herself before she said *rebellion*. ". . . these trying times."

The princess arched a golden eyebrow. "Hmm." Then the royal mouth curled into a delicate smile. "Unfortunately, our accommodations have been severely strained by the current difficulties." Her tone became condescending. "It seems that half of Paris has turned up on my doorstep since the regent's troops headed this way. I'm afraid the only room I have left will be here in the salon, Corbay." She laid a finger beside her mouth. "I think there are still some cots about. You shouldn't be too uncomfortable."

Annique heard Châtillon snicker, but she remained impassive. Lack of reaction was her only weapon.

The Great Mademoiselle turned a scowl on Châtillon, erasing the duchess's smug expression with, "As a matter of fact, I have decided that it would be safest for *all* my ladies to sleep in the salon until the siege is resolved."

Madame Fiésque, the princess's aged chaperone, bolted upright in her chair. "*All?* Surely you don't mean me?"

A wicked gleam lit the princess's eye. "I especially mean

you, madame. After all your years of unrelenting vigilance, I'm only too happy to return the favor."

The formidable old woman sputtered, "But, dear mademoiselle, my room's just down the hall. Surely I'll be just as safe there."

The princess raised her hand. "You are too precious to risk, even by so short a distance." She paused to consider. "But perhaps your maid should remain in your room to protect your belongings. We're too shorthanded to spare a guard."

So the maid would pass the nights in comfort and privacy while her mistress shared a room with two other women and slept, unattended, on a cot. The irony was not lost on Annique. In spite of herself, she had to admit that there was a certain elegance to the princess's subtle tortures.

The Great Mademoiselle turned back to Châtillon. "I know the lack of privacy will be an imposition on some of you, but it can't be helped. These are treacherous times. I dare not let any of you out of my sight."

The remark seemed to have a chilling effect on the duchess.

Suddenly Annique became aware of the unspoken tension in the rest of the entourage. Surely Philippe must have realized he'd placed her at the very center of the rebellion. But why would a man sworn to uphold the regent place his wife in the care of the enemy?

Annique hid her confusion behind carefully arranged features. Perhaps he was playing both sides, hedging his position in case the regency failed. A more cynical voice told her she was merely being used once again, this time to humor her husband's secret lover. Or was her presence here part of an even darker purpose?

So many questions. At least she was in the right place to find the answers.

But Annique found few answers during the next week. The revelations of Court life were more mundane. Frontenac had little or no personality; Châtillon complained incessantly; and Madame Fiésque snored all night and constantly, explosively, passed gas.

Annique got through the long, hot days by watching and listening. Rumors flew through the Court. The rebellion was heating up even faster than the city in the unseasonably warm June weather. The gnawing tension of the rebel siege shortened tempers from the gutters to the highest councils of the capital, but the Great Mademoiselle remained the same as ever: imperious, emphatic, and above all, in control.

And though there was no hard evidence, Annique still believed the princess was somehow secretly helping to orchestrate the rebellion. Sometimes in the deep of night, shadows flickered under the Great Mademoiselle's door and the Marquis de Flamarin's high, nasal voice could be heard from the princess's boudoir, but that was of no concern to Annique. And occasionally a grim-faced princess had retreated to her room after a whispered conversation with a messenger or her nursemaid. But there was no proof of the princess's direct involvement in the rebellion.

Yet as the days rolled on, Annique realized she was becoming immersed in a world of lies and deceit. Court life was maddeningly indirect on its surface, and dangerously deceptive at its core. No one said what she really thought. No one did what she really wanted. The truth was kept in secret, far too precious and dangerous a commodity to be shared. Annique hated secrecy, hated dishonesty, yet she had little choice but to go along with the elaborate charade, hiding her true feelings behind the mask of mild obedience she had perfected at the convent.

After the freedom and independence she had tasted in Sèvres, this rigid existence felt as desperate and confining as any dungeon's deepest pit. But she was determined to survive and to taste freedom once again. Somehow, she would find an honorable way to return to Maison Corbay.

More than a week of hot summer days crawled by, most of them spent indoors. On the rare occasions when the princess ventured out of the Tuileries, Annique was left behind in the grudging company of Châtillon. Evenings were taken up with sodden, listless gatherings. Almost all of the Court had fled the city with Louis and the regent, leaving the Great Mademoiselle to preside nightly over a salon filled with ambitious social climbers and sycophants. Only rarely did the Prince de Condé or one of his marshals turn up at a reception, and then the conversation ran to wine and wenches, not politics. Annique endured such gatherings sitting by the window with her fan and wishing everyone would go home so she could go to bed. More than once she woke up the next morning still in her chair.

Then, abruptly, the Marquis de Flamarin was gone, without explanation or farewell. Two days after his disappearance, the Great Mademoiselle swept into the room, Fiésque in her wake. "I'm off for a ride, ladies. Don't bother to get up. You shall remain here." Despite the heat, she was decked out in velvet and feathers and dripping with jewels.

Châtillon pushed the needle through her embroidery frame. "It seems a shame to waste such a lovely dress on just your chaperone. Perhaps your highness will meet someone."

The princess was not amused. "Whom I meet and where I go is no concern of yours, madame." She looked at Annique. "Or yours. Good afternoon."

After she had left, Châtillon shook her head. "Gracious. I do believe the heat has deprived her highness of her usual good humor. *You* know I meant no harm by my remark, don't you, Corbay?"

Annique smiled. "Your intention was perfectly clear to me."

The duchess eyed her suspiciously. "Of course. Ah, well, I should count myself fortunate. At least her highness isn't as unpleasant to me as she is to you." Then she returned to her needlework. "What is the date today, anyway? These last few weeks have been so boring I've lost track."

Annique sighed. "June twenty-seventh." Ten long, lonely days she had been away from Maison Corbay.

Châtillon retrieved a glass of chilled wine from the table beside her. "I hope this rebellion's over soon. My maid said the ice house is almost empty. If that happens, I shall have to leave, no matter what her highness says. A lady of gentle breeding can endure only so much." She took a sip, then rattled on. "Speaking of endurance, have you heard the latest news from St. Germain? I understand our poor young king put his toe right through the ragged sheets the other night! Such a scandal, our monarch reduced to living in such terrible conditions. I hope the king of Spain doesn't get wind of it. How embarrassing."

Annique concentrated on her needlework, shutting out Châtillon's incessant gossip.

Hours later, the salon doors burst open to reveal an exu-

berant Great Mademoiselle. "There's a day's work done,
ladies! Never let it be said that a woman's only way into
history is through matrimony." She removed her bonnet
and sailed it across the room into Annique's lap. The princess's eyes narrowed. "A wise woman can use even the
foolishness of those around her. Think about *that,* Corbay,
sitting there so quietly with your pious face, always watching, always listening."

A charge of fear shot through Annique. Something had
happened, something that had renewed the princess's hostility toward her. But what? Smooth as smoke, an insidious
thought crept into her mind: *Philippe.* With the marquis
gone, had the princess sought another diversion? Had she
spent the afternoon with Philippe?

The Great Mademoiselle paused at her chamber doorway and spoke loudly without looking back. "I shall not
receive anyone tonight. Order the household to bed early.
I do not wish to be disturbed."

When the door closed behind her, Annique could hear
the bolt sliding into place. Everyone knew what that
meant. As soon as darkness fell, the soft sound of voices
would come through that locked door, and one of those
voices would be male.

After she was certain everyone else in the room was
asleep, Annique moved, inch by agonizing inch, until she
escaped her cot without so much as a creak. She carefully
pulled her cotton lawn dressing gown over her sleeveless
nightgown, then blew out the single candle that illuminated
the salon.

A familiar voice rumbled from behind the princess's
door, then fell silent.

Philippe? It sounded like him.

Blood rushed to her face. She shouldn't care, but she
did. Annique told herself it was only because he was hers,
by right and the laws of God and man. But the pain she felt
at the prospect of Philippe's holding another woman in his
arms—that came from deep within the guarded recesses of
her heart. She would not admit she loved him, but she had
to know if the man on the other side of that door was her
husband.

Once her vision had adjusted to the darkness, she knelt
beside Marie's pallet and whispered into the sleeping girl's

ear, "Marie. Don't cry out. It's me. I need you." Marie's eyes fluttered open. Annique placed a finger gently across her lips. "Shhh. Is there another way into the princess's room?"

Marie shrugged and shook her head.

"What about a back way to Nourrie's room? It leads into the princess's."

Marie nodded yes.

"Can you show me?"

Again, she nodded in silent confirmation. Quiet as a cat, the maid rose and padded through the darkened salon. Just as Marie's hand touched the knob of the anteroom door, Fiésque snorted loudly and turned over.

Both Annique and Marie dropped reflexively into the shadows, crouching tensely until the room fell silent once more. Then Annique straightened and slowly turned the knob, every hair on the back of her neck standing on end for fear the mechanism would squeak. It didn't. By the time they were both safely in the antechamber with the door pulled shut behind them, she was drenched with perspiration.

Marie knew exactly where to find the concealed doorway that led into a musty servants' corridor, lit only by a distant torch. Annique followed her maid down the narrow hallway, her heart beating so fast she felt dizzy.

She couldn't believe she was doing this. Had she changed so much in the past few months? Before, she never would have taken such a risk. But watching the princess had taught Annique the value of taking risks, of seizing the moment. If she didn't do this now, she would always be tormented by doubt.

Nearing the door to Nourrie's room, she motioned for Marie to stop so she could regain her equilibrium. She whispered, "You haven't asked what I'm up to, Marie. Aren't you curious?"

The faint yellow light of the torch flickered across Marie's face, revealing a shy smile. "I know you'd never do any evil, your grace. Whatever you're up to is your business."

"Bless you, dear Marie." Annique gave her arm a squeeze, then murmured, "Now let's see if you can get me into the princess's room without anyone's knowing."

Once inside Nourrie's room, Marie stood sentinel beside

the old woman's bed. Nourrie's deep, even breathing remained undisturbed while Annique crept across the darkened floor.

She halted at the door to the princess's chamber and
listened. The voices were louder now. Holding her breath,
she turned the knob. Slowly, she drew the door toward her
and leaned into the narrow opening. The man's voice
drifted in her direction from the alcove beyond the princess's bed, but she couldn't make out the words. The
rhythm and timbre of his speech was almost identical to
Philippe's, but the bed hangings obscured her view. Determined to find out for certain if it was Philippe, she crept
into the princess's room.

Two candles glowed from the table on the far side of the
bed. Seated in the alcove beyond with her back to Annique, the Great Mademoiselle leaned toward her visitor,
the earnest murmur of her voice barely reaching Annique's
ears. Only a knee and the top of her companion's boot
were visible.

Debating whether or not to close the door behind her,
Annique decided she dared not risk leaving it open. The
princess's voice might wake her nursemaid. Gingerly, she
closed it, then slipped into the shadow of a tall chest
nearby.

The Great Mademoiselle's voice grew louder. "Don't be
silly. Infidelity is like murder—given the proper circumstances, *anyone's* capable of it."

Annique's hands clenched into fists. She saw the black-
clad leg straighten. The princess's visitor stood to his feet
and stepped into the light. Her heart skipped a beat. It
wasn't Philippe, but *Condé,* leader of the rebel armies!

Annique felt as if she'd stepped into a puddle and ended
up falling into a black, bottomless well. What had she gotten herself into? Unless she could escape without being
detected, her impetuous spying might end up costing her
life! They'd never believe the truth. She eased herself
backward toward the door, halting when Condé's fist
struck the table.

He declared, "We're betrayed at every turn! I warned
you that the Duke of Lorraine's allegiance was shaky. We
should have gone to him sooner, not waited until today."
She could hear him pace the cramped corner. "The very
moment I got back to Paris from our meeting, I received

word that he was withdrawing and needed reinforcements. Reinforcements! *He* and his mercenaries were to be our reinforcements! Without him, Turenne has us outnumbered two to one!"

The prince slumped back into the chair. "I outrode my escort getting back to Lorraine's camp, and do you know what I found? Lorraine acted as if we'd never been there today. That same fellow who charmed and fawned and joked with us this afternoon, two hours later treated me like I was born on the wrong side of the sheets! He said he'd signed the treaty with Mazarin days ago!"

Annique didn't want to hear this. Every word placed her deeper in jeopardy. Her heartbeat thundering in her ears, she shifted closer to the door. Her retreat was cut short when the Great Mademoiselle jumped to her feet and began pacing. Annique froze, certain that any moment the princess would turn and see her.

But she didn't. The Great Mademoiselle was too wrapped up in her own crisis. "Why would he lie, swear allegiance to both of us this afternoon, then tell you about the treaty only hours later? It doesn't make sense."

The prince's voice was bitter. "Because *you* were there this afternoon, that's why."

Annique saw a look of perverse satisfaction slide across the princess's features.

Condé went on. "Obviously, he would not risk offending *you*. Of course, he had no compunctions about insulting me and betraying your father, his own sister's husband!"

Even in the dim light, triumph was evident in the Great Mademoiselle's eyes as she stared past her beleaguered cousin. "So he doesn't dare offend me. A wise man. You could take a leaf from his book, Monsieur le Prince."

Condé snorted. "And what do you propose we do now?"

The princess sat and faced him. "You must go to my father. Tonight. And I must find out who in my own household has betrayed us. I've been warned before that someone close is spying for the regent. I should have acted sooner, but I have no taste for torture."

The prince leaned forward, his voice tight with anger. "I *told* you, it's Châtillon."

"You're just saying that because she's closed her boudoir to you and gone back to de Nemours. You men! You'd rather believe a woman a traitor than an unfaithful lover.

No. I don't think it's Châtillon." The Great Mademoiselle's tone became pensive. "I think it's Corbay."

The back of Annique's knees stung as if someone had struck her. Surely the princess didn't think she was a spy . . .

Condé growled, "Haven't you heard a single thing I've told you in the last half hour? It can't be Corbay. What could that simple child have possibly found out?"

The Great Mademoiselle interjected grimly. "I assure you, she is neither a child, nor simple."

A sudden chill racked Annique. If she didn't get out of there, her life wouldn't be worth a sou. As she eased toward the door, she heard Condé say, "This business has been going on long before Corbay turned up. Our traitor's connections are at the highest level. My sources say it's Châtillon, and they have witnesses. She sold us out to the regent for a hundred thousand francs."

After a pause, the princess said, "The fool. I'd have paid her twice that to keep quiet." Annique could hear the disappointment in her begrudging admission. "All right. So it's Châtillon."

A wave of silent relief washed through Annique. Now, if only she could escape undetected. She crept to the door and began to inch it open.

Behind her, Condé's voice grew softer. "I know you're well-equipped to handle Châtillon's interrogation. Feel free to use whatever methods you wish to get the truth out of the slut. I only regret I can't stay and watch." She heard him rise. "I'm off to your father's. Unfortunately, I came here straight from Lorraine's camp, and I have no messengers to spare. We need to send word of this latest development to our camp. But who can we trust to take the message?"

The door was almost open far enough to slip through when one of the hinges let out a shattering squeak. Annique heard the princess and her secret visitor leap forward.

Caught. At the sound of their approaching footsteps, Annique made a desperate decision. She turned and faced them boldly.

The Great Mademoiselle gasped. "You! How long have you been here? What have you heard?"

His sword half out of its scabbard, the prince looked

Annique over with a mixture of suspicion and hunger, his gaze lingering on her open robe and thin gown.

Annique knew her only hope lay in showing no fear. "I heard what you said about the Duke of Lorraine and Châtillon."

The Great Mademoiselle hissed, "You *are* the spy!" She turned to the prince. "What more proof do you need? I was right all along!"

Annique drew her robe together. "Your highness, I did not come here to betray you. I came, rather, because I thought *you* had betrayed *me.*" She looked to Condé. "I thought her highness was with someone else, someone she and I both know."

Her manner suddenly guarded, the princess crossed her arms. "And why should I believe that?"

"Because it's true." Annique could see the Great Mademoiselle wanted no further mention of her other nocturnal visitors.

Condé threw up his hands. "Mademoiselle, I have told you there is *proof* of Châtillon's treachery. But this is another kettle of fish. Perhaps Châtillon is not the only traitor." He shook his head at Annique. "What in perdition are we to do with you?"

Annique remained deadly calm on the outside, but inside her mind was racing. "The way I see it, you have three choices: trust me, kill me, or send me back to my bed."

The princess arched an eyebrow in surprise, then a cold smile curled her lips. She circled Annique. "You're a cool one, aren't you? I vow, Corbay, it's hard not to like you." She ran her folded fan down Annique's backbone. When she continued around to confront Annique, there was a disturbing hunger in her cold blue eyes. "Why shouldn't we kill you? That would simplify things immensely."

Annique decided to bluff. She smiled. "Hardly. If I disappeared, there would be all kinds of talk. People are already wondering why you invited the wife of a captain of the Queen's Guard into your retinue in the first place."

Condé cocked his head. "She has a point."

The Great Mademoiselle seated herself at the table. "That's no one's business but my own."

The subtle indication of retreat encouraged Annique to go on. Perhaps Condé didn't know about Philippe, and the princess didn't want him to find out. That gave Annique a little leverage, at least. And she was certain neither the prince nor the Great Mademoiselle would dare to expose their clandestine meeting by summoning the guards.

She directed her appeal to the woman in front of her. "It's true I have watched you, Mademoiselle, but not as a spy." Annique sank to one knee in supplication. "I've witnessed firsthand the fierce pride with which you protect what is yours. Would you kill me for doing the same thing—trying to protect what is mine?"

When the princess looked away, Annique knew she had a chance. "You yourself brought me here, Mademoiselle. I didn't want to come, but you insisted. And once I came, it was you who drew the battle lines, not I." She pointed to the locked door. "Your highness, *you* were the one who bid me sleep just outside your door. When I heard the prince, I thought he was someone else. How could I lie there listening, when I thought you were with—"

"Enough!" The princess gripped the arms of her chair. "Not another word." She turned to Condé. "Send her to the camp with the message. If we're lucky, one of Mazarin's men will finish her off for us."

The prince's fingernail stroked his oily beard. "You're willing to trust her?"

"Hardly. But someone has to take the message. It might as well be Corbay. By now, our troops are probably the *only* ones in Paris who haven't heard about Lorraine's defection." The Great Mademoiselle extracted a bundle of coarse clothing from a nearby chest and hurled it at Annique. "Put these on."

Annique's relief was tempered by embarrassment. "Now?" She glanced anxiously at a bemused Condé.

The Great Mademoiselle smiled. "Now."

Annique turned her back and removed her robe. She slipped the peasant blouse over her gown and pulled the simple skirt over her head. Only by tightening the drawstrings at the skirt's waist and the blouse's neckline could she keep the garments from falling off.

"You make a most convincing serving wench, Corbay." The Great Mademoiselle scribbled a message, waxed it shut, thrust it into Annique's hand, then gave her an embroidered handkerchief that reeked of the heavy scent she wore. "When you deliver the message, show this handkerchief." She opened a hidden panel and motioned toward the darkened passage beyond. "Monsieur le Prince will lead you to the outer gate and provide a horse and directions to our encampment."

Annique murmured weakly, "A horse?"

"Our regiments are more than five miles away. You can't very well walk." The princess paused. "Oh, that's right. Someone told me you don't like horses."

And they both knew who *that* would be. Annique straightened. "On the contrary. I find horses far more likable than most *people* I've met in this city." She marched past the princess, then turned back to the opening. "Monsieur le Prince, I await your convenience."

Just before dawn, Annique slid off her mount and staggered to the secret gate to the Tuileries, her thighs aching painfully from the bobbling, pell-mell ride to the rebel encampment and back.

The ordeal of this night had left her exhausted, but more than that, changed. In a matter of hours she had become a stranger to herself. She had seen, done, and learned things that took her forever beyond the narrow horizons of yesterday's childish perspective. Now she felt old, yet oddly strengthened. She could never go back to the ignorance, or the innocence, that had protected her.

She didn't want to. Not after what she'd seen and heard tonight.

Wearily, she limped to the secret door. At her knock, a yawning Nourrie admitted her, then lifted her lantern to lead the way through the dank, musty maze. The old nursemaid stopped just short of the princess's suite and grumbled, "Make your report brief. Her highness hasn't had a wink of sleep all night."

Annique nodded, then pushed the secret panel into the room.

The princess stood staring out the window at the river. When she turned, Annique could see that her eyes were red and puffy. "Well?"

Annique curtsied. "They kept me waiting for over an hour, but finally I delivered your message to the commander. He didn't like what he heard. He shook me, accusing me of lying, but when I showed him your handkerchief, he put his head on the table and told me to go."

"And that was all?"

"Yes, your highness."

The princess turned her gaze back to the river and murmured absently, "I knew it was risky to count on Lorraine, but we needed him. He's a real *soldier*—one of France's best. Now we not only fight without him, we fight *against* him."

Annique moved closer. The past few hours had given her an entirely new perspective on the princess. It was hard to imagine how the woman functioned at all under such tremendous pressures.

The Great Mademoiselle murmured bleakly, "Leave me."

Annique looked at the floor. It wasn't easy to say what she was thinking, but after what she'd witnessed this night, she could no longer remain silent. "I will leave, your highness, but there's something I'd like to say first. I fear I've misjudged you."

The Great Mademoiselle snapped, "I've far more important things to think about than how you feel about me, Corbay."

"I know. Tell me how I can help."

The princess rose, the fire returning to her eyes. "Help? And how, pray tell, do *you* plan to help *me?*"

"That's up to you, but I want to." Somehow, she had to make the princess understand the profound experience she'd just gone through. Her voice became earnest. "Until tonight I thought of the Fronde as someone else's problem—a senseless confrontation that inconvenienced me and interrupted my life. I wanted no part of it. But tonight as I waited to deliver your message, I walked among the Frondeurs, and what I saw changed everything."

Even in the breathless heat, the rebel cookfires had been surrounded by sleepless, distant-eyed men, their firelit faces forming ghostly circles of tension in the small hours before dawn. "The battle will be soon. I could see it in their faces. Feel it in the air."

The princess stared sightlessly beyond her. Was she listening? Annique went on, "I heard the soldiers speak of their homes, the women and children they left behind. Some bragged about the battles they'd already fought. Some spoke of the courage of their commanders. They're particularly fond of your highness. Over and over, I heard tales of your bravery at Orléans and how it inspired them."

The Great Mademoiselle only sighed.

"I began to understand what those men were risking, and why. I thought about what would happen to our country if all the wealth and power of so many great lineages were turned over to the regent, or to Mazarin." Annique shivered. "Then I understood what you're trying to do."

The princess's eyes narrowed. "Don't flatter yourself, madame. No one really understands fully what I'm trying to do, not even my father."

"Perhaps not. The point is, I want to help make it possible for those men to go back to their farms and their families. I'm through with merely watching. Let me help."

"You, a Frondeur? Somehow I find this midnight conversion more than a little suspect." The princess toyed with a lock of her own hair. "What about your husband? His loyalties lie with the other side."

Annique stiffened, her voice growing hard. "Take care, your highness. It would be most unfortunate for us to discuss either Philippe's loyalties or his lies."

"Ha!" A surprised smile took years from the Great Mademoiselle's face. "I always knew there was acid under that mild facade."

"Will you let me help you?"

"And how do I know you're not working for the regent, only pretending to help me?"

"You don't."

A haughty gleam sparked the royal eyes. "So there it is; I have no reason to trust you."

Annique's voice dropped. "But you need me, whether you're willing to admit it or not. There's no one else in your entourage besides Préfontaine who's loyal, and he's too well-known to be of use to you in certain situations. You need a woman, one with wit, one who can keep her mouth shut." Absolute calm radiated as she spoke what both of them knew to be the truth. "Frontenac can do you no good; she's too timid. Fiésque reports your every move to your father, and she's very clumsy about it. There's no telling how many people read her messages before they're delivered to the Luxembourg. And Châtillon—she's the most dangerous of all."

A look of contempt congealed the princess's features.

"You've told me nothing I don't already know. These people have been useful to me, but I've never been foolish enough to trust them. And I'm certainly not foolish enough to trust you."

"Then don't trust me. But *do* use me."

The princess chuckled mirthlessly. "Corbay, you're either the bravest fool I've ever met or the most convincing liar. I can't decide which."

Annique curtsied. "Mademoiselle, I am neither. Right now, I am the weariest lady-in-waiting in all of France." She glanced at the first rays of sunrise brightening the window. "I have completed the task you gave me and said what I had to say. May I be excused?"

The Great Mademoiselle thought for a moment, then gestured toward the bolted door. "Very well. You may leave."

"And about the matter we've been discussing?"

"We shall see, madame. We shall see."

❊ CHAPTER 19 ❊

1:30 A.M.—July 2, 1652

*L*ong past midnight, the Great Mademoiselle pushed open the window of her bedchamber and inhaled deeply, trying to catch some hint of coolness stirred by the Seine's silent currents below, but the air was as humid and stagnant as a cellar. Frustrated, she leaned across the stone sill, only to find that it, too, was unrelenting in its warmth.

Then her ear picked up the faint clink of metal against metal, the rumble of wood on stone, the scrape of leather against flesh, and the muffled passage of hooves upon the pavement. She knew those sounds, and what they meant could spell disaster. A tingle of foreboding raced down her neck and into the backs of her arms.

After blowing out all the candles in the room, she groped back to the window. Since the siege, no torches lit the outer walls of the Tuileries, and no light escaped from the shuttered structures across the Seine. Her eyes strained into the darkness toward the furtive, ominous procession along the far bank of the river.

An army was on the move. But whose? She must find out. Préfontaine could be trusted, but summoning him now would attract too much attention. She knew better than to rouse Fiésque, and Frontenac wouldn't know a Frondeur from a farmer. There was no one else. Unless . . .

Louise hastened to the outer chamber, then picked her way through the maze of sleeping women to the cot set slightly apart from the others. The instant she clamped her hand over Corbay's mouth, her lady-in-waiting's eyes flew open in silent alarm. Louise pressed harder against the soft resistance of Corbay's lips and whispered urgently, "Come with me, and don't make a sound. I need you."

Corbay obeyed.

Once back in the bedchamber, Louise threw the bolt on the door and drew Corbay to the window. "You wanted to help. This is your chance." Outside, the darkness was oppressive.

Despite a lifetime of hiding her true feelings, Louise could not conceal the tension in her voice. "Listen. They're on the move. If those are our regiments, we're still safe. But if that's Turenne, there's not a minute to waste. We must get word to Condé, warn him."

Corbay peered at the shapeless column that shuffled along the far embankment. When she turned, her voice was low, but resolute. "It must be Monsieur le Prince. Look closely. They're headed toward Charenton. If the regiment were Turenne's, they'd already have encountered our encampment. There would have been a confrontation—an alarm, at the very least."

"Yes . . . and Turenne has never mounted a night attack." Relieved, Louise collapsed onto a nearby chaise, her ostrich feather fan pumping vigorously. Corbay's evaluation confirmed her own hopes, but there were still a few loose ends nagging at her. Louise wondered aloud, "Yet I was not notified of this movement. Surely Monsieur le Prince would send word of his intentions."

How could she prevent disaster if they didn't keep her informed? Then the fan stilled.

The young messenger's dying words echoed through her thoughts. Perhaps her secret communications had been disrupted by betrayal.

Louise regarded the silent woman beside the window, a lingering suspicion tugging at her vitals. Had she made a grave error in bringing Corbay into this? She decided not. For all Corbay's quiet, watching ways, Louise sensed no fear in the younger woman, felt no scheming undercurrents. For now, it would suit her purposes to take Corbay at her word and use her. Though their conflict over Philippe added a tantalizing element to the equation, Louise reminded herself that Philippe's wife was better suited for the needs of this night than any of the others.

The fan resumed its silent rhythm as Louise's face relaxed in the darkness. She spoke casually, as if remarking on nothing more substantial than the heat. "If Condé is on the move, Turenne must be close to the city."

Now all they could do was wait, and waiting was what she hated more than anything.

Corbay paused, then voiced what Louise, herself, was thinking. "So the battle will take place tomorrow."

"Yes. Tomorrow." A seductive blend of pain and exultation twisted low inside Louise. *Tomorrow.* There was something great and nameless hiding in that word, some momentous event she had been anticipating all her life. She knew it.

For a split second, Corbay's profile was illuminated by a flutter of heat lightning. The image lingered in Louise's consciousness, a flash capturing the statuesque girl's erect posture, her fine bone structure, the tendrils of dark hair framing her face and curling softly down her shoulders. Strange that such arresting qualities had gone unnoticed until now.

Faintly silhouetted against the open window, Corbay spoke into the gloom. "What time is it? Your highness is usually sound asleep by so late an hour."

In the darkness Louise permitted herself an unguarded smile. "When Préfontaine brought my usual draught, I refused it. How could I waste this night in sleep, knowing that tomorrow I might be called upon to repeat what happened at Orléans?"

Corbay moved through the darkened room to the dresser where she fumbled for a flint, then struck a solitary candle to light. The shadows cast by the single flame transformed the room into the dim landscape of a dream, like some ancient tomb, the faint light more sinister, somehow, than the darkness. Corbay set the candle beside Louise, then crossed to where she was sitting.

Louise kept her face blank as Philippe's wife gently drew the fan from her grasp and began to fan them both. The feathers' currents stirred an acrid, familiar smell from Louise that had less to do with the heat than with survival.

Corbay spoke. "You are afraid?" It was more a statement than a question.

Usually, Louise permitted only anger to escape untempered by artifice. But in the dark portent of this breathless night, she allowed herself the luxury of honesty. "Afraid? Only enough to sharpen every sensation, every sound. I like it." Her gaze followed the motion of Corbay's slender arm. Back and forth, back and forth, bringing the scent of lilacs from Corbay's direction as she fanned.

Louise focused on the woman beside her. The thin fabric of Corbay's gown was limp in the heat, hiding little. Philippe's bride always made such a subtle show of modesty, keeping herself covered even among the women. Yet Louise had not been fooled by that pretense of innocence. She knew that there was fire beneath Corbay's cool, aloof exterior.

Her eyes shifted downward from Corbay's bosom to the swell of her abdomen. Bitterness threatened to override the tug of desire that twitched through Louise. She had never envied or hated a woman more than she did Corbay at this moment. Why should this . . . chit, this *nobody* have what Louise wanted but had been denied?

Jealousy twisted at her heart and left the taste of brass in her mouth. Louise escaped the pain by looking ahead to the greatness that awaited her. This night was too precious to waste on regret.

Tomorrow would bring glory once again, and perhaps death. She closed her eyes and relived the roar of the crowds at Orléans, the surge of power that had washed over her with the breath of the mob, the delicate balance of danger and opportunity that had distilled, crystallized, heightened every sensation. An exquisite frisson of desire rippled through her at the memory of her triumph, and her breathing quickened. Almost as if it had a will of its own, her hand reached out and stroked the smooth ivory skin of Corbay's arm. Louise's voice was husky. "I have always found fear a powerful aphrodisiac. It awakens, clarifies. Don't you agree?"

Corbay abruptly withdrew her arm and retreated to the window. "On the contrary, your highness. The Scriptures teach that love casts out fear."

"Who said anything about love?" Louise's chuckle was thick with irony. "I speak of lust."

Leveling a candid stare at her, Corbay declared, "Lust is far too demanding a mistress for me; she has too many mouths to feed. When one *does* find satisfaction, it's gone in an instant, and then one is left hungry again."

Was Philippe responsible for the bitterness in the last?

Louise rose and crossed to within a foot of her attendant. Tendrils of Corbay's dark hair clung moistly to the creamy flesh of her bosom, where a sheen of perspiration released the sweet, musky scent of her. A perverse smile curved Louise's lips as she considered taking her pleasure from Philippe's wife just as she had taken it from him. The idea had a certain elegant complexity, particularly in light of what her spies had told her just this afternoon about the young duchess.

Louise felt Corbay's muscles stiffen beneath her touch as her fingertip traced a winding tendril from the base of the girl's neck to her chemise.

"If that is all, your highness, I beg your leave to retire."

The Great Mademoiselle smiled. What good was *willing* prey? Where was the sport in that? Thick with desire, her voice rolled from her lips. "Can you not sense the power all around us? The forces of destiny are moving out there, huge and unseen in this night. Tomorrow we will be at the very intersection of those forces. Does the prospect not stir your blood?"

Corbay stepped back, her dark eyes fathomless and guarded in the feeble light. "It stirs me, but not to lust. I do not share your highness's hunger for confrontation. The costs are too dear. This time tomorrow night, how many Frenchmen will lie dead or maimed? And for what? Even if we win, the king's mother will still be regent, dancing to whatever song Mazarin sings."

A surge of anger replaced Louise's desire with contempt. "My, my. Such cynicism. Does this mean you've repented of your decision to work for our cause? What about the faces of the Frondeurs, the stories that touched your heart and moved you to join us? Perhaps you've misled us."

"My loyalty is with the Fronde. I have no love for the regent or Mazarin. But I can't silence the questions inside me that ask if tomorrow will be worth the cost. And I can't help wondering if any of it will make a real difference in the end."

Surprised and unsettled by the artless honesty in Corbay's words, Louise withdrew slightly. Her voice hardened. "It *must* make a difference. We *must* believe that it will, fight to the last man and woman. Otherwise, France will be lost in the end. Perhaps not tomorrow, or next month, or even next year, but if Mazarin wins the day, the cost will be our autonomy and our hope for the great king Louis might one day become." She straightened beside her attendant. "Do you think for one moment that Mazarin will allow Louis out from under his thumb? Of course not. The queen is so besotted with the man that she probably wouldn't suspect a thing if Louis were to sicken and die."

Corbay recoiled. "Poison? He wouldn't dare."

Louise shook her head. "It wouldn't be the first time France lost her king to a 'convenient' illness." She leaned against the windowsill, her attention shifting to the distant remnants of the Frondeurs' retreat. A renewed sense of anticipation tingled through her. Her next words escaped as if they had a will of their own, propelled by some irresistible compulsion to document her plan. "Tomorrow we will rid France of Mazarin and his Spanish whore. Then I shall marry Louis." She turned the intensity of her gaze to her lady-in-waiting. "His own mother spoke the prophecy, the first time I saw my cousin the king. He was just a few days old. The queen, herself, said that I should marry him one day, and I shall. Then the throne will be mine as well as his, and no mere man can take it from me. *I* shall be queen, and Bourbon blood will rule France undiluted." Her words hung in the hot, still air. "I was born for tomorrow. No bullet can strike me, no arrow find me. God will be my armor, and the throne of France my prize."

Wide-eyed, Corbay murmured, "God save France."

The princess clutched the stone ledge, her gaze lifted to the few faint stars twinkling through the haze that hung over Paris. "He shall, and I will be His instrument."

* * *

Philippe watched the dice land inside the ring of yellow lantern light on the blanketed table.

Some men slept the night before a battle. Others drank and boasted. Others sat alone staring into the campfires, even in the heat of summer.

Philippe gambled. He always had.

There was something comforting in the element of chance, the arbitrary shift of luck that governed the roll of the dice. When he won, he won big, leaving the table with a full purse and the assurance that Lady Luck would go with him. When he lost, he considered the cost some sort of sacrifice to whatever forces of fortune left one man dead on the battlefield and the one beside him whole and safe. Either way, the gambling spared Philippe hours of tossing on his cot, haunted by questions he couldn't answer.

Tonight, the air was stifling inside the officers' tent, despite the fact that the tent walls were rolled up to admit the night air. Beyond the halo of lantern light on the makeshift gaming table, more than a dozen officers slept in varying states of undress on cots.

Philippe shook the ivory cubes and cast them on the table. "Seven. I win." He scooped the gold coins from the blanketed surface.

The elder Guitaut, Commander of the Queen's Guard, arched an eyebrow. "Don't you know it's dangerous to beat your commanding officer at the gaming tables the night before a battle, Corbay? Though I only outrank you by a little, my seniority gives me the power to avenge my luck in most unpleasant ways." A lazy smile accompanied the threat.

Philippe yawned, then stretched on his camp stool. "Despite what you say, sir, I know you're a good sport, one who bears his losses with dignity. Otherwise, I'd have left the game when you joined us."

"You've seen right through me." Guitaut stood, prompting the others to rise. "I've lost enough gold for tonight. After I check in at headquarters, I think I'll retire." He stepped between two cots, then paused to peer toward the eastern horizon. "It will be dawn in a few hours." He motioned Philippe to him. Out of earshot of the others, he murmured, "Your father asked after you this evening. Why don't you go by and see him? The light's still on in his tent. I'm sure he'd like to speak with you before tomorrow."

Philippe stiffened. He'd found it difficult enough to win the respect of his men on his own merits. The last thing he wanted was to be seen cozying up to his father, the marshal, just before a battle. Not to mention the fact that he had no stomach for his father's inevitable lectures. "I appreciate your concern, sir, but I'd rather return to my game."

"What is it with you boys?" Guitaut sighed. "Why can't you take a moment to talk to your old fathers, especially in times such as these? I haven't heard from Georges in over a week, myself."

Philippe's eyes moved to the marshal's tent across the field. It might as well have been on the other side of the world, for the gulf that separated them. "My father and I have little to say to each other, sir."

Guitaut shook his head and smiled into the distance. "It is the same with Georges and me, I fear, but I wish it weren't so." Then the older man's voice lowered. "Cardinal Mazarin was with us at dinner. He asked about you, too."

Philippe's concerns about his father were immediately overriden by this new development. He tried to keep his tone casual. "Really? Why would the cardinal be interested in me?"

Guitaut shrugged. "Who can say? He questioned me about your service record. I told him you were one of my most trusted officers, the best strategist I've ever had."

"And?"

"That's all. Then he changed the subject. Your father seemed disturbed by the questions, but he said nothing."

Forewarned was forearmed. Or at least Philippe hoped so. It was an open secret that his father owed his position to the cardinal. Philippe hated to think by what subterfuge the marshal had earned Mazarin's favor.

So Mazarin had asked about him, and his father had been visibly disturbed. Had a rift formed between the two? Did the cardinal's inquiry serve as some sort of indirect threat to the marshal? Worst of all, had some word of Philippe's past involvement with the princess leaked out? If it had, no amount of bravery on the battlefield could remove the mark of suspicion from his career.

Philippe felt his senses sharpen, but nothing in his manner betrayed the alert. He extended his hand to the captain. "Thank you for telling me."

"These are trying times." Guitaut's face hardened. "One can no longer tell an enemy from a friend." He squeezed Philippe's shoulder. "Why don't you go talk to your father? Tonight's as good a time as any to settle your differences. Especially in light of what we face tomorrow."

Philippe forced a slow smile to his lips, but his eyes remained cold. "If men could settle their differences, there would *be* no battle tomorrow, and we'd all be safe at home in our beds right now."

A chortle escaped Guitaut. "A point well taken." He clapped Philippe soundly on the back. "Good night, my boy. May you live long enough to spend the purse you won from me."

An easy grin flashed across Philippe's face. "And may you live long enough to regret losing it!"

When Philippe returned to the officers' tent, only one person remained at the gaming table. Tomas Verigny drained the last whiskey from the cup in his hand. "I thought the Old Man would never leave." He frowned. "Try as I might, I can never seem to get drunk the night before a battle. It takes a full pint of hard liquor just to shave the edge off my nerves." He lifted his bottle to eye level and shook it, only to discover it was empty. "But since we've taken to killing our friends, I need *two* bottles to take the edge off."

Philippe snatched the bottle from his hand and hissed, "Shut up, Tomas. This is no time or place for such talk."

Despite Tomas's claims to the contrary, the man was indeed drunk. His next outburst put them both in jeopardy. "Hell, I'm only saying what we all think, and you know it!" He lurched to his feet, the camp stool toppling beneath him. "We trained to defend the throne from foreigners, not to fight against Frenchmen who swear true allegiance to the Bourbon king!" He tugged his sword from its scabbard and held the blade to the lamplight. "This steel was meant to skewer the Hun or to drink Spanish and English blood! Not the blood of men who were my hunting companions, my gambling fellows, my cousins, my friends." He pointed it unsteadily toward the cardinal's tent. "And for what? Who are we fighting for, anyway? Our queen was born a Spaniard, the daughter of our enemy! She doesn't love France. She only loves that ambitious Italian scum who controls *her* with his—" His free hand gestured toward his crotch, but he was interrupted before he could finish.

"Shut your mouth before you get us all hanged for treason!" Philippe snatched the saber and propelled Tomas onto an empty cot. There was a subtle tensing throughout the tent. Most of the men had probably been awakened by now and had clearly heard the drunken man's ramblings, but no one moved. Though Tomas had only spoken what they all felt, none of the others had been stupid enough to voice such dangerous sentiments.

No purpose was served by such talk, anyway. Their duty lay in fighting, and fight they would, to a man.

Suddenly the odor of sweat and whiskey in the tent seemed overpowering. Philippe escaped into the hot, breathless night. He stared into the heavens and tried to force the nagging paradox of loyalties from his mind, wishing for the night to be over and the battle joined. If only he could make it to that moment of confrontation, when everything was reduced to elegant simplicity: kill or be killed. Then it wouldn't matter *why* he was fighting, or who he was fighting for. The thinking, questioning Philippe would be safely closed away, lost in the trained reflexes of a soldier.

Duty, obedience, honorable death or survival. There was no dilemma there.

Or was there?

His nerves coiled as tightly as a clock spring, Philippe lowered his eyes toward the sleeping hulk of Paris spread below them. Condé's campfires no longer glowed near St. Cloud. Turenne's advance must have forced them to move.

Philippe's eyes searched out the few telltale lights burning in the city, and his mind flashed with the image of his wife, her auburn hair cascading across the pillows. Was she sleeping now?

Hard as it was to admit, he longed to smell her skin, to bury his hands in the silky tangle of her hair, to lose his anger and pain in her own as their bodies locked in a battle of passion that left neither victor and neither vanquished.

He stared at the distant, indistinct outline of the Tuileries. Did Anne-Marie wait and wonder in this night, fearful that tomorrow would find her a widow?

Philippe chuckled ruefully. Perhaps she prayed for such

a fate. He had no way of knowing. The woman was a cipher, passionate and distant at the same time, a creature of secrets just as he was.

His loins stirred at the thought of her. She had won her way into his heart with her anger as much as with her moments of childlike vulnerability. He closed his eyes and relived the memory of her straddling his hips—riding him like a mythical Fury. Groaning softly, he started walking to ease the fullness that strained against the front of his cotton breeches.

Philippe jumped at the unexpected sound of his second-in-command's voice. "Tomas finally passed out, sir. I would have hit him over the head with that liquor bottle right away if I'd known he was about to start spilling his guts in front of all the other officers. What if Guitaut gets wind of it?" Etienne Granville mopped the perspiration from his neck with a lace handkerchief.

"I thought you were asleep."

"No more than any of the others."

Philippe frowned. He liked Granville well enough, but the man always asked too many questions. There was something that didn't quite fit about him, something that put Philippe on his guard. In these times, that was good enough reason not to be seen talking in the shadows. Philippe tried to come up with some reason to terminate the conversation without arousing the other man's suspicions. Thirty yards away, lantern light still illuminated Marshal Corbay's tent. He bowed slightly. "If you will excuse me, I was on my way to speak with my father."

Granville arched an eyebrow. "I thought you two avoided each other."

Philippe leveled a piercing stare at him. "I have always considered my family relationships a private matter."

Granville stammered, "I beg your pardon, sir. I intended no offense." Dragging his kerchief across the neck of his open shirt, he backed away and muttered, "I'll just see if I can find a game of dice."

Philippe hadn't really intended to go into his father's tent. He started walking in that direction only to be rid of Granville. But the familiar, solitary image silhouetted on the canvas prompted him to move closer.

"Who goes there?" His father's aide rose from his cot

outside the open tent flap. When he saw who it was, he saluted. "Oh. Sorry, your grace. I didn't see it was you."

"As you were." Philippe stepped inside, then halted in surprise at what he saw. Clad in a damask doublet and satin breeches, Marshal d'Harcourt peered through his lorgnette at a massive book on the table in front of him.

Philippe murmured, "The Bible? I never knew you read it."

His father laid down his reading glasses and pinched the bridge of his nose. "There are many things you don't know about me, Philippe." He smiled, motioning toward an empty camp stool. "It's good to see you, my boy. Have a seat."

Philippe bridled at the word *boy,* but obeyed. He was caught off-guard by his father's uncharacteristic mellowness. But then he remembered that in all their combined years of military service, they had never been on a campaign together. Perhaps the specter of impending battle had softened the marshal. Philippe leaned over and read the Latin superscription. "Second Chronicles?"

His father translated from the text, "The Lord saith unto you: Do not be dismayed by this great multitude, for the battle is not yours, but God's." A cynical smile curled his lips. "The campaigns of Israel and Judah make fascinating reading." He closed the book. "And there is a certain comfort in the assurance that Divine Providence will be served, no matter what we mortals do."

Philippe knew perfectly well his father didn't believe the last. The man's whole life was devoted to one scheme after another in an unending quest for power and wealth. He sat down, folded his arms across his chest and extended his legs under the table. "So the battle is God's. . . . And whose side will God be on tomorrow, Father? Ours, or the men we've pinned against the walls?"

The marshal placed two silver goblets on the table, then poured a generous measure of strong spirits into each. "You always were an insolent know-it-all, Philippe. Maybe that's one reason I never liked you." He set one of the cups in front of his son. "But you are my son, blood of my blood. Let's not quarrel this night. I know you will acquit yourself honorably tomorrow, regardless of whose side God is on. That is all any father can ask of his son, or any marshal of his officer." He lifted his own cup in a toast. "To the victor . . . whoever that might be."

Philippe returned the salute, then downed the burning contents with a gulp, his eyes boring into his father's. He knew the toast encompassed more than tomorrow's battle.

What a fool he had been to come here, thinking to make peace. He had only opened himself, again, to the brutal bluntness of the marshal's rejection. Philippe had always known his father didn't like him, but the words had pierced, sure and deadly, to shatter whatever fragment remained of the child who had once hungered in vain for a father's love.

The marshal twirled his goblet, then sniffed the amber contents' aroma. "I paid the price of a good stallion for this brandy. It's older than both of us combined, and you gulp it like cheap wine."

Philippe allowed a sardonic smile to escape. At least he had succeeded in irritating the old man.

The marshal's face congealed. He countered, "And how do you find married life, Philippe? I trust you approve of my choice for your wife. I understand you did a little Bible reading of your own on your wedding night." A lecherous sneer deformed his aristocratic features.

The languid stretch of Philippe's posture froze. He struggled to control his anger, but he could feel a telltale glow creep up his neck. Had his own father peered through the cracks into the wedding chamber, or had he delegated some spy to do it for him? The thought filled Philippe with revulsion. Then he remembered the darkness within the drawn bedcurtains, and thanked Providence for the privacy they had afforded.

He forced a smile. "Be assured, sir, that was the last night either I or my wife shall ever spend under your roof." He picked up the brandy and poured a double portion, then gulped it down.

Red-faced, the older man snatched the decanter away from him. "As usual, Philippe, I find you ungrateful as well as disrespectful. You wouldn't even *have* a home, were it not for my intervention. Maison Corbay isn't much, but it's quite good enough for a second son. And clumsy and plain though she may be, Anne-Marie is quite good enough for your wife. Her dowry bought her back a fitting home, one where she belongs. *She* owes me a debt of gratitude for that as well."

Philippe's eyes remained guileless, but his response was just above a whisper. "What do you mean, bought her *back* a fitting home? That sounds as if she owned it in the first place, then lost it."

A flash of consternation betrayed the marshal's thoughts, and Philippe realized he had struck upon the truth. "So the house was hers. The title has distaff rights, so it would be rightfully hers, as well, and any treasury." He wondered aloud, "Why didn't you go after the treasury yourself?" A brief flicker of anger in his father's eyes told Philippe he'd struck a nerve, but he couldn't imagine what might have come between the marshal's greed and the duchy he wanted. Something formidable, no doubt, but what?

Philippe shifted his approach. "Or why not have Henri sue for the estate? He's always been so . . . pliable." He fixed an ironic stare on his father. "But as firstborn, Henri already has all he wants. Why should he bother with a lawsuit? He must have dragged his feet so long you finally gave up and brought me into it." Philippe took some small comfort from the thought of his older brother's balking, for once, at the marshal.

Bitterness swept through him. How gullible he had been to hope that his father's attention to the lawsuit had sprung, at least in part, from genuine concern for Philippe's welfare. Suddenly everything made perfect sense. "Now I see why you arranged the marriage. It tied up quite a few loose ends."

The marshal merely blinked and sipped his brandy, but Philippe knew the old duke was seething. "Must have cost you the price of *several* good stallions to find our dear Anne-Marie, and the money that went with her." If Anne-Marie knew anything about this, she probably thought Philippe had been in on the marshal's plan from the very beginning. Was that the source of her anger? If so, she had a lifetime to take her revenge against the husband who had stolen her birthright. No wonder she had left him bound and humiliated. Philippe shuddered inwardly. "How much does my wife know? Did she go along willingly to recover what was rightfully hers, or did you use her the way you did me?"

The marshal sighed. "You're drunk, talking pure non-sense. Go back to your tent and sleep it off."

Philippe smiled coldly. "Your plan almost worked, Father, but you didn't take one thing into consideration. *I* am now the master of Maison Corbay. The title and the dowry have given me the means to independence. And I will *never* be a party to any more of your plots. You won't get your hands on one penny of that dowry, nor one square foot of our land. I swear it on my soul."

"You're always so certain of everything, aren't you?" The marshal swirled his brandy. "Swear what you will, Philippe, I generally get my way."

Bowing briefly, Philippe prepared to leave. "Perhaps tomorrow's battle will deprive you of the chance."

"Perhaps tomorrow we shall fall together. After all, we fight under the same banner. If we both die, does that mean God is on the side of our widows?" The marshal let out a dry chuckle, then raised his chalice in a farewell salute. "A disconcerting thought."

❈   CHAPTER 20   ❧

Sunrise—July 2, 1652

*B*y the time the horizon was white with the promise of dawn, Philippe and his men had checked and rechecked their armor, weapons, and their mounts. The horses sensed the edge of fear and anticipation in the air and stamped impatiently.

"Captain Corbay! Captain Corbay?"

"Whoa, Balthus." Steadying the beast, Philippe turned toward the sound of his name. "Here! What is it?"

A messenger approached and handed up a missal stamped with Guitaut's seal. Accepting it with a tingle of foreboding, Philippe broke the seal and read. It took a few moments for the words to sink in. He couldn't believe his father had done this to him! Relieved of his command, at such a crucial hour. The shame of it almost cost Philippe his self-control. "Granville! Front and center!"

His second-in-command reined in beside him and saluted. "Sir?"

Philippe showed him the orders. "As you can see, I have been reassigned to Turenne's Third Cavalry. We lead the first offensive. Take over here." The announcement prompted a shock wave of agitated whispers among the troops.

He turned his horse toward the cavalry massing below them, then swung back and clasped Granville's forearm against his own. "I doubt we shall meet again this side of heaven. If you're alive at the end of this day, the company will be yours to command. They're fine men. Try to be worthy of the responsibility." Then he grinned and whispered, "And never cast dice with Flaubert. He cheats."

Granville held onto his arm. "They've sent you to the Third Cavalry? Surely there's been some mistake . . ."

"There is no mistake." Now Philippe knew why he had always stopped short of openly challenging his father. Last night's confrontation would probably end up costing his life.

Pulling free of Granville's grip, he took a deep breath and scanned the confusion of men and horses on the trampled ground.

Every smell, every sound, every sight came into distinct focus, despite the haze of dust and heat.

Today was as good a day as any to die.

He chuckled bitterly. "Who knows? Perhaps God will preserve me, even though I am to be sent into the lion's mouth. Stranger things have happened."

As Philippe rode away, every man in the company bade him farewell with a rigid salute.

The pale and blistering circle of the sun had just cleared the horizon when trumpets sounded the first charge. Saber extended, his pulse thundering as loudly as the hoofbeats beside him, and a primal cry exploding from his lips, Philippe de Corbay galloped full-speed into the waiting mouths of the Prince de Condé's cannons.

Annique felt as if she had barely closed her eyes when Frontenac's worried voice roused her. "Hurry, madame! Get up! It's after six, and her highness has been summoned to the Luxembourg Palace by her father. She wishes us to

accompany her." Her summons delivered, Frontenac went
back to her own hurried toilette.

The day of battle had come at last. Annique sat up and
drew her robe from the foot of the bed. The morning had
dawned so hot that even her thin cotton dressing gown felt
clammy and restricting. She leaned down to the pallet beside her and shook Marie. "Wake up, Marie. You must
dress me right away."

Marie's eyes were wide with concern as she silently
obeyed, but Annique said nothing more. Her mind was
miles away, somewhere across the Seine. Was Philippe
mounted on the heights of Charonne, ready to fight in the
oppressive heat of this dawn? Did he think of her, of Maison Corbay, or simply of the task ahead?

There had been so many waiting, dangerous days, but
this one was different. A certain dreamlike sense hovered
over the entire city. This was the day when Frenchman
would turn against Frenchman at the very heart of the nation. If the regent's armies prevailed, France might find
itself a pawn of Spain or the Papacy. Victory for Philippe's
troops could spell the end of autonomy.

Annique inhaled deeply, then coughed and reached for
her perfumed handkerchief. Ironically appropriate, she
thought, that on this day the overwhelming stench of Paris
permeated everything, tainted every breath. The capital
rotted in the heat, a corrupt core for a nation eaten from
the inside out by dissent, perversion, and decay.

Perversion. The thought roused the disturbing memory
of the Great Mademoiselle's overture last night. Though
Annique had only a murky comprehension of what the
princess had intended, she knew she wanted no part of
such things. Was every highborn person in Paris corrupt?
The dark thread of dissolution wove its pervasive pattern
through the Court, and she despaired of seeing her own
life tangled in its malignant web.

Her stomach fluttering unsteadily, she frowned and
stared into space as Marie completed her toilette. There
would be no peace for her this day. And what about tomorrow? Would tomorrow's dawn find her among the living? Or Philippe? Somehow the thought of her own death
seemed abstract, too unreal to frighten her, but Philippe's
was another matter. Though an inner voice told her wid-
owhood would mean freedom, something raw and power-

ful contracted at the thought of losing him. She shut her mind to the wrenching conjecture.

This was not the time for thinking; it was the time for being. All Annique's instincts told her that the events of this day would propel the Great Mademoiselle—and all those with her—to a moment of desperate decision, and Annique meant to be there when it happened.

Twenty minutes later Marie buttoned the last fastening on Annique's lightweight silk overskirt just as the Great Mademoiselle, gowned in white and gold, strode resolutely from her chamber, her bodice encased with a solid-gold breastplate, and a golden helmet modeled after that of Diana upon her head. The Bourbon princess looked every inch the goddess queen she imagined herself to be. She announced, "I have just received word from the Comte de Fiésque that Monsieur le Prince has been attacked outside the walls near Montmartre and refused entry into the city gates. The situation is most dire. I had hoped my father would go to the city council to persuade them to open the gates, but he is ill and cannot leave his house, so I must go to him. You will all accompany me."

"Blessed St. Jude, watch over us," Annique breathed softly, conjuring the patron of lost causes. She turned to Marie. "Stay here. If word—any word—comes of my husband, send a page immediately to find me. I'll be with her highness."

As they settled into the gilded carriage outside, Annique saw dumb panic on Madame Fiésque's face, apprehension on Préfontaine's, and drawn concern on Frontenac's, but the Great Mademoiselle gave no sign of fear, even when her musketeers were forced to clear a path for the carriage in the crowded street beyond the gates.

Annique lifted her handkerchief to her mouth against the haze of dust and powdered dung stirred by the terrified Parisians clogging the way. Their cries were almost drowned out by the clatter of wooden carts laden with belongings. Underneath it all rumbled the deadly sound of cannon fire. Yet despite the panic that surrounded them, Annique felt a curious sense of detachment.

She felt her gaze drawn to the Great Mademoiselle, whose somber face seemed as rigid and impenetrable as the detailed breasts hammered into the golden armor she wore. Remembering the pale fire that had lit the princess's

eyes when she had spoken of this day, Annique saw
through the princess's studied aloofness. God help her, she
felt the same hungry expectation. So she watched and
waited, her heart beating a drumroll that called her not to
fear, but to destiny.

I understand. The thought formed with such conviction
Annique could almost see it cross the carriage.

The Great Mademoiselle returned a long, penetrating
look, confirming a bond too deep, too momentous for
words, a kinship that briefly silenced the conflicts between
them and erased the differences in their stations. Then she
looked away, and the spell was broken.

Despite their escorts' efforts to clear a path before them,
it took more than fifteen minutes to cross the Seine. Their
driver shouted to the pages and musketeers in front of
them, "Make way! Make way! Her highness has threatened
to take to the street if we don't move any faster." At this,
their efforts trebled, but the progress was still maddeningly
slow. The rear entrance of the Luxembourg was blocked
off by a hopeless snarl of traffic, forcing them two blocks
farther to the side gate. Once inside the palace grounds,
the driver tried to make up for lost time by galloping the
horses, then reining them to a bone-jarring stop at the
front entrance. The Great Mademoiselle bounded out of
the carriage and hurried inside, her stride rivaling any
man's and her golden armor glimmering in the sun.

Annique was right behind her. She arrived in the foyer
to hear the princess demand, "Where is Monsieur?"

The butler pointed to the landing above, where a disheveled Gaston paced erratically. Despite the heat and the
restrictions of her cuirass, the princess took the stairs two
at a time, making it difficult for Annique to keep up. When
they reached the landing, the Great Mademoiselle wasted
no time in confronting her father. "By all that's holy, Monsieur! I thought you were too *sick* to stir from your bed,
and instead I find you wringing your hands!"

Trying to be as inconspicuous as possible, Annique
stepped into a corner and stared at the old king's brother.
He really did look like a rat, just as everyone had whispered.

The soiled, disheveled little man didn't seem to notice
her. His attention was focused on his daughter. "Guard
your tongue, young lady! I remind you that you are speak-

ing to your father." He flicked open an ebony fan and stirred the thin wisps of yellowish gray hair that straggled beside his haggard cheeks. "I *am* ill, too ill to go out. But I'm well enough to be out of bed."

The only disease that appeared to afflict Gaston, duc d'Orléans, was fear. Annique wondered how such a weak and indecisive man could have spawned a woman-child as fierce as the Great Mademoiselle.

Disgust flickered across the princess's features. She closed her eyes, her breathing labored and her knuckles white on the scabbard of her sword from the visible effort to regain her composure. "Father, less than a dozen years ago, you had the courage to openly challenge your brother for his throne to rid the nation of that devil, Richelieu. Where is that courage, now? Our troops are dying—men who have pledged their lives to make you regent! How can you stay in your house, when you could go to the Council and save them? Do you *mean* to sacrifice Condé to Mazarin? For that is what you'll be doing if you don't take control of the situation. Please, sire, you cannot abandon Monsieur le Prince now. He is depending upon you to save him. Go to the Council, while there's still time."

Monsieur looked away, his full lower lip working petulantly. "I told you, I am too ill to venture into the streets under these circumstances."

The princess flushed. "Retz is behind this, isn't he? He'd like nothing better than for you to remain holed up here while our cause is lost. Don't listen to him, Father."

"Not everyone shares your affinity for rabble-rousing. At least Cardinal Retz has shown a proper and most touching concern for my welfare. *He* hasn't asked me to leave the safety of my home to risk the mob. A battle's one thing, but a mob's another." Monsieur's beady eyes leveled on his daughter. "But then again, you'd probably like nothing better than to see me torn to bits by the rabble."

"Neither one of us has anything to fear from the people of Paris, sir. You must speak to the City Council. Your position *demands* that you go to the aid of our allies."

When he made no reply, agonized frustration bloomed across the princess's features. "Even now, our troops are dying. In the name of honor, go to the City Council and demand that the deputies allow our regiments safe passage through Paris. Delay will mean certain defeat, and France will never be rid of Mazarin or the queen."

The plaintive scene was interrupted by pounding footsteps from the foyer below. Annique recognized the Duc de Rohan and the Comte de Chavigny from several of the princess's receptions. The two men bounded up the stairs and strode past to bow to Monsieur and the princess.

Rohan spoke. "Monsieur. Mademoiselle. Excuse the interruption, your highnesses, but we have most urgent news." He fell to one knee before Monsieur. "Twenty musketeers and a carriage wait outside to escort your highness to the Hôtel de Ville. The situation is most dire. The regent's troops have massed at the heights of Charonne. We're surrounded. We *must* gain entrance to the city and retreat. Every moment we delay, lives are lost."

All eyes turned expectantly to Monsieur, but he responded by collapsing into a nearby chair. "Impossible, impossible. I am far too ill. I've told you that already."

Annique watched with a sense of morbid detachment. If she had witnessed such a scene in any play, she would have rejected it as improbable and hopelessly exaggerated, but there Monsieur Gaston sat, cringing in fear and indecision, reducing his daughter to pleading while his subjects and allies perished. Why had he ever raised an army against the regent and Mazarin in the first place, if he meant to give up so easily?

Her gaze rested on the Great Mademoiselle with a new understanding of that lady's rashness and even her cruelty. What must it have been like to grow up under the domination of such a cowardly, selfish, indecisive man?

A strangled moan escaped the princess. She turned to the emissaries. "It's useless to try to convince him. To my everlasting shame, he means to hide here until the danger is past." She recoiled upon her father and spat out, "At least have the decency to take to your bed, Father! I shall die of humiliation if one more soul sees you fit enough to stand!"

When he said nothing, she spun and paced to the edge of the landing. Her hands gripped the railing. "We must do *something* to save them! Would to God I could go to the Council in my father's place."

Annique was the only one who saw the princess's eyes cut aside to gauge the response of her audience.

So that's how it was. She'd probably planned all along to represent her father.

Rohan and Chavigny exchanged meaningful glances. Chavigny moved closer to Monsieur. "Perhaps that might be a solution, your highness. If you command it, I am certain our Great Mademoiselle would act as your envoy to the Council. In light of your poor health, it seems the most logical course of action."

Monsieur leaned forward and plucked nervously at his lip. "But she is hardly more than a child. What if they refuse to listen to her?"

The princess crossed to kneel at his feet and take his hand. "They *must* listen to me, for I shall speak in your name. All of France listens when Monsieur speaks."

Her intensity seemed to bring her father back to some semblance of responsibility. "Very well. Speak in my name. They will obey. You have my leave to go."

The Great Mademoiselle dropped his hand as if it were leprous.

Annique could see that this was no game of pride, no charade, no childish plot. Pale and grim, the princess was ready to enter the cannon's mouth. The golden war goddess swept down the stairs and Annique followed, propelled by a surge of admiration. "Wait, your highness."

The princess didn't stop. "No. Go back to the Tuileries. My father will provide a coach."

Annique had no intention of being left behind. "Your highness, wait!"

The Great Mademoiselle paused for a heartbeat, allowing Annique to shorten the distance between them. Annique caught up to her just as the princess lifted her foot to the carriage step. "Mademoiselle, please don't send me away to wait for word in some darkened room. Let me come with you." Her voice dropped to a choked whisper. "Let me be there to see if my husband lives or dies."

Wordless, the princess blinked at her, then stepped into the waiting carriage. Rohan and Chavigny were already mounted beside it. Her silence was all the permission Annique needed. She barely had time to scramble aboard before the carriage began moving.

The Great Mademoiselle leaned forward and grasped Annique's wrists so hard her nails carved shallow arcs in the flesh. "Who gave you leave to accompany me? I do not wish it! I shall have you put out at the first opportunity. One of my musketeers will escort you back to the Tuileries." Something bitter and unspoken loomed behind her words.

Annique jerked her hands free. "Let me stay! I can be of use. I'm not afraid. You know it."

"Your safety is of little enough concern to me, but I will not have the death of Philippe's child on my head."

Stunned, Annique repeated, "Child? What do you mean, child?"

Fiésque and Frontenac rolled their eyes.

Disgust marred the Great Mademoiselle's features. "Don't play ignorant with me, madame. I have my sources, even on your own hearth. We both know full well you haven't passed blood for two months now, and any fool can see the signs of nausea and fatigue."

Annique stammered, "But my monthly penance didn't come because I was sinful and would not confess. Mother Bernard told me God would visit the penance of blood on me every month, and if I confessed and repented, the bleeding would go away for another month. She told me." Confusion compounded the effects of the jarring coach ride, and Annique broke into a cold sweat. "After I . . . sinned, willfully gave myself to the flesh, my penance didn't come because I failed to confess, to repent." The moment the words were out, she heard how ridiculous they sounded.

Annique saw a flicker of genuine surprise in the princess's face. "You stupid, ignorant girl. I have overestimated you. Don't you know *anything?*"

Shrewd looks from everyone else in the carriage told Annique she was the only one there who hadn't been aware she was carrying a child. How could she have been so blind, so thick-headed? She'd believed Mother Bernard's explanation about her monthly "penance" without question. Why hadn't she sought confirmation from Sister Thomas? Or asked Marie when the cycles had stopped?

Suddenly Marie's recent shy comments and admonitions made sense. She knew, too, but had misinterpreted her mistress's monumental ignorance for secrecy.

A child. Dear heaven, if only Annique had known, she'd never have set foot in Paris, no matter what Philippe did. If

Philippe had known, he wouldn't have forced her to leave the country in the first place.

Philippe's child. She was carrying Philippe's child.

Her hand slid across her abdomen. She should feel different, changed, but she didn't. The idea of life within her was too fresh, too shocking to seem real.

The princess spent a sad, bitter look on Annique. "You really *are* ignorant, aren't you?" The older woman shrank slightly, a fleeting look of regret the only betrayal of her own long-ago loss of innocence. For the briefest instant, Annique thought the princess would cry. Then the royal jaw stiffened. "Fool girl. You should never have left the Luxembourg."

The coach slowed to enter the Place de l'Hôtel de Ville. Cheering crowds passed the word of the Great Mademoiselle's approach.

Annique scanned the unbroken confusion surrounding the carriage. "Perhaps I should return to the Tuileries."

The princess motioned Rohan close and asked him to arrange it, but he shook his head. "I'm sorry, Mademoiselle, but your safety must be our first concern. We can't spare an escort for the duchess. She must remain with us until we reach a more secure area of the city."

The princess leveled a trenchant stare at Annique. "I told you not to come. Now it's too late. Whatever happens from here on in, you may lay to your own doorstep, not mine."

❧ CHAPTER 21 ❧

*S*till numbed by the revelation that she was with child, Annique was caught up in the rushing current of destiny that flowed around her.

The square in front of the Hôtel de Ville was packed with jostling, howling citizens. As the golden carriage wedged its way into the crowd, Annique could smell the powerful odors of fear and drink mingled with the acrid stink of spent powder. Angry faces and raised fists focused on the carriage's aristocratic occupants. Beyond the circle of beleaguered musketeers, coarse voices shouted blame and curses. No wonder the princess's father had been afraid. Annique was afraid now, too—not of mere injury, but of being torn apart by the enraged mob. She sat rigid, her gaze glued to the chaos that crushed against the guards on every side.

Thirty yards short of the Hôtel de Ville, the entourage reached an impasse.

The mounting danger had an incredible effect on the Great Mademoiselle. As if she drew strength from the raw power of the mob, she rose majestically to stand on the seat, her feet rock-steady on the upholstery. She raised her golden sword and scabbard above her head and silenced the crowd with a look as fierce as God's own wrath.

The princess's words, surprisingly deep and resonant from such a diminutive woman, echoed faintly from the surrounding buildings. "Loyal subjects . . ."

A roar of acknowledgment rose in response.

Annique shrank back into the seat as the press of bodies closed tighter around the carriage. There would be no escape if things went amiss.

Yet the princess's every motion, her every word spoke absolute confidence. Another wave of her golden weapon stilled the crowd. "Men and women of Paris! You know how I love this city and its people. I come among you now, freely, without fear, because of that love."

A brief tide of approval swelled from the mob.

"Thank you, my people. I am deeply touched by your loyalty and your affection." The golden curls bowed, the royal cheeks flushed on cue with convincing humility. Then she scanned the sea of expectant faces, her eyes resolute. Like a mother soothing a frightened, willful child, she reached out to them. "I have left the safety of my home today as an emissary from my father, sent to plead with the Council to stop the bloodshed."

A mutter rippled through the crowd.

Slowly, deliberately, her gaze engaged every sector of the assemblage. "Even as we speak, Frenchmen are dying outside the walls of the city! Unless the Council acts, the Seine will run red with the blood of our brothers, our fathers, our children! Do I have your support in asking an end to this killing?"

The thunderous reply of the mob drowned out the distant sound of battle. "Peace!" "Aye, we're with you!" "Stop the killing!"

The driver surrendered his seat as the princess sought a higher perch. She straightened to her feet and shouted, "Bless you, good citizens, for your support! Now pray God's guidance and protection as I go to the Council. And wait, ready to come to my aid if they refuse to listen to reason! Are you with me?"

Again, the mob bellowed its assent to the golden vision above them. Annique marveled at the aura of glory that radiated from the princess. With mere words she had channeled the crowd's fears to her own purposes, harnessing their brutality to her own ends, cementing a bond of loyalty between herself and thousands of nameless citizens. Their Great Mademoiselle could do no wrong.

This was how it must have been when Antony spoke on the steps of the Forum after the death of Caesar. But today the single, fearless voice that rose to shape the force of history was a woman's voice, and Annique was there to hear it.

The Great Mademoiselle descended to the floorboards. "Rohan! Chavigny! Come with me." She turned her attention to her entourage, her face registering contempt at their fear until she saw the admiration in Annique's eyes. "You, too, Corbay." She strode to the edge of the driver's platform. Without hesitation the princess flung herself off, hurling herself into the sea of uplifted hands as confidently as a bird commits to the wind. Her gesture of reckless trust heightened the mob's devotion to the edge of frenzy. Cheering wildly, they passed her hand-to-hand to the front steps of the Hôtel de Ville, then set her gently to her feet. She mounted the narrow terrace and turned to await the others.

Her knees shaking, Annique rose and crossed to the open carriage door where Rohan and Chavigny were trying vainly to clear the way on foot. Suddenly, as if on cue, a narrow passageway opened between the carriage and the waiting princess. Annique's heart fluttered like a trapped dove's as she climbed down onto the pavement, but she kept her head high and walked with the two men between the walls of jostling humanity.

Upon reaching the Great Mademoiselle, Rohan and Chavigny shepherded them inside and up the stairs to the assembly room. At the landing Chavigny pushed aside a knot of surprised spectators blocking the doorway. Undisguised dread followed the look of recognition as the men realized who had come to call. Once inside the Council chamber, it was the same. Though the common citizenry might adore her, the Great Mademoiselle was not welcome among the city fathers of Paris.

An uneasy silence followed them into the packed assembly. Despite the open windows and tall ceilings, the hall was stifling. Annique stayed close in the princess's wake, a tide of angry murmurs following them. Their progress halted in front of a small, meticulously dressed little man wearing the chain of office. The mayor's agitation was obvious from the outset, but protocol was meticulously observed. Once the formalities were completed, he cleared his throat in a vain effort to quiet the Council.

The Great Mademoiselle raised her voice above the buzz of whispered comments. "Honored deputies, councilors, gentlemen—" The room fell silent. "I come in the name of my father, who is too ill to stir from his home. Monsieur commissioned me to address you most urgently." Her cold blue gaze shifted boldly from face to face. Invariably, those she looked upon glanced away. "This conflict has brought us to a point of dire decision. Anarchy threatens to overtake the streets. Listen to the sound of the frightened citizens below." She paused as the ominous rumble filled the room. "No one in Paris is safe. We must immediately mobilize all militia in every sector of the city to maintain order."

The mayor bowed slightly. "It has already been done, your highness. Four thousand troops stand at the ready."

Annique breathed easier. She listened as the golden princess eloquently pleaded for two thousand of those troops to be sent as reinforcements to relieve Condé outside the St. Cloud gate. The deputies and commissioners agreed without hesitation, obviously anxious to be rid of the princess. When the doors opened for the messengers dispatched to direct the reinforcements, the waiting mob sent up a cheer of encouragement.

The Great Mademoiselle pressed further, explaining that a protective guard was needed in the Place Royale. The Council agreed to deploy four hundred troops straightaway. Again, messengers were dispatched through the waiting crowd.

Now only one request remained, the most important.

The Great Mademoiselle paused, then spoke with the authority of a royal edict. "Monsieur le Prince has been cut off. My legions are pinned against the city walls and are being slaughtered. There remains no choice but to open the gates of the city and allow the Frondeurs free passage through the city."

For several heartbeats, there was silence. Then pandemonium broke loose. The shouts of the Council clashed above the tumult of the mob outside.

"What? Invite the battle to our streets, our very doorsteps?"

"Are you mad? Turenne would turn his guns on us all!"

"No! The city would be destroyed!"

"Never! Madness!"

The mayor staggered backward, then turned, red-faced, upon the princess to shout, "Turenne would never have come so close to the city in the first place, had Mademoiselle not brought her regiments to our very doorstep! Surely your highness cannot expect us to invite her armies into the city, bringing the battle to our homes, our streets!"

In response to the ugly shift of atmosphere in the packed room, Annique stepped closer to the princess. Yet she need not have worried. A flock of bureaucrats and politicians held little threat for a woman who had faced the mobs of Orléans and tamed the desperate, drunken throng that jammed the square outside.

A chilling smile curled the princess's lips. Without warning, her tiny, immaculate hands snatched the front of the mayor's jacket and jerked the shocked official forward, wrenching him from his feet with an ease that stunned everyone who saw it, Annique included. Sputtering, he scrambled to regain his footing while the Great Mademoiselle, her face mere inches from his own, shouted, "You worm! You coward! Men are dying out there, better men than you, and you hide inside here wringing your hands!"

For a split second, Annique imagined the Great Mademoiselle's father in place of the terrified mayor.

The princess looked past him. "You'll not play your usual games with me, gentlemen! No foot-dragging, no delays!" She released the mayor and spun to confront the rest of the Council, her pointed finger marking them, one by one. "All of you! If you refuse this, you're not fit to call yourselves Frenchmen, much less deputies! Some of the finest men of France have risked everything to protect us from Mazarin's foreign schemes, and I will not see them slaughtered!" Her creamy skin bloomed crimson with rage, the contrast adding even more menace to the pale blue glitter of her eyes.

A tide of exultation rose in Annique. Never in her life had she seen such a display. No wonder the princess had spoken as she had the night before. This moment was no abstract of history. It was real, alive—breathing treachery and glory in the same breath, granting life or death to thousands by the force of a single will. The Great Mademoiselle met these men on their own ground and would bend them to her designs, with sheer force, if necessary.

When the Council made no move to respond, the Great Mademoiselle went further. Quick as lightning, her fingers threaded into the mayor's beard and clamped into a fist. She jerked downward, ignoring the startled little man's yelp of pain. Glaring straight into his eyes, she thundered, "If you don't open those gates, and *soon,* I shall tear the beard from your puny face and then kill you with my bare hands!"

Every soul in the room knew she was fully prepared to make good the threat.

Visibly struggling to maintain her self-control, the Great Mademoiselle growled, "You *will* open the gates. Now." Her hands shaking, she released him.

"Pardon, Great Lady, pardon," the mayor gulped. His trembling fingers smoothed the crimped beard back into place, then he bowed to the fierce apparition before him. "If your highness will allow us to discuss the matter—" The princess bristled menacingly, and he put forth his hands in appeasement. *"Briefly,* your highness. We need but a moment to come to agreement, I assure you."

A hundred anxious faces turned to gauge the royal response.

Her features cold as stone, the Great Mademoiselle nodded almost imperceptibly. "Very well. You have five minutes. We shall wait in the carriage." She glared balefully at the silent assembly. "If you do not bring the answer I want, I shall return, but not alone. Deny my request, and I'll come back with the mob." Her voice carried to the farthest man. "The people of Paris love me, as I love them. A word from me, and they would burn this building down around you, or drown the lot of you in the Seine!" She smiled. "Rest assured, gentlemen, you've far worse to fear from my loyal subjects outside than you do from the regent. Think about *that* as you reach your decision!"

With that, she swept from the room, Annique and a smug Rohan and Chavigny close behind. Outside, the adulation of her subjects accompanied the Great Mademoiselle.

Rohan winked as he handed Annique back into the carriage behind her. "That will be a story fit to tell your children, and your children's children."

Annique glanced about them, then shook her head. "If we live to tell it, sir."

He stared past her to the princess and murmured, "We'll live to tell it. She's charmed today, and all of us with her. Mark my words."

Annique thought of the child within her and whispered, "I hope you're right."

Rohan and Chavigny climbed into the coach behind Annique, and the waiting began. The musketeers' mounts shifted nervously as the guards kept their weapons to the ready.

Annique could see that most of the mob seemed drunk, either with wine or with the heady passion of the moment. How little it would take to turn their adoration to brutal, senseless killing.

Slowly the seconds ticked by. Her face pale and rigid, the Great Mademoiselle whispered, "What time is it, Rohan? Are the five minutes up?" Her eyes never left the mob.

Rohan looked at the clock on the tower. "Only two minutes have passed, your highness. The Council will agree. They must."

She faced him, her expression almost trancelike, but formidable in its intensity. "I meant what I said. I'll turn the mob on them if they dare refuse. Page!" A messenger sprang to the carriage platform. "Tell them to hurry!" The boy scampered into the Hôtel de Ville.

The princess lowered her head and clenched her hands in prayer. "Dear God, make them hurry. I can almost hear the cries of my troops dying. I can smell their blood."

Annique saw genuine admiration in Rohan's concerned expression as he offered comfort to the princess. "This day has proved your highness as good a general as any I've ever fought beside. I shall count it a privilege to die in Mademoiselle's service, if need be."

For an instant the Great Mademoiselle looked younger and more vulnerable than her twenty-four years. "I shall remember your loyalty, sir." Then grimness stole her youth again. Her hands flexed compulsively on the sheathed sword across her lap. "Page!"

Another boy appeared, this one younger than the last and visibly frightened.

"Tell them I said if they wish to live to the end of this day, they must give me the answer I want. Tell them."

Eyes wide, the boy bowed and scurried through the crowd.

One minute before the deadline, the mayor appeared at the doorway. Annique tried to read his face, but all she saw was fear. He halted, obviously afraid to venture farther.

When the princess saw him, she rose, but made no move to leave the carriage. The mayor was forced to descend into the hostile mob and come to them. Looking up from the pavement beside the coach, he stood below the princess like a suppliant.

A simple lifting of the princess's hand stayed the escort from admitting the mayor to the coach. She spoke first, her voice stilling all others. "And what is the decision of the Council, sir? Have they agreed to open the gates of the city as I requested?"

The mayor hesitated, his eyes darting nervously to the thousands surrounding him.

The indecisive gesture sparked a cry from the depths of the crowd. "Drown him! Throw him in the Seine!" Other voices took up the threat, until it grew to a malignant crescendo. The coach shook as the throng pressed closer, forcing the alarmed mayor to seek shelter behind one of the musketeers.

The small hairs rose on the back of Annique's neck. What if the mob killed him, right before their eyes?

The princess lifted her scabbard. "Silence, loyal subjects! Let him speak. The people must hear his answer." At her command, the angry shouts ceased.

The mayor's voice croaked dryly. "Yes! Let the gates be

opened. Monsieur le Prince's troops shall be given free passage through the city."

Annique covered her face with her hands and murmured, "Thank God. Thank God." Perhaps Philippe would not have to fight today, after all. But she knew the danger wasn't over.

In the roar that followed, the Great Mademoiselle shouted down to the terrified little man before her, "I suggest you hurry back to the safety of the Hôtel de Ville, Mayor, while I am still here to protect you." He retreated just as a panting emissary worked his way from behind the carriage and waved for Rohan's attention. After a murmured conference, Rohan leaned close to the princess's ear and relayed the message.

She nodded curtly, then rose. "Loyal subjects! Clear the way! We must make haste! Grant us passage to the Bastille!"

❦ CHAPTER 22 ❦

*N*ever in her darkest imagination had Annique conjured sights such as those which awaited them on the way to the Bastille. Two short miles of crowded avenue took them from reality to the mouth of hell.

The sound of cannon fire was no longer distant. Errant cannonballs struck all around them. Every few minutes, shards of iron sizzled across the air above their heads. Bits of stone, tile, or mortar rained down on them, littering the streets. Thick columns of smoke rose from burning buildings set afire by the deadly assault. When the fitful breeze panted from the south, the acrid, burning odor of powder overpowered all else.

At the sound of a screaming whine overhead, Annique bent double, her arms protectively sheltering her head. A red-hot chunk of cannonball struck the roof of a nearby building, loosing a slab of slate that just missed the driver.

Silently, she prayed for the safety of the child within her.

Despite the efforts of their escort, the carriage slowed to a crawl. Now Annique no longer watched the skies for bits of stone or red-hot iron. Her attention shifted to the clogged streets where frightened shopkeepers and house-wives gave way to a shuffling exodus of wounded.

She watched in morbid compulsion as a footsoldier stumbled past, his good arm cradling a mangled stump that left a trail of bright red blood along the cobblestones. Close behind followed an officer of the Guard, his face downcast and his head bandaged with a blood-soaked shirt. Annique noticed a lock of raven hair straggling from beneath the bandage, and her heart lurched.

Philippe? A small cry escaped her. She leapt to her feet and reached out toward him. A stranger's face looked up at her without recognition. He stumbled out of the car-riage's path.

No, thank God. Not Philippe.

Annique sank to the seat. Silent tears bathing her cheeks, she crammed her handkerchief hard against her mouth to keep from crying aloud. All around them, dead and dying were carried past on boards, ladders, anything that could supply a makeshift litter. Part of her wanted to leap from the carriage and offer what little help she could, but she knew such a gesture would be futile. Something told her she would be of greater use later, alongside the princess.

Spoke by spoke, the wheels carried them deeper into madness, deeper into danger.

Fiésque covered her face with her hands, her shoulders shaking, the sound of her sobs drowned out by the noise. But the Great Mademoiselle remained pale and erect, her eyes upon some unnamed objective in the distance.

The sound of the fighting grew louder. Exchanging omi-nous looks, Rohan and Chavigny took to their horses and joined the escort, leaving Préfontaine in the carriage with the four women. Soon after they entered the rue St. An-toine, the Great Mademoiselle looked into the crowd ahead of them and cried, "Guitaut! My God! Are you dy-ing?"

Sieur de Guitaut, Captain of the Royal Guard, staggered toward them, his hands clutched to the blood-soaked tan-gle of clothing at his abdomen. Hatless, his clothes unbut-toned, his skin pale as candle wax, he reached out in answer to the princess's cry. His head shook in silent denial of the mortality of his wound.

The Guard! If Philippe's commander had been so

gravely wounded, what did that bode for him? The muscles of Annique's throat tightened, and tears rose, unbidden, to cloud her vision. If Philippe died, their child would lose not only its father, but a part of its mother, as well. She watched Guitaut stumble away. *Please God, spare my husband!* In the face of this horror, she could no longer deny how much of her heart she'd given to Philippe. God help her, she cared deeply for Philippe, and she could not bear to think of him wounded or dying like Guitaut.

She turned her eyes forward.

A horse meandered toward the carriage, its rider slumped forward against its neck. The horseman's arms limply bracketed the animal's foreflanks, which glistened red in the glaring sunlight. Annique could not tell if the blood came from the rider or some wound to the snorting, frightened creature. But when the beast skittered sideways, both she and the princess saw the look of surprise in the dead man's vacant, staring eyes, and the blood still oozing from his mouth.

Rohan kicked the animal's flank and deflected its grisly journey. Only then did the Great Mademoiselle seem to falter. Annique imagined a craze of tiny cracks blooming across the marble goddess. A sharp blow would reduce her facade to rubble.

But the worst was yet to come.

One of the musketeers in the escort choked an oath, and all eyes followed his gaze to a grim procession only yards away.

The Duke de la Rochefoucauld rode toward them, supported on either side by his son and his adjutant. A musket wound through the temples had knocked Rochefoucauld's eyeballs from their sockets. Snorting loudly to keep himself from drowning in the blood that poured over his nose and mouth, he rode past without acknowledging their presence.

It was more than Annique could endure. She turned her face against the princess's shoulder and moaned. She felt the Great Mademoiselle gag, but the royal posture remained erect. A brusque sideways shove forced Annique away, restoring the envelope of bleak solitude that surrounded the princess.

Several blocks before they reached the Bastille, the princess ordered the carriage to stop beside a two-story building whose entrance was guarded by a sentry wearing the uniform of her regiment. Her colors hung limply from his lance.

The Great Mademoiselle was out of the carriage before it stopped moving completely. As Rohan and Chavigny dismounted, the others hastily piled out and followed her inside. Annique couldn't help noticing the small sign beside the entrance that incongruously identified the structure as an accountant's office.

Rohan escorted the four women past several rebel soldiers and into a dim, shuttered parlor, then left. The princess sat down, her hands in her lap. Annique shot a questioning glance to Frontenac, who shrugged and shook her head.

They were not kept in suspense for long. The soldiers in the hallway snapped to attention, and one announced, "His highness, the Prince of Condé."

The desperate man who careened into the room was a far cry from the arrogant aristocrat Annique had met in the princess's chamber. His unbuttoned shirt was splattered with blood, and his shaking hand still grasped the hilt of his naked sword.

The women stared in open shock.

Sweat matted tangled hair to his skull. Mud stained his face and clothes. Grass stuck to the fabric of his torn shirt. Dirt clogged the nails of the hand that thrust his sword, hilt-first, into Annique's grasp. "Here. Take this." The blade glistened red and smelled of iron. Condé swayed, and Annique saw that his cuirass was dented and flecked with blood.

"Monsieur le Prince!" The Great Mademoiselle rushed forward to support him. "Are you hurt?"

He fixed a haunted stare on his cousin. "You behold a man in despair. I have lost all my friends." Then his features crumbled. "Forgive me." He flung himself into a chair and wept.

No accusations. No asking why the Duke of Orléans had not come to his aid. No shouted indictment for Gaston's cowardice and betrayal. Only the tears of a broken man, his head in his hands.

The Great Mademoiselle dropped to her knees before him. "Do not weep, dear cousin. All is not lost. Guitaut is only wounded! De Clinchamp is well, as is de Vallon. I saw them myself on the way. But that is not the best news. I have just come from the Hôtel de Ville. Even now, word is being sent to open the gates."

The prince lifted his face. "Your father—?"

She averted her eyes. "No. Father is ill. I begged him to go, but he could not. I went in his place. They listened to me." She smiled wryly when his head snapped up in surprise. "Remember Orléans. The people love me. They stood behind me, gave me the power I needed to sway the Council."

He leaned back and closed his eyes. "Too late. So many killed. What shall I do?"

She gripped his arms. "Dear cousin, collect yourself. Our men are counting on you. You must go to them immediately, start the retreat."

Condé's eyes shot open at the word *retreat*, his arrogance returning. "Retreat? In broad daylight, in front of Mazarin and all the others? No! Never!"

The Great Mademoiselle blinked in astonishment, then rose and turned so he would not see the brief flash of disgust on her face. When she turned back to speak, her tone was calm but firm. "It's the only way. Think. If we move quickly, even the baggage carts can be saved. Our men will be alive and provisioned to fight another day. We must retreat, and *now*. Otherwise, all is lost. You know I speak the truth."

"I don't know." He threw himself back into the chair. "Retreat? How could I live with such shame?"

Only the Great Mademoiselle's clenched fists betrayed her frustration. Seeing the prince's indecision, Annique shared that same frustration. Why was it relegated to women to wait for men to act? If only the princess had the power to direct events! The choice was clear. Would this man spare his own pride at the cost of thousands of lives?

After minutes that seemed like hours, the prince rose, his face haggard but composed. "Of course, Mademoiselle. What could I have been thinking? I shall go immediately."

"I understand your first impulse, dear cousin, and I forgive it. This day, you have endured more than any man should be called upon to suffer." The princess placed a subtle emphasis on the word *man*, her eyes meeting Annique's for a split second. Then she was once again all concern for the prince. "Send the provision carts here. I shall attend to them after I return from the Bastille."

The prince straightened. "The Bastille? But they'll not let you in—"

"Councilor Broussel's son is keeper of the fortress. He will not dare to refuse me, not after the Council's vote of confidence." She ushered him to the door. "The parapet provides a perfect place to follow the fighting. I'll send word the minute I discover how the battle goes."

The prince kissed both her cheeks. "We are all in your debt."

As he walked away, Annique heard the princess murmur, "Indeed you are, sir. Indeed."

Thirty minutes later, the Great Mademoiselle turned all her charms on young Broussel at the Bastille. "I merely wish to see the battle, monsieur. Surely you would not begrudge me that? My dear cousin, the king, is across the river. I cannot draw another peaceful breath until I know he's safe." Having removed her golden armor on the way over, she now appeared the very soul of maidenly concern.

Annique remembered Broussel's petulant, self-important manner from the first time she'd met him at Maison d'Harcourt.

A little power made big trouble of small men, and this fellow seemed to be enjoying his authority now. Arms crossed and feet firmly planted, the diminutive Broussel glared obstinately at Rohan, Chavigny, and the waiting musketeers. "Perhaps I could allow Mademoiselle and her ladies inside—just to watch, mind you. But no soldiers." He cast a skeptical eye at Préfontaine. "And no gentlemen, either. Only the ladies."

The Great Mademoiselle granted Broussel a warm smile. "How very kind of you, sir." Six armed guards barred Chavigny and Rohan's way as the princess and Annique led Fiésque and Frontenac into the fortress's courtyard. Once inside, the princess fairly sprinted for the spiral stairway to the parapet.

Fiésque called after them, "I'm too old to take those stairs in this heat. I'll wait for you here."

All three women were panting by the time they reached the top, but the Great Mademoiselle did not stop to rest. She made straight for the long line of waiting cannons along the battlement. Hurrying after her, Annique covered her ears against the constant, explosive din from the battle below. She noted that the Bastille's cannons were silent, their muzzles turned backward into the city. Obviously, the city fathers wanted no part of the confrontation taking place on their doorstep.

Annique had almost caught up with the princess when a musket ball whizzed by so close it stirred the air on her cheek. She crouched down in alarm. "Your highness, take care! There are bullets!"

"Of course there are. This is war." The princess calmly peered over the stone ledge to the tumult of dust, smoke, humanity, and horseflesh below them.

Annique crept close and tugged at the royal skirts. "Please come away from the edge, your highness." A crossbow arrow landed nearby and skidded along the stones. "And arrows! In the name of all that's holy, step back!"

Her royal patron merely swatted Annique's hand away. "I can hardly see a thing." The princess turned back to the sullen garrison and fixed on a nearby cannoneer. "You there! Hand over that spyglass."

After a questioning glance at his compatriots, the soldier shrugged and obeyed.

The princess aimed the lens at a cluster of tents and coaches across the battlefield on the high ground of Charonne. "Just as I thought. Mazarin's there."

From the far end of the battlement, a steady stream of profanity heralded the approach of a blustering sergeant. He strode past cannon after cannon, his men grinning in his wake. "Here now! What in bloody blazes are *you* doing up here?" Arms akimbo, he halted in front of the elegantly dressed intruders. "Can't you see there's a battle goin' on down there? This is no place for *any* lady, much less a handful of 'em! This ain't a garden party! Those are real musket balls flyin' by, not dragonflies!"

The Great Mademoiselle drew herself to her full height, her eyes narrowing dangerously. "I am the Duchess of Montpensier, the king's cousin and princess of the realm. Your insolence explains why these men have failed to properly acknowledge our presence. If you do not apologize immediately, I shall feel compelled to report this affront."

The sergeant faltered. "No insult intended, yer highness. None at all." His agitation returned when a chunk of stone sailed between them. "At least take cover, yer highness! I can't answer for yer safety unless you and the ladies keep behind the battlements."

She dismissed him with a wave of her handkerchief. "Pay no attention to us. I'll take full responsibility for the safety of my party. You may return to your duties."

"But—"

"And since you brought it up, this looks more like a garden party than a proper garrison, I must say. Are your men always so lax in their duties? My cousin the king will be most interested to know that he's paying his troops to gamble and sleep."

Already red and sweat-streaked in the blazing sun, the sergeant's face flushed purple. "As it so happens, these men haven't received a single sou from his majesty in months, and neither have I!" Then he stalked away to issue a dressing-down that sent a sluggish ripple of activity through the ranks.

Having disposed of the sergeant's opposition, the princess stepped to an opening in the battlements for a better look at the conflict below them.

Annique heard the rustle of silk beside her, followed by Frontenac's ragged whisper. "Dear heaven, Corbay. Her highness has come unhinged." Her bonnet askew, Frontenac crumpled beside her and whimpered, "Mademoiselle can't know what she's doing, endangering herself and us so recklessly." Desperation lighting her eyes, she gripped Annique's sleeve. "You're clever. She respects you; I've seen it. Bring her back to her senses so we can return to the carriage. Otherwise, who knows what will become of us?"

"I'll see what I can do. But I don't think she's mad. The princess came here for a reason. Everything she does is for a reason." Annique crept to the princess's side and raised up for a look at the battle below. Grim fascination made her forget her fear. Through the haze of smoke and dust, she could see the explosions as cannon fire pounded the Frondeurs entrenched outside the locked gate of the city walls. To the right, ranks of opposing cavalry disappeared into a cloud of noise and confusion. Beyond that on the heights of Charonne, fresh troops massed under the regent's banner.

Annique could easily see that Condé's troops were outnumbered more than two to one.

The princess trained her spyglass on Charonne. "There, by those coaches! The king's standard. Look." She thrust the brass instrument into Annique's hands.

It took Annique several moments to focus the device and locate the familiar Bourbon insignia hanging limply near the elaborate tents of the high command. "I see his flag." She returned the glass. "But does that mean he's there? Would the regent risk his safety?"

A wry smile accompanied a nod of approval from the princess. "An excellent point. I doubt the regent would expose the king to such a risk. But Mazarin's there. I've seen him."

A subtle shifting drew their attention downward to the dusty chaos below. Annique scanned the battlefield, her gaze coming to rest at the far side where a line of cavalry massed like a slowly writhing snake. A tingle spread from the backs of her arms to the base of her skull. She stepped closer to the princess and pointed. "Mademoiselle! Look! The gates are still locked, and Turenne is massing troops to cut Condé's only avenue of retreat. Your regiments will be annihilated."

The princess turned her spyglass to the area Annique had indicated. "I don't know how you spotted that troop movement, but you're right." She bent down and snatched Frontenac to her feet. "Quickly! As fast as you can, run to Rohan. Tell him to take word to Monsieur le Prince that the trap is tightening. Tell him they're massing a fresh attack to cut off his retreat. Have him send Chavigny to hurry the destruction of the barricades. Those gates *must* be opened!"

Frontenac tried to crouch back down. "But . . ."

Her skin mottled with heat and anger, the princess screamed, "Do it! Now. If you fail, you're no friend of mine. Repeat the message!"

Frontenac stammered the message to the princess's satisfaction, then bolted for the stairway, her footsteps hastened, no doubt, by the prospect of the relative safety of the carriage.

Annique turned back to watch the battle. Desperation was as thick as the dust in the glare of midday—she inhaled its acrid presence with every breath. As she watched the nameless soldiers crumple and fall, the image of Philippe's face formed in her mind, and the struggle below lost all anonymity, all distance.

Philippe was out there, perhaps dead or dying. The conflict was suddenly reduced to the taking of life, blow by blow, wound by wound, shot by shot, man by man. Philippe was one of those men. Annique turned toward Sèvres. She wanted to go home, back to the security and familiarity of Maison Corbay.

The princess had other ideas. She paced between two of the cannons, her arms gripped tightly across her chest. "By all that's holy, there must be *something* we can do to stop this massacre! Think, Corbay."

Annique knew she was right. The barricades couldn't be torn down before the regent's troops reached the Frondeurs. Unless the attack could be stopped or delayed, a massacre was inevitable.

Yet what good could they do up here, so far removed from the fighting? Years of Father Jules's meticulous tactical training were reduced to a senseless jumble as Annique ransacked her brain for a solution, any solution, but no flash of insight came. She couldn't focus. Her thoughts were fragmented by the thunder of distant cannons, the ringing reports of musket fire, and the urgent shouts of the Frondeurs outside the walls. She ground the heels of her hands into her eyes and tried vainly to shut everything out so she could concentrate, but gave up in anguish. When she opened her eyes again, her gaze lit upon the long row of silent guns that lay shimmering in the July heat before her.

"The cannons!" But the moment the words were spoken, she wished she could call them back. What was she thinking? That would mean firing on the regent's troops. Philippe was among those troops. Philippe, her husband— the man who had wakened her to herself, then betrayed her. The man who had given her a home, only to abandon her. The man whose devil's touch had stolen her soul. The man she hated. The man she loved.

The Great Mademoiselle's eyebrows shot up. "Of course! The cannons." Then her gaze followed Annique's to the distant banner of the Royal Guard. Both women watched in morbid fascination as the ranks of Turenne's flanking force moved downward toward the plain. If they reached the rebel lines, all was indeed lost.

This was not the hour to think of only one life—not her own, not Philippe's, not even their unborn child's. Annique fixed a look of sheer agony on the princess. "Yes. The cannons. Only you can do it, your highness. Have the guns turned and order the men to fire. If they act quickly, the garrison can lay down a barrage in advance of the charge, stalling the charge without killing anyone."

The Great Mademoiselle kissed Annique's cheeks. "By my soul, you've served me well this day, Corbay. Stay here. I command it." Then she hoisted her skirts and strode toward the cannoneers. "Soldiers! Citizens of France! Hear me!"

Resentful of the trouble she'd brought them, the men seemed to be doing their best to ignore the flamboyant woman who moved among them. Annique bent low and crept closer so she could hear every word.

The princess's voice swelled. "Good soldiers! The fate of France is in *your* hands, not on the battlefield below!"

Two or three stopped what they were doing and listened.

"You have it in your power to save France from the domination of this foreigner who has bewitched our queen! Hear me! Your king needs you."

Elbows nudged to attention those who had not stopped to listen, but the men remained surly and suspicious.

Then the Great Mademoiselle did something that riveted every eye to her presence, every ear to her uplifted voice. She planted a silk-slippered foot upon the lip of a cannon brace, then another atop the pocked steel of the cannon shaft, then hopped nimbly to the top of the stone battlement. Her eyes scanning the twenty men just below her, she took a deliberate step backward toward the sheer dropoff.

A dozen soldiers reached out reflexively, gasping. "What's she doing up there?" "God's blood! Get her down before she falls!"

The sergeant lunged foward and bellowed, "Princess or no princess, I'll not be held accountable for such foolhardiness! Come down from there, yer highness, or I'll drag you down myself."

The princess's sword sang against its golden scabbard as she unsheathed it. She swung its tip to the sergeant's chest. "Hear me first, good soldier! Then decide if you wish to bring me down."

He stopped cold at the menace in her eyes.

She addressed the cannoneers. "Ask yourself, loyal subjects of France, who is at the root of these terrible troubles? Why would noble men of France take arms against the regent? Have you never wondered what forces compelled your fellow Frenchmen to risk everything they own, even their lives, in this struggle?"

Puzzled glances were exchanged.

The princess paced the parapet as confidently as if she were walking a garden path. "Have you not heard the street ditties? Our queen, daughter of our sworn enemy, the king of Spain, has been seduced by that devil Mazarin!" She waved her sword toward the beleaguered rebels. "Those men pinned against the gates are not foreigners! They are loyal Frenchmen who love their king, just as you do! Will you let Mazarin fill the Seine with their blood then seize for himself their wealth and their titles? Is that what you want?"

A murmur of denial rippled through her spellbound audience.

Encouraged, the princess spread her arms in supplication. "You have the power to save our nation from such a tragedy! You can stop the slaughter, and only you! The fate of France is in *your* hands, but you must act quickly, with great courage."

A nearby soldier cried, "Us? We're not rebels!"

She responded fiercely, "The Frondeurs do not rebel against our king or his mother. They have risked their lives and fortunes to stop Mazarin, for they know that he will not rest until all of France is under his thumb!" She thrust her fist into the air. *"He's* the one who has turned Frenchman against Frenchman, to weaken our nation, then bend it to his own devices!"

The response now was no dull murmur. The men answered her upraised fist with their own. "She's right! He's a foreigner, and he's got us fighting against ourselves!" "Everybody knows he controls the queen!" "He's probably an agent for the Vatican! Rome is always poking its nose into our affairs!"

The Great Mademoiselle shook loose her blond curls into a gleaming corona around her flushed face. The blade of her sword swept toward Charonne. "Then strike, and strike now! Free France from his sedition!"

"What shall we do?" "How, Lady?"

Pacing the parapet like a great golden lioness, she urged, "Turn the cannons toward the battlefield! Aim them in front of Turenne's advancing troops! The city fathers have already agreed to open the gates and allow the Frondeurs to retreat."

Stunned, the men looked to their sergeant. He exploded. "Fire on the regent's troops, our own cavalry? Do I look like a madman? Only a fool would do such a thing!"

She crossed to stand above him. "No one's asking you to fire *on* them! Merely block their way, so they can't prevent the retreat! If you move quickly, no one need be harmed."

He looked to his men, then back. "But . . ."

"Hesitation will cost France the blood of her best and finest leaders! Turn the cannons! Now, before it's too late! Otherwise, history will lay the death of our independence at *your* feet! This is your moment of greatness! Seize it! Do not be cowards!"

After a moment of silence, a single cannoneer shouted, "Turn the cannon! She's right!" His crew began to shift the muzzle.

The Great Mademoiselle brandished her blade. *"There* are loyal men of France! Godspeed, good soldiers! Who else has the courage to join them?"

Caught up in the desperate drama of the moment, the soldiers rallied. One by one, the crews redirected the barrels of their cannons and loaded them.

The princess looked to the sergeant. "And you, Sergeant. How say you? Shall you save our nation, or die at the point of my sword?"

A quick look to his men was all the convincing the sergeant needed. He fell to one knee and bowed his head. "We are at your command, your highness."

She pointed toward a boy of not more than fourteen. "You there, boy! Come here!"

When the sergeant nodded, the boy advanced in awe.

"Go to my carriage outside the gate of the fortress. Tell my men to send word immediately to Monsieur le Prince of what we are doing. Quickly now!"

"Yes, your highness." He disappeared down the stairs.

The princess turned back to the troops. Torches at the ready, their guns were aimed for the clearing in the path of Turenne's advance. Her exhortation trumpeted above the tumult of the battlefield like the shriek of a mythical harpy. "Now fire, men! For the sake of France and our king, fire!"

The first few cannons exploded to life, shaking the stones beneath their feet and almost causing Annique to jump out of her skin. The volley that followed threatened to shake the parapet apart. Her head ringing from the percussion, Annique stuck her fingers in her ears and stepped back from the battlement, but the Great Mademoiselle stood firm, like a heroic figure on a ship's prow, her sword stretched toward the advancing cavalry.

Then, as if time had slowed, great plumes of dust slowly bloomed from the bare earth in front of the troops. At first, it seemed the regiments were still advancing.

Barely able to make out the princess's words for the ringing in her head, Annique heard the Great Mademoiselle urge the men, "Again! Quickly! We must stop them before the gap is closed, so no blood will be spilled!"

Annique braced herself for the deafening report of the guns, but she still jerked spasmodically when they thundered to life.

The shots landed closer to the face of Turenne's ranks this time, and Annique watched in horror as men along the front lines crumpled and fell, the advance slowing to an uneven flux of foot soldiers and horsemen.

Annique's heart twisted. Blood *was* shed. Dear God, please don't let it be Philippe's, she thought, then reminded herself that every man who fell was someone's husband or someone's son.

In a matter of moments, a hail of arrows and musket fire thickened the air on the battlements. Annique could see the regent's forces nearest the Bastille turning to counter the fusillade from atop the walls.

"Mademoiselle! Your highness! You must come down." Annique reached for the swishing gold-embroidered skirt as it rustled past, but the princess was too quick for her.

The Great Mademoiselle moved out of reach, her attention directed to the royal encampment on the heights of Charonne. "And how do you like *that*, dear Cardinal? Did you think you could so easily best a Bourbon princess?" She was manic now, her breast heaving as she dropped the spyglass and rallied the men to her bidding. Her voice was hoarse, but the cannoneers seemed to have no difficulty hearing her. Annique read the Great Mademoiselle's lips more than heard, "The advance has stopped! Let's put them to rout! Fire again, men! In the name of France, fire!" Fearless, she gave no sign of coming down, oblivious to the musket balls and arrows that sizzled by her.

Annique picked her way to the princess's feet. Flinching every time a cannon roared, she reached up and caught hold of the princess's skirt. "Come down, your highness! You've done what you set out to do! It's over."

The Great Mademoiselle jerked the fabric free. "No! It's not over. I'm not ready for it to be over." She stepped closer to the edge, a demented grin distorting her features. "I have no need to hide! God will not allow me to be stricken! Look out there . . ." She gestured toward the aborted advance and the flood of Condé's forces moving through the now-opened gates. "All my life, I have waited for this moment. Orléans was a mere portent of this day. Until now, life has been a shadow, a reflection. *This* is the only true reality!" Madness glittered in the princess's pale eyes, along with triumph. "Thousands are meeting their deaths before us. God, the power of it! Can't you feel it?"

Frontenac had been right. The princess had gone completely mad. After vainly trying again to catch hold of her skirts and pull her down, Annique realized there was but one way to stop her.

Annique closed her eyes and muttered a prayer, then clambered up on the stone ledge and approached her. "I beg you, your highness, abandon this dangerous place." Not daring to look down, she pleaded, "Please, let me take you to safety."

The Great Mademoiselle responded by grabbing Annique and turning her to face the conflict. "Don't be afraid of it! Embrace the moment, the power. It will lift you higher than the arms of any lover! It is glorious!"

"No, lady, it is not! It is *dangerous!* Do not tempt God, your highness." Annique pulled herself free just in time to see an arrow heading straight for them. Without a moment to consider the consequences, she thrust her right hand outward in a protective gesture, while using her left to shove the princess to safety.

The next thing she knew, an impact to her chest hurled her backward atop the Great Mademoiselle, who sputtered, "Oof! What are you doing! Get off me, you fool! How dare you . . . ?" The princess's protests stopped abruptly when she pulled herself free of Annique and rose to her knees.

As if through a mist, Annique saw a look of horror replace the princess's anger. Movement brought a blinding flash of white-hot pain, but when she rolled into the princess's lap, the pain changed to coldness.

Eyes wide, the princess breathed, "Dear God, Corbay."

Annique couldn't seem to move her right hand. She glanced downward to her bodice. The arrow had pinned her hand, palm outward, to her chest. The weapon's stubby shank rose and fell with every painful breath. Blood spread a growing blot of scarlet across her chest and onto the Great Mademoiselle's magnificent dress.

Jarred back into her senses, the princess said, "Corbay, you saved my life." Then she shouted, "Sergeant! Help us! I need a stretcher!" Her arms cradled Annique gently. "You mustn't worry. We'll get help. *Sergeant!* Don't die, Corbay! I never meant for you to die. Oh, God, you're bleeding so badly."

Annique could see the crimson pulsing from her wound with every heartbeat. She was so cold. Blackness hovered around the edges of her vision. Everything sounded so far away, even her own voice as she said, "My lady, I fear it is my heart's blood."

✢   CHAPTER 23   ✢

*P*hilippe drifted in numbing darkness, his slumber soothed by the high, clear hum of a distant lullaby.

Or was it a hum? No. A ringing. That was it. One resonant tone that filled the darkness like the sound of a hundred tiny silver bells fused into a single note. Beyond that he picked out the faint rumble of muffled voices.

And then there was nothing. That was best. No pain, no straining to make sense of the echoing siren song.

A shining image floated toward him: Anne-Marie, her dark eyes sultry, her thick russet hair unbound and streaming against the blackness, the ivory skin of her outstretched arms luminescent. It was she who sang to him, who called to him across the void.

Then the vision evaporated at the sound of a harsh male

voice. "Your grace! Wake up, sir! I have orders from the commander!"

Philippe squeezed his eyes tighter to ward off the misery that came with consciousness. A thick moaning nearby irritated him, stirred him from oblivion.

As he drifted back into oblivion, Philippe heard the intrusive visitor say, "Officer, are you certain he hasn't roused since they brought him in? I have orders for the Duke of Corbay from the commander."

Orders. Can't sleep now. Must respond to orders.

The moaning shaped itself into a single word, and Philippe recognized the sound of his own voice. "What?"

"That's it, sir. Please wake up. You must."

Philippe opened his eyes to the shifting double image of a dirt-smeared page who couldn't have been more than fifteen. When he shook his head to clear his vision, an explosion of pain ripped through his skull. He felt as if he had been hung upside down in the big bell at Notre Dame and used for a clapper. "Holy Mother! My head! Where am I?" He grabbed the page's tunic to pull himself upright. The effort sent a thundering pulse through his temples.

The boy's voice barely overrode the ringing in Philippe's ears. "I searched all over for you, your grace. The adjutant of the Queen's Guard sent me to the Third Cavalry tent, and they said to look here."

A few hard blinks brought the double image of the boy's anxious face into clearer focus. Slowly, Philippe swung his legs free of the canvas cot and looked around. He saw now that he was in the hospital tent. He closed his eyes and cradled his head in his hands. When he was still, the throbbing receded.

The page tugged at his sleeve. "Please, your grace. Rouse yourself. I have urgent news and orders from the commander." The words had become a litany.

This time when Philippe opened his eyes, there was only one of everything. Dead and dying lay all around him. Beyond the rolled-up sides of the tent, long shadows cut the afternoon sun. He must have been unconscious for hours. Still weak, he swayed slightly. He needed a moment more to collect himself. "Is it still today? How did I get here? What happened?"

The page answered, "The cavalry commander said you were blown from your saddle when cannon fire hit a powder keg just as you reached the prince's lines. I've been trying to revive you for almost an hour."

"And the battle? Speak up, boy. I can barely hear you over this cursed ringing in my head." Philippe didn't realize he was shouting, but the wounded men nearby were beyond noticing.

"The battle is over, sir."

Philippe stilled. "Who won?"

Eyes alight, the boy leaned closer. "There was no clear victor, your grace, but a slaughter was averted. When the regent's troops tried to cut off the prince's retreat into the Porte St. Antoine, the Great Mademoiselle stopped the end run with cannon fire."

"What!" The damage to his ears must have been worse than he'd thought. Surely he hadn't heard the last correctly. "Cannon fire? Where in hell did she get hold of cannons?"

A look of panic crossed the messenger's face. "Your grace, please keep your voice down."

Philippe's eyes narrowed. For the first time, he noticed that no crest or regimental colors marked the page's clothing. Something was amiss. He covered his suspicions with an apology. "Sorry. Go on."

The page leaned close and spoke softly but distinctly, his words cutting through the maddening tone. "Her highness scaled the battlements of the Bastille and ordered the cannons turned against the regent's troops. The barrage gave the Frondeurs time for a safe retreat into the city."

Philippe closed one eye at the pain that came with his wry smile. "She turned the queen's cannons on their own troops?" He knew the princess well enough to believe it. She was probably the one person in the world who *could* pull off such an outrageous scheme. He studied the boy's earnest features. "Who sent you?"

The page cleared his throat and spoke loudly in a rehearsed manner. "I bring orders from Commander Guitaut." He withdrew a sealed message from his pouch.

Philippe unfolded the thick, ivory-colored paper. No imprint marked the wax closure, the handwriting was unfamiliar, and the signature bore little resemblance to Guitaut's. An obvious forgery, and a clumsy one at that. He threw the paper into the boy's lap. "What is this nonsense?"

The messenger shifted uncomfortably and glanced from side to side. Then he unfastened a single button of his jacket and retrieved a gold signet ring. The last time Philippe had seen that ring, it had been on the Great Mademoiselle's right hand. She was never without it.

What mischief was the princess brewing now? Philippe retrieved the paper and read the words requesting his presence in the city. Did she think him an idiot? He still remembered all too well what had happened the last time she'd sent for him. And only a fool—or a traitor—would follow false orders into the camp of the enemy. Despite the torment of divided loyalties this rebellion had spawned in him, Philippe was no traitor, nor was he a fool.

He jerked the boy closer and growled into his ear, "Tell whoever sent you I'm not stupid enough to fall for this. I have no intention of exposing myself to charges of treason by going with you." He shoved him roughly away. "Put *that* in your pouch and deliver it!"

The page's voice was tight with urgency. "You *must* come, your grace."

Pain intensified Philippe's snarl. "Get out, before I call the guard and have you arrested as a spy."

The boy's tongue darted nervously across his lips, but he persisted. "Sir, it's your wife . . ."

Anne-Marie? But she was safely back at the Tuileries with the Great—

Philippe's heartbeat skipped. "What about my wife?"

The boy wouldn't look him in the eye. "She was with the Great Mademoiselle on the battlements of the Bastille. Monsieur le duc's wife has been gravely wounded, sir."

The memory of Anne-Marie's image floating in the darkness came back upon Philippe full-force, now sinister instead of poignant. Was the dream a portent of death, a last farewell from a soul linked to his by anger as well as sacrament? Had he lost her?

Only in that moment did Philippe realize how much of himself would die with her. He gripped the messenger's upper arms. "How badly was she wounded?"

The boy grimaced. "Very badly, sir. Her grace has been taken to a house in the rue de Rivoli. I will lead you there." He folded the "orders" and proffered them once again. "Her highness bid me say that Commander Guitaut was injured, as well, and has summoned you to his side."

He pressed the message into Philippe's hand. "With my own eyes I saw Commander Guitaut stumbling into the city, wounded. That much I can swear to." He stood. "Only Commander Guitaut himself could prove that those orders are *not* from him."

Anne-Marie, dying! The pain in Philippe's head found a dull echo deep in his chest. It had never occurred to him that something might happen to *her.* He was the soldier, the one who lived with the threat of death, not she.

He must go to her. Yet his own innate caution combined with years of military training to hold him back. The inward battle of impulse and duty threatened to split his aching skull. Indecision was as alien to him as inactivity, but he didn't know what to do next. He couldn't simply lie back down. Separated from his regiment already, he might not be reassigned for days.

Why *shouldn't* he leave? The fighting was finished for now, and no one would miss him for hours, maybe days. He fingered the orders and weighed the consequences of taking them at face value. Even if their authenticity later came into question, he could convincingly plead confusion.

Nothing compelled him to stay; he was no use here— he'd been relieved of his command. And Anne-Marie might be dying.

He struggled to his feet. His balance unsteady, he fought down a surge of vertigo. After a few tentative steps, his footing became surer.

Exiting the tent, he handed the counterfeit orders to the sentry standing outside. "Guard! Have these orders delivered to headquarters and inform them of my whereabouts. I have been summoned to assist Commander Guitaut."

"Very well, sir. But are you certain you're fit to travel?"

Philippe squinted into the glaring sunlight. "Fit enough to try."

The guard pointed out a line of horses tied nearby. "Your horse is over there."

"Balthus!" Strange what comfort came with the sight of his faithful mount. The messenger in tow, Philippe walked over and inspected the animal for injuries. Except for a glazed look in the creature's great, black eyes, Balthus appeared unscathed. "Poor beast. You've probably got a worse headache than I do."

At the sound of his master's voice, the horse's ears

pricked up. Balthus tugged at the reins that anchored him
to the tie-line.

"Easy, boy. Easy." Philippe untied him, then swung his
boot into the stirrup. Hoisting himself into the saddle set
loose a jolt of pain that threatened to drive every hair from
Philippe's head, but this flash of agony was shorter than
the last. He was grateful for even that small bit of progress.
He needed his wits about him now more than ever. Philippe asked the page, "Do you have a horse?"

"No, sir."

"Then mount up behind me and show the way." He extended a hand, noting that the boy's gray eyes were weary
far beyond his years.

"Yes, your grace."

Philippe winced as he heaved the lad up behind him,
then his expression softened. "You've done well, boy. Now
take me to my wife."

"Across the battlefield to the wicket gate, sir."

The cannons were silent now, the only movement in the
scattered destruction that of litter bearers collecting the
dead and dying. Golden motes of dust hung suspended in
the thick stench of blood and sulphur and excrement. Flies
swarmed everywhere.

Philippe felt the page shudder and gag when they rode
past a headless, legless corpse. "Close your eyes, son, and
breathe through your mouth." Fixing his own gaze on the
battlements ahead, he tried not to look, either. No matter
how many times he had experienced the aftermath of battle, he'd never been able to harden himself to its horrors.

By the time they'd picked their way through the debris
and reached the walls of Paris, the ringing in Philippe's
ears had ebbed. His mind was clearer now, the pain settling to a dull ache in his temples. Less than half an hour
after he had awakened in the hospital tent, he rode unchal-
lenged through the wicket gate and directed Balthus onto
the rue de Rivoli.

What awaited inside the walls was more wrenching, in a
way, than the devastation outside. The once-familiar sector
of the city had been turned into a charnel house. A shuffling cortege of wounded soldiers and civilians moved
through the littered streets. Some were carried on ladders,
some on charred, broken boards, some on the arms of
their comrades. Here and there, crumpled bodies lay mo-

tionless on the cobblestones just as they had fallen. The air was thick with smoke and the shouts of frantic citizens who scrambled to rescue a few belongings from burning homes and shops.

When Balthus's hooves slipped on the blood of a soldier sprawled in the gutter, the page's strong young arms tightened so hard around Philippe's middle he could hardly gasp, "Easy, lad! I'll be of no use at all if you break my ribs before we get there."

"Sorry, sir. I was afraid—I didn't want to be thrown into the blood, sir."

"No one wants to be thrown into the blood, boy." At the sound of his own words, Philippe realized that was exactly where the regent and her ambitious paramour had thrown *him*—into the blood.

Before them in what had once been a prosperous, tidy neighborhood, Philippe now found no safe place to look, no haven from the destruction he had been a part of. He kept a close rein on Balthus to avoid trampling the bodies stretched onto the simmering pavement. They passed an alcove where a soot-stained young woman in flowered silk sat propped against a doorjamb. Sheltered from the hazy, broiling sunlight, she stared with empty eyes across the limp body of her lifeless child.

Philippe's throat tightened.

Children. They were killing children now. When would this madness end?

"Steady, Balthus." He urged the frightened animal forward.

Each block of progress seemed like a mile now, each minute stretched interminably by the suffering around them. Finally the page pointed ahead and to the left. "There it is, your grace, just beyond the next side street."

The accountant's house had obviously become a command center for the retreating Frondeurs. Condé's baggage carts jammed the entire block, and wounded soldiers in rebel uniforms were everywhere.

Forced to dismount, Philippe led his horse through the maze of men and supplies. Ignoring the shocked and angry expressions provoked by his uniform, he resolutely paced through the hostile troops. Finally he reached the stairway guarded by sentries whose lances bore the banners of the Fronde.

One look at his uniform and the guards blocked his way with their lances. The page stepped forward. "It's all right, men. He's been sent for." He pulled the signet ring from his doublet and offered it for their inspection. "This should grant us entry."

One of the guards took the ring. "Wait here." Still wary, he disappeared inside.

Philippe stepped into the narrow band of shade beneath the eaves, grateful for the shelter from the sun as well as for something to lean against in his weakened state. He scanned the congested street. If only they hadn't brought her here, to their headquarters. Crossing that threshold could cast his loyalty forever into question. Then he straightened. This cursed rebellion had erased the line between friend and foe, but not the vow that bound him to his wife. He had no choice but to go to her.

The guard returned empty-handed. "All right. Come in."

The walls of the cramped foyer fairly shook from a confusion of shouted orders and cries of the injured. Men sprawled over almost every inch of floor. Every uniform was splattered with blood and dirt, making it almost impossible to tell the wounded from the merely exhausted.

Philippe's inquiries about Anne-Marie and the princess brought only sullen denials or outright indifference. Discipline seemed to have broken down completely among the Frondeurs. No one was in charge. How in blazes was he supposed to find his wife in this madhouse? The page's efforts to locate the princess were fruitless, as well.

Then a new commotion drew all eyes to the closed doors of what must have been the parlor. Philippe recognized Condé's voice, shouting at the top of his lungs, followed by the angry shriek of Monsieur Gaston. Under different circumstances, Philippe would have paid a month's wages to listen in on *that* exchange. But the fact that he didn't hear the princess's voice told him she must not be there, so he continued to search. If only he could find someone who had seen the Great Mademoiselle or Anne-Marie.

Then he spotted a familiar face.

He picked his way across the room. "Bosarge! Where is the Great Mademoiselle? Have you seen her?"

The gray-haired captain looked up with hollowed eyes. "Why should I tell you? Or have you finally decided to switch sides? If so, your timing's wretched. I always thought you were smarter than that. A clever man doesn't hitch a ride on the executioner's cart."

Philippe had fought duels over lesser insults, but he refused to let Bosarge's slur stand between him and finding Anne-Marie. "Mademoiselle sent for me. My wife was with her highness at the Bastille and was injured. Have you seen them?"

Sympathy erased some of the bitterness from the older man's face. "That was your wife? I'm sorry, lad. I spoke out of turn." He jerked his thumb upward. "They brought her in some time ago, bleeding badly. She's upstairs." Bosarge struggled to his feet and hailed the guard who blocked the bottom of the stairs. "Let Captain Corbay pass. I'll vouch for him."

Philippe bounded past the sentry, but his progress halted when he saw the track of blood, its edges congealed on the dusty oak treads that led up to the landing. So much blood. Anne-Marie's blood.

He took the stairs two at a time.

Even his fears did not prepare him for the macabre sight that waited in the bedroom. The scarlet trail led across the threshold and all the way to the high mahogany bed the princess paced beside.

The Great Mademoiselle turned and swept toward him. "Philippe! Thank God you're alive."

Philippe barely registered her presence. He walked past her to the bed, his gaze locked on his wife. Pale as the sheets beneath her, Anne-Marie lay frozen in a grotesque pose, her hand twisted palm-out and pinned helplessly to her breast by the shaft of a crossbow arrow. Blood soaked the stiffened, padded silk of her yellow bodice. The sight turned him inside-out. "Dear God. Is she dead?"

Then he saw that with each heartbeat, the pool of blood in her palm glistened afresh. And with each rapid, shallow breath, the feathered shaft rose and fell slightly.

The princess sank into a chair beside the bed. "She lives, but I don't know for how long. What shall we do? We must help her, but there are no doctors." Her voice echoed the intensity in her pale blue eyes. "She saved my life, Philippe. We *must* help her."

An agonized groan escaped him. Anne-Marie had risked her own life to save the princess—the very woman she saw as a rival, the same woman who had publicly embarrassed and taunted her. And now she looked as if every fragile breath might be her last. But she couldn't die. Life was too precious to this woman for whom every new day was a sojourn of discovery. He had to try to save her.

Philippe pointed at Frontenac, who cowered by the door. "Go to the kitchen. Find something metal, something long, about the thickness of my thumb—a poker or a honing rod. Put it into the coals and fan the fire until the tip of the metal glows red. Then put the coals and the rod into a kettle and bring them to me. And see if there's any whiskey in the house." Frontenac obeyed only after the princess nodded her assent.

Philippe turned to the Great Mademoiselle. "Where's that page who brought me here? Send him to my town house to fetch Suzanne. Have her bring my medicine box. It contains potions to slow the bleeding and prevent putrification."

Completely unaccustomed to taking orders, the princess stiffened, but Philippe cared nothing about denting her vaulted ego. He crossed to the window and looked below. "He'll need an armed escort. The streets are a madhouse." When he returned to the bedside, his hand recoiled at the coldness of Anne-Marie's fingers in his own. Her short, buffed nails had taken on a faint bluish hue. "If we can keep her alive until he gets back, I might be able to save her."

The princess stepped to the doorway. "Page!" The boy appeared and accepted her murmured instructions. Then she returned to the bedside. "Your box should be here within the half hour."

But no sooner had Philippe returned to the window to reassure himself that the lad was on his way, than Anne-Marie's breathing became erratic.

The princess leaned close to Anne-Marie's ear. "Don't die, Corbay. Do you hear me? Don't give up." The intensity in her voice amazed Philippe. What had passed between the two women to merit such emotion? The Great Mademoiselle looked over at him. "Perhaps if we bled her . . ."

Philippe struggled to keep his composure. "Bleed her? Can't you see she's bleeding to death already?"

The princess responded with uncharacteristic meekness,

uttering two words Philippe had never thought to hear from her lips. "I'm sorry." She straightened and took a step backward. "I only meant to help."

So there was some shred of humility in the woman. He bowed slightly. "Forgive me, your highness. I know you meant well."

Philippe looked back at his unconscious wife. Long wary of the European custom of bleeding the ill or injured, he had adopted the healing arts he'd learned from the Moors in his youthful travels. Yet his potions were desperate minutes away. He couldn't wait. Dangerous though it was, he'd have to proceed without the powdered herbs.

A muffled thump against the door preceded Frontenac into the room. Extended before her, an iron pot held glowing red coals and a smoldering honing rod.

"Good. Put the pot on the hearth." He followed, the princess in his wake, her hands clenched white. Philippe fanned the coals and shifted the poker within them. Returning to the bedside, he addressed the Great Mademoiselle without ceremony. "Send Frontenac down to await my medicine box, then close the door."

Under ordinary circumstances, the princess would have had his head for such presumption. Now, concern etching her features, she relayed Philippe's instructions to her lady-in-waiting, then took up her place beside him. "What can I do?"

"I *do* need your help, Mademoiselle, but I can't have you fainting on me. If the arrow has pierced an artery, the blood will spurt when I pull the shaft free. I can't waste a second in sealing the wound."

She answered with a challenging stare of her own. "I've seen the same carnage this day as you have, sir, and I haven't fainted yet." She pointed to Anne-Marie's chest. "That arrow was meant for me. Your wife deliberately stepped into its path to spare me. I'll do whatever is needed to help you save her. You may depend on it."

For the first time, he noticed the wild disarray of the Great Mademoiselle's hair, the streaks of dirt and perspiration on her porcelain skin, and the blood that stained her torn gown. But there was absolute, cold calm in her blue eyes. He nodded. "Very well. Tear some bandages from the sheet, then hold her down tightly." Philippe shrugged out of his jacket as the princess began tearing neat linen strips.

He bent closer to inspect Anne-Marie's damaged hand. He was not at all certain that his efforts wouldn't make things worse, but there was no time to waste. He could see the life slipping from her with every beat of her heart.

The Great Mademoiselle made short work tearing apart two pillowcases, then deposited a folded stack of bandages within easy reach on the bed. "There." She circled the bed, unceremoniously hiked up her skirts, and crawled across the pillows above Anne-Marie's head. Leaning forward, she secured the unconscious woman's shoulders and gripped the limp, uninjured hand.

Philippe retrieved the glowing poker from the coals. "Ready?"

She nodded.

First he must smooth the shaft. At the touch of the rod's orange-red tip, the feathers crackled and burned away in a puff of noxious smoke. "Her hand is pierced clear through. I'll begin by pulling it free and cauterizing that wound first. Hold her tightly. She's liable to thrash when the poker hits her flesh."

He threaded his fingers under her pinned hand and tugged upward. The blood was warm and sticky, but after an initial resistance, the hand slid smoothly up the shaft and free. A red stream spurted across his shirt from the hole in her palm. Steeling himself, Philippe thrust the smoking rod clear through the wound. Unexpectedly, her fingers curled inward into a searing, spasmodic grip on the poker.

Deep and huge as the very soul of suffering, Anne-Marie's brown eyes flew open, and her lips parted to emit a strangled cry. Then her irises rolled upward into descending lids, and she went limp. The smell of scorched flesh spewed sickly sweet across the bed, bringing with it the memories of a dozen battles.

A wrenching sob escaped the princess, but she did not abandon her post.

Philippe pried the poker free of Anne-Marie's grasp, but her fingers remained drawn toward the blackened crater at the center of her palm. Deep blisters had risen across the base of her thumb and the tips of three fingers. In trying to help her, he had scarred her further. As he lifted the maimed, clawed hand before him, he remembered the look of satisfaction on her face when she had finished a piece of intricate needlework at Maison Corbay. No more.

When he saw that no blood issued from the blackened puncture, his fingers gently probed the hand near the injury. The arrow had snapped a bone and obviously torn open an artery, but the poker had done its work. He laid Anne-Marie's hand on a strip of torn sheeting. "That's stopped the bleeding there. Leave her hand uncovered, so I can check it after I deal with the arrow."

For the next, he needed a clear field to work in, but he dared not raise her up to cut the laces at the back of her bodice. Instead, he drew his dagger and carefully began to cut through the stubborn layers of stiffened, padded material surrounding the arrow's point of entry. Sweat drenched his whole body. Philippe stopped to wipe his hands on the bedclothes. If the dagger slipped, he might cut past the fabric to her flesh. "Why in heaven must you women truss yourselves in these cursed contraptions?"

Acid edged the princess's response. "We wear these 'cursed contraptions' to please our men, sir."

When the last bit of crimson-soaked cloth was removed, Philippe had uncovered a palm-sized patch of skin around the shaft in the center of Anne-Marie's chest. Rusty coagulated flecks bordered the red-glazed valley between her breasts.

He crossed back to the pot of coals. The poker sizzled when he returned it to the glowing heart of the embers.

Philippe lowered himself into a chair to wait for the tip of the honing rod to glow red once again. A thousand images crowded his brain, Anne-Marie the center of all of them. Despite the complications she had brought into his life, he wondered if he would ever be whole without her. And he wondered if his efforts to help her would only hasten her death.

Twisting the honing rod in the coals, he spoke frankly. "Now comes the most difficult part. I can't tell whether the arrow point is lodged in her breastbone or has gone clear through. If the head of the arrow has pierced to her heart, she'll die the moment I pull it out." Philippe released the honing rod and leaned forward, placing his aching head into his hands. "Perhaps we should wait, leave her alone. Maybe I could find a doctor."

The Great Mademoiselle eased herself carefully from

the bed, then crossed to stand beside him. She spoke with resignation. "We both know she won't last until we can find a doctor." Her voice became almost tender. "Don't torment yourself, Philippe." Then she was once more in command. "You must remove the arrow. It's her only chance. If her heart is pierced, she'll die anyway, no matter what we do. At least we will have tried."

No matter what plots or plans or secret revenge she might be working even now, Philippe saw that what she said made sense. He had to try to save his wife.

The Great Mademoiselle looked at him strangely, then returned to her post above Anne-Marie's head. "I am ready. Do what you must, Philippe."

He drew the smoldering instrument from the iron kettle and moved to the bed to hand it to the princess. "Hold this. I'll have to use both hands to free the shaft. Pray the arrow's tip isn't barbed."

He grasped the shank and gave it a tentative tug. The pool of blood at the point of entry spilled out to one side as her flesh rose with the arrow. "It's imbedded too tightly to come free. I'll try twisting it." He applied pressure to rotate the shaft, but it refused to move. Another, more forceful try shifted the shank several degrees. Now in response to his gentle tug, the arrow gave slightly.

"I'll have to twist and pull at the same time. Have that poker ready and use your free hand to hold her shoulder down. I'll pull on the count of three." The fingers of both his hands interlocking around the stubby shaft, he counted aloud. "One . . . two . . . three!"

Anne-Marie's entire torso rose as he lifted upward with all his might and twisted the stubborn shaft. Her back was completely clear of the bed before the arrow surrendered its grasp. As she collapsed limply back onto the mattress, he dropped the scorched arrow beside her and reached for the honing rod. The dull red tip crackled when he eased it into the wound, but it stopped just below the surface.

This time Philippe didn't notice the revolting odor that smoked from the wound. "It's shallow. The tip must have been lodged in the bone." He hurled the poker into the fireplace, then lifted the arrow to the light. It was only an inch longer than the portion that had protruded from her hand.

By the mercy of God, he hadn't killed her.

He placed his ear gently to her breast and heard the faint, rapid drumming of her heart. "She may live." The words were thick with emotion.

Feeling as if he were underwater, Philippe sank into the chair by the bed. He slumped forward and braced his elbows on his thighs. His bloodied fingers threaded into the hair at his temples as he sent up a prayer of thanks.

Careful not to jar Anne-Marie, the Great Mademoiselle eased from the pillows and crossed to the window. She looked down on the chaos below and sighed. "It's not over yet. After what happened today, no one around me is safe. You must hide her, take her to safety—at least until I know how Mazarin plans to retaliate."

A sudden rapping at the door caused them both to jump.

The princess answered. "Who is it?"

"Frontenac, your highness. I have the captain's medicine box. His servants came, as well. They wish to speak to him."

Philippe stood and gently covered his wife's bodice with a square of torn sheeting. "Send them in."

The princess raised an eyebrow.

"Don't worry. They can be trusted."

A cold smile curved her lips. "They can't be bribed. That much I know."

Before Philippe could respond, Jacques barged in, the rattling box of potions in his arms. He halted abruptly when he saw the bed. "Oh, master! Is she . . . ?"

Marie followed, bursting into tears at the sight of her mistress, but Suzanne would have none of that. The housekeeper gave Marie's arm a not-too-gentle pinch. "Hush, girl. You're only making things worse." Suzanne granted the princess and Philippe only a brief bob on her way to the bedside. "Your highness. Your grace." All business, she staked her claim on the patient like a mother lioness protecting her cub. But when she lifted the bandage to expose the charred crater in the center of her mistress's chest, her kind eyes filled with tears.

Weary beyond thinking, Philippe could only stare at the motionless form on the bed.

The princess stepped directly in front of him. "Philippe, you can't stay here, and neither can she. There's no time to waste."

He nodded numbly.

The princess turned. "Frontenac, go downstairs and tell Monsieur le Prince I shall join him straightaway." A futile pat to her bedraggled coiffure testified to the resilience of feminine vanity. "My troops need me now."

There she stood, bloodstained, dirty, wrinkled, and perspiring, her hair a tangled ruin, yet obviously convinced that her beauty and dignity could be restored by that single, useless feminine gesture. Tired though he was, Philippe couldn't help smiling. He had to admit, he liked the woman revealed in this room. Despite her affectations, the princess had shown herself this day to be brave and practical.

Gathering her dusty skirts, she moved toward the door. "I must go help with the baggage carts and the rest of the wounded. Let me know what you decide to do." But before she reached the landing, a panting emissary rounded the corner and knelt at her feet.

He offered a folded letter. "Highness, an urgent message from behind enemy lines."

The princess took the note and motioned to Jacques and Marie. "You two follow the messenger downstairs and put yourselves to good use. And close the door behind you."

Jacques hesitated, but after a nod from Philippe, he begrudgingly led Marie outside. The door closed emphatically.

It was no surprise to Philippe that she should receive word so quickly from her spies in Mazarin's camp. He leaned back in his chair and closed his eyes to conceal his interest. His ears picked out the faint sound of the wax seal tearing loose and the paper unfolding. Then something in the silence that followed caused him to open his eyes.

Her profile in sharp relief, the Great Mademoiselle stared unseeing and uttered a strangled exclamation of disbelief tinged with hysteria. "No. No." The face that turned to Philippe bore the shocked expression of a dueler who had just been run through. She shifted backward, then caught her balance.

Philippe rose. "What is it?"

There was no command in what came next, only thoughts escaping aloud. "I never thought . . . there was no time, just do what must be done. This had *nothing to do* with Louis. Surely his majesty will realize that." She closed her eyes in anguish. "But how could he understand? He's only a child. That Spanish witch of a mother will twist everything and use this against me." She reread the message, her pale bosom rising and falling rapidly.

Philippe took a step toward her, but she raised a hand as if to ward off an attacker. "No!" Crumpling the paper into her clenched fingers, she bent forward like a doll broken at the waist, muttering, ". . . Some way to convince him . . . I only wanted to save my troops . . . I . . ." A single tear traced a track through the grime on her cheek.

She straightened. "Perhaps God was on the cardinal's side, after all." Her voice came out tight and dry. "Ever since Louis was born, I've consecrated myself to a single destiny—taking my rightful place as queen beside him. Everything I've done has been to that end, even my involvement in the Fronde. How could I let that Spanish whore carve up France between herself and Mazarin?"

The Great Mademoiselle carefully smoothed open the message and read it again, as if the words would change. Then she stared past Philippe. "When I saw Turenne's men advancing to cut off our retreat, I had to do something to stop them. I couldn't just stand there and watch thousands of my troops die.

"Mazarin first mistook our cannon fire for his own." A look of bitter satisfaction momentarily broke the bleakness of her expression. Then her eyes glazed over, her chin jerking twice, spasmodically, before she went on. "But when he found out what had really happened and saw me through the glass, he shouted, 'She has killed her royal husband with that cannon fire!' "

Tears welled in her eyes. "Funny. I never imagined that at such a tender age I would look back, too late, to see that the zenith of my life had already passed." She stared once again out the window. "If only I could have realized when it was happening. I never would have come down from that parapet." She reached out into the empty air. "I would have embraced death with open arms—glorious death, a fitting conclusion! Now all that's left is anathema."

Her hands dropped to her sides, her voice to a whisper. "Perhaps God is punishing me. When the doctor told me what the pox had done, I knew I shouldn't marry Louis, but I couldn't let go of my dream." Philippe saw the barrenness of a thousand deserts in her eyes. "And now God is punishing me for my ambition. The cruelest punishment of all, to go on living deprived of the station I was born to attain."

Philippe tried to comfort her. "France still needs your courage. You must not give up, your highness."

Her answering look was one of infinite dignity and pain. Then she gazed past him to the still, white figure on the bed. "Did you know about—" She halted, keeping something back.

"About what, your highness?"

"Never mind. It's in God's hands now." She touched Anne-Marie's cheek. "So much has been lost already; I pray you will not lose her, too. Your wife is a clever woman, Philippe, and exceptionally brave. She won my respect long before she saved my life. Take care of her."

He nodded.

A small, wistful smile made the princess look very young and very vulnerable. Minutes passed before she spoke again. When she did, her voice was flat. "I must go. They're expecting me downstairs. I'll send your servants up."

Philippe rose and escorted her to the landing. He bowed farewell. "May God go with you, your highness."

Only the mute desolation in her eyes betrayed the loss of all she'd planned for. Sympathy tightened Philippe's throat as he stepped backward and slowly began to shut the door between them. Just before it closed, he caught a narrow vignette of the princess alone in the hallway. He paused, transfixed by the sad, solitary figure.

Her hands covered her face, her shoulders sagged, and a sigh as heavy as the world shivered through her. But she shed no tears.

Philippe was seized by the oddest feeling that she somehow knew he was watching. In a flash of insight, he realized she *always* thought someone was watching, even when she was alone. That would be the saddest, most isolating thing of all—never to have the comfort of a single, honest, unmanipulative moment.

He closed the door as the Great Mademoiselle slowly descended to her waiting penance below.

CHAPTER 24

Philippe knew the moment he sat down he shouldn't
have. Bone-deep weariness crept through his limbs and
fogged his mind. Oblivious to his servants' quiet, worried
presence, he leaned forward in the chair beside Anne-
Marie's bed and massaged his temples. He couldn't rest
yet. He must think, decide what to do next.

One thing was certain: The princess's warning could not
be ignored. No one who had been with her at the Bastille
would be safe from Mazarin's brutal interrogations. The
Great Mademoiselle's status might protect *her* from imprisonment and torture, but that protection didn't extend
to Anne-Marie. Mazarin would want blood for being
cheated of his chance to crush the rebellion.

Appealing to the marshal for help would be useless. After all, hadn't he had Philippe stripped of his command
and placed in the front line of the cavalry attack? There
was nothing left but to escape, and quickly. Yet after all
these years as a soldier, Philippe balked at quitting without
a release from his commander. But asking for leave would
surely betray his plans to Mazarin. Anne-Marie's only
hope was for them to disappear without a trace.

Disappear? Why didn't he call it what it was—what
Guitaut would call it—desertion.

Philippe's head throbbed afresh. Unwilling to face the
fact that the choice had been made the moment he had
crossed the threshold into Condé's headquarters, he agonized over the obvious course of action.

The harder he tried to concentrate, the louder the con-
flicting voices became inside his pounding head. Should he
risk everything—his career, his reputation, their homes,
their fortune—to save a woman so close to death? Such a
course made little sense. And she was so weak. A journey
of any length could easily finish her off. Where would he
be then?

His gaze lifted to the bed, where Suzanne and Marie
hovered anxiously beside their mistress. Anne-Marie lay so
motionless that her classic profile seemed carved of alabaster, her grip on life as tenuous as the barely perceptible
pattern of her breathing. Why must he choose between her
and all he'd worked for?

Still, he couldn't turn her over to Mazarin. Philippe had

seen firsthand the results of the cardinal's interrogations. Mazarin was absolutely without mercy or conscience. Ironic, that Philippe should now find himself at odds with the same vicious, evil man he had served, no matter how indirectly, for the last two years.

A wave of shame washed over him, summoning up the image of the dead child he'd seen in its mother's arms. If he fled Paris now, he'd also be leaving behind that specter of senseless violence—the chaos and corruption that was tearing France apart, tearing *him* apart. Since he'd been relieved of command, he probably had no career left to protect, anyway.

One by one, the strident inner voices fell silent. In the quiet that remained, he asked himself if anything he owned was worth risking Anne-Marie's life.

No.

The conviction behind the realization surprised him. Deep within the guarded recesses of his heart, Philippe closed one door and opened another. Odd how easily he made the decision that would change his life forever. Odd, too, how that decision left him feeling he was moving *toward* something. No longer would he allow himself to be swept along by circumstance or the schemes of others. From now on, Philippe would be master of his own destiny.

He motioned Jacques over and murmured, "Balthus is tied outside. Take Marie back to the town house, then pack enough supplies for a fortnight's journey. Bring all the gold from my strongbox. We must get the duchess far away from here, and quickly. The baggage wagon isn't very large, but it will have to do. And watch out for Mazarin's men. They're probably looking for the duchess already." He laid a hand on his servant's shoulder. "There's only one place where we can be safe. I just wish it were closer."

Jacques' brows drew together, then shot up in recognition. "The secret place?"

Grateful that he didn't have to risk speaking their destination aloud, Philippe nodded.

Jacques gathered the medicine box. "Shall we bring the wagon back here?"

Philippe shook his head. "No. That would make it too easy for them to trace us." He paused, his hand scraping across the stubble on his chin. Then he had an inspiration. He whispered into Jacques' ear, "Remember where I had

you deliver the picnic luncheon last spring? Meet us there.
The safest way out of the city tonight will be the Seine. I'll
find a boat somewhere. Now go, and waste no time."

Philippe watched out the window until Jacques led
Balthus, with Marie in the saddle, through the departing
baggage carts and out of sight.

He crossed to the bed and inspected Anne-Marie's
wounds. No new blood stained the bandages, and a faint
tinge of color had crept back into her skin. "I think it's safe
to move her now. Let's get her out of those filthy clothes."
The armoire in the corner yielded a freshly laundered
man's nightshirt. He handed the garment to Suzanne, then
drew out his dagger. "I'm going to roll her onto her side to
cut her out of her bodice. Hold her there, and keep an eye
on her chest wound. If it starts to bleed, let me know."

"Aye, your grace."

Fortunately, there was no fresh bleeding. After Philippe
had helped Suzanne strip his wife down to her chemise, he
turned his attention to his own appearance while the
housekeeper finished bathing and changing her.

Philippe looked down at his stained uniform. He
couldn't very well go nosing around for a boat dressed as
he was. The uniform was bound to raise suspicion. Busy
with her mistress, Suzanne didn't even notice when he removed his boots, then peeled off his bloodied, sweat-
stained shirt.

There was barely enough water left in the pitcher on the
washstand to rinse Anne-Marie's blood from his hands and
the grime from his face. That done, he returned to the
armoire and rummaged up a pair of cotton breeches and a
linen shirt. "Turn around, Suzanne. I need to change."

Suzanne looked up to find him bare-chested, and
gasped. "See here, your grace. I may be only a servant, but
you might have warned me you were goin' to shuck off
your clothes!"

Women! No matter how dire the circumstances, they
clung to their precious proprieties. Philippe reached purposefully for the buttons of his breeches. "Well, I'm warning you now. Turn around, or you'll get a good look at the
rest of me."

"Sir!" She spun around, her back rigid.

Philippe wasted no time changing into the borrowed

clothes. The fit was snug, but presentable. Donning his boots, he said, "You can look, now. I'm decent."

He extracted a small leather pouch from his uniform and took out two gold coins to leave on the shelf of the armoire. "That should cover the cost of the clothing." Tucking the pouch into his shirt, he crossed to the door. "Don't open this door for anyone but her highness until I get back. If I haven't returned by morning, seek out the Great Mademoiselle. She'll be your best help if I'm killed or captured. Contact my father only as a last resort."

Suzanne blanched. "You're going to leave us . . . ?"

"Don't worry. I'll be back."

Finding a boat took longer than he had expected. By the time he tied the flat-bottomed skiff underneath a dock near Ile St. Louis, darkness hovered over the city. Twenty minutes later, Philippe found the ground floor of the accountant's house deserted. A shiver of alarm ran through him. His long legs quickly covered the distance to the bedroom door, but he stopped with his hand on the knob.

Please let them be there, and please let them be all right. The door wasn't locked. Slowly, he pushed it open. Across the room, a single candle lit the bed. Thank God. Atop the covers, Anne-Marie lay in the white nightshirt.

At the sound of a breath behind him, Philippe spun around to find Suzanne lying in wait with a bed warmer raised threateningly over her head. When she recognized him, she lowered her weapon and issued a whispered scolding. "Why did you sneak up on us like that, your grace? I almost bashed your brains out."

Closing the door behind him, he countered, "Why did you leave the door unlocked? *Anyone* could have walked right in!"

"I couldn't very well lock it without a key, could I?" A superior look on her face, she propped her makeshift bludgeon against the wall. "I was ready for whatever came."

"I never knew such fierceness lay beneath those dimples." Three strides took him to the bed. Suzanne had bathed, bandaged, and changed her mistress, but the nightshirt looked too much like a shroud. "How is she?"

The housekeeper leaned past him to smooth Anne-Marie's cheek. "Her hands are a bit warmer now, and her breathing's deeper. I only wish we didn't have to move her."

"We have no choice." Philippe unfolded the dark green bedspread from the foot of the bed, then transferred Anne-Marie onto it as delicately as he would a sleeping baby. Despite the heat, her skin felt clammy, so he bundled her securely before lifting her into his arms. His wife never stirred. He couldn't even hear the sound of her breathing.

Concerned, he bent his ear to her slightly parted lips. The faintest current of air told him life had not left her. He closed his eyes in relief and buried his face in her hair, only to inhale the lingering odor of spent powder.

Though he knew she couldn't hear him, he murmured into her ear, "Fight for your life. In just a few days, we'll be away from all this. Then we'll be safe. If you can just hold on for a little longer, everything will be all right."

If only he believed it.

Holding his wife, Philippe stood ankle-deep in mud while Suzanne crawled into the rowboat and settled herself.

Suzanne reached out to accept her mistress. "Lay her head in my lap, here at the back. Then there'll be room for your grace to row." She added matter-of-factly, "And take care not to rock the boat. I can't swim."

Once Anne-Marie was safely in Suzanne's embrace, Philippe shoved the skiff away from the riverbank and heaved himself aboard. The Seine flowed slow and sluggish, offering little resistance when the oars bit into the water to carry them upstream. As they glided along, Philippe watched the faint, familiar silhouette of Notre Dame grow smaller and smaller above the trees and wondered if this would be the last time he ever saw it.

He pulled harder on the oars to chase the melancholy thought from his mind, focusing on the positive, instead. There was much to be grateful for. Once he had located a boat, things had gone almost too smoothly. The boatman hadn't asked a single question, just pocketed the windfall price and handed over his skiff without a word. Lucky, too, that no one had remained to challenge Philippe when he'd returned to collect the women. And they hadn't encountered a soul in the darkened streets between the house and the river.

So many favorable coincidences. Or were they coincidences? Philippe focused on the starry sky over Paris. He dared not think that Providence was, at last, on their side.

The river curved and the last lights of the capital disappeared. No campfires lit the banks of the Seine now. No horses whinnied or stamped, no wagons rumbled. The only sound heard over the chorus of frogs and insects was the rhythmic splash of the oars on the water. If his arms didn't give out, they would meet Jacques within the hour.

By the time he directed the boat to the shore and the bottom scraped into the river grass, Philippe could feel nothing from his shoulders to his fingertips. He eased himself into the shallow water, then tugged the prow toward the bank. When the craft would go no farther, he whispered, "Jacques? Are you there?"

A familiar rasping voice answered from the bushes. "Over here, your grace."

Philippe tried to whisper, but nothing came out. Weary beyond caution, he spoke aloud. "Well, come and help me, man. I haven't the strength to lift the duchess."

Two figures scuttled across the clearing. Marie waded in to help Philippe out of the mud while Jacques and Suzanne carried the duchess ashore.

The wagon, with Balthus tied behind, was hidden in a nearby copse of trees. Exhausted though he was, Philippe looked the conveyance over with satisfaction. Jacques had erected the wooden roof and canvas curtains on the load bed, then neatly stowed their trunks and some of the provisions inside, leaving room for a thick stack of mattresses to lie on. Barrels of wine and staples were lashed to the outside. Except for the presence of Philippe's magnificent stallion, the little caravan looked exactly like that of a farmer journeying home from a buying trip to the capital.

His soaked boots feeling like lead, Philippe leaned against the wagon and numbly watched the servants settle Anne-Marie into her maid's lap on the mattresses. When they'd finished, he took Jacques aside. "You've done well." His voice dropped to a cracked whisper. "Where did you put the gold?"

Jacques whispered back, "I made a false bottom for the turnip barrel. Most of the gold is there." Even in the darkness, Philippe could see him smile. "I put a few rotten turnips on top of the good ones in the barrel to discourage anyone who might get curious." He motioned to the front of the wagon. "The rest of the money is under a board I nailed to the floorboards."

Philippe sagged slightly. "Good. Now all that's left to do is shove the boat out into the current, and we can be off."

"Aye, your grace." Jacques hurried back to the river, then returned and helped Suzanne into the driver's seat.

At the shaking of the wagon, Marie looked up from chafing her mistress's uninjured hand and asked, "Will you be riding alongside, your grace?"

Suddenly light-headed, Philippe heard a bitter laugh escape his lips. "No. I just haven't the strength to climb into the wagon." With that, he felt himself falling.

It wasn't the swaying of the wagon that woke Philippe at last, but thirst and ravenous hunger. He opened his eyes to daylight and his sleeping wife's face less than an arm's length away. A faint touch of pink in her cheeks indicated she was improving. Beyond her on the far side of the crowded load bed, Marie snored loudly, her head bobbing to the irregular jostling of their passage.

Philippe stretched slowly so as not to disturb the two women, then raised up on one elbow. Flexing his free arm, he realized he could barely form a fist. Must have been all that rowing last night. He crawled forward and poked one of the ample backsides that hung over the rear of the driver's bench.

Suzanne bounced clear out of her seat with a whoop, then spun around to find herself face-to-face with her master. "Saints, your grace! You scared the life from me."

"Sorry. I only wanted to let you know I'm fit enough to take my turn at driving."

Suzanne rubbed her husband's arm. "Jacques could use some rest. He's only let me take the reins a few hours at a time in the last two days."

"Two days!" Philippe straightened in surprise just as they hit a bump, and his head bounced against the wooden roof of the load bed. "Ouch! Where are we?"

Jacques' haggard face appeared in the opening. "A day's ride from Dijon, sir. We've only stopped to minister to necessity or spell the horses." He offered a weary smile. "I'm glad to see your grace up and about. I feared you had

fallen into a stupor like the mistress, but thought it best to
let you sleep it out."

Philippe rubbed the aching muscles in his back. No wonder he was so stiff. Two days! "Pull over. Both of you need
some rest, and I need a trip to the bushes. And some
food."

Jacques directed the team into a small wood and
stopped beside a clear, slow-running stream. Philippe
eased out of the wagon and paced stiffly toward the under-
brush to answer the urgent needs of his body. That accomplished, his state of well-being improved immensely. He
fetched two buckets from the wagon, then climbed down to
the stream. After he'd filled the buckets, he bent and
drank his fill, then splashed cool water over his face. By the
time he set the pails down in front of the horses, he was
feeling almost human.

Suzanne appeared with a fresh change of clothing. "I
thought your grace might like to have his own clothes."
She handed them over. "Jacques is already inside, asleep.
I'll get out something to eat."

Philippe stepped behind a nearby tree and changed. Despite the oppressive heat, it felt good to be back in his own
clothes. When he returned, Suzanne was waiting with a
wooden bowl full of plums, cheese, and dried beef. After
he had eaten, Philippe stepped onto a wheel spoke and
raised the side curtain to find Jacques asleep on the far
side of the load bed while Marie patiently dripped liquid
from a small flagon into the corner of her mistress's
mouth.

The maid offered a hopeful smile. "I've managed to get
quite a bit down her. I think it's helping."

He leaned in and took his wife's uninjured hand, noting
that it felt neither cold nor fevered. "Has she roused at all,
eaten anything?"

Marie shook her head sadly. "No, your grace. Every
hour or so, I drip a little weakened wine into the side of
her mouth, but she never stirs." Her face brightened. "But
she does swallow."

"You've done well, Marie. Keep it up." He gently laid
Anne-Marie's hand across her stomach. "I checked her
bandages earlier, while you were sleeping. There's no sign
of infection in the wounds." He frowned. "If only she

would wake up. I grow more worried with every hour she remains unconscious."

Marie sighed. "So do I."

Suzanne's practical voice interrupted. "Put away those long faces. Her grace hasn't waked up because her body's too busy healing to waste energy being awake. Every day her color improves. We must just be patient, that's all. Now make way for me beside Jacques. It's our turn for some sleep."

Four road-weary days and three nights later, Philippe felt Jacques shake his arm. Blinking at the darkened road ahead, he realized he must have dozed off while he was driving.

"Master, Suzanne says we must stop. Her grace has taken a turn for the worse." The urgency in his voice threw a chill into the warm night.

Philippe reined the horses to a halt alongside a stand of scrubby pines. By the time he dismounted and reached the rear of the wagon, Jacques was waiting to intercept him. "Wait, your grace. The women are tendin' her." The lantern hanging inside silhouetted Suzanne against the canvas curtain as she knelt at her mistress's feet.

Philippe heard her croon, "There's my lady. It's almost over. We just have to make sure everything's out, so the fever won't come." He reached to raise the curtain, but Jacques stayed his hand.

"Please wait, your grace. It's no place for menfolk right now."

Philippe's eyes narrowed. Jacques obviously knew something he didn't. He said quietly, "Stand aside."

Reluctantly, Jacques obeyed, averting his eyes.

When Philippe entered the cramped space, Suzanne turned, her hand abruptly concealing something she had been inspecting in the lantern light. Cradling his unconscious wife, Marie held Anne-Marie's knees bent and spread apart. The hem of the nightshirt swagged between her legs was soaked in blood. Philippe's eyes shifted lower to the damask coverlet beneath her hips. It was black with blood.

"What has happened here?" He grasped Suzanne's wrist and pulled her hand forward. "What are you hiding?"

Keeping her fingers closed, Suzanne tried to pull free.

"Please don't, your grace, leave us for a little while longer. I know she wouldn't want you to see this."

His grip unrelenting, he crawled nearer his wife and smelled an unfamiliar, cloying odor. A formless suspicion took shape in Philippe's mind. He raised Suzanne's bloodied hand to the light. "Show me what's in your hand."

Her features congealed, but she obeyed, opening her bloodied palm to reveal a pale curl of flesh half the size of her finger.

Philippe drew closer. It took a moment to identify what she was holding, but when he did, his stomach lurched.

It was a baby.

His baby.

Dead.

Suzanne whispered, "Poor bit of a child. So newly made, yet already a son."

Every fragment of Philippe's consciousness focused on the tiny corpse. Only ten weeks after their wedding night, the child was recognizably human.

Bile rose in his throat, but he couldn't tear his gaze from the splayed little legs and intricately formed feet, the minute hands, the transparent lids that sealed dark orbs in the tiny skull.

Suzanne pleaded, "Please go with Jacques, your grace, so I can finish here. I must see that everything's out, so there can be other children."

Other children!

He released her hand. An overwhelming sense of rage and betrayal propelled him from the wagon and into the darkness of the nearby woods. The thick carpet of pine needles was resilient under his steps and then under his palms as he fell to his hands and knees. When wave after wave of nausea ripped through him, he surrendered willingly in hope that he would be purged, somehow, from what he had just seen.

A child! She had been with child—*his* child, and she hadn't told him! She should have told him. No matter what had come between them, she owed him that, at least.

When the heaving subsided, Philippe dragged his sleeve across his mouth and leaned against a nearby tree trunk. His son. Anne-Marie had not only placed her own life at risk to save the princess, but that of his unborn son.

Years of pent-up disappointment, unacknowledged

hope, and bitter rejection rose up within Philippe and
threatened to explode. He had wanted a son more than
anything in life—a son of his own, one he could love as he
had never been loved.

Such a simple thing to want. Was it so selfish a wish that
God had taken his child before he even knew of its existence? Wasn't it enough that he'd lost his career, his reputation, his position at Court, his newfound financial
security, and his duchy?

He'd turned his back on everything to save his wife, only
to face this final desolation.

It was more than Philippe could bear. A dreadful, guttural wail tore from the depths of his soul and echoed
through the night. Denied even the comfort of tears, he
keened not only for the loss of his son, but for all he had
left behind.

❦ CHAPTER 25 ❦

$\mathcal{I}$t was the tapping that finally brought Annique back to
the world of the living. Again and again, without pattern or
predictability, the distant tapping echoed hollowly into her
consciousness. The sound was faintly metallic. Persistent.
Annoying.

Annique inhaled deeply and stirred. She was hot. Too
hot. Why couldn't she throw off the heavy covers that
weighted her down?

The tapping stopped.

Her eyes blinked open to an unfamiliar blur of white
ceiling and oddly reflective pale green walls. Drawn by a
flutter of motion at the edge of her vision, she turned her
head and saw wide white curtains billowing inward, granting brief glimpses of slender columns and brilliant sunshine beyond.

She had never seen such a place. The room, its Spartan
furnishings, the strange plants she glimpsed through the
curtains—everything looked foreign. Even the light had a
different quality, an unusual glare.

Where was she? And she could barely move. A quick
assessment revealed that only a sheet covered her, not the
heavy quilts she had imagined. The strange inertia deep-

ened as part of her cautioned, *Don't ask questions. Sleep. Sleep is safe. Hide.* But why should she hide? Another, stronger, part of her demanded that she concentrate, told her something important had happened. Something terrible. Oh yes, the battle.

And something else . . .

Philippe. It had to do with Philippe. The thought of his name brought a spasm of fear. Was he dead? Was that it?

She tried to push herself upright, but the effort sent pain blasting from her right palm all the way to her shoulder. Her hand throbbed as if it would explode with every heartbeat. When she raised it closer to see why, a shiver of disbelief shot through her. She stared at the mangled claw as if it belonged to someone else. Her fingers were drawn inward around a deep, blackened indentation in the center of her swollen palm. Annique turned her palm outward to find a corresponding cavity darkly indenting the swollen back of her hand. She tried to straighten her fingers, but the effort brought only agony.

Maimed.

Her eyes slammed shut. *This can't be real.* A dream. Yes, that was it! A nightmare. Mustering all her strength, she willed the dream to change, yet when she looked again, everything was the same.

She wanted to curl into a miserable ball, but when she tried to roll over, something pulled painfully at the center of her chest. Using her left hand, she tugged at the ribbons of her gown until she worked open the neckline.

Annique looked down and gasped. A crusted disk of dried blood and scar tissue spoiled the indentation between her breasts.

Afraid to look further for fear she would discover more, she crumpled the fabric closed over her chest.

Suzanne's voice came from the open doorway. "Praise heaven! Her grace is awake!" Almost spilling the contents of the bowl she was carrying, she leaned back into the hallway and cried, "Jacques! Marie! The mistress is awake!" then hastened across the room to Annique's side.

When Annique hurriedly covered her scarred hand with the other, Suzanne's smile faded to a sympathetic frown. The housekeeper drew up a chair and leaned close. "It's good to see you awake, your grace. The worst is over. Everything will be all right now."

Annique heard the words but didn't believe them. Shoving her maimed hand under the sheet, she closed her eyes in a vain effort to avoid reality.

Suzanne had no intention of letting her escape so easily. The gentleness disappeared from her voice. "Open your eyes, madame!" When Annique obeyed, relief smoothed the housekeeper's worried features. "Thank goodness. I was afraid we'd lost you again." Her tone softened. "You mustn't worry about your hand, your grace. The master has a special balm that will fade those scars. And massage will restore the use of your fingers." She nodded emphatically. "The treatment works. His grace proved that after his last Spanish Campaign."

At the mention of Philippe, Annique's attention shifted from her own injuries. "My husband . . . the battle. Is he all right?"

Before Suzanne could reply, she was silenced by a clatter of hurried footsteps and Jacques' anxious voice from the hallway. "Suzanne? What's happened? Marie and I heard you yellin' all the way in the kitchen, but we couldn't make out what—" He halted abruptly in the doorway, his look of surprise followed by a wide grin. "Praise be! The mistress has come back to us." He and Suzanne exchanged knowing looks, then he nodded and bowed. "I'll tell the master at once." With that, he left them.

The master. So she hadn't killed Philippe, after all.

Annique paused. *Killed him?* Why on earth would she think such a thing? She tried to find the answer in her jumbled recollections, but her memory stubbornly refused to cooperate. "My husband?"

Suzanne's gentle smile was reassuring. "His grace was knocked unconscious during the battle and woke with a royal headache, but he's fine now."

"What happened to me?"

Suzanne glanced nervously toward a closed door in the corner of the bedchamber. "The master said you were injured at the Bastille."

"How?" Her speech came almost as slowly as her memory. "I remember leaving the Luxembourg Palace, but nothing after. My mind's a muddle."

"Perhaps that's for the best." Suzanne busied herself with the soup. "You should be using your energy eatin', your grace, not askin' questions. There'll be plenty of time for questions later, when you're better." She lifted a spoonful of the salty-smelling liquid to Annique's lips. "Here. Try some broth."

Annique's memory might not be functioning properly, but her powers of observation were intact. She could tell Suzanne was hiding something. Turning her head away from the spoon, she said, "I'll eat, but only if you tell me what happened. The truth."

Suzanne's eyes shifted from the spoon to the closed door in the corner, then back to her mistress. "You don't know what you're askin', your grace. The truth can be painful, and you've suffered so much already."

Dread tightened Annique's stomach. "I still want to know. Where *are* we? How was I injured?"

"We're at the master's villa near Savoy. On the coast."

Savoy! "The Mediterranean? So far . . . How? Why?"

The housekeeper shifted uneasily. "We came by wagon, stoppin' only when we had to. The journey took two weeks, and you never woke up once."

Annique was more confused than ever. Why would Philippe risk such a journey, with her so ill? What could possibly have prompted such a decision? "Start at the beginning and tell me all you know."

After a long, agonized pause, Suzanne let out a sigh of resignation. "Very well, your grace. If you insist. I had hoped to wait until you were stronger." She set the soup aside. "The Great Mademoiselle's lady-in-waiting told me what happened. She said you were in the carriage with the princess . . ."

Annique listened as Suzanne related Frontenac's account of that fateful morning. The story triggered dark fragments of memory: crushing tension in the Place de l'Hôtel de Ville, the deafening roar of cannon fire, the macabre sight of Rochefoucauld on his horse. Beneath each recollection lurked something sinister, something as formless and heavy as a blanket of wet snow. Something Annique wouldn't let herself remember.

Forcing herself to concentrate, she heard Suzanne say, "After the princess made them turn the cannons, she wouldn't come down off the wall, so you went up after her. You saved her life, your grace." Suzanne went on, telling how the princess had taken Annique to safety and summoned Philippe, and what he had been forced to do to stop the bleeding. She concluded, "We didn't want to move you, but her highness said no one who had been with her at the Bastille would be safe. She said Cardinal Mazarin's men would torture you if they found you, so the master arranged for our escape."

Suzanne glanced around the sparsely furnished bed-chamber. "They'll never find us here. The master won this place in a game of chance when he was travelin' abroad with his tutor. Not even the Duke d'Harcourt knows about it."

Jacques appeared in the doorway. "Pardon, your grace, but might I have a word with Suzanne?"

Annique nodded.

Suzanne rose, straightening the covers. "Rest now. I know I've worn your grace out with all my talkin'."

Though Annique's mind churned with unanswered questions, she was almost too exhausted to respond. Nodding, she closed her eyes to the sound of Suzanne's footsteps retreating to the hallway for a whispered conversation.

But this was no house for secrets. The servants' voices reflected off the marble walls and through the open door-way, and Annique heard every word.

Suzanne whispered, "Where's the master? I thought sure he'd come, once she woke up."

Jacques' gravelly response was hardly discreet. "No. He never even looked up. Just stopped his writing, thanked me for telling him, then asked if she knew about you-know-what."

"Shh. Keep your voice down. She'll hear you."

Annique could almost hear Jacques squirm as he whis-pered, "Sorry. Well, did you tell her?"

"No, and I don't intend to, not unless she asks me straight-out."

What were they hiding?

Suzanne continued, "Now off with you. I'm sure Marie could use some help in the kitchen."

Abandoning his efforts to whisper, Jacques muttered, "There is no help for *that* woman's cookin'. I'll be glad when she's back tendin' the mistress and you're back at the stove, where you both belong." His footsteps faded as Su-zanne's grew louder.

Annique opened her eyes. "Where is my husband?"

Suzanne faltered. "His grace keeps to his books, madame, except for his early-morning ride."

"He hasn't come to see me?"

A dejected shake of her head was Suzanne's only reply.

"Why?" Annique's voice softened. "The truth, Suzanne. I've had enough of lies."

After a long pause, Suzanne relented. "I don't know. He was so worried about your grace at first, so tender. Then—" Her brows drew together.

"Then what? The truth."

"He grieved so over the babe, your grace. It was like something broke inside him. And you were so near death. I think he'd have gone mad if he'd lost you, too."

The babe? A subtle note of warning sounded within Annique, but she had to know. "What babe?"

"You don't remember?"

The curled fingers of Annique's damaged hand tightened beneath the covers. "No, I don't remember. What baby? For mercy's sake, Suzanne, *tell me.*"

Suzanne's kind eyes met Annique's. "Your grace had a miscarriage six days into our journey."

Annique sat bolt upright, face-to-face with the terrible, hidden thing that had lurked behind her lack of memory. Shattered pieces of recollection fell into place with devastating accuracy, and the truth came flooding back. She remembered finding out she was with child. She was in the carriage again, rolling toward the battle, hearing the scorn in the princess's voice, feeling the shock of realization, the shame at her ignorance, the humiliation of being told by her husband's mistress. She remembered everything, right up to the moment on the parapet when she turned and saw the arrow.

The arrow, coming at her.

Her vision glazed as she relived those few, fateful seconds—her mind recreating the inexorable sequence of recognition, fear, then nothingness. "No!" Annique covered her face with her hands. If only she hadn't hesitated, wasted precious time with a useless gesture of protection. If only she had stayed behind the wall. If only . . .

An ache deeper than her soul bloomed inside her. Her child, miscarried. Gone, almost before she knew it existed. This was the truth she'd asked for, but it brought no cleansing, no catharsis—only ashes.

She asked dully, "Who told my husband about the baby? Was it the princess?"

"You hadn't told him?" Suzanne looked away. "I feared as much."

Annique closed her eyes. "*I* didn't know, not until just before I was hurt."

Suzanne laid a reassuring hand on her arm. "I didn't know, myself, until I discovered you were bleeding, and how much. Then I suspected. I begged the master to stop the wagon. He was so worried about your grace I couldn't keep him away, and he saw—" Her voice dropped. "His grace made me show him the poor tiny babe." She heaved a pensive sigh. "He lifted my hand into the lamplight and stared at the wee thing, then dashed into the woods. He took it so hard. We heard him keening in the darkness until his voice was hoarse. I feared he'd come unhinged."

The words struck Annique like blows. Philippe hadn't even known he was to be a father until it was too late. No matter what he'd done to her, she wouldn't have wished him to find out that way.

Suzanne's voice reflected the grim recollection of that terrible night. "It seemed like forever before he came back to the wagon, and when he did, the life had gone out of him."

So he had grieved the loss of their child alone. Now it was her turn to lie comfortless.

Suzanne shook her head, a faraway look in her eyes. "I don't think the master could face losing you, too. You were so near death, and so much had been lost already. He just . . . closed up, somehow." She sighed. "After about an hour, he came back and took the reins from Jacques. Drove for days without sleepin' nor sayin' a word, nor once lookin' into the back of the wagon." Her focus cleared. "When we finally got here, his grace shut himself into his study and has stayed there ever since, except for his mornin' ride every day." She glanced toward the corner. "I'd hoped he might come out when your grace woke up, but . . ."

Annique's gaze followed Suzanne's to the closed door that separated her from Philippe. No wonder he had shut himself away from her. She had cost him everything—their child, their homes, his career, all his plans. Remorse, cold and wrenching, knotted her vitals.

Suddenly Annique couldn't bear the presence of another human being. She choked, "Leave me."

"But, madame—"

"Please."

"Very well. But I'll be right outside, if you need me." Suzanne backed into the hallway, drawing the heavy door ajar behind her.

Alone, Annique began to shake, her body racked with silent spasms of guilt and grief. She closed her eyes and pulled her arms tight against her, but the shaking wouldn't stop.

From beyond the door in the corner, the tapping started up again.

Philippe laid aside his mallet and brushed the chips from the stone plaque. Almost done.

Unable to concentrate enough to read more than a few sentences at a time, he had begun the project as a mindless distraction. But now, with just a few letters remaining, he felt his numbness fading, and that frightened him.

He couldn't lose his numbness. It was his refuge, his last remaining protection against caring for his wife, and by caring, letting her take the last thing that remained to him—himself.

He could not love her. He *would* not love her. Look what she'd cost him already.

Angling the chisel into the precise groove he had carved, he fed his bitterness with yet another strike of the mallet. The blow struck true, but not the blame. Instead, dark questions swooped into his mind like angry crows, driving him from the comforting numbness of his task just as they had driven him from the solace of his books.

Anne-Marie had lost as much as he. More—she was maimed. And their child had been brutally expelled from her body, not his. They'd lost their home, but Maison Corbay had been hers by right, not his.

Philippe hammered more swiftly, as if the sound of the chisel could drown out his thoughts.

He couldn't even blame Anne-Marie for his desertion. Philippe's mind shaped the haunting image of the dead child in its mother's arms—a child he had helped to kill. What honor remained after that? What reputation mattered? He could still see the child's vacant, staring eyes, the smudge on its cheek, its slightly parted lips. The stunned anguish in its mother's face.

Escape had saved more than Anne-Marie's life; it had saved what was left of his soul. He could never have taken up arms against innocent women and children again.

Laying the tools on the desktop, his hands stilled, and in the silence his mind formed the most terrible question of all, the one he'd avoided facing until that very moment: Was that the real reason his own child had died? Some divine accounting for his part in the death of other innocent children?

Fitting retribution from a just God.

Philippe rested his forehead in his palm, the fingers of his hand digging into his temples. Regret, cold and pervasive as a winter fog, rolled through him. All his life, he had faced the consequences of his mistakes without flinching, never looking back. Now everything had changed. He was no longer alone. Anne-Marie and his unborn child had borne *his* penance.

He could not risk her further, any more than he could erase the hold she had on him.

Philippe stared past the marble bookshelves crammed with books and scrolls that no longer brought him any peace. His gaze was drawn to the locked door that connected the library to the bedchamber where Anne-Marie lay. He'd bolted the heavy, metal-studded door to shut himself away from her, but neither of them could escape what had happened. They were trapped here, his once-peaceful retreat now a prison for them both.

Philippe picked up his tools to complete the last few letters on the marble tablet. When he was done, he brushed the surface clean and carried the book-sized piece of white stone to the locked door behind his desk. Beyond that door lay his most secret retreat, a covered Roman bath and adjoining garden completely hidden from the rest of the house.

He unlocked the door and strode through the humid enclosure, the slight echo of his footsteps softened by vapor rising from the hot spring waters of the first pool. He followed the marble walkway past the tepid central pool and into the sunlight, then crossed to a narrow strip of garden along a low wall that overlooked the sea far below.

Philippe knelt in front of a small statue of a child nestled among the flowers. On the rare occasions when he'd been able to come to the villa in the past, he'd always been drawn to the perpetual serenity of that little face. Now he could scarcely bear to look at it. Shifting the marble tablet to one hand, he pushed aside the flowers to reveal a patch of bare dirt at the statue's base.

Philippe settled the plaque atop the dry earth. It just fit, but the bright, unweathered marble looked garish and out of place beside the ancient statue and the crumbling stucco of the wall.

In time the plaque would mellow, its rawness fading until it blended into its surroundings. If only the aching void in Philippe's soul would do the same. He breathed a prayer, then rose, turning his back on the inscription he had carved:

HERE LIES
A SON
AND A
FATHER'S HOPE

❧ CHAPTER 26 ❧

"Ouch!" Annique tried to pull her injured hand out of Suzanne's grasp. "That hurts."

Suzanne kept right on working, stretching the drawn tendons, massaging the tissue with aromatic oils. Three times a day, every day, it was the same, rousing Annique from her sodden sleep. But this particular morning Suzanne didn't offer her usual murmured apologies. She responded with the firmness of a mother counseling an intractable child. "I know it's painful, your grace, but that's the way of healing. When you've been hurt, badly hurt, there's no runnin' away from the pain. Avoidin' it only cripples you, makes things miserable for that much longer."

Annique's throat tightened. "You're not talking about just my hand, are you?"

"No, your grace."

As she had so many times in the last few days, Annique turned her face to the reassuring blankness of the wall beside her bed. "It hurts so much to feel, to care, to think." She sighed. "Things would have been simpler for everyone if I had died."

"You mustn't talk that way, your grace." The housekeeper calmly straightened her finger to the brink of agony. "Like it or not, the good Lord's seen fit to spare you. Your grace is young yet, and will soon be strong again. There can be wonderful things ahead."

"But you don't understand . . ."

"Don't I?"

Annique tugged her hand free and curled on her side. "I've lost everything. Everything." If only Suzanne would go away and let her sleep.

Fists planted firmly on her ample hips, the housekeeper stepped into Annique's line of vision. "May I speak freely, your grace?"

"You always do."

Suzanne tilted until her face aligned with Annique's. The words poured out. "Four years ago, I thought I'd die when Jacques was sentenced to hang for poachin' deer. He's a good man, and he'd not have broken the law if a storm hadn't ruined our crops. He only poached to keep us from starvin'."

Suzanne straightened, unshed tears brightening her eyes, her voice thick with emotion. "It tore my heart out of me to see them take him away to wait for his execution. But I didn't give up. I asked God to save my husband, and lo and behold, the master arrived and bought him out of prison. It was a miracle."

Dabbing the moisture from her eyes with the corner of her apron, she regained her usual brisk manner. "Jacques sent us everything he made, but it was barely enough for food, with nothing left over for clothes or goods or rent, and there was no work in the village for me or the children—"

Annique rolled onto her back. "Children? What children?"

Suzanne looked down at her and calmly said, "*Our* children, Jacques' and mine. Seven of 'em. It's been three years since we've seen 'em. The youngest is five, now, and she calls my sister 'Mama.' She doesn't remember me at all."

"Seven children?"

Suzanne nodded. "Seven. I didn't want to leave them, but I had little choice. Jacques has no family. My sister in Orléans had taken us in, but their farm barely makes enough to feed their own brood." She stared into the distance, her eyes clouding. "I didn't know what to do. Then the master told Jacques to look for a housekeeper, one who could cook." She patted Annique's hand. "It was another miracle. Together, our wages would feed the whole lot.

"But I couldn't bring my babies with me. His grace had no use for a houseful of children. My sister agreed to look after them as long as we could send enough money for food and clothes." Her face softened. "They're good children—hard workers, right down to the smallest one. I knew they'd be all right, but it hurt so much to leave them that I crept away before they wakened, without saying good-bye. I hope they've forgiven me for that."

Annique was dumbstruck. She had accepted Suzanne and Jacques' presence, relied upon them, grown fond of them, without ever suspecting their secret pain.

Suzanne picked up a cloth and began wiping the oil from Annique's hand. "My sister's husband comes to Paris twice a year with things to sell. He brings us word of the children and takes back the money we've saved." She smiled sadly. "Not a day goes by that I don't think of my babies." Then she was all business again, meeting Annique's incredulous stare with resolution. "It hurts, bein' separated from them. But even with that pain, I thank God for every day I'm granted and every sou I can send them."

Annique stammered, "I . . . you . . . Does Philippe know of this?"

Suzanne shook her head. "Oh, no. We dared not tell him at first. After we'd gotten to know his grace and found him to be a good man—a kind man—we realized that the little he paid us was all he had. The household scraped along on almost nothing until the marriage. After that, there was money, but we weren't sure how either of your graces would feel about . . . Well, we decided it would be best to leave things as they were."

Annique thought back to those first few weeks at Maison Corbay, before Philippe had taken Suzanne and Jacques back to Paris. She remembered how Suzanne would look to the south and sigh, but the faithful servant had never complained, never wept, never been cross. She'd kept right on working, ministering to the household and Annique's needs while her mistress looked right through her.

Ashamed, Annique sat up. "Suzanne. Dear Suzanne. You could have come to *me*. I'd have sent for your children."

A wry chuckle escaped the housekeeper. "And a fine barrel of brine they'd be in *now*, if they'd been brought to Maison Corbay or to Paris. We couldn't very well have escaped unnoticed with seven children trailin' along with us. And if we'd left them behind, who would look after them? Paoul?" She lifted an eyebrow at the impossible thought. "Madame Pleuris? Hardly."

"I see what you mean." Annique's brows drew together. What would happen to the children now? Would they, too, become innocent victims of her impetuous decision at the Bastille?

Suzanne rose and smoothed her apron. "So you see, it was best that they were with my sister when all the trouble came. Things have a way of workin' out to the good. That's why I don't give up. And your grace mustn't either."

"And all this time . . . Why didn't I see?" Sinking back against the pillows, Annique whispered, "I'm so sorry, Suzanne." How self-absorbed she had become, never thinking past her own needs, her own problems, her own pain. She blurted out, "You have my word that I'll do everything in my power to see you reunited with your children." Her voice faltered. "I don't know what I can do, but I vow to try."

Suzanne folded her arms in challenge. "Does your grace intend to keep that promise with sad faces and sleepin' all day?"

Annique surveyed the wrinkled bedclothes. Suddenly she saw how small a prison she'd made for herself. "No, I've slept long enough."

"Then it's time to get on with the business of livin'. Pain and all, you'll find it well worth the effort, and that's a promise from *me*." With one good tug, Suzanne whipped off the sheet Annique had been hiding under for a week. "I think your grace is strong enough to get dressed and sit outside for a bit today." She crossed the room and opened the curtains.

Beyond the shady peristyle, a cloudless blue sky presided

over the courtyard. The early-morning sunlight bore only a trace of the ferocious heat that would take over by late afternoon. "Ah, and what a fine day it is." She motioned toward the low wall at the end of the garden and tempted Annique with the one thing certain to lure her outside. "The breeze is lovely by the wall, and the sea sparkles like a thousand diamonds."

"The sea?" Surfacing from her self-recriminations, Annique cast a wishful glance at the flowering vines that trailed over the low wall. She confided, "All my life, I've read about the sea, imagined what it looked like, longed to see it for myself." She inhaled deeply. "The smell of it is so strong here that it's invaded my dreams."

"Well, that's one dream that *can* come true." Suzanne motioned toward the garden. "I'll set up a chair, and Jacques will carry you outside. You won't even have to walk." Without waiting for Annique to agree, she bellowed toward the hallway, "Marie! Come at once! Her grace is getting up!" That done, she crossed to the foot of the bed and opened Annique's trunk. "Now, let's see. There's the aqua silk, the apricot lawn, the russet damask, the green—"

Annique quailed at the mere thought of being trussed into one of her dresses in this heat. "Surely you don't expect me to get dressed?"

The housekeeper's face appeared over the trunk lid. "But yes."

"But no. It's far too hot to be laced and buttoned and smothered. I've endured *enough* discomfort in the last few weeks. I'm not willing to suffer anymore."

"Then what does madame suggest?" Suzanne lifted Annique's robe from the bed. The cotton lawn was almost transparent against the sunlight. "I'm afraid this wouldn't be appropriate for the garden."

"No, but surely—"

Marie's arrival cut the discussion short. As usual, a torrent of words came with her. "Oh, I'm so glad your grace is feeling enough to sit up. I've prayed that your grace would soon be needin' me again. I don't think I could have survived another day in that kitchen." She reddened. "Oh, dear, that didn't come out right, that part about the kitchen. That's not the main reason I'm glad. I mean, mostly I'm just glad your grace is better. I—"

Annique couldn't help smiling. "I know what you meant, Marie. I'm glad to be better, too."

Suzanne glared at Marie. "Don't be wearin' her grace out with a lot of chatter. And be careful of her grace's wounds when you dress her." After retrieving the remains of Annique's half-eaten breakfast, Suzanne headed for the kitchen. She paused in the doorway for a final admonition. "Call Jacques when her grace is ready. And remember— no jabber."

Marie aimed a haughty glance at Suzanne's back. Once the housekeeper was safely out of earshot, she muttered, "Back to your pots and pans, Suzanne. I ought to know how to dress her grace. *I'm* her maid." Marie nodded smugly to her mistress, then turned her attention to the contents of the trunk. "Which gown would your grace like today? I'm afraid there isn't much to choose from. We packed in such a hurry, and your grace's coffer took up most of the trunk—"

"My coffer!" Annique's heart leapt. "You brought my books?"

Marie straightened. "But of course. Just as your grace said—always, her coffer must accompany her. Jacques tried to make me leave the coffer behind, but I wouldn't." Looking down into the trunk, she shook her head. "I'm afraid there wasn't room for much else. Only a few summer gowns and nightclothes, some undergarments, and several pairs of satin slippers." Obviously, Marie had no idea of the wonderful gift she had given her mistress.

For the first time since she had awakened at the villa, Annique smiled without sadness. "Thank you, Marie. I can't tell you how much it means to me to have my books. You've done well." The contents of that wooden chest provided her with an anchor. No longer did she feel rootless, completely cut off from her past. She still had her father's books.

Basking in her mistress's approval, Marie lifted a stiff bodice of sprigged apricot cotton from the trunk. "How about this one, your grace?"

Annique shook her head. "No." Even her most comfortable dress would be a torture rack in this climate and her condition. But Suzanne was right; she couldn't go outside in her nightgown. And she found herself wanting very much to go outside, to feel the sun on her skin, to be once again among the living.

Annique glanced from the filmy robe draped over the trunk lid to the padded bodice in Marie's hands. A wickedly appealing notion crept into her mind. She cast an appraising glance up and down her attendant. "How many of my gowns did you bring, Marie?"

"Six. I tried to select your favorites, the coolest, most comfortable ones, but—"

"And how many changes of your own clothes did you bring?"

After a puzzled silence, Marie answered. "Three—this old one I'm wearing, and the two outfits given to me when I came into your grace's service."

A slow smile bloomed on Annique's face. "I have a proposition for you. I'll trade any two of my gowns for one of yours."

The maid looked at her as if Annique had lost her mind. "Your grace?"

"Very well, then. Three. Or will you hold out for more? Shame on you, Marie, for taking advantage of your mistress this way."

"No, mistress, two will be plenty! I mean, two's far too many. I mean, why on earth would your grace want—"

Annique spoke frankly. "I never could get used to those fancy gowns. It would suit me just fine never to be trussed into silk and satin again. We're not at Court anymore, nor are we likely ever to be, so there's no reason for me to dress like a courtier." Strange, how liberating honesty could be. Annique glanced around the spacious, utilitarian room. "This is a simple house. Simple clothes would be far more appropriate, and far more comfortable in such a place. Will you agree to the trade?"

Marie responded in the same tone she might use to humor a lunatic. "If that's what your grace wants."

"Good. And another thing—no more curling irons and fancy hairdos. I'll wear my hair in a chignon or a braid from now on."

"As you wish, your grace." There was that tone again.

It felt good to exercise some control over her circumstances, no matter how small. "Now run fetch my new clothes." As Marie sidled toward the hallway, Annique added, "And telling Suzanne won't do any good. I haven't lost my mind, and I don't mean to change it."

The maid blinked in astonishment. "No, your grace. I mean, yes, your grace."

Twenty minutes later, a skeptical Marie laid a simple white linen blouse with a drawstring neckline, a sturdy blue linen skirt, and an unboned bodice of black homespun across Annique's bed. "Here you are, your grace. My best uniform, all clean."

"How kind of you to offer your best." Annique reached out to finger the fabric, but halted when Marie averted her eyes from the blackened scar and curled fingers. A hot tingle spread up Annique's throat as she tucked the injured hand out of sight. She used her other to examine the fabric.

The bodice's cotton weave felt substantial but pliant. "This will be perfect." Laying it aside, Annique slowly swung her legs over the side of the bed. "I'm afraid dressing me will take a lot of patience. I'm stiff as an old grandmother."

A hopeful smile lit Marie's face. "Perhaps a warm bath would help. There's a hot spring right beside the house, with a trough of running water right in the kitchen! Your grace has always been so partial to her baths. I'll be glad to bring water."

Despite the heat, the prospect of soaking away her stiffness had its appeal. "I'd *love* a long, leisurely soak, Marie."

The maid's face fell. "Oh, dear. I meant a sponge bath. I'm afraid there's no slipper tub." She cocked her head. "Odd, that we don't have one, seein' as how the master's so fond of soakin' himself." She shrugged. "When I asked Jacques and Suzanne about it, they just looked at me funny and told me there's no slipper tub and don't ask about it again." She offered apologetically, "I can bring a nice pitcher of warm water in no time."

Annique tried to conceal her disappointment, reminding herself that she'd managed for nineteen years without a tub. She could get used to doing without one again. At least there was plenty of water, and hot water, at that. "No thank you, Marie. Suzanne bathed me this morning. Let's just get me dressed."

"Very good, your grace." Marie withdrew a clean chemise and a silk petticoat from the trunk.

"No petticoat. It's too hot. The skirt is quite thick enough to be decent without one."

Marie shot her a sideways glance and muttered, "As you wish."

But when the maid stepped closer to unfasten the ribbons that closed her nightgown, Annique pulled back from her and said, "Wait. I'll do that. Just lay the chemise on the bed and turn your back. I'll let you know if I need help."

Marie blushed, her eyes resting for a telltale second on the intricate pleats covering Annique's wounded chest before she obediently turned away. "Sorry, your grace."

Slowly, Annique inched out of her gown, and just as slowly, into the clean chemise, then the peasant blouse. She managed fine until she attempted to tie the drawstring on the blouse. She could grasp the cords to draw the neckline discreetly above her scarred chest, but tying a bowknot presented an almost impossible challenge.

Again and again, she tried, but her crippled fingers refused to cooperate. Her frustrated efforts quickly ate away at what little strength she had left. Finally, she settled for a haphazard knot instead of a bow. Annique barely had the energy to lift the skirt over her head and settle it loosely to her shrunken waistline. That done, she slid leaden arms into the black bodice before flopping, exhausted, back onto the mattress. "You'll have to finish for me, Marie. I can't manage the button on the skirt, and I haven't the energy to lace the bodice shut."

Marie turned around, her face reflecting real concern. "Your grace should have let me help more." Her hands gentle, she fastened the skirt and laced the front of the bodice closed.

Annique sat up and inhaled deeply. "Much better than my other dresses. I can breathe." Though the fabric was coarse, the outfit was cooler than her summer habit had been. If only the blouse's puffed sleeves weren't so short. Annique self-consciously hid her maimed hand behind her back.

Marie looked away. After a moment of awkward hesitation, she disappeared behind the trunk lid, rummaging through the contents until she emerged with a pair of lace gloves in one hand and a pair of white kidskin gloves in the other. "I thought your grace . . . that is, I packed these so that . . ." She stopped, at a loss for words, the gloves proffered limply.

Flushing in humiliation, Annique inwardly recoiled from the pity in Marie's eyes. Was this how it was to be from now on, covering her infirmity from others to spare herself that inevitable look of sympathy, or worse still, veiled revulsion? Annique's vision watered, but her right hand was steady as it closed on the white kidskin gloves.

Marie leaned forward. "May I help—"

Not trusting herself to speak without breaking down, Annique waved her away. She swiveled to conceal her clumsy efforts to don the glove. The process was difficult and painful, but the supple leather accommodated her swollen hand, though the raised scar stood out in clear relief on the glove's smooth surface. The second glove was almost on when Annique stopped. Suddenly she saw the absurdity of what she was doing. "No."

"Your grace?" Marie turned back to face her.

Annique stared at her hands. "This is ridiculous. I can't wear kid gloves with this clothing. Look at me!" A ragged, hysterical giggle escaped her. "Don't you see? Covering up won't change anything." She pulled at the gloves, suddenly desperate to get them off. When she was free of them, her right hand dragged down the neckline of her blouse, exposing the hated scar. "Won't change anything! It happened, all of it, and it won't go away!"

Marie's eyes widened.

Annique had run from the pain long enough. Now she reached out and seized it to her. She spoke as much to herself as to Marie. "Look at me! These scars are part of me. We might as well get used to them. Both of us. All of us." She extended her mangled hand, turning it before her. "Nothing can change what's happened." The words cut, but this pain was different, not like the dull agony of denial. Here was the healing Suzanne had spoken of.

She took Marie's hand in her own damaged one. "What good will it do to hide these wounds? All my life, I've had to hide things, but not anymore." She glanced up, her voice calm now. "First I pretended to be a good, obedient novice, but I wasn't. Then I pretended to be a lady, the Duchess of Corbay, mistress of a great house. But I wasn't a lady. I had more in common with you and Suzanne than I did with my husband. Then I pretended to be the Great

Mademoiselle's brave attendant, but I wasn't brave; I was only foolish, and all of us are still paying the price."

Odd, how saying it aloud gave her strength. "I've pretended for so long, I'm not even certain who I really am anymore. But I know this—I'm through with pretending and through with hiding. No more secrets. No more lies." She thrust the gloves at Marie. "No gloves."

Marie accepted them, her fingers carefully straightening the wrinkled leather. When she looked up, there was no pity in her eyes, only admiration. "Your grace *is* a lady. The finest, bravest lady I've ever known."

A sigh as cold as ashes shuddered through Annique. "Please fetch Jacques, now. I'm ready to go outside."

The sea was waiting.

❀ CHAPTER 27 ❀

*A*nnique set small goals at first: to eat more, to sit up longer in her chair, to stand, to take a few steps, to walk all the way around the peristyle. By the time two weeks had passed, she felt steady on her feet and was able to cover short distances without growing faint. Soon she was able to read whole chapters of her father's books before exhaustion forced her to rest.

As a girl she had dreamed of an existence like this— warm, pampered, free to read as much as she wished—but reality was not as she had dreamed it. She chafed under the enforced idleness, and contentment eluded her because of the locked door in the corner of her room and the man behind it.

Philippe was on the other side of that door. Did he grieve, as she, for their unborn child? Did he hate her for what she'd cost them both? Did he feel trapped, uprooted, diminished by the loss of Maison Corbay?

Her only answer was a locked door.

Every time she heard the slightest stirring from that direction, she stopped what she was doing and listened, hoping that the next sound would be of the bolt sliding back and the door opening. But it never did, and day after day, she nursed her wounded heart alone, telling herself to let go of the past and all its hopes and disappointments.

She was alive. She was safe. Soon she would be strong again. That should be enough.

Yet every day, she had to fight harder to push aside the feelings that washed over her when her body stirred with remembered passion. Try as she might to purge herself of that exquisitely tortuous hunger, she could not, any more than she could be content with the solitude she had once wished for.

The garden became her observatory and salon, its tiny arbor her dining place, its paved paths her walking course, its shady peristyle her sitting room. She retreated to her chamber only for long naps during the heat of midday.

Every evening found her sitting at the low garden wall, watching the quiet death of another day and the birth of another lonely night. As sunset came, she looked far down the mountain to the women turning toward home from their work in the orchards and olive groves. Farther down, the fishermen left their nets beside the sheltered harbor and trudged upward to reunion in their village. By twilight, the distant, anonymous dots of humanity met in the streets and paired off as smaller dots surrounded them. Soon the streets were empty, and the windows of the village glowed softly. Only then could Annique turn her eyes to the vast, placid face of the sea and try to drown her sense of incompleteness in its peace.

Every morning she found herself in the garden again, listening for the sound of Balthus's retreating hoofbeats that carried over the rooftop as Philippe escaped for his morning ride. And still, he did not come to her. Despite the servants' solicitude, Annique grew more and more lonely—more and more conscious of the locked door that represented all her unanswered questions and her failures.

One hot August afternoon, she had had enough. After tossing restlessly through the midday heat, she rose from her bed and strode purposefully to the library door. Why had she been so sure the door was locked? What if it wasn't? What if Philippe had been waiting, all these weeks, for her to open it? She pulled the handle.

Locked.

Annique leaned miserably against the polished wood, her strength disappearing in the face of Philippe's continued rejection. As she felt herself slipping into despair, a spark of determination stopped her. No. She wouldn't retreat meekly to her bed. She had to know how things stood between them. Inhaling a quavering breath, she set off for the kitchen.

When Philippe realized he was reading the same line for the third time, he let out an exasperated sigh and lifted his eyes to the patch of blue sky visible through the high windows of the little library. His attention span had been reduced to that of a fidgety schoolboy.

Was he to have no peace, no refuge left, not even his books?

First Anne-Marie had invaded his dreams, robbing him of even a decent night's sleep. Now he couldn't even read without some word or image causing his mind to wander— either into the misty landscape of remembered passion, or the dark and terrifying constructions of his nightmares. His gaze dropped, focusing on the locked corner door that led to her room.

Perhaps he would regain his peace of mind if he opened the door and confronted her. Yet a healthy sense of self-preservation held him back. What if she asked questions he did not want to answer? Philippe had learned all too well the cost of bringing ugly truths to light. Confronting his father had cost him his command and put him in the frontline of the charge.

No. He would not walk through that door when she was awake. Only when the house was still, in deepest night, was it safe. When Philippe had begun his midnight visits, he'd told himself he went because of his nightmares—twisted, terrifying recreations of their flight so real that he woke, sweating, his mind blazoned with the dream image of her dead, her hips in a growing pool of red. When that terrible vision had first invaded his sleep, he'd gone to her bedside, driven by an overwhelming need to hear the reassuring rhythm of her breathing and see with his own eyes that she still lived. But lately, now that the nightmares had abated, another reason drew him to her side in darkness: He was lonely.

Yet despite his loneliness, he held back from openly seeking her companionship. Anne-Marie was dangerous. If she were to discover that he loved her . . .

Life had taught him that love and manipulation were synonymous. Anne-Marie had turned his existence inside-out, as it was. He would not risk losing what was left of himself by letting her know what a powerful hold she had on him. And so he stayed away from her.

By day, he tried to distract himself with riding, with swimming, with study, with drink. But by night, nothing could fill the emptiness for long. And nothing but seeing her could still the troubled turnings that kept his mind from slumber. So, night after restless night, he went to the corner, painstakingly eased back the bolt, inched the door open, then slipped into her darkened chamber to linger in the shadows and watch her sleep.

Sometimes she stirred, a flicker of pain briefly tightening her features. Other times, he saw the shadow of her own bad dreams rob her sleeping face of its composure. Then it was all he could do to keep from gathering her into his arms, waking her with soft words, sharing his own grief, his own loss with the woman who had lost as much as he.

But he couldn't. He'd hoped to leave the past behind when they'd fled Paris, yet a cloud of secrets still hung, dark and deadly, between them. He dared not tell Anne-Marie about Maison Corbay. How could he expect her to believe he hadn't knowingly stolen her birthright? The truth seemed improbable, even to him.

So much had been lost. Philippe was still angry—at himself, at his father, at Mazarin and the God who allowed such men to ravage nations with their greed. Anne-Marie was the only innocent in all of this. Her scars remained, indelible reminders of everything that had gone wrong. How could she hold anything but bitterness in her heart?

No. The door should remain locked, the secrets unspoken. Perhaps in time . . . .

Closing his eyes to the cramped room that surrounded him now, Philippe massaged the knotted muscles at his temples. Maybe he'd feel better if he wrote another letter to his father—another letter that would never be sent. He dipped his quill into the inkstand and began to write.

Entering the kitchen, Annique inhaled the savory aroma that wafted from the kettle Suzanne was stirring in the corner of the enormous fireplace. "Smells good in here."

Suzanne straightened in surprise. "Good morning, your grace." She motioned to the pot. "It's just a vegetable stew. Nothing fancy."

Annique looked around the cozy room. How many times in the last few days she had wanted to come here, but remained in lonely solitude rather than intrude upon the servants' privacy. She'd disrupted their lives enough, as it was. But today was different. Today she came into the kitchen with a purpose. Trying to appear casual, she reached up and broke off a fragrant twig of dried rosemary from the bundle hanging overhead, then strolled toward the center of the room, where a tray lay beside a basket of pears, a round of pungent cheese, and two loaves of fresh bread.

Annique spotted the entrance to a narrow corridor that should, by her reckoning, lead to the room adjoining hers. "Has my husband eaten his midday meal yet?"

Suzanne glanced at the empty bowl on the tray, then back to her mistress. Her brows lowered in suspicion. "No, your grace. I was just about to dish it up for serving."

Annique stood very straight, her words resonant with calm authority. "Good. I've decided to take his grace's tray to him myself. Please prepare the plate."

Suzanne bit her lip in misgiving. But after an appraising look at her mistress, the cook sighed and relented. "As you wish, your grace."

Annique's mouth twitched. She found it ironic that the servants invariably treated her as if she'd lost her reason when, in fact, she was finally beginning to use it. Undaunted, she watched Suzanne serve up the simple, hearty meal, then half-fill the goblet with wine.

The housekeeper hesitated, shot a pregnant glance at her mistress, then added another generous dollop of the strong vintage. When the tray was ready, she paused, concern furrowing her wide brow. Her eyes darted nervously to Annique's damaged hand. "This is a might heavy, your grace. Please let me carry it for you."

Annique's cheeks stung with embarrassment, but she kept her voice light. "That won't be necessary. Thanks to your therapy, I can manage quite well by myself." She slid the tray from the table, balancing the right side atop her right wrist. Her left hand firmly gripped the other side of the tray. A tiny bit of wine slopped over the rim of the goblet, but the rest of Philippe's lunch was undisturbed. "See?" She headed toward Philippe's study.

Fortunately, the door at the end of the hall was slightly

ajar. Annique used the corner of the tray to tap out notice of her presence, then pushed it open. Philippe never even looked up. He remained bent over the cluttered desk that dominated the center of the room, his quill busily scratching away. "Just set it anywhere, Suzanne. I'll eat when I get to a stopping place."

Annique couldn't see his face, only the top of his head. His neatly tied hair gleamed blue-black in the diffused light admitted by high, clerestory windows that lined a raised section of ceiling.

She stepped closer, her eyes drawn to the corner door she'd seen so often from the other side. The bolt was nestled securely in place. A third door behind Philippe bore similar hardware, but it was not bolted. She glanced back at Philippe, still lost in his work, then she scanned the small, cluttered room. Floor-to-ceiling, books and scrolls jammed the marble shelves that lined the walls between the room's three doors. Philippe's desk took up most of the floor, leaving barely enough space to pass between it and the narrow cot shoved against the bookshelves beside it.

How could he bear being cooped up in this tiny place, day after day? Unless that door behind him led into another, larger room. But if that were the case, why would he sleep in these cramped quarters?

Annique's curiosity was diverted by a rude pang from her injured hand, prompting her to speak. "Unless you clear your desk, I'll have to set this on your bed."

At the sound of her voice, his head snapped up, his dark brows drawing together in consternation. Philippe rose, looking her up and down as if she were a creature from another world.

Annique felt her breath catch in her throat. She had forgotten just how handsome he was. Despite the rustic austerity of their circumstances, Philippe was simply but elegantly dressed, his shirt of the finest white cotton, his breeches plain black silk, his soft black boots burnished to a genteel patina. She saw a new gauntness in his clean-shaven face, but even that was becoming. And his eyes. They were darker blue than she remembered, more compelling.

Annique had prepared herself to meet his anger, but not for the impact of his physical presence. She had spent the last three weeks trying to forget how just being close to him could make her hands grow cold and her inmost parts shiver. Perhaps she shouldn't have come. She hesitated, her right wrist shifting slightly under its burden. "This is rather heavy." She hadn't meant to make reference to her infirmity, but Philippe's gaze moved instantly to her crippled hand.

His face rigid, he transferred an armful of scrolls and papers from the desk to his cot. "Here. Put that tray down. You shouldn't be carrying anything."

Still rattled by the undeniable current of physical attraction his closeness generated, Annique paid an inordinate amount of attention to sliding the tray onto the desktop. How could she do what she had planned, when just being next to him made her feel this way?

But she must. She must let go of the past and move on.

His next words took her completely by surprise, the tight intensity of his voice belying its quiet tone. "Why are you dressed like that? Have you forgotten who you are?"

Caught off-guard, Annique looked down at herself and replied, "I coaxed these clothes out of Marie because mine were so uncomfortable. This place is so remote, I thought it wouldn't matter what I wore."

She was merely being honest, but her reference to their circumstances seemed to anger him further. Eyes narrowing, he gestured to the tray, his words clipped. "Must you act like a servant as well as look like one? If you mean to insult me, you have succeeded."

A mixture of embarrassment and defensiveness caused Annique to bristle. Did he actually think she had dressed this way just to humiliate him? *Men. Always accusing women of being overly emotional, then allowing their pride to completely distort their own perceptions.*

Reminding herself of why she'd come, she squelched the urge to fire off a stinging retort. Instead, she spoke frankly and evenly. "It was never my intention to offend you. I came at mealtime so as not to interrupt your studies unnecessarily. I brought your tray myself because I didn't want an audience for our . . . meeting."

She smoothed the folds of her skirt. "As for my dress, the choice was dictated strictly by a selfish concern for my own comfort. I confess it never occurred to me that you would take it as an affront." Annique met his gaze without flinching. "I apologize for such thoughtlessness. Would you prefer I change into something more suitable?" There was no sarcasm in the last. She had come to make peace.

She could have sworn a flicker of shame passed across his face before he muttered, "Wear what you please."

What was behind that glimpse of emotion? Was Philippe ashamed for imagining some vindictive motive that didn't exist, or merely embarrassed by her impropriety? Or did her very presence as his wife humiliate him? Suddenly the marble floor felt hard and unforgiving beneath her feet. "Excuse me. I must sit down."

Frowning, he sprang forward to grasp her bare forearms and guide her to the edge of the narrow cot. His hands, huge and warm against her skin, lingered for a heartbeat before he stepped back. Her husband's famous elan seemed to have deserted him. She could readily read confusion and suspicion in his eyes.

Philippe struggled to regain control of the emotions warring within him. Blast the woman for invading his sanctuary. And blast her for dressing like a domestic. Regardless of her reasons, the sight of her in such coarse, common clothing struck him like a blow—a stinging reminder of how far they'd fallen—wounding his pride more deeply than any of the embarrassments he'd endured in years of genteel poverty.

Yet she seemed so frail, so young in those ridiculous clothes. Philippe felt a surge of protective concern in spite of himself. Her face was pale, her nails white as she sat, the effort required to maintain her erect posture evident in an occasional, brief waver of her torso. He should never have let her stand there with that heavy tray for so long. Despite Jacques' glowing reports of her progress, Philippe wondered if she shouldn't be in bed.

But something in the calm directness of her manner stopped him from sending her back to her room. Her brush with death had changed her. He could sense it. He settled back into his chair and stared at his wife.

Anne-Marie made no effort to avoid his scrutiny. She simply said, "It feels good to sit down. I tire easily these days." The statement wasn't a bid for sympathy, merely a fact.

Those enormous brown eyes steadily returned his gaze. Where Philippe had once sensed concealment, now he saw stillness. And sadness . . . for her lost child? For the hopelessness of their exile? For her injuries?

Or was hatred hiding in those depths, or blame? He'd expected both. Now as she sat before him in the library, he caught himself glancing at her wounded hand and a surge of remorse engulfed him. It should never have happened. He should never have turned her over to the Great Mademoiselle, no matter what.

Something died inside Annique when she saw Philippe's thoughtfulness turn bitter as his gaze settled on her maimed hand. It was all too easy to mistake his veiled anguish for revulsion.

So that's how it is, she thought. Not only was he chained to a wife lacking in the qualities necessary for her station, but also one whose scars repelled him. Though she had tried to prepare herself for this, his reaction almost stole her composure. She looked away, not wanting him to see the power his rejection had to wound her.

It took all her strength not to run, weeping, from the room, but she steeled herself and retained the illusion, at least, of calmness. Annique reminded herself that they were two adults, not children, and both their futures were at stake.

She had to do something, anything, to show him that she had accepted her infirmity, as must he. Deliberately using her injured hand, she reached out and retrieved one of the scrolls from the heap beside her. The faded Greek inscription on the outside was barely legible. She read aloud, *"The Peace,* by Aristophanes. One of my favorites."

Philippe's expression shifted abruptly to one of surprise. "You read Greek? But I thought you told me you couldn't."

Annique smiled slightly, glad that the change in subject had diverted him. "No. I did not say I couldn't read Greek. I merely asked why you would ask such a question." He studied her now as if seeing her for the first time. She carefully unfurled the ancient vellum. "I am fluent in Latin, as well, but I prefer Greek. It's far more colorful." She expertly scanned the opening passages of the fifteen-hundred-year-old political satire. She'd love to read it again, now that she'd experienced the insanities of Court politics firsthand. "I must have read this play twenty times, huddled by my stolen candle in the middle of the night in the forbidden room of the convent library." A quick side-long glance revealed that Philippe found her little confession intriguing. At least he hadn't responded with another storm of disapproval.

Tracing the bottom of his lower lip with his finger, he asked, "Was that the only forbidden book you read?"

Annique lifted her chin defiantly. "Hardly." She rolled up the scroll and placed it firmly on his desk. "I wonder if France would be any different if everyone at Court had read this play as often as I did."

Dry humor colored her husband's reply. "Hardly."

Encouraged by his smile, she abandoned small talk. "Philippe, there are things I must tell you."

The humor faded from his face. "I didn't think you came here to discuss Aristophanes."

Curse that brittle sarcasm he always hid behind. She continued, "About what happened back in Paris . . . I want you to know the truth."

He leaned back and crossed his arms tightly at his chest, his voice weary. "I see no purpose to dredging all that up. What difference does it make now?"

"It matters a great deal. As it is, we each have only fragments of truth and hearsay. Look what that's done to us, to the whole household. Can either of us have any real peace until we know what really happened? That's all I'm asking, Philippe. Truth between us."

When he didn't answer, she went on, "Like it or not, we are still man and wife. Like it or not, we're both trapped in this place, for who knows how long. We can't go on avoiding each other, living under the same roof in self-imposed isolation. It will destroy us both." She ignored the flicker of bitterness in his eyes. "I'm not asking for forgiveness, or even companionship. All I'm asking for is honesty between us. Heaven knows there was little enough of that before."

Philippe rose and stepped past her, taking two long strides toward the service hall. For a moment, she was afraid he'd keep on going, through the hallway and out to the barn for Balthus, to ride away without looking back. But he stopped short, his wide shoulders flexing. "The truth."

When he turned back around, his face was old, the lines deepened, his eyes dead. He spoke barely above a whisper. "Perhaps some truths are best left buried, along with the past. Along with . . ." His gaze bored into hers. ". . . our child. Why didn't you tell me about the child, Anne-Marie? Why didn't I know about him until I saw his unformed body in Suzanne's bloody hand?"

The words pierced Annique straight through, sending a quaking shudder up her spine. "Oh, Philippe."

He saw the pain in her face and wanted to comfort her, but some hurt, hidden part of him was desperate to push her away. His voice hardened. "Why didn't you tell me?"

She closed her eyes. "I didn't tell you because I didn't know. Not until the princess told me in the carriage on the way to the Bastille."

"The princess? That's preposterous."

Annique looked up at him and said flatly, "Mother Bernard had told me my monthly bleeding was a penance from God. I didn't know what to think when the cycles stopped." Seeing that he didn't believe her, she repeated woodenly, "I didn't know about the baby until the Great Mademoiselle told me, the day of the battle. If you don't believe me, you can ask her yourself." How could she convince him, heal that one wound, at least?

Bracing his fists on the desk, he bent forward. "So you say, knowing full well that neither one of us is likely ever to set foot in Paris again, much less see the Great Mademoiselle."

"I'm telling you the truth, Philippe, although I don't see how I can expect you to believe me." She shook her head, offering up a sad smile. "You gave up everything to save me, yet you didn't even know me." Annique's hands tightened in her lap. "I admit I never gave you a chance to know me as I really am. I was afraid. Afraid you wouldn't want me, or that you'd use me. But I'm through pretending. It only hurt us both." She rose. "That's why it's so important for us to be honest now. I want to put lies and secrets and half-truths behind us and make something of what's left of our lives."

"What's left of our lives . . ." Philippe gestured to the cramped room, his voice resigned. "This is all that's left. This house, and a few hundred francs. Assuming Mazarin's men don't find us, we can look forward to several years of penurious exile before the money runs out. And then what?" The dark circles under his eyes seemed to deepen. "Where can a deserter go to hide when he has no money?

What kind of life will there be then, for either of us?" Desolate but unbowed, he stood.

Annique wanted to reach out and comfort him, put her arms around him and tell him that everything would be all right, but that would be the cruelest lie of all. Instead, she said, "We'll manage, Philippe. It will be harder for you than for me, but I'll do everything in my power to make it easier. I promise." Unable to bear any more, she stepped past him to leave.

She paused at the threshold of the service hallway, her eyes turning to the bolted door in the corner. "You needn't bother to lock that anymore. I won't disturb your privacy again. But if ever you want to talk . . . about books or science or philosophy—anything—I would be honored to have your company."

She felt her throat tighten. "This is a beautiful house, but it can be a very lonely place with no one to talk to."

Philippe watched her go in silence, barely able to breathe for the weight of sadness in his chest. Dear heaven, he hurt. And he had hurt her, too, but somehow she had borne her own agony with dignity. He wanted to call her back, to pull her into his arms and take comfort from the peace she seemed to have found. He wanted to bury his face in her hair and feel the resilient warmth of another body close to his, but all he could do was stand there, alone, and stare at the empty doorway where she had been.

❦ CHAPTER 28 ❦

$\mathcal{T}$wo days later when Annique returned to her room from the garden, she found a neat pile of scrolls on her bed. She lifted the top cylinder. Her quizzical frown turned to a smile as she translated the Greek characters of the outer inscription: *The Peace*, by Aristophanes.

She shook her head in amazement. This, after all Philippe's distance, his pain.

She settled beside the pile of scrolls. It didn't surprise her that he had reached out with his mind and not his heart, but the gesture was a beginning.

Looking over the other titles, she wondered if all Aristophanes' plays were as wickedly amusing as *The Peace*. Annique hoped so. It seemed a lifetime since she had laughed. Suddenly days that had loomed long and lonely before her didn't seem so empty.

When Marie entered with an armful of clean linens, Annique gestured to the scrolls. "Marie, do you know how these came to be in my room?"

"His grace brought them to the kitchen on his way out this mornin'. He told Jacques to put them on your bed after you went to the garden." Her brows drew together in apprehension. "That was all right, wasn't it?"

"Of course it was all right." Annique carefully transferred the scrolls to the table beside her bed. "Has his grace returned from his morning ride?"

"No, your grace. He's not expected for at least another hour."

"I see." She hid her disappointment. "Thank you. You may go. And please tell Jacques I quite enjoyed my surprise." Jacques would waste no time in telling Philippe.

Alone again, Annique glanced at the manuscripts. A sense of bittersweet longing tugged at her chest. If only there were some way to repay Philippe's kindness, something special that would reinforce the tentative bridge he had extended over the gulf that separated them. But she'd promised not to intrude upon his privacy, and she had no gift—

Or had she?

Philippe loved books, and she owned a set of them— brilliant, provocative, politically dangerous books that any serious scholar would give his soul to read.

Philippe had reached out, mind to mind, and she would reciprocate in kind.

She opened her coffer and ran her fingers over the gilded inscriptions on the richly tooled spines. Annique took out the first two volumes of Machiavelli's commentaries. They would whet her husband's appetite for the remaining volumes. There were ten more in the set—ten more chances to strengthen the bridge between them.

She hurried to the hallway and called, "Jacques! Please come at once! I want you to take something to his grace's study." As she waited for the valet, she smiled again, picturing her husband's surprise when he returned from his morning ride to find what Jacques had left on *his* bed.

* * *

An hour later Annique was so engrossed in reading *The Peace* that she almost didn't hear Philippe return from his morning ride, but the faint sound of Balthus's hoofbeats pulled her back to reality. Her hands tightened on the scroll. Ears straining, she rose from her bed and crossed to the library door. No sound emanated from the room beyond.

Excitement fluttered through her as she imagined his reaction to her gift. She leaned closer. Still no sound from the library. Then the faint but unmistakable rhythm of Philippe's long strides carried through the wood.

Annique jumped back. Strangely flustered, she retreated to her bed. She settled against the pillows and tried to focus on the scroll still gripped in her hands, but she couldn't concentrate. Her mind was twenty feet away, in a room whose literary treasures had been increased by two precious volumes.

Suddenly a dark thought stirred her. Philippe had so many books already. What if he didn't appreciate her offering, or didn't like it?

Before she could consider such a thing, the corner door flew open and Philippe burst through, his face flushed and her books gripped in his hands. He crossed to her bedside and stood towering over her, the books thrust forward. "Where did you get these?"

Annique straightened. "They're mine. My father left them to me when he died." She stared up at his sweat-stained shirt and windblown hair. Saints, but he looked gloriously fierce in his disarray!

Philippe broke into a grin and dropped to the edge of the bed, his eyes greedily scanning the opening pages of the first volume. "I saw a set of these in Savoy years ago, when I was there with my tutor. I'd have killed for a chance to read them, but our host kept them under lock and key." He handled the books as reverently as a knight entrusted with the Grail. "They're very rare, you know, and quite controversial."

Annique could only stare, amazed at the transformation in him.

He looked up, his eagerness as ingenuous as a ten-year-old boy's. "Do you have any of the other volumes?"

She hesitated, then answered, "All of them. I have all twelve volumes."

A hint of misgiving returned to his face. "But how? Where? I didn't see them in the wagon."

"They were in my trunk." She shifted, suddenly self-conscious. "The books and the coffer that holds them are all I have left of my parents. Marie knew how precious they were to me, so she packed them." By heaven, he was close to her. She could smell the tang of exertion and sea air his clothes gave off.

"It seems Marie knows more about you than I do." Philippe cocked his head. "And you share them with me? I am honored." He granted her a bemused smile.

The glow of that smile wakened all the longing she had so carefully suppressed. She felt herself smiling back, but an inner whisper of warning countered the stirrings within her body. *Tread lightly. You must put away the passion that once passed between you.* Mind to mind. Philippe, himself, had set the terms.

She tried vainly to focus on intellectual matters. "I've read the entire series twice, some volumes three times. Though I disagree with many of Machiavelli's conclusions, I find his insights fascinating."

Philippe frowned and hefted the books in his hands. She could see that he wanted very much to talk with her, but something held him back. He had sacrificed so much to save her—his career, his family, his honor, his home. She could hardly blame him for wanting to lick his wounds in solitude.

She ventured, "Perhaps we could discuss them after you've read them."

He leveled a thoughtful gaze at her. "Yes. We could. At your convenience, of course."

Fearful that she might betray the hope that welled up within her, Annique glanced at her lap and murmured, "I would like that very much." If only they could be friends.

Philippe stiffened, causing Annique to wonder if he had somehow sensed what she was thinking.

He motioned at the scroll she was holding. "I see you've been reading."

She hadn't even thanked him for the plays! Annique stammered inanely, "Yes. The play. I mean, *The Peace.*"

"Are you enjoying it as much as you did in the convent?"

Spurred by the note of amused challenge in his question, she lifted an eyebrow and said coolly, "The premise is unbelievable, the setting impossible, the theology worse than heresy. All laws—divine and natural—are suspended. This play has no basis in reality." Philippe's congealed expression told her she'd gone far enough. She grinned. "In short, it's perfect, just what I needed. Thank you, Philippe. You've given me the gift of laughter."

He rose abruptly, his manner suddenly smooth and distant. "I'm glad you like the play. And I agree with your assessment." Gauging the thickness of the books in his hands, he added, "It will take me several days to read these. Shall we talk on Sunday, perhaps over lunch?"

Annique nodded. "Very good. I'll tell Suzanne."

Philippe looked pointedly at the open hallway door. "She probably knows already." An audible exhalation echoed from the hall, followed by a swish of fabric. Chuckling, he retreated toward the library. "I shall look forward to Sunday."

Only after he was gone did Annique realize that during their entire exchange neither of them had noticed her maimed hand.

Philippe did come on Sunday, and on the Wednesday after that, then again on Friday. Despite a certain awkwardness in the beginning, they soon settled into a companionable routine. Their sessions together became an odyssey for Annique, an unpredictable sojourn into the mind of a man whose depth of education far exceeded even Father Jules's. Philippe had not merely found refuge in his books; he had found a world that extended far beyond the boundaries of France and the sensibilities of his era. And every discussion with him took Annique into that wider world.

Yet although Philippe seemed to enjoy their exchanges as much as she did, he never stayed for more than an hour or two, and he deliberately kept the subject matter impersonal. Even so, Annique learned a great deal about him from his comments on history, politics, and philosophy. And he was learning about her.

With each passing week she meted out her precious

commentaries, one at a time, as she had promised. Philippe reciprocated with works of Caesar, Plato, Cicero, Aristotle, and Socrates.

By late September, the hurts and deceptions that had once come between them seemed like a distant, bad dream. Annique liked her husband now. More than that, she liked the way he made her think, the way he made her feel. And Philippe liked her. She could see it in the subtle gleam of approval in his eye when she argued him to an impasse. She could hear it in the warmth of his laughter when she surprised him with a deft twist of logic or amused him with a witticism. By the time autumn was upon them, neither made any effort to hide the fact that they enjoyed their time together.

But he never stayed to sup with her, never invited her into his library, never spoke of personal matters. Obviously, Philippe meant to keep their relationship as it was—safe, distant, and narrowly defined.

If only she could do the same. Though she struggled to conceal it, being near him sometimes drove her almost mad with longing for his touch, the taste of his lips, the feel of his silky black hair, the reckless passion they had once shared. Yet she dared not jeopardize their friendship by letting him know. So night after night she dined alone, then sat alone and watched the sunset. And night after night, she went to her solitary bed and dreamed that Philippe, her husband and now her friend, would join her there.

One morning early in October, Annique breezed into the kitchen and nodded to Suzanne. "I heard Jacques mention that there are some berries just on the other side of the peak. I think I'll go pick them."

Suzanne's spoon stilled in the batter she was mixing. "I'm afraid that'll have to wait till this afternoon, your grace. There's no one to accompany you." She frowned apologetically. "The master's still out riding, I'm in the middle of making bread, and Jacques and Marie won't be back from the village until suppertime."

"I haven't been outside the compound alone since we got here. It's not that I don't enjoy your company, but today I feel as if the walls are closing in on me. I need to walk free."

Annique crossed to the open window and leaned out, her lungs filling with crisp air as she scanned the faultless azure sky overhead. Was it the promise of fall that made her so restless, lately? Or was it the fact that she could no longer be content with the meager portion of himself Philippe doled out to her every day? She sighed and pulled back inside the kitchen. Scooping up a straw basket, she headed for the door. "I won't be gone more than an hour or so, and I won't go far."

"Please wait, your grace." Suzanne put down her bowl. "I'll go with you. I can make more bread later." When Annique frowned, she added apologetically, "The master left strict orders that—"

Annique cut her off. "*I* am ordering you to stay and finish the bread. If it's safe for Philippe to go out riding alone every day, surely it's safe enough for me to pick a few berries by myself. I won't go far." Feeling stronger than she had in months, she was determined to have a taste, at least, of liberty. Her voice softened at the genuine concern in Suzanne's face. "Nothing will happen to me, Suzanne. We've walked together a dozen times without seeing a living soul. If my husband should ask why you allowed me to go alone, just tell him I ordered you to remain behind. He knows how stubborn I can be." Before Suzanne could reply, she escaped into the courtyard, her sudden appearance sending the chickens flying.

The housekeeper rushed to the doorway and called after her, "Your grace! Come back!" When Annique kept going, she shouted, "Take care that no one sees you!"

Annique lifted the crosspiece to open the door in the outer wall. She looked back at Suzanne and grinned. "Don't worry. The devil himself couldn't find us in this place." As Suzanne crossed herself, Annique waved and said, "Why don't you make a pie crust while I'm gone? If his grace returns before I do, tell him we'll have berry pie with our lunch."

With luck, Philippe would never know she'd gone.

Annique followed Balthus's hoofprints along the dusty road, then down a path into the shadow of the rocky summit that loomed fifty feet above the compound. For weeks she had wondered what lay on the other side of that crag. Now, at last, she felt strong enough to see for herself.

The sound of the sea grew louder and louder as she

climbed upward toward the narrow pass. Reaching it, Annique straightened. The wind caught her full force, whipping her clothes and tugging loose a corona of curls from the thick braid that trailed down her back. She gasped, transfixed.

Before her, a wide plateau stretched to steep cliffs embracing the turbulent waters of an enormous bay. No evidence of humankind spoiled its natural splendor. Shielding her eyes from the sun, she scanned the plateau to the headland on the other side of the bay. There was no sign of anyone, not even a distant fishing boat.

Good. She was safe. Annique made her way between patches of herbs and low clumps of wind-stunted bushes to a broad carpet of sea-scrub where she sat, her weight releasing a pungent cloud of resinous scent. Relishing the hint of coolness in the wind, she stretched her arms wide, her shawl fluttering behind her like a banner. What a glorious sensation. This must be how a seagull feels, she thought. Annique closed her eyes and imagined herself in flight, free of sorrows, free of regret, free of human desire.

She wasn't sure how long she remained there, soaking up the sunlight, solitude, and the sound of the waves. It seemed like only a moment, and yet forever. When she opened her eyes, she saw that the light had shifted. Suzanne would be frantic if she didn't return to the villa soon. She gathered her basket and set out to find the berries.

Barely twenty yards away, she spied a cluster of bushes along the edge of the cliff. Plump berries weighted down the low-growing branches. Jacques hadn't said anything about their being on the edge of a cliff! She moved cautiously to within a few yards of the berries. The ground looked solid, but she'd have to move closer to see over the edge.

Inching forward, her heart pounding almost as loudly as the surf, she peered over the drop-off, only to discover a wide ledge just a few feet below. Another, narrower, ledge extended beyond that, reassuring her that she could safely fill her basket.

Letting out a long, relieved breath, Annique flexed her injured hand. Thanks to Suzanne's ministrations, her fingers moved almost naturally now, and the once-purple scars had faded significantly. She settled to the mindless task of stripping the bushes of their sweet-tasting bounty.

An hour later, her basket laden with enough berries for two pies, she had almost forgotten where she was and who she was when two black-gloved hands clamped onto her upper arms and jerked her backward.

Dear Father! Suzanne was right. Mazarin's men have found me!

Struggling frantically to free herself, Annique dug in her heels, but her assailant dragged her with almost superhuman strength and speed. Then he stopped, and she was spun around to face a livid, breathless Philippe.

He shouted, "What were you doing so close to the edge? Have you lost your mind entirely? Don't you know those cliffs are a thousand feet high?"

A heartbeat of pure relief was replaced immediately by anger. Annique wrenched her left arm free of his grasp, spilling most of the berries from her basket in the process. "Saints, Philippe! You almost frightened the life out of me!"

Coming dangerously close to his face on the cross-swing, she whacked the empty basket against the hand that still gripped her right arm. "Let me go! If you'd bothered to look, you'd have seen that there's another ledge just below this one. I was perfectly safe!"

Instead of releasing her, Philippe jerked her closer, the lines beside his mouth deepening. "Where is Suzanne?"

She faced him defiantly. "She had work to do, so I ordered her to stay at the villa. I made certain no one was about before I ventured into the open. I'm a grown woman, Philippe, perfectly capable of picking a few berries by myself." Her eyes narrowed. "Or do you plan to punish me by keeping me under guard for the rest of my life?"

Philippe growled, "You *need* a guard. If I had been one of Mazarin's men, you'd be in a sack in the back of a wagon by now, on your way to Paris and torture." His eyes held hers as the wind whipped dark tendrils about his face.

She met his gaze without flinching, and when she did, the dark fire that hid behind his anger took her breath away.

He wanted her. She could see it.

All the longing she had tried to suppress rose up and blotted out her self-control. In an instant, her arms circled his neck and she kissed him, long and hard. He tasted so good, felt so strong against her.

Philippe remained rigid for only a moment. Then his arms were around her, lifting her from her feet and crushing her to him. Nothing existed but that moment. No past, no future, no motive, no consequences. Only the ravening hunger fed by his kiss.

She didn't stop until she grew faint for lack of air. Only then did she tear her lips from his. She hid against the hollow of his neck, her hair brushing his chin. She could hear the galloping pace of his heartbeat, as strong and wild as her own, but his posture remained stiffly erect, his muscles knotted with tension. Or with anger.

The thought brought Annique back to her senses. Dear heaven, what had she done? With one impulsive gesture, she had risked the trust that had grown between them. Annique couldn't bear it if she'd ruined everything.

His embrace slackened, allowing her to regain her feet. Annique was afraid to look into his face, afraid of what she'd see. Still leaning against him, she turned her forehead to his chest, prolonging the feel of her body against his, even if only for one last moment.

He did not respond. Annique sighed and tried to withdraw, her voice harsh against the wind. "We can go back, now."

Philippe's left arm tightened around her, pulling her against him with such force she could hardly breathe. His right hand slid roughly up her neck to clamp her jawbone in his grasp, forcing her face back until those glittering blue eyes bored into hers.

"No." His breath was hot, his grip so powerful she realized he could snap her neck as easily as a child breaks a twig. But he didn't hurt her. Instead he stared into her eyes, his own face betraying lust and need and confusion and, underneath it all, a desperation borne of vulnerability. He whispered raggedly, "We can never go back. Only forward."

He kissed her again, a searing, probing kiss that threatened to consume her. Eyes closed, she tasted the sweet insistence of his mouth and reveled in the pleasant roughness of his chin.

Then, abruptly, the iron reassurance of his encircling arms disappeared. Wobbling to regain her equilibrium, Annique opened her eyes to see Philippe mount Balthus, then shift forward against the saddle, an odd, half-lidded look momentarily claiming his features.

He nodded toward the empty basket hanging on her arm and grinned. "Perhaps you should stay and pick those berries. Suddenly I have quite a taste for pie." He spurred Balthus across the plateau and disappeared through the pass.

Annique stared after him, her shock slowly replaced by dawning hope. Their kiss had shattered forever the illusion that they could keep their relationship neatly confined within the limits Philippe had set. Both of them knew that now.

Smiling, she touched her lips. Unless she was badly mistaken, she and Philippe would share more than pie at lunch.

❧ CHAPTER 29 ❧

*A*nnique was humming when she breezed into the outer courtyard with her basket full of berries, but the melody died on her lips at the sight of the wagon, back hours before Suzanne had said it would be. Jacques was leading Balthus into the barn. He acknowledged Annique's presence with a brief nod, then averted his eyes.

It wasn't like Jacques to be so curt. Annique's stride lost its bounce as she approached him. "Something's wrong, isn't it?"

Before he could answer, Philippe's voice interrupted. "There you are!" Annique turned to see him approaching from the kitchen doorway. "I was just about to set out to fetch you." He took the basket from her grasp, then led her into the house, his tone low. "Come. We must talk."

Inside the kitchen, both Marie and Suzanne were hurriedly wrapping food, but they stopped when Annique walked in and saw Philippe's saddlebags lying open on the table. He was leaving. Her breathing tightened as he led her into her bedchamber.

He closed the door behind them, then turned to face her. "There's been a development."

She shot back a tight, rather sour smile. "Obviously."

For just a moment, her barb erased the tension in his

face. "Obviously." Then he grew grave. "When Jacques went to the village for supplies, the priest approached him in the square and asked if he had seen any strangers in the area. Being a stranger, Jacques was understandably wary."

Fear coiled in her chest. "And?"

"Jacques shook his head no, but the priest spoke on. He said that there was a message waiting for a certain stranger from Paris at the Convent Sacre Coeur in Provence."

Annique felt her blood turn to ice. "If this priest knows we're here, it's just a matter of time until Mazarin does."

Philippe began to pace. "Not necessarily. If the priest had wanted to find us and report back to the cardinal, why bother speaking to Jacques? Why not simply follow Jacques and see for himself?" He paused. "The message was very carefully worded. For all we know, every priest in the south of France might have said the same thing to every stranger in the region."

"Someone might be trying to contact us. But who?"

"It could be anyone. Neither of us has made any secret of your background." He stroked his chin. "The convent's a logical point of contact."

She straightened. "*I've* never discussed my 'background' with anyone."

Deep in thought, he didn't seem to hear her. "The princess, perhaps?"

At the mention of the Great Mademoiselle, Annique's sense of warning grew even stronger. "It might be a trap, Philippe." She could no longer keep the fear from her voice. "Don't go. It's too dangerous. Let's run, while there's still time. We could go anywhere. Spain, Greece, the Holy Land. Even the New World. I don't care."

He stopped pacing and straightened to his full height. As she watched, a subtle transformation stole the Philippe who had become her friend. She'd seen that look of bravado before, when he'd left her at the Tuileries. It was the look of a warrior girding for battle. "I find I have no talent for the fox's life—hiding, living in fear. Sooner or later, I'd have had to go back. Perhaps this message is destiny's way of choosing the time."

What a fool she'd been to think they might have a future. Now—just when she had begun to see light—they were being pulled back into darkness.

Philippe approached her, his smile as unconvincing as

his reassurances. "Don't look so worried. I won't leave until dark, and I'll make sure no one follows me. Jacques is
readying the horses. With a spare mount, I'll be able to
reach Sacre Coeur in just a few days." He cupped her chin.
"Once I get there, I won't go *near* the convent until I'm
certain it's safe."

She grasped his hand, savoring the warm roughness of
his skin. "We both know there's no way you can be certain
it's not a trap until you're inside. Then it will be too late."

A wry half-smile cocked his mouth. "You underestimate
me, madame." He bent down and surprised her with a kiss,
the brief pressure of his lips ending far too soon. "I would
love to linger for a more memorable farewell, but I'm
afraid there isn't time. I have much to attend to before
dark. I only hope I'll have a chance to steal a little sleep."

A dozen questions hovered at the tip of her tongue as
she watched him head for the library door. "Wait. I—"

Philippe silenced her with a lifted hand. "We'll talk tonight before I leave. I promise." Once again, the cursed
door closed between them.

Determined not to let him escape so conveniently, she
hurried after him, but her fingers paused on the iron handle. What good would it do to confront him? He would go,
no matter what she said. In just a few hours he would ride
away, leaving her to wonder if she'd ever see him again.
And she, for all her talk of honesty, would watch him go
without telling him the one thing she wanted more than
anything to reveal.

"Don't leave me, Philippe," she whispered. "I love you."

Three days later while the nuns were gathered in the
chapel for evensong, Philippe adjusted a thick coil of rope
over his shoulder, then scaled the enormous oak that over-
hung the refectory. So far he'd seen no sign of the cardinal's men, but he hadn't expected to. If they were inside,
he only hoped that their days of waiting had made them
lax.

Hidden by the tree's browned leaves, Philippe settled
into a high crotch of branches to pass the hours until night-
fall. He tried not to think of Anne-Marie and how dangerously close he'd come to surrendering to the growing
attraction between them. If Jacques hadn't been waiting
with the message when he'd ridden into the compound

. . . Philippe thanked Providence once more for the timing of this distraction, but knew full well that he would desire Anne-Marie just as deeply when he returned to the villa.

If he returned.

He tucked his arms beneath his dark cloak and willed himself to sleep.

When he awoke it was night and his senses were poised, razor-keen. He scanned the sleeping convent below. What had wakened him? Philippe listened, barely breathing until a flutter of wings from the branch above him caused him to flinch. An owl swooped from the shadows overhead, the moonlight silvering its feathers as it swept down to pluck a hapless creature from the cloister garden. Philippe heard a strangled, high-pitched squeak as the prey was carried away, its dark silhouette writhing helplessly in the owl's grip. He shivered, hoping the incident wasn't an omen of what awaited him in the convent.

He'd left the horses safely hidden almost a mile away, but on a night as still as this, the sound of a twig snapping underfoot would carry like a musket shot. Smooth as a cat, he climbed down to the thick branch that overarched the refectory. After inching his way out as far as he dared, he secured the end of his rope to the branch, then lowered himself into the stark pool of shadow on the tiled roof below.

At the soft crunch of his boots on the clay tiles, he froze, listening for any motion within the convent, but there was none. Philippe made his way painstakingly to the edge of the roof, then eased himself down into the cloister. The moment his feet touched the ground, he retreated into the relative darkness of the columned walkway that bordered the garden. One by one, he tested the doors along the covered walkway and found them locked. He was halfway around the cloister before he found one open.

Philippe held his breath and slipped inside. The hallway beyond was deserted, illuminated by only a small patch of moonlight that slanted through the grille of a heavily barred entrance at the opposite end. At a faint swishing sound from the direction of the cloister, Philippe ducked into the first room he came to and closed the door behind him. From the sound of his own breathing, he sensed that the chamber was a large one.

With but a frail shard of indirect moonlight seeping under the door, it took almost a minute for his eyes to adjust. When they did, Philippe discovered a grid of heavy iron bars separated his end of the long room from the only other exit. Except for a few benches and chairs facing each other on opposite sides of the bars, the room had no other furnishings.

He grasped the iron bars and tugged, but they were firmly imbedded in both the floor and the ceiling. Propelled by a sudden uneasiness, he turned back toward the hall door. There had to be a better place to hide than this dead end. But as he reached for the door's iron handle, he heard the unmistakable sound of a key turning in the lock, then the rasp of a heavy bar settling into the braces on the other side of the wood.

A thrill of alarm shot through him. Philippe jerked with all his might, but the door wouldn't budge. Swiftly, he felt along the doorjamb, but no hinges broke the snug intersection.

It was a trap, and he'd walked right into it! Philippe withdrew his sword from its scabbard and backed into the center of the room. He snarled into the darkness, "All right. You have me. Why don't you show yourself?"

A woman's voice spoke calmly from beyond the bars, startling him. "Not until I know who you are, and why you've broken the peace of this community."

Philippe turned and took a step closer to the bars. The voice seemed to have come from the door on the other side, but Philippe could tell from the dim reflection of its handle and metal studs that it remained closed. The room had been empty when he'd entered—he was certain of it—and he still sensed no presence but his own within the stuccoed walls. A cold chill tightened his skin. "Who are you? *Where* are you?"

After a pause, the disembodied voice spoke again. "I am Mother Bernard, abbess of this convent. And unless you tell me who *you* are and why you've come here, I shall be forced to wake Father Jules and send for the *cardinal's* soldiers, whom the Lord has so providentially brought to the village nearby."

Philippe's mind raced. What was going on here? If Mazarin's men were behind this, why hadn't they simply come forward and placed him in irons? And why the subtle emphasis in the abbess's threat, unless she suspected who he was?

He began to hope. When he spoke, his voice was disarmingly casual. "I come on behalf of a certain gentleman from Paris who was given reason to believe there might be a message for him here."

"So you broke into our convent while we were sleeping? Odd manners for a messenger, sir."

In spite of himself, he smiled. Her cool sarcasm indicated anything but fear. "These are troubled times. One never knows what sort of reception might be waiting."

He heard the soft scrape of wood against wood, then the rattle of hardware from the door at the opposite end of the room. When it opened, the nun's shrouded lantern revealed the small peephole through which she had been speaking. Lifting the lantern before her, the abbess glided silently into the room, a second nun cowering in her wake. As they drew closer, Philippe noted their bare feet, skewed veils, and capes thrown over coarse cotton gowns.

Without warning, the abbess opened the front of the lantern cover, blinding Philippe for a few seconds. After looking him over thoroughly, she ordered her companion away. "Leave us, Sister Thomas. Wait outside the door. If you hear anything amiss, or if I do not return within five minutes, send for Father Jules immediately and summon the soldiers." The plump sister nodded, then scurried out the door and pushed it almost closed. Mother Bernard set the lantern on a bench against the far wall and sat beside it, her features cast into eerie shadow.

Philippe turned his attention to his side of the room. This visiting salon had obviously been designed to do more than protect the sanctity of the cloister. Glancing at the door on his side of the grid, he saw deep gouges in the wood that made him wonder how many others had been detained here.

The abbess straightened her veil. Even in disarray, she was a formidable woman. "I must ask that you remove your cape and toss your weapons through the bars, sir. I do not hold conversations with armed men."

When he hesitated, she lifted an eyebrow. "They will be returned to you." She smiled coldly. "*If*, of course, you are the gentleman we seek."

He had little choice. Feigning frustration, he shrugged his cape from his shoulders and stuffed it through the grid, then unbuckled his scabbard and sheathed his sword. The hilt barely fit between the bars. He lowered it to the floor, then shoved it toward Mother Bernard. His dagger followed. The small dirk hidden in his boot would be weapon enough.

She nodded. "Thank you. And now your boots, please."

Philippe bristled, his resistance real this time. After a moment's hesitation, he flopped onto the bench, pulled off his boots, and hurled them through the bars.

The nun remained expressionless. "And the other dagger."

With an exaggerated bow, he surrendered the dagger tied to his calf. The cold from the stone floor penetrated his silk stockings. Philippe felt ridiculous. He'd been trapped and disarmed by a nun—*a nun!*—and now he stood squirming like a schoolboy in his stocking feet. "I am defenseless, madame."

She lifted an eyebrow. "I am hardly fool enough to believe you defenseless, sir, even without your weapons." Her face settled into an impenetrable mask. "You still haven't told me who you are."

"You told your companion to raise the alarm in five minutes. The time's almost up. Give me five more, and I'll tell you."

He could have sworn her face softened before she stepped to the door and called, "Five more minutes, Sister Thomas." Then she crossed to stand just beyond his reach on the other side of the bars. She stared, hawklike, into his eyes. "Well?"

Through gritted teeth, he muttered, "And I thought Anne-Marie was exaggerating."

A look of shock flashed across her face. "What did you say?"

Philippe lifted his chin. "My wife told me you could be as stubborn as a bulldog and twice as disagreeable, but I thought she was exaggerating. I stand corrected."

"Your wife?" She took a step forward. "Answer me honestly, sir, on pain of your immortal soul. Are you the Duke of Corbay?"

He bent with a flourish. "At your service."

Mother Bernard gripped the bars. "Annique! How is she? We heard she was gravely injured."

"Annique?" Philippe's brows drew together. "You mean Anne-Marie?"

"Yes, yes. But we always called her by her pet name, Annique." Her face grew suspicious. "She never told you that?"

Philippe shook his head. "No. But she did mention dear Sister Thomas and cruel Sister Jonah, and—"

Mother Bernard dropped all pretense of superiority. "For pity's sake, tell me. Is she all right?"

At last, he had some leverage. "Let me go, and I'll tell you."

The abbess thrust a staying hand through the bars. "Wait there." She scooped up his boots and heaved them at the grid that separated them. "Put those on. We can't have you catching cold." She gathered the rest of his belongings, then disappeared, closing the door behind her.

Philippe pulled on his boots and was waiting when she unlocked the hallway door and pushed it open. Mother Bernard shoved his cape and weapons into his arms and whispered, "Here. Quickly. Follow me. Mazarin has spies everywhere, even in the convent, but there is one place where you'll be safe."

Keeping close behind her, he buckled on his scabbard, whispering, "The secret room behind the library? The one with the forbidden books? Anne-Marie *did* tell me about that."

Mother Bernard murmured grumpily, "I might have known she'd find that room. And *tell* somebody."

Philippe grinned at the substantial figure beside him. "We can discuss that later, once I'm hidden."

Her lantern safely shrouded, the abbess moved with absolute assurance through the darkened hallways. Philippe suspected she could have found her way blindfolded through the maze of corridors that ended in what looked like an abandoned storeroom. She crossed to an empty cabinet and reached inside. With the click of a latch, one side of the cabinet swung free, revealing a low passageway behind it. She handed him the lantern. "The secret room is at the end of that corridor. You'll find your message in the large Bible on the table, chapter one of the book of Ho-

sea." She handed him the lantern. "I'll be back soon with
food and drink."

"Thank you." Philippe ducked into the cramped passage
and made his way to the opening a dozen feet beyond.
Once inside the secret room, he straightened and removed
the shroud from the light to reveal a table and chair occu-
pying the only area in the twenty-by-twenty room not taken
up with closely spaced shelves crammed with books.

He placed the lantern beside a dusty Bible on the table
and opened to the book of Hosea, as instructed. The light
fell across an unaddressed letter, its wax seal indented with
the familiar pattern of his father's crest.

Philippe sat heavily in the chair. Knowing his father, he
had little doubt what the marshal would have to say to his
son, the deserter. Fingering the heavy paper, he toyed with
the idea of burning the letter unread. Then he sighed and
broke the seal. He read:

> August 15, 1652
> My son,
>   Your disappearance did not become known to me
> for several days following the battle. Only then did I
> discover that you had gone missing under circum-
> stances that can most charitably be described as
> questionable.
>   We have had our differences, Philippe, but never
> in my worst imaginations did I conceive that you
> might disgrace our family by abandoning your duty.
> Though rumor has it that you were lured away by
> false orders, then kidnapped in an effort to discredit
> me, however indirectly, I can hardly give credence to
> such a story, especially since the rumors originate
> with a certain highborn rebel sympathizer with whom
> you are now known to have been involved.

Of course, his father would believe the worst of him.
Philippe had known he would. He read on.

> Regardless of the cause, your disappearance has
> forced me to exercise all my influence and consider-
> able expense to avoid scandal. I have given out the
> story that my own men rescued you from the rebels
> and took you and your wife to recuperate, incommu-

nicado, at a location which I dare not reveal for fear that further attempts might be made on your lives.

As for the truth, I think I can piece that together for myself. The first thing my inquiries uncovered was Mazarin's treachery in relieving you of your command and placing you in the forefront of the charge. No matter what suspicions your romantic liaisons might have aroused, I count the cardinal's act against my own blood as a strike against me. He will come to regret his treachery. As for your part in this, I am told that you accepted his orders with dignity and courage, and acquitted yourself most honorably in the charge. I try to think of that, and not the shame I feel when I consider your subsequent abandonment of your duty.

Philippe lifted his eyes to the ceiling. If only he could believe that his father hadn't ordered him into the front of the charge. He read on,

Reliable informants have told me that you entered and left the Frondeurs' command center of your own accord. I am aware of your head injury and of your wife's wounds and how she sustained them. Giving you the benefit of the doubt, I have reached the conclusion that your actions are mitigated, at least in part, by those circumstances.

I cannot, however, maintain indefinitely the ruse that protects us both. Sooner or later, someone will discover that you and your wife are not the couple "recovering" at my estates in Bordeaux. Though I have deflected offers by both the queen and Cardinal Mazarin to send their personal physicians to attend you, they grow more suspicious with each passing week. I don't know how much longer I can avoid either producing you in the flesh, or announcing your deaths. The choice is yours.

It was a choice Philippe had never expected. So the old man had covered for him, after all. He read further.

I adjure you, though, to consider one thing above all others in making your decision: I will not endure dishonor on your account a second time. You'll die by my own hand, first.

> Henri, duc d'Harcourt
> Marshal of France

P.S. Two days after you disappeared, the Hôtel de Ville was burned and many were killed by a mob of rebel sympathizers. Such barbarism has turned all of Paris against the Princes of the Fronde. Mazarin is stronger than ever. Though a certain princess continues to make a fool of herself by parading about the city at the head of her troops, her sun is set, and soon she, along with her seditious allies, will taste banishment. That is how the wind blows now, Philippe.

When he had finished reading, Philippe sat staring at the precise letters penned in orderly lines on the heavy paper. . . . *abandonment of your duty . . . disgrace . . . scandal . . . You'll die by my own hand, first.*

Philippe's gaze lost focus. In protecting himself, the marshal had accomplished the impossible. All that Philippe had thought lost—his home, his wealth, his reputation, his position—remained his. He could return to Maison Corbay and resume his life as if he'd never left. He could resign his commission, retire to the country with Anne-Marie, and start a family.

But the cost would be dear: He would be forever in his father's debt, suffering the marshal's contempt until one of them died.

Philippe sighed. It might already be too late. In the time since the marshal sent this letter, his ruse could have been discovered, or he might have been forced to feign Philippe's death. Either case would make for a most awkward homecoming. Philippe would have to proceed with caution.

At a sound from the corridor, he crushed the letter in his fist.

Mother Bernard emerged from the passageway with a tray bearing bread, cheese, and a tankard of wine.

He stood. "When did you receive this message, Mother Bernard?"

She placed the tray on the table. "Three weeks ago. The cardinal's men arrived in the village soon after."

An unsettling sequence of events. Could the message be a forgery? A trick by the cardinal to trap him into returning to torture and disgrace? He glanced at the seal. If the letter was meant to trap him, his own father was party to the scheme. The writing was in the marshal's own hand, and the wording, as well as the seal, bore his unmistakable stamp.

No. Philippe's father was too proud a man to bring down shame on his own house, no matter what the cardinal did. The letter had the ring of truth.

He must act, and quickly. Philippe seized the tankard and gulped down a stout draught. The raw red wine insulted his palate and burned his throat. He stuffed the food into his shirt for later. "Thank you for the food, but I have no time to eat now. I must leave."

The abbess's hand clamped down on his forearm. "You'll go nowhere until you've told me of Annique. Does she live?"

Philippe flashed an ironic grin. "More than that. She thrives and has turned my household upside down."

The nun's grip relaxed. She peered into his eyes. "You care for her?"

Afraid that she would see just how much he did care, Philippe busied himself with buckling his scabbard, then looked up in challenge. "She's the most contradictory creature I've ever known."

Mother Bernard actually smiled. "From what I've seen of you, sir, the two of you deserve each other. Tell her I said so. And tell her to write me."

He paused at the entrance to the corridor. "I'll do better than that. I'll bring her here on our way back to Paris."

❧ CHAPTER 30 ❧

The first five nights Philippe was gone, Annique slept fitfully, but the sixth was worse than all the rest. Maybe it was the full moon. Maybe it was an omen of watchfulness for his safety, but sleep escaped her.

If all went well, she would only be alone for a few more

nights. But what would happen when he *did* return? Would he still want her as he had before he left? Or would he once again close the library door that she had kept open since he had ridden away?

What if he never came back at all?

Long past midnight of that sixth night, she turned in her bed and stared through the draperies at the dim, shifting images of the moonlit garden. Even that could not calm the questions that churned through her mind this night. After another restless hour, she rose and pulled on her robe against the occasional breath of wind that stirred the curtains. The polished marble floor felt chilly beneath her bare feet as she padded across the room and into the library. Annique told herself she was looking for a book to read, but in truth, she sought the comfort of Philippe's presence among his belongings.

In the library she crossed through a shaft of moonlight and sat on Philippe's cot. Drawing his pillow close against her chest, she caught the faint scent of his skin on its linen cover. Annique closed her eyes and buried her face into the soft, smothering resistance, the smell of him awakening a vivid memory of his lips on hers as they had stood on the windswept plateau. She could almost taste him, feel his hands upon her. Saints, how she wanted him.

She lifted her eyes to the high windows overhead and stared into the night sky, wondering, *Where are you, Philippe? Are you in danger?*

Suddenly restless, she rose and scanned the books on the shelves, her fingers grazing the bindings. The moonlight was so bright she needed no candle to read the titles, but none of them interested her. She reached the door behind his desk and paused, her eyes drawn to the key protruding from the age-scarred lock. She'd been tempted to turn that key uncounted times since Philippe had left, but hadn't out of respect for his privacy. Tonight, her curiosity got the best of her. Annique never had been able to resist a chance to open what was closed, to search beyond rules and permission, to know what was forbidden. She grasped the smooth loops of the key and turned.

The mechanism released with a satisfying clunk, and well-oiled hinges moved silently as the door opened to reveal a short corridor hewn from the same limestone rock that towered over the compound. Along the unbroken wall of the dim room beyond, a long stone bench looked as if it, too, had been carved from the mountain's face. She caught a whiff of sulphur, like the smell of the spring water that trickled endlessly through a trough in the kitchen, but stronger. Drawn by the same curiosity that had lured her to find the convent's secret library and devour its contents, she stepped into the hallway and pulled the door closed behind her.

The stone floor felt strangely warm beneath her feet. She moved toward the dusky enclosure of the grotto beyond.

When she got there, Annique gasped at what Philippe had kept hidden all this time.

She gazed across the surface of a warm artesian spring, almost twenty feet wide, carved by man and nature from the mountain's peak and sheltered from the elements by a deep, columned portico. The center of the spring bubbled restlessly, and wisps of water vapor danced across its surface. Beyond that, the hot waters spilled downward twice into two man-made pools that stair-stepped out into the night. Annique's eyes scanned past the descending pools to a tiny moonlit garden beyond, its lush border of flowers interrupted only by a small statue gleaming white against the seaward wall.

Everything was in perfect proportion—the rippling rectangular pools, the wide marble walkway that hugged the water's edge, and the slender columns that framed the second spillway at the edge of the portico.

She rose and tried to orient herself. The high wall to her right must be that of her bedroom and the central garden. A gust of sea breeze from the far end of the enclosure lured her beyond the middle pool and into the open air.

Annique stepped to the border of flowers, where a small paving stone in front of the little statue provided footing for her to lean over the low wall and look beyond. The hidden enclosure shared almost the same view of the distant Mediterranean she had seen every day from the main garden. Only the stout buttress at the end of the wall had kept her from suspecting that this secret retreat lay on the other side.

No wonder Suzanne had acted so strangely about the slipper tub. Who needed a tin tub, when he had this? Suzanne, and Jacques as well, must have known about this place all along and never said a word. Annique couldn't help feeling a little angry and more than a little betrayed by their keeping this place a secret.

Secrets. The harder she fought to eliminate them from her life, the more she uncovered.

All this time, she'd never even suspected . . .

Philippe must have ordered them to keep it from her. The disturbing thought sent a stab of jealousy through Annique. Perhaps this was Philippe's refuge for memories of another lover. Had his secret longings summoned the Great Mademoiselle to this hidden place—and to his heart?

Annique felt her own heart tighten painfully at the thought. She shook her head, as if doing so would chase away the jealous memories. All that was past now. She reminded herself that fate had relegated the Great Mademoiselle to the past. Ironic, that exile had been the means of their liberation from the princess's schemes and manipulations.

A muffled thump brought Annique abruptly back to reality. Had the sound come from the main house? Tensing, she peered into the deep shadow beneath the portico, barely able to make out the empty opening to the hallway.

No one there.

Philippe wasn't due back until tomorrow evening, at the earliest, and the servants were sound asleep. At least, she thought they were. Annique rose and crept back into the library, her ears straining. Minutes passed, and all she heard were the quiet sounds of the night. Relieved, she pulled the library door closed behind her and returned to the grotto.

Curious now, she crossed to the back of the hot pool and crouched to peer into the turbulent, cloudy water. Just below the surface, wide stone steps had been carved into the limestone all the way across the end of the pool. She scooped up a handful of the hot water; as it escaped between her fingers, its warmth chased a path of gooseflesh up her arm.

How glorious it would be to immerse herself in that warmth, shutting out everything except the muffled sounds of the spring and her own movements. The prospect was irresistible.

A carved stone niche held stacks of neatly folded cotton

homespun. Annique shook loose one of the towels and dropped it at the edge of the pool, then allowed her robe to slip free of her shoulders and fall to the ground. She untied the ribbon between her breasts and raised her chemise over her head. Even in the shelter of the grotto, the night air felt cool on her bare skin.

She loosed the braid that bound her hair and shook free a curtain of auburn waves. The stone cherub at the far end of the garden was the only witness as she slowly descended into the rippling water.

Step by step, the warmth claimed her. The deeper she got, the warmer it became, but not unpleasantly so. She proceeded cautiously, making certain of her footing as the stairway led her into the heart of the spring. Her toes curled around the edge of the step, and she lowered herself farther, allowing the water to swallow her breasts. Tiny shivers radiated through her as the warm bubbles licked over her nipples, then covered them completely. Annique stepped even deeper, her hair spreading into the water like a diaphanous cape of dark silk. She had reached the end of the submerged stairway, and her head and shoulders were still comfortably above the surface. Wary because she couldn't swim, she inched forward, her feet feeling along the slightly abrasive stone until she was certain that the bottom had leveled.

Just as carefully, she explored the remainder of the pool, saving the bubbling center for last. Once she had reassured herself that there were no unexpected drop-offs, she glided freely through the effervescent resistance of the water, her scalp tingling pleasantly at the tug of her hair trailing behind her.

She waded happily around the pool's perimeter, twisting and turning so that she could feel the soft caress of her hair floating against her skin. So much wonderful warm water, so much room to move and stir its currents. Growing more confident, she left the security of the edge and circled the roiling center of the spring. When at last she stepped into the midst of the rising column of warm water, it surged all around her, scrubbing her body with millions of tiny bubbles.

A burble of pure delight escaped her lips. The force of the artesian spring was so powerful that it almost lifted her off her feet. She moved in and out of the current, experimenting with its effect against her weight. Smiling, she returned to the submerged stairway to sit, her thoughts turning to the erotic possibilities of such a place. What pleasures she and Philippe could enjoy here together. The prospect sent her blood surging through her veins as hot and agitated as the spring itself.

Annique smoothed a strand of wet hair from her shoulder, and was surprised to feel that her fingertips were wrinkled like dried grapes. She'd bathed long enough. She climbed out and scampered for the towel. Warmed by the thermal effect of the stone, the fabric felt almost seductive against her skin. Annique dried herself slowly, savoring every sensation. When she was done, she twisted as much moisture as she could from her hair, then wrapped herself in a fresh towel, draping the excess length over her shoulder like a Roman toga.

Feeling expansive and more than a little wicked, she strolled to the far end of the garden and looked out over the Mediterranean. A sword of glistening silver pointed westward to the enormous moon that hovered above the horizon. She closed her eyes and listened. The murmur of the spring pulsed and trickled behind her. Before her, a gentle southerly breeze brought the rhythmic crunch of distant waves upon the shore.

Annique inhaled the scent of the sea mingled with the mineral fumes of the spa. Soothed by the quiet voices of the waters, she surrendered to the joy of pure sensation, feeling as if she were disappearing, becoming a part of all that surrounded her. Trancelike, she swayed slightly in the warm wind and allowed the towel to slip from her body.

At the feel of the breeze against her bare torso, she scooped the towel up, but halted before she covered herself again. Who was she hiding from? All her life, she had been taught that nakedness was a sin, and she had accepted that teaching, but now she couldn't help wondering if it wasn't a greater sin to be ashamed of the way God had made her. Why, she scarcely knew what her own naked body looked like, much less how it was made.

Emboldened by the intimate seclusion of this place, she lowered her gaze and looked at herself as if for the first time. Ignoring a surge of embarrassment, she let her fingers glide smoothly where her gaze had been, feeling the textures of her own body.

Her explorations were interrupted abruptly by the sound of a sharp intake of breath from the shadows of the grotto. Annique's heart almost stopped beating. Covering herself, she pivoted to see a darkened figure beside the pool. The silhouette of his naked body was as perfect as any Greek statue. For a fleeting moment, Annique wondered if her self-indulgent games had conjured some dark spirit from the waters. She froze. "Who is it? Who's there?"

After three days and two nights of unrelenting travel, the only thing that had kept Philippe from collapsing into his bed was the prospect of a long, hot soak for his saddle-weary bones. He'd exhausted the last of his strength stripping off his grimy clothes, but what he saw when he reached the grotto literally sucked the breath from him, instantly evaporating his fatigue.

There in profile stood a luminous vision of feminine seductiveness, her downcast face in shadow, a graceful drape of white fabric on her arm her only covering.

Was she real, or was she a phantom? Then he saw the dark indentation on her right hand and between her breasts.

Anne-Marie.

Transfixed, Philippe felt his heartbeat quicken, the thundering pulse in his loins rivaling that in his chest. Watching her, completely unaware of his presence, was one of the most tantalizing, erotic experiences he had ever known. He saw her hands slide, slowly and deliberately, over the contours of her torso, her head turning away in silent pleasure. A gasp of pure lust escaped him.

At the sound, she spun toward him, fumbling to pull the fabric over her nakedness. "Who is it? Who's there?"

Why hadn't he ever realized how beautiful she was, how perfect the line and curve of her body? She was exquisite, even now, poised like a frightened doe in the moonlight. Barely aware of his own nakedness, Philippe took a step forward. "Welcome to my garden. I trust you've found it pleasurable."

Anne-Marie clutched the towel tighter to her chest and whispered, "Philippe."

For an instant, he wondered if she was disappointed, but then she looked up at him, her frank gaze piercing the shadows where he stood. The raw hunger in her eyes sent an answering shudder through him. Her next words rocked him further.

"Welcome home, husband. Come, let me greet you properly." She opened her arms to him, allowing the fabric to fall to the ground.

He answered her summons, stepping into the moonlight. Anne-Marie's gaze pivoted to the evidence of his arousal, but she did not look away. He reached out, his hands cradling her ribs. "When I first saw you there I wondered if you were real, or if you were made from the moonlight itself, and your dark hair woven from the night sky."

She murmured huskily, "When you appeared in the shadows, I thought you were Neptune himself, called from the depths by my desire."

"Perhaps I am." Philippe swept her into his arms. "Come, let me show you what pleasures the waters can bring." He carried her to the hot spring and descended into its bubbling warmth. Gently, he lowered her to her feet. "Wait here. I must wash first." He slipped below the water, shook his head slowly back and forth, then rose, smoothing his wet hair against his scalp.

When he extracted a clay pot filled with perfumed bathing oils from a niche in the lip of the pool, Annique pulled the container from his grasp. "Let me."

His faint smile faded to a look of searing intensity as he watched her scoop out a dollop of the aromatic oil. Annique smoothed a glistening arc across his chest, her hand grazing the taut points of his nipples.

Philippe grasped her waist and drew her closer. Her fingers moved lower, sending shock waves through him as her touch lingered on the deep indentation that slashed across his ribs. His lips brushed tantalizingly near her mouth, then grazed her cheek to whisper hot into her ear, "We both have battle scars. I have more, but none so brave as yours."

"Let me see if I can find them." Anne-Marie's fingers followed the dark, silky trail that led downward from his chest. The oil released an incandescent film on the surface of the spring. Her touch moved lower until she encountered the evidence of his arousal. That, too, she caressed, savoring the look of blissful agony that washed over his face at her touch.

His hands slid down to cup her buttocks and lift her hard against him.

She wrapped her legs around his hips, the seat of her desire enfolding his as he began to move slowly through the water. His mouth claimed hers, gently at first, then more insistently, moving away just when she was hungry for more. She felt his lips trace a feathery track across her shoulder, then down the side of her neck. Every place he kissed set up a pulsing echo to the beating of her heart.

They were moving constantly now, shifting with the evanescent currents of the water. The moonlight revealed every flicker of passionate agony that fluttered across his features. In taking her own pleasure, she pleased him. She could see it. Annique had never dreamed that there could be such power in surrendering to the untempered wisdom of her own body.

Philippe spoke above the murmuring of the spring. "Wet your hair. I want to see it floating in the water."

She arched her back until her head was almost touching the surface, her legs tightening around Philippe as he pulled her through the water. He bent over her, his mouth caressing her breasts. Annique thought she would die with pleasure when his teeth closed gingerly on one nipple, then another. Straining against the water's pull, she raised upright against Philippe and pressed herself to him, the burning void inside her too hungry now to be ignored.

He lifted her, then lowered her again, their bodies linked almost weightlessly in the surging waters of the pool. Annique gasped again with pleasure. Her hands gripping his shoulders, she arched against him, meeting every thrust with a buoyant rhythm of her own. And then his mouth covered hers almost brutally, their tongues entwining, searching, probing.

Annique's heart beat so loud and fast she could barely hear the ragged staccato of her own breathing. Or was it Philippe's? She could no longer tell where she left off and he began. Hot. She was so hot.

Faster and faster, he plunged. Deeper and deeper, she felt the heat of his presence within her, until at last the stone walls echoed her sharp, wrenching cry of exultation.

The next thing Annique knew, she was lying in her bed and Philippe was sitting beside her, chafing her wrists. He smiled down at her. "You gave me quite a fright. We generated so much heat, I fear the spring was too much for you."

The very sight of him hovering over her was enough to send a tremor of remembered ecstasy through her. Here they were, just as she had dreamed it—side by side in the same bed, both of them wanting to be there. Annique reached up to touch him, her fingers rasped by the faint stubble on his cheeks. This was real, and what had happened in the pool, that was real, too. Her fingers threaded into his hair and pulled him toward her. "Maybe we ought to try it again, here."

❀ CHAPTER 31 ❀

*P*hilippe rolled onto his side and gazed at his sleeping wife. Anne-Marie's lips were parted slightly, her breathing deep and easy. In the faint light before dawn, he could see a hint of gold in the dark russet hair scattered recklessly across the pillows. How could he ever have thought her anything but beautiful? He couldn't believe that he'd once considered her plain, any more than he could now deny the tenderness that swelled within his chest at the sight of her.

She looked exposed and vulnerable. Gently, so as not to wake her, he replaced the covers she had kicked off in the lingering heat that followed their lovemaking. Then, sliding close beside her under the sheets, he cupped her body with his own. The soft skin of her breast was cool in his palm, but her buttocks felt hot and slightly moist against his abdomen, stirring a whisper of remembered passion.

This night he had lived every man's fantasy. Anne-Marie had come to him without haste or inhibition. Gone was the anger that had tainted their lovemaking in the past. She'd been tender one moment, hungry the next. He had answered her passion and, to his amazement, felt his own jaded senses born anew.

Until tonight, a part of him had always stood back, analyzing everything, protecting some safe remnant of himself from those who would use him. Anne-Marie had opened the door of that inner prison, and in that moment become a part of him, as inseparable as the blood that coursed through his veins.

He knew now that the past had worked a strange purpose between them. Their souls had been heated white-hot by the fires of anger and passion, then painfully hammered together on the anvil of adversity. Remembering how desperately he had resisted that fusion, Philippe smiled. All those months, he'd fought so hard to stay whole by remaining separate. Yet when in her arms the line dividing them had disappeared at last, he had lost nothing of himself. Rather, he had gained.

Peace had come with her into his heart, and a strange sense of a burden lifted. The world was new again, full of possibilities. Philippe nuzzled the back of her neck and pulled her even closer. She smelled so good, felt so good in his arms.

There was no use denying it any longer. He loved her—even though it gave her the power to destroy him.

Long after the sun had risen, Annique was no longer observed, but observer. She'd never had the opportunity to inspect a naked man at her leisure in broad daylight, and she was enjoying the opportunity immensely. If Philippe would just sleep a little longer, there wouldn't be a freckle or a curl she didn't know by heart. On his front, anyway.

She smiled, happier than she could ever remember feeling. Something had changed last night, though she wasn't certain how. She only knew that Philippe had let go, at last, and broken through an inner barrier that had kept him from her. Now they belonged together.

She stared brazenly at the muscular symmetry of his uncovered torso and the elegant relaxation of his arms and legs. By Heaven, he was beautiful—perfectly proportioned, with just the right amount of silky black hair on his limbs, his chest, and surrounding the part of him that had given her so much pleasure. Her stomach did a little fillip when she saw that he seemed more than ready to do so again.

Perhaps she should wake him after all. She cleared her throat and was rewarded by a flutter of dark lashes.

He smiled up at her and reached out to stroke her bare back. "Good morning."

The gentle friction of his hand on her skin awakened every nerve in Annique's body. Her response was unnaturally high and breathy. "I think good *afternoon* is more in order." She watched with pleasure the play of muscle over bone and sinew as he stretched, slowly and deliberately—

for her benefit, she was certain. Her gaze drifted downward and settled on his arousal. "I hope you've been
dreaming of me."

A wry half-grin hoisted one side of his mouth. "Well,
actually, that's not exactly—I mean, I wake up this way
every—"

His words halted abruptly when she reached out and
traced the length of his desire. It leapt to her touch. Fifteen minutes later, both of them lay panting in a tangle of
arms and legs and auburn hair.

A loud growl from Annique's belly prompted her to giggle. "Maybe we ought to eat some breakfast. I seem to
have worked up quite an appetite."

He glanced at the sunlight filtering through the drapes.
"You mean lunch. Maybe even dinner." Philippe stood up
and rubbed his taut, flat belly. "I'm starved." Oblivious to
the fact that both of them were unclothed, he strode to the
hallway door, flung it open, and bellowed, "Suzanne! Bring
us food! Lots of it!"

Laughing, Annique scrambled to cover herself with the
sheet. "Philippe!"

Suddenly preoccupied, he turned and headed back
across the room, but when he reached the foot of the bed
he kept on going, muttering, "Now where in blazes has
Jacques put my robe?"

When he reached the library door, Annique felt her
smile fade.

Almost as if he, too, had felt the cold splash of remembered isolation that washed over her, Philippe halted.
"What's the matter? You've gone white as . . ." Then
dawning comprehension smoothed his features. "Oh. How
thick of me." He strode back to the bed and sat beside her.
"Don't worry, Annique."

She looked up in surprise. He had called her by her
nickname! Her *real* name!

He continued, "I'll be right back. My clothes are still in
the other room, but not for long. From now on we shall be
together. I promise, I'll never leave you again. Unless you
ask me to. My word on it."

Annique had prayed for so long that he would say those
very words. Now that he had, she should have been
overjoyed to hear his promise. Instead, fear hovered over
her, reminding her of past rejections. "I know it's not ra-

tional, but I don't want you to leave me, not even for a moment. Not yet." Her arms slid around him, and she nuzzled against his chest. The solid, reassuring warmth of his flesh gave her the courage to speak truthfully. "I have the strangest feeling that if I let you out of my sight, something terrible will happen."

"Ah, *Ma Coeur,* how can I convince you?" He sighed deeply. "I've shut you out so many times—too many times—but those days are over. I swear it. Like it or not, you're stuck with me. No more locked doors between us. No more separate rooms."

"I want us to stay just as we are, naked in this bed, forever."

Philippe looked down at the tumbling cascade of ruddy curls beneath his chin. He wished they could stay naked in the bed forever, too. He couldn't remember ever being happier than he was now in her arms, but even this moment's happiness was not without its shadows. He had to tell her. "Does it matter what bed we're in, as long as we're together?" He felt her tense, but he went on, "We cannot stay here."

She pulled back and searched his eyes. "The message at the convent."

"Yes." He tried to put the best possible face on things. "The message was from my father, of all people. It seems he's managed to spare himself—and us—disgrace by claiming that we were rescued from the rebels and taken to his country estate to recuperate."

After a long silence, she whispered brokenly, "We have to go back, don't we?"

"Yes. Right away. But everything will be all right." He drew her close again, as much to reassure himself as to comfort her. "The rebellion is over, crushed. At last we can be free of wars and politics, both of us. If all goes well when we reach my father, I can resign my commission. Then we'll retire to Maison Corbay and live out our lives in peace." As he heard himself say it, Philippe began to believe that they could.

Anne-Marie's arms tightened around him. "And what if we get there only to find that things have gone wrong?"

"Actually, we're better prepared than you might think." Resolution strengthened his voice. "When the rebellion heated up, I shifted as many of our assets as I dared into holdings even my father couldn't trace. Most of our assets are safe, but I had no way to get to them when we fled the city." If she was impressed by his foresight, she gave no indication. "Should we find trouble waiting back in Paris, we'll just take the money and run, anywhere you want. Asia. The New World. Here. It's up to you. But we'll be together, and we'll have enough to offer our children a comfortable future."

Anne-Marie's expression was grave. "I almost wish we *could* run away—anywhere but Paris. I'm afraid, Philippe. Afraid that if we go back to Court, I'll lose you for good."

"That won't happen, I promise. I'm finished with the Court and everyone in it." He meant it. Giving her a quick squeeze, he kissed the top of her head. "We will start preparing for our journey tomorrow. I'd like to leave the next day."

"So soon." She looked longingly around the room. "Very well. I'll be ready."

Philippe heard the sad resignation in her tone. He urged, "We must go back. You deserve more than this, Annique. Maison Corbay is a great house, and you are its rightful mistress. You belong there, not hidden away in this tiny place."

The intensity in his voice surprised them both. Her eyes narrowing, she murmured, *"Rightful* mistress?"

Philippe recoiled inwardly at the dangerous slip. He'd let down his guard and almost ruined everything. Perhaps one day their love would be strong enough to bear the whole truth, but now the trust between them was too new, too fragile for such a burden. He changed the subject abruptly, knowing he could count on her insatiable curiosity to distract her. "I've planned a special stop on the way home, one I think you'll like."

Five days later, Annique stood beside her husband as he rapped on the main door of the convent. When she'd left Sacre Coeur less than a year ago, she'd never dreamed she would return—or that she'd want to—but now she could hardly wait for the door to open.

Marie hovered close. Her gaze cut from the gray cobbles to the formidable stone walls and iron bars that enclosed the courtyard. "Looks too much like a prison to suit me."

Seeing the utilitarian structure as it must look to Marie,

Annique realized it *was* forbidding, but she could only think of it as home. She patted the maid's arm. "These walls don't keep the sisters in; they keep the World out. Wait till you see inside. There can be great beauty in simplicity. The chapel and the gardens of the cloister are lovely." When a luggage-laden Jacques and Suzanne joined them, Annique leaned closer and confided to Marie, "His grace and Jacques, of course, will have to remain in the public rooms, but you and Suzanne and I shall be free to roam wherever we wish. I'll show you the dairy where I worked for seven years."

With that, the peephole opened, and Annique heard a familiar voice exclaim, "They're here! They're here!" Sister Thomas threw open the massive door and enveloped Annique in a well-cushioned embrace. "Thanks be to the Blessed Mother for bringing you safely back to us!" She thrust Annique to arm's length for inspection, her eyes lingering briefly on her scarred hand. "Look at you. So thin. We'll have to feed you some of Sister Matthias's good yeast rolls and pancakes to fatten you up."

Without so much as a word to the others, she dragged Annique toward the refectory. "Come. Everyone's been on swords' points awaiting your arrival."

Laughing, Annique pulled back. "Wait, Sister. Allow me to introduce you to my husband."

"Oh, dear, I forgot myself. But his grace and I have met, of course." Sister Thomas aimed a perfunctory curtsy in Philippe's direction. "Pleased to see you again, your grace." Then she hustled Annique along, motioning the others after her. "Come in. All are welcome."

The weary little group followed her across the hall and into the reception room. Philippe cocked an enigmatic smile at the sight of the iron grid that divided the chamber. He motioned to the mums and cedar greens gracing the center of a large table. "I see you provide most hospitably for your *daytime* guests."

Sister Thomas shot him a look that could only be described as insolent, but she kept smiling. "This time we knew you were coming." The nun went on briskly, "One of the sisters will bring food and drink directly. Mother Bernard will greet you properly after you have refreshed yourselves. Your rooms will be ready shortly. Until then, please make yourselves at home." She glanced apologetically from Jacques to Philippe. "The ladies are free to visit wherever they wish, but I'm afraid we must ask monsieur le duc and his manservant to remain in this wing of the building."

Annique didn't miss the spark of mischief in Philippe's eye when he replied, "That's fine. I've already seen the cloister, anyway."

Sister Thomas colored. "Yes. Well, fortunately the circumstances of *this* visit are more conventional than your last." She smoothed her veil as if to make up for the dishevel of their first meeting. "And now, your grace, may I beg leave to take Ann—I mean, *her grace* to the refectory for just a little while? The sisters have gathered to greet her."

Instead of answering the nun directly, Philippe turned and spoke to Annique with open affection. "Take all the time you need, my dear. I know you're eager to see your family." He nodded to Suzanne. "You and Marie may attend your mistress. I'll wait here with Jacques."

Sister Thomas beamed. "Bless you, your grace." She motioned the women back into the hallway. "Come along." She led them down the hall and into the cloister, then turned and locked the door behind her.

Annique knew it was routine to do so when there were men staying in the visitors quarters, but she felt a brief spasm of disquiet. Philippe had promised there would be no more locked doors between them.

Sister Thomas cocked her head and frowned. "Is something the matter?"

Suddenly Annique felt foolish. "Nothing. It's nothing." She turned her attention to the cloister garden. Warmed by the fall sunshine, its intricate hedges released a sour tang of boxwood into the air, sharpened by the pungent smell of cedar and sage. "Everything looks the same. Not a leaf out of place, as usual."

Annique pointed to the covered walkway at the opposite side of the deserted garden. "Suzanne, the kitchen is over there, at the end of that hallway. I'd like for you and Marie to go get something to eat. Sister Thomas and I will be along in a few minutes."

Obviously grateful for the opportunity to refresh themselves, the two servants curtsied and scurried away.

Sister Thomas waited until they were alone to speak. "I

know it's selfish, but I had hoped we'd have a moment alone, just the two of us. Come. Let's go where we can find a little privacy." She led the way to a secluded bench sheltered by cedars. Sister Thomas sat down and pulled Annique to the bench beside her, like a mother hen gathering her chick.

Annique relaxed against her familiar bulk and sighed. "Oh, Sister Thomas. How many times in these last few months I've longed to put my head on your shoulder and tell you everything like I used to when I was a little girl."

"Well, now you can. I want to hear it all. About your wedding, your husband, Paris, the rebellion . . ."

Annique drew back. "You know about the rebellion?"

Sister Thomas said matter-of-factly, "You'd be surprised what sins I've committed because of my lack of faith concerning your welfare." She grinned without a hint of penitence. *"Mea culpa.* So tell me what has happened since we left you in Paris. I want to know everything."

Everything. How could Annique tell her everything? The early months of her marriage had been so dark, so complicated. She didn't even feel like the same person as the naive girl who had left here only months ago, and this place no longer felt like home.

Annique's words came slowly. "I never knew how safe I was here until I left. The real world, the one outside these walls, can be a treacherous place. It can be beautiful, too. Exciting." She sought the comforting innocence in Sister Thomas's wide, guileless face. "Reality has changed me— made me harder. Stronger." Annique looked away. "Better."

"Forgive me, precious child." Sister Thomas lifted Annique's injured hand to her lips and bestowed a motherly kiss upon the scar. "I know there have been . . . problems. It was thoughtless of me to ask you to relive painful memories. Perhaps what is past is better forgotten." Her arm tightened around Annique's shoulders. "All that really matters now is that you're here, and you're well. And from what I can see, you're happy." Her tone warmed. "I like your young duke. He's quite a rascal, and very handsome. And kind—we all appreciate his bringing you back to us. What a blessing, when I thought I'd never see you again this side of heaven."

Annique smiled. "Philippe and I have grown very close.

It wasn't easy at first. There were . . . complications. But somehow we've both gotten past them."

How could she explain the conflicts that had pushed them apart or the force of passion that had pulled them together? Sister Thomas wouldn't understand; she knew almost nothing of the flesh. She had married Christ at the age of twelve. How could a nun—committed to dying daily to self—understand Annique's struggle to find her own identity, or her triumph in succeeding? It wasn't possible.

Both women had known and accepted the differences in their natures, but now a vast chasm of experience stretched between them. The realization made Annique feel old inside and sad, in a resigned sort of way.

At least she could put Sister Thomas's mind at rest. "Philippe is a complicated man, but I love him. And he loves me. I think we can face anything now, as long as we're together."

"Then my prayers have been answered." Two tears of quiet joy dropped into soggy circles on the nun's wide collar.

The tightness in Annique's chest eased. "I always knew you were praying for me, you and the others. I felt it, just as I could feel your arms around me, like they are now, whenever things got . . . terrible."

Sister Thomas pulled a large square of coarse homespun from behind her scapula and loudly blew her nose. Then she rose. "Come. I've kept you to myself long enough. The others are waiting. We can talk again at supper." Her brows drew together. "Unless, of course, you'd prefer to dine with your husband in the reception hall."

Annique took her arm and strolled toward the refectory. "Philippe and I have the rest of our lives to sup together. I'm sure he can spare me for one evening."

Arm in arm, they walked to the refectory and entered. As she stepped inside, the scent of beeswax and fresh-baked bread greeted Annique, along with an explosion of familiar voices. The entire community was waiting to envelop her. Surrounded by black and white habits, Annique suddenly felt garish and bare in her green silk gown. And she couldn't help noticing how everyone tried not to look at her scarred hand. The wave of warmth and affection that surrounded her soon dissolved her self-consciousness, though.

Searching the crowd of familiar faces, Annique located Mother Bernard at the edge of the gathering. The abbess nodded in acknowledgment, but made no open show of emotion. Annique reminded herself that it would be foolish to expect otherwise. Still, she had hoped that Mother Bernard would be glad to see her.

All the sisters were talking at once, admiring Annique's gown, telling her how they had prayed for her recovery from her "illness," and asking so many questions that she could hardly single any one out to answer. Yet despite the chatter and attention, Annique felt separate, set apart—acutely aware that she was now an alien presence in this closely knit community of souls.

The convent hadn't changed. She had.

Annique's unease grew, as if she could sense the weight of a hostile stare from somewhere in the room. Her gaze was drawn to a solitary figure in the corner. Sister Jonah glared at her with undisguised hatred. Annique had seen such malice only once before—in the Great Mademoiselle's eyes the night Annique had worn the princess's altered gift.

Such darkness was concentrated in Sister Jonah's eyes, and all directed at her. Annique abruptly turned away, glad for the buffering presence of the nuns who surrounded her. Then she stilled. She had no reason to be afraid. After all, Sister Jonah was merely a trapped, dried-up creature who no longer had the power to hurt her.

Slowly and deliberately, she pivoted for a long look at the woman who had once taken such pleasure in tormenting her. An unexpected wave of pity drowned out her fear. Poor Sister Jonah. She *was* trapped, not by this cloistered community, but by the bitterness that made an impenetrable dungeon of her own skin. Annique felt the old resentments melt away, replaced by pity.

Across the room, Sister Jonah reacted as though she had been slapped. She spun on her heel and exited through the kitchen.

Mother Bernard's voice brought instant quiet. "Back to work, Sisters. We'll have plenty of time to talk with Ann—madame la duchesse at supper. Sister Thomas, remain with me." Twenty-three heads bowed obediently as the nuns silently dispersed.

After the others had left, Mother Bernard addressed

Annique with such impeccable formality that her words
bordered on sarcasm. "I pray we have not overtired madame la duchesse with our welcome. Your grace must be
exhausted from her journey. We have provided food for
monsieur le duc and his grace's manservant. Would your
grace care to eat something, as well?"

Annique chose to accept her deference at face value.
"You are very kind, Mother. I'm looking forward to some
of Sister Matthias's good yeast rolls and pancakes. And a
cool mug of our sweet spring water."

"As you wish." A hint of humor softened Mother Bernard's rigid expression. "Though I seem to recall you used
to complain of such simple fare."

Annique smiled. "Life at Court has taught me the value
of simplicity."

Mother Bernard nodded in approval. "Sister Thomas,
please bring her grace's tray to my study. And a cup of
wine for each of us."

"Yes, Mother." Sister Thomas hurried away.

Mother Bernard stepped to the door, pulled it open, and
waited. "After you, your grace."

Standing very straight, Annique glided through before
her. Things had changed, indeed.

Twenty minutes later, Annique stifled a yawn as she and
Mother Bernard watched Sister Thomas disappear into the
hall with the empty dishes. "Goodness. Forgive me,
Mother. Now that I've eaten, I can hardly keep my eyes
open." Perhaps her fatigue would provide a refuge from
the questions Mother Bernard was sure to ask.

Never one to waste time with preliminaries, the abbess
leaned back in her chair and spoke as if she had read Annique's mind. "You needn't worry about explaining what's
happened since you left here. I knew most of it before your
husband came for his message. He only confirmed what I
had heard." She used the familiar voice. Quite obviously,
Mother Bernard considered Annique's rank worthy of recognition only in public. She had dropped all pretense of
protocol the moment they were alone.

Deciding that this might be her only chance to ask
Mother Bernard a few questions of her own, Annique rose
and strolled to the window. She peered through the bars to
the cloister garden below and spoke frankly, "I've always
admired your hauteur, Mother. You never used it as a

weapon to make other people feel small the way Sister Jonah does. You're different." She turned a probing stare on the abbess. "Oh, you say the right things, and you kneel and bow with the rest of the sisters, but always with an unshakable air of superiority. I used to think it came with your office, but now I rather suspect it was bred into you."

Mother Bernard's eyes narrowed. "So you *have* learned something in the last year, Little Sister."

"Yes, my lady. Or would 'your highness' be more appropriate?"

"I see you're still jumping to insupportable conclusions, Annique, just as you always did." A look of deep weariness crossed Mother Bernard's face. "My only title now is abbess of this house. That is how I think of myself, and so should you."

"What about Sister Jonah? She wears a crucifix inscribed by a king. How should I think of her?"

Mother Bernard rose to stand beside her. Staring across the compound, she sighed. "Think of Sister Jonah with compassion. You needed hardening, and she was the perfect one to do it." She faced Annique. "Before she came to us, Sister Jonah spent eight years in our Mother House near Paris. She did not go there willingly. It was forced upon her."

Annique had known all along that Sister Jonah was somehow different from the others. "And yet she took her final vows. Why?"

"I don't suppose there's any harm in telling you. Perhaps knowing the truth will make it easier to forgive her." Mother Bernard shook her head. "She was highborn, powerful, and ambitious. Her family married her off to a very old, very wealthy man who obliged her by dying only a year after the wedding. Free to use her money as she pleased, she became the darling of the Court and plotted her way into the old king's bed. Before long, she became his favorite mistress. She openly flaunted her status, even to the queen." The abbess tucked her hands behind the bib of her scapula. "But all that changed when the queen, at last, managed to conceive. She insisted that the king get rid of her rival before the dauphin was born. Sister Jonah was given a choice: take the veil or lose her head. She picked the convent."

The abbess shrugged. "Then the king died and the

queen became regent. Sister Jonah's only protection lay in taking her final vows. I often think she would have been better off choosing the headsman."

A cold feeling invaded Annique's chest. Such was the world she and Philippe must return to. She chafed a sudden chill from her upper arms. "Thank you for telling me the truth."

Mother Bernard looked up sharply, a shadow of guilt crossing her features before she announced abruptly, "Father Jules has been looking forward to seeing you. If you're not too tired to wait, I'll go see if he's returned from his rounds in the village."

Annique stilled. The thought of her mentor aroused a flood of contradictory emotions. Love. Disappointment. Gratitude. Suspicion. "Yes. I'd like to see him." Maybe this time they could make a proper parting.

"I won't be long." Mother Bernard left her alone.

Annique strolled back to the windows and stretched, afraid to sit down lest she fall asleep. She heard the door swish open and turned, a smile of greeting on her face. "Goodness, that was quick. I—" Her words were cut short by the sight of Sister Jonah closing the door and bolting it.

She turned to look Annique over. "I see your adoring subjects have left you all alone. Pity." Her usual icy control had been replaced by a lurid, almost wanton, expression.

Annique never had felt comfortable around Sister Jonah, but now she sensed something brittle and dangerous in the older woman. Struggling to maintain the illusion of calm as a thrill of alarm raced through her, she kept her voice even. "Hello, Sister. Did you wish to speak with me?"

Sister Jonah mocked Annique's tone, exaggerating it into a simpering whine. "Yes, I wish to speak with you." She crossed to stand so close their toes touched, close enough for Annique to see the stains that marred her usually immaculate habit. The stench of neglect filled the air between them, prompting Annique to take a step backward.

Sister Jonah pushed against her. "Dear little Annique. Everybody's pet. Everybody's darling. Our precious little sister who dreamed of escaping all these years." Her fingers plucked randomly at the fabric of Annique's gown as her tone intensified. "Now you have lots of money . . .

and a title . . . and a home in the country . . . and a handsome, hot-blooded young husband." Madness hovered in her cold gray eyes.

For a fleeting moment, Annique wondered if Sister Jonah meant to kill her. The nun backed her against the windowsill. Annique felt the cold, unrelenting imprint of the iron grille against her back. She had to get away, but all the windows were barred. If only she could get past Sister Jonah and beat her to the bolted door. She sidestepped abruptly, but Sister Jonah matched her movements, blocking her escape.

The nun executed a chilling parody of a smile. "Now, now, Little Sister. Don't run away. I only want to talk." Keeping her eyes on Annique, she backed away to block the door with a heavy chair. She draped herself across the massive chair, propping one calf on its arm. "Now we can chat."

The woman was insane. Annique could see it now, and she knew better than to try to overpower her captor. Madness had its own unnatural strength.

Why was Sister Jonah doing this?

Trying to act casual, Annique stepped back into the slanting sunshine at the open window. If anyone came through the cloister below, she'd cry out for help, but for now she was trapped, and her best defense lay in taking the offense. She spoke to Sister Jonah as if she were addressing an insolent child. "What do you want?"

The nun let out a disconcerting chuckle. "I've come to give you a wedding gift, Little Sister. The truth will be my gift to you."

Lolling like a concubine, she pulled her crucifix from her belt and dangled it between them. "You asked about this once. It was a gift, a remembrance from the old king." She turned a feral smile on Annique. "I was his favorite. I knew how to please his majesty, and I knew how to get him to talk. When he was in his cups, he told me things, things Richelieu wanted kept secret, things no one else at Court knew. I know a lot of secrets, some of them about you."

She hung the crucifix on the arm of the chair, then looked up, her eyes challenging. "As I recall, you always were insufferably curious. Haven't you ever wondered about yourself—who you really are, how you came here?"

Part of Annique warned her not to listen, but a bigger

part of her could not resist. She took the bait. "What secrets? What do you know?"

Sister Jonah bounced the foot dangling over the arm of the chair. As her sandal flapped to the floor, Annique saw that she wore no stockings. "Why don't we start with your parents?"

"What about them?" A fresh wave of warning rose within Annique. "They died of the plague."

"That's rich." The older woman kicked off her other sandal. "Plague! Did you really believe that?" She pulled off her veil. "They didn't die of the plague. They were murdered, shot through with a dozen arrows as they rode along in their carriage." Slowly unlacing the cowl that covered her skull, she mused, "Nice assassination, that. Clean, quick, quiet. Very well done, except for one thing." She sighed, the way one might when having to turn down a dinner invitation. "They didn't kill everyone. Botched it with you." She tapped her heart. "You were shot, of course. Right here. But you didn't die."

Annique's breathing quickened, her hand flying instinctively to the fresh scar that throbbed between her breasts. "You're insane, making this up! It *can't* be true! There was no scar there when I was a child! I don't remember any—"

Sister Jonah interrupted. "Unfortunately for everyone concerned, you were only stunned, saved by a little book of poems your mother had stuffed into your coat."

The book of Latin poetry in her coffer! The hole that pierced it was just the right size . . . But how could Sister Jonah know about . . . ?

Unless she was telling the truth.

All her life Annique had prayed for a past, had longed for an end to secrets and lies. Now that she had the truth, it came as something huge and dark, swallowing her self-control and leaving her helpless and exposed. Suddenly she felt like a little child, terrified and alone in the midst of chaos.

The whinnies of panicked carriage horses echoed inside her head. In an effort to drown out the phantom cries, Annique covered her ears and cried, "You're making it all up, trying to punish me because I'm happy now. I don't have to listen to this." Eyes squeezed shut, she lifted her face into the strong rays of afternoon sun. The light filtered through her eyelids, flooding her vision with a red haze.

Red, everywhere. As red as the blood that had spurted into her face from her mother's chest. Blood. The smell of it filled her nostrils. She spun back around and stared wide to banish the vision, but the metallic stench remained, as real as it had been to the three-year-old who had vainly tried to awaken her blood-soaked parents in the careening carriage.

Annique forced herself to remain upright despite the crushing weight that lay like a gravestone upon her chest.

Sister Jonah seemed curiously indifferent to her reaction. For the moment she was preoccupied with removing the linen cowl that covered her skull. Once the laces were free, she pulled it off, exposing a plaited coil of pale blond hair that uncurled from the base of her neck. She dropped the wrinkled cowl to the floor beside her discarded veil.

Annique gasped. "Your hair! But they must have cut it when you took your final vows! How—"

The nun gave her braid a loving stroke. "Every day, it grows." Then her eyes narrowed as she focused on Annique. "You needn't be so sanctimonious. I know what goes on at Court, and I know what a hypocritical little wanton you are. How dare you judge *me?*" She sat up straight in the chair, her bare feet firmly planted on the floor. "You don't like the truth, do you? Well, there's more, yet.

"Your parents were murdered in broad daylight, and I know who was behind it." A cunning smile shaped her lips. "It was your father's first cousin, Marshal Harcourt."

Annique felt as if something had sucked all the air out of her lungs. Philippe's father! If that were true, then Philippe . . . No, he couldn't have known of this treachery! Or could he?

Sister Jonah continued pouring out her poison. "Always was a greedy fellow, Harcourt, and very jealous of your father. The marshal never forgave him for being the one who inherited the duchy, not to mention their grandmother's jewels." As she spoke, she jerked off the starched collar of her habit. "Such a stupid, inconsequential little duchy." She flung the collar toward the window, but it drifted aimlessly to the floor. "Harcourt wanted your mother, too, but she rejected him. He didn't give up, even after she married your father, but still she spurned him. Of course, Harcourt wasn't a marshal then; he was just a sneaky little schemer who did Richelieu's dirty work. Now that Richelieu's dead, he does Mazarin's dirty work."

She seemed to lose her train of thought, then picked it up again. "I can't fault your mother for rejecting his suit in favor of your father's—after all, the title was his—but she was stupid not to oblige Harcourt with a harmless liaison. Instead, she spat in his face." Sister Jonah smiled in triumph. "That little bit of arrogance cost her her life."

She shifted forward. "And you. He thought he had gotten rid of you, too, but you were only stunned, saved by that little book of poetry. I guess that's what you'd call poetic justice." Her humorless laugh echoed through the room.

Annique leaned heavily against the table. She wouldn't give Sister Jonah the satisfaction of seeing her collapse.

Sister Jonah's fingers fumbled with the knot that secured her rope belt to her waist. When it finally loosened, she dropped the cord to the floor. All the while she kept talking, her manner detached one minute, deadly the next. "I don't think Harcourt cared as much about the title as he did about the jewels. And the treasury. The funny thing is, he never found the treasury *or* the jewels. Turned the place upside down after the assassination, but the gold and the Corbay emeralds were nowhere to be found." She stood and pulled her apron off over her head. "Of course, he hadn't realized how many powerful friends your father had at Court. There was such an outcry over the killings that Harcourt dared not take over the duchy himself, for fear of arousing suspicions. So he waited. The marshal is a very patient man."

The woman was coming unraveled before Annique's eyes, yet everything she said made perfect sense. Every revelation was a weapon, lethal and accurate. Annique had to stop her, or she might go mad herself. She uttered, "Please stop. This accomplishes nothing. I don't know anything about any treasury, or any jewels."

Sister Jonah exhaled impatiently. Then she gripped the neckline of her coarse gown and ripped. Like a butterfly leaving its cocoon, she stepped—naked and preening— free of the last vestment.

Morbid fascination prevented Annique from looking

away from the pale perfection of the body that had once captured the heart of a king. Sister Jonah's white skin was unmarred by a single blemish or freckle. Her breasts were full and firm, almost like a girl's, and her elegant limbs retained a pleasing roundness.

The nun executed a coquettish pirouette before settling her crucifix around her neck. She lifted the cross to her lips and kissed it, then dropped it between her breasts. Her voice hardened. "Where do you think your dowry came from, you impertinent little fool? Do you really believe that anyone, even Harcourt's second son, would have considered a marriage without one?" She slid her hands seductively down her hips.

Ashamed for both of them, Annique looked away. The cloister was still deserted. Where was Mother Bernard? Surely Father Jules was back by now. Surely they would discover the door locked and put an end to this travesty. She choked out, "Philippe couldn't have known. Not about my parents."

Sister Jonah advanced, the sour smell of her unwashed body causing Annique to gag. "Of course Philippe knew! He told me so when he came here. When he came into my room. Into my bed." Her chin lifted in sly triumph.

Annique's heart beat faster, her mind shaping a hideous image of Philippe's hard, hungry body intertwined with Sister Jonah's. "You're lying! Philippe would never do that!" She retreated a step. "I don't know why Philippe's father arranged the marriage, but Philippe couldn't have known about my parents. He's not that kind of man."

Sister Jonah hissed, "He's *just* that kind of man. Like father, like son. They're users, both of them. Philippe has secured his title, but he still hasn't found the jewels. He needs you for that. But once he's gotten what he wants from you, he'll throw you away. Just as I was thrown away." She stopped abruptly and shook loose her braid, then ran her fingers through the wavy blond curtain that spilled across her shoulder.

The gesture seemed to calm her. She looked up with renewed clarity. "Now where was I? Oh, yes. The assassination. When the carriage returned to Maison Corbay bearing you and your dead parents, the servants found you covered in blood. They hid you away and sent for your only remaining close relative, an uncle." She began to pace back and forth, keeping between Annique and the door. "Harcourt hadn't bothered to eliminate him, because he couldn't lay claim to the estate. He was a priest, you see. He brought you here, where he could watch over you."

As if in divine confirmation, Father Jule's voice followed a dull knock on the door. "Annique? Are you there?"

Father Jules. Her uncle!

❧ CHAPTER 32 ❧

*S*ister Jonah sat back down in the chair. "Aren't you going to answer him? After all, he's your uncle—the same man who arranged your marriage to the son of your parents' murderer."

The truth cut through Annique like the blade of a rusty sword—jagged, tearing, and mortal. Father Jules—her mentor, her teacher, her confessor and friend—her uncle, and her betrayer.

For more than a decade Annique had longed to fill the aching void of her unknown past. Now Sister Jonah had done it for her, not with comfort, but with a legacy of treachery, greed, manipulation, and deceit.

More knocking preceded Mother Bernard's voice. "Sister Jonah! On peril of your immortal soul, let me in at once!"

When the naked woman failed to react, Annique shouted past her, "Sister Jonah has gone mad! She's locked the door and taken off all her clothes. She won't let me out!"

Heavy thumping accompanied both the priest's and the abbess's renewed commands for Sister Jonah to open up, but the nun took her own sweet time in responding. She stretched, then rose and slowly began to collect the scattered pieces of her discarded habit. As she neatly folded each item of clothing before draping it over her arm, she raised her voice to be heard through the door. "And how will you punish me this time, Mother?" She rolled her eyes. "Do you really think I *care* what you do to me? My soul has already been damned." She glanced derisively around the room. "I began serving my sentence in hell twelve years ago. Nothing you do to me will make it any better. Or any worse."

With that she shoved the chair aside, stepped to the door and threw open the bolt, then aimed a look of satisfaction at Annique. "I've enjoyed our little *tête-à-tête.*" Then she pulled open the door and stood—brazen and unbowed in her nakedness—confronting a shocked priest and mother superior.

Father Jules turned his face to the wall. "Merciful Father! Woman, have you no shame?"

Mother Bernard's reaction was more pragmatic. She snatched the folded clothing from Sister Jonah's arm. "I might have known something like this would happen!" Directing her anger at the priest, the abbess shook loose the torn dress and draped it front-to-back over Sister Jonah's shoulders. "I *told* you she was unstable. We should have sent her back to the Mother House months ago."

Now compliant, Sister Jonah stared vacantly into space. But as Mother Bernard led her into the hall, she turned a last look of triumph on the priest. "I told her everything, Jules. She knows who you are, and what you did to her."

Father Jules's features contorted. He rushed into the study, his arms outstretched. "Are you all right? Did she harm you?"

Annique recoiled. "It's true, then, what she said. All of it. I can see it in your face." The agony in his eyes only confirmed what she already knew.

He went very still. "I wanted to tell you, but you were safer not knowing. Lying to you all those years was the hardest thing I've ever done. But I'd do it again, even knowing that you would hate me for it, if that was what it took to keep you safe."

His eyes begged her to understand, but Annique was still suffering the searing effects of what she had heard. Like the red-hot poker that Philippe had plunged clear through her hand, the truth had pierced her to the core, scarring her forever. She was numb now, but soon the pain would come. She had to know everything before then. "Why? Why would you ally me to the family that killed my parents, killed your own brother?"

He sank into a nearby chair. "What else could I do? When I learned that Harcourt had discovered you were alive, I knew it was only a matter of time until he found you here. He'd have gone to Mazarin, and the cardinal would have made short work of locating you. I had to do something to assure your safety, and quickly."

He rose and began to pace. "The marriage seemed to be your only hope. Merging the bloodlines gave Harcourt the satisfaction of seeing the title and estates brought into his own lineage at last—legally and indisputably. And the alliance protected your birthright, restoring you to the home you'd lost." He stopped pacing. "Philippe's father is an evil man, but shrewd. Finding and eliminating you would have been costly, and not without risk. So he agreed to the match, instead."

"And Philippe?" The very mention of his name awakened a stab of pain inside her. "Did he know who I really was, what his father had done to my parents?" Her voice tightened. "The truth!"

Father Jules looked at her with infinite compassion. "The truth is, I don't know. I'd like to be able to tell you he didn't, but there have been enough lies already. I won't add the weight of another to my soul." He sighed deeply. "He might know nothing. He might have been aware of everything from the beginning."

The last remnant of feeling died within her. "He knows. I've sensed it hanging between us like a shadow. I've seen it in his eyes, pulling him away from happiness." Her voice sharpened. "Sister Jonah says Philippe slept with her when he was here last. Is that true, too?"

Father Jules recoiled. "Don't be absurd! Mother Bernard had him watched from the moment he entered the convent. She'd never have allowed anything like that to . . ."

"Never say never, Father. You taught me that. And you taught me that anyone is capable of anything, given the right circumstances." The room had gone cold and airless. Annique clutched her arms tightly against her chest and stepped to the sunlight at the open window.

She heard the priest approach behind her. "Philippe isn't like his father. I would never have proposed the alliance, otherwise. He had as little choice in the matter as you did. It was his father who agreed to the match and obtained the queen's approval." He extended his hand. "Give him a chance. Mother Bernard tells me that you love your husband, and he loves you. That's a rare blessing in marriage. Hold onto it. Don't let the past destroy your happiness."

She turned, an anger cold as ice stealing the life from her bones. "Philippe doesn't love me. He was only using me to get to the jewels." She let out a bitter chuckle. "But the joke's on him. There are no jewels." The irony of that one truth appealed to her greatly.

Her uncle shook his head. "But there are."

"What!"

"There are, and you've had them all along. The Corbay jewels are hidden in a secret compartment of the chest containing your father's books. I had hoped you would find them after reading my note. You did not realize there was a hidden message?"

"No," Annique confessed flatly.

He scanned the room, his priestly calm slipping slightly. "You still have the coffer, don't you?"

Annique had thought herself beyond further pain, but this last revelation still had the power to sting. "Jewels hidden in my coffer? Secret messages?" She glared at him. "Do you mean to tell me that you *left* me—without a word of warning or farewell—in the care of the very man who had my parents assassinated, without telling me something as important as *that?* For all you knew, I might have sold the coffer, or given it away!"

He folded his hands and said quietly, "I knew you wouldn't." A hint of worry crept into his voice. "You didn't sell it, did you?"

"No! I didn't sell it! I still have it." She lifted a shaking fist in frustration. "Coward! How I despise you for leaving me like that, and for the way you've used me, all of you! My whole life is a lie—everything I thought I'd gained, everything I thought I was!" Mindless fury boiled up inside her, taking her beyond words, beyond accusations.

Now she understood the hate in Sister Jonah's eyes. Now she knew why human beings murdered each other. The black tide of rage left her light-headed and queasy. Annique staggered sideways and sank to an upholstered bench.

Father Jules—Uncle Jules—hastened to her side. "Hate me if you must, but don't hate Mother Bernard. All she did was try to protect you from those who would harm you."

She retorted, "By subjecting me to Sister Jonah's cruelty?"

"That was *my* mistake." The priest shook his head, his shoulders sagging. "Mother tried her best to talk me out of putting you under Sister Jonah's tutelage, but I wouldn't listen." He sighed. "We had so little time to prepare you for your rightful place in society. Mother Bernard couldn't do it; she had to run the convent. Sister Jonah seemed the logical choice." Suddenly he looked small to her, and very old. "I had no idea she was so cruel, so unstable."

Annique snuffed out a last twinge of sympathy by withdrawing even further into the burned-out shell of what had once been her heart. She turned away. "Perhaps I should go mad, as well. It seems to excuse a multitude of sins."

Before the priest could reply, there was a commotion in the hallway. Philippe appeared outside the doorway with Sister Thomas tugging vainly on his arm. She and Sister Matthias tried to block his way into the study. She cried, "Your grace, this is most improper! I must insist that you return to the common rooms at once. Your presence here violates the hospitality of this community and—"

He silenced her with a growl. "Let go of me, woman. I'll not leave without the duchess." He shoved past them and into the study, then looked from the priest to his ashen-faced wife. "Anne-Marie, Suzanne just told me that some lunatic had barricaded herself in here with you. Is everything all right?"

Sister Thomas pushed Sister Matthias back out into the hallway and dispatched her with a whispered, "Quickly! Fetch Mother at once!" Then she started toward Annique but was stopped in midstride by a scalding look of warning from Philippe. The nun backed away. "I'll just wait for Mother Bernard here by the door."

Annique tried to speak, but her throat had gone dry. She choked out, "Go away, Philippe. Leave me alone." She fixed an unfocused stare on his puzzled face. "All of you. Just leave me alone."

Father Jules stepped between them. "Come, my son. Perhaps we should do as she asks."

"Why? What's happened?" Philippe shoved past him and knelt on one knee in front of Annique, taking her cold hands into his warm ones. "Why are you looking at me that way?"

She snatched free of him. "I know the truth, Philippe, all of it." When she saw fear dawn in his eyes—and guilt along with it—a strange aloofness settled over her, making it easier to speak. "Sister Jonah told me everything—how your father had my parents murdered and tried to kill me. How you took *my* title and estates, and when the two of you found out I was alive, you married me to assure your claim to *my* heritage."

A shocked whimper escaped Sister Thomas.

Annique's eyes narrowed as she studied the effect of her revelation on Philippe. If she didn't know better, she might have been swayed by the stunned incredulity she saw.

He stammered, "Your parents murdered? By my father? I've heard nothing of this! Who's told you such a thing?" She could almost see him piecing together what had happened. He flushed, his dark brows drawing together. "It was Sister Jonah, wasn't it? You told me she'd always hated you. And you believed her. But why? How could she possibly know the first thing about what happened to your parents? She'd been locked away in a convent for the past—"

Annique cut him off. "Sister Jonah just happened to have been the old king's favorite mistress when my parents were killed. She was privy to secrets at the highest level. And Father Jules, or should I say *Uncle Jules,* has confirmed her story."

Philippe pivoted to gape at the priest. "Your *uncle?*"

"Yes, my sole surviving kinsman, who kept me ignorant of my identity and my heritage, then arranged for me to marry the very person who'd stolen my birthright." She leveled a cool stare on her husband. "You, Philippe. The son of the man who thought he'd killed me along with my parents. But why am I telling you? I'm sure you already know the details."

Philippe's eyes darkened dangerously. "I know nothing of such a plot!" He grasped her upper arms, as if by taking hold of her he could make her believe him. "You don't have to tell me what kind of man my father is. I'd be the last to deny him capable of such a thing. But on my immortal soul, I swear my ignorance of this crime." He faltered. "I suspected he was up to something when he proposed the match, but for once, I decided to go along with him."

Annique wasn't listening. Her mind had turned inward, finding refuge in numbness.

Philippe didn't give up. "I needed the money, so I didn't ask any questions. I didn't know that Maison Corbay was rightfully yours until my father told me the night before you were injured. I swear it." He searched her face for some sign that he was getting through to her, but she acted sluggish and detached, almost as if she'd been drugged.

He spoke louder in an effort to rouse her. "That night I found out how my father had used us both. I hated him for it, and I told him so." Annique remained unresponsive. He was losing her. He kept talking. "The next day I was transferred to the front line of the battle. I thought Father had ordered it, to punish me for standing up to him at last. Even if I'd wanted to, I had no chance to tell you what I'd learned. The next time I saw you, you were almost dead, and I gave up everything in an effort to save you." He shook her slightly. "I'd do it again. But I couldn't let you know how much I cared for you."

Philippe didn't care that the priest was listening, or the silent nun who lingered near the hallway. He spoke his heart as if only he and Anne-Marie could hear. "You'd cost me my home, my career, my reputation. We'd lost our child, a son I wanted more than anything in life. And I was afraid I'd lose you, too. I couldn't bear to watch you die."

He might as well be talking to himself. Annique stared straight through him. His voice dropped. "Perhaps you did die, in a way." He remembered how she had come back to the living like a butterfly emerging, frail and trembling, from its shrouded cocoon to spread its wings for the first time. "The woman I came to know at the villa was not the angry, willful child I married. You had a new stillness, a confidence, an openness I'd never seen before. Was it grief that changed you so, or was it suffering?"

"Both." The tone of her unexpected response was as flat and dull as her eyes. "But that was when I still believed in life. And in truth. I don't anymore."

If he didn't do something to stop what was happening, nothing would remain of the woman he loved. His fingers dug into her flesh. "Believe in this, then: I love you. Don't throw away what we've found."

Annique knew the strength of his grasp should have hurt her, but she felt nothing.

Philippe went on, "I love *you!* It's the only good and honest thing to come from this terrible mess. Look at me. Hear what I'm saying. I love you." He didn't realize he was shaking her until Father Jules grabbed his wrists.

"Stop. You're hurting her! Can't you see she's insensible?"

Philippe released her and lurched to his feet.

Annique looked from him to the priest and spoke without emotion. "The only two men I ever loved, and both of you betrayed me."

Father Jules put his arm across Philippe's shoulders and tried to guide him toward the hallway. "Come, my son. Nothing will be solved by continuing this confrontation. Sister Thomas will care for her. If we stay, we'll only provoke her to say things she might regret later."

"Regret?" Annique's chuckle was as dry as dead leaves. She blinked at Philippe, resentful that he had pulled her from inner oblivion. She was tired, so tired, and she didn't know what to believe. Part of her wanted to take Philippe at his word, but the greater part warned that such trust would be fatal. How could she trust him, after what she'd learned? "My only regret is that I was so gullible. So many lies, from the beginning."

A single thought grew in her mind, a thought that smothered out the last embers of her anger and her pain. She could be safe alone. She would be safe alone.

Annique clung to the peace that came with that thought. She didn't have to decide what was true and what was not. She only needed to be alone, away from Philippe, the convent, Sister Jonah. Only then would she be safe, depending on no one, loving no one.

She faced Philippe calmly. "Please, just leave me alone. I won't tell you where the jewels are."

Philippe shrugged free of the priest. "Jewels? What jewels? What is she talking about?"

She felt a small sense of satisfaction at the pain and denial that flashed across his face. "I gave you my heart, Philippe, even when I thought you'd betrayed me with the Great Mademoiselle. Even when you rejected me, I loved you." She rose stiffly. "But you'll never have the Corbay jewels. They're my insurance. As long as I know where they are—and you and your father don't—I can make a life for myself alone." Her gaze pivoted to the priest. "Unless you plan a final betrayal by turning that last remnant of my heritage over to my loving husband."

Father Jules never took his eyes from Annique. "I would rather die than hurt you any further."

She knew better than to trust that look of abject sincerity. As soon as she could, she'd hide the jewels where only she could find them.

Philippe's hands clenched into fists at his side. "Anne-Marie, I know nothing of any jewels, just as I knew nothing about your parents' death."

He was a man unaccustomed to pleading. He had no skill for it, even when the thing he treasured most hung in the balance. The emptiness in her eyes told him that he had lost already. Begging would accomplish nothing. He lapsed into agonized silence.

The priest crossed himself. "May God forgive us for what we've done to you."

Annique exhaled raggedly. "Perhaps He shall, but I won't."

❈ CHAPTER 33 ❈

*F*our months later, a rare afternoon of late February sunshine brightened the bedroom of Annique's rented town house in Paris. Arms extended, she stood in the center of the carpet while Marie knelt beside her, tugging and pinning at the bodice of her ball gown. She glanced down. "I don't know how much longer I can stand like this. My arms are getting heavier by the minute."

Marie's frown of concentration deepened. "Just a few moments longer, your grace." She inserted one more pin. "It seems to me we could find at least *one* dressmaker in Paris who could keep her mouth shut. I fear I'm not much of a seamstress." She reared back on her haunches to survey the results of her efforts. "You can lower your arms now, madame. The sides are done. I'll try to be quicker with the back."

A long sigh escaped Annique as she let her arms drop. "You're doing a fine job, Marie, and I am most grateful." Careful pressing should remove the evidence that the bodice had been let out. "I dare not hire a seamstress. I think they *all* supplement their incomes by peddling gossip to the highest bidder." An involuntary shudder rippled up her spine. "It would be disastrous if word of my condition got out before I've told the duke."

Marie cocked a skeptical eyebrow. "He doesn't know yet? I thought your grace was going to tell his grace last week."

Annique glanced away from the mild reproach in Marie's eyes. She needed no reminder how dangerous it was to put off telling Philippe. "I was going to. I even sent Paoul to St. Germain to fetch him, but Paoul came back with word that my husband had gone to the country for a house party." Even now, Annique's cheeks burned with jealousy at the thought. She chided herself inwardly. Why should she care if Philippe had found companionship elsewhere? She was the one who had insisted he leave her.

After the disaster at the convent, the two of them had journeyed back to Paris in strained silence, returning to find that the marshal had arranged for Philippe to be appointed bodyguard to the queen at St. Germain. For once, Annique was grateful for her father-in-law's interference. The appointment restored Philippe's reputation while allowing her to put things in order at Maison Corbay alone. She'd come to Paris for the Season alone, as well.

But now Providence had intervened, forcing her to break the uneasy silence with Philippe. Annique sighed and rubbed her hand across the strained fabric at her waist. "I'll tell him. Soon."

She had no choice. Soon her figure would give her away. The news *must* come from her, not from the gossips. He had a right to know about the baby, even if telling him put an end to her autonomy.

Tomorrow. She'd write a note. That would be the simplest, least painful way to handle the matter.

But for now, she needed to concentrate on finishing the alterations to her gown in time for tonight's ball. Annique fingered the lace Marie had added to her collar, then smoothed her hand across the scattered pearls she herself had sewn to the green velvet overskirt. The dress wasn't new; she'd worn it to a ball in December. If anyone saw through the changes she and Marie had made, she'd be laughed at behind her back, but Annique couldn't bring herself to waste money on another ball gown that she would outgrow in just a few weeks.

She needed new clothes, ones that would see her through until her confinement. She'd have to sell more jewelry; that was all there was to it. Renting this apartment on the fashionable Place Royale and maintaining appearances had already gobbled up the small fortune she'd gotten for the few loose gems she'd found among the treasures crammed beneath the false bottom of her coffer. Annique hated to part with any of the sparkling heirlooms, but there were still the Corbay emeralds, plus two gold crucifixes with jeweled chains, twelve jeweled necklaces with matching earrings, six bracelets, seven ropes of pearls, a dozen jeweled brooches, and twenty-three rings left besides a handful of loose pearls and several unusual pieces whose function remained a mystery.

Perhaps the odd bits would generate enough money to pay for her clothes. Letting even those go was painful, for they were part of her birthright. But she'd sell the lot if she had to, rather than ask Philippe for a single sou. Not that her independence had turned out to be as satisfying as she'd hoped. The past few months had been lonely and restless, but safe. Perhaps she had been childish to expect more.

Annique spoke over her shoulder. "Marie, do you remember the jeweler's shop by the river? The man I sent for last November right after we moved to town for the Season?"

"Yes, your grace. The short fellow who wears spectacles?"

"That's him. When you've finished with my dress, please go to his shop and arrange for him to come here tomorrow at eleven. And remind him to use the back door. I don't want everyone on the block knowing my business." The truth was, she didn't want *Philippe* to know her business. Let him wonder how she was managing so well.

Was she managing so well without him? Even as she asked herself the question, Annique knew the answer was no. How could a person mistrust a man so much, yet ache with longing for him at the same time? It made no sense and left her soul-sick.

Every time she thought she'd purged herself of him, their paths would cross at some Court function, and the

sight of him with another woman would rip open wounds
that had never had a chance to heal. At least she had never
faced Philippe without a handsome man on her own arm.
She took some comfort from that. But she doubted her
husband even noticed—much less cared—that she had become the darling of the Season, pursued by every male at
Court with a bent for assignation. Philippe's response to
their unexpected meetings had always been cool and civilized.

He was nothing if not civilized; she had to give him
credit for that. And she had to give him credit for leaving
her alone, as she had asked. He hadn't even taken Jacques
and Suzanne with him to St. Germain.

Against her conscious will, Annique's mind conjured up
the image of his face as he'd bid her a stiff farewell at
Maison Corbay, the grim set of his jaw making him more
handsome than ever. She'd watched him go in bitter triumph, but all the while some perverse part of her had
wanted to call him back. Back to her arms, back to her
bed, back inside her. God help her, she still ached for him,
even while her lips cursed him.

Her life with him now seemed like a distant dream—or
nightmare, depending on which memories haunted her as
she lay alone in her bed.

In the last few months she'd had ample opportunity to
fill that empty bed with men far more honest about their
motives than Philippe had ever been. But she hadn't been
able to bring herself to consummate a single flirtation.
Something always stopped her at only a few kisses or a
fleeting embrace.

That part was the worst of all. No other man's kisses had
the power to move her as Philippe's had. No other man's
touch set her senses afire. No other arms could shut the
world away. He had ruined her for anyone else.

A peculiar flutter in her abdomen reminded her of the
one source of happiness she now clung to. She pressed her
hand over the life within her. She and Philippe had done at
least one thing right. They had made this child.

Marie spoke up from behind her. "Are you all right,
your grace? You're weaving back and forth."

"I'm fine, Marie. Carry on."

Carry on. That's what Annique had done for the last
four months. She'd made a place for herself at Court,

shamelessly cultivating relationships with the rich and powerful, quietly and relentlessly collecting secrets that could be of use to her one day. Already, she had made influential friends in every faction and learned enough to protect herself and her child no matter which way the political winds blew.

Her child. She would do nothing to risk this precious life. Annique turned slightly to consider her silhouette in the cheval mirror. Her once-slender torso had thickened noticeably, and her breasts swelled immodestly above the low collar of her blouse.

Marie let out an exasperated sigh. "I'll never finish, your grace, if you keep shiftin' about. And I'll not be able to let this dress out again. There's barely enough seam to hold the stitching."

"Perhaps you'd better stitch it twice then, just to be safe," Annique declared. One more look in the mirror only confirmed what she already knew. "This ball will have to be the last of the Season for me. I can't hide my condition any longer. My dress is so tight, I'm wondering how I'll manage tonight. Heaven help me if I sneeze! The seams will explode, and there I'll be, standing in my chemise in front of the entire Court."

Marie chuckled at the prospect, and Annique joined in, dislodging a pin that pricked her side. "Ouch! Oh, quickly, get me out of this blessed bodice! I can hardly breathe."

"Right away, your grace." Marie deftly unhooked the hidden fastenings.

When the last closure was loosened, Annique inhaled deeply. "Whew! That's a relief." She began unbuttoning her blouse. "If all goes well with the jeweler, we'll start packing tomorrow afternoon. I can have my new clothes made in the country."

A smile of pure delight transformed Marie's plain face to almost pretty. "Back to Maison Corbay? Oh, I'm so glad!"

Annique knew why Marie was so eager to return to Maison Corbay: Pierre, Suzanne's oldest son. She couldn't resist teasing, "On second thought, maybe it would be better if you remained here to see to the town house."

"But . . . but . . . won't you need me more in the country? I mean, with no one here, what will I have to do?

I can cover everything up with dust cloths before we leave, and Paoul will make sure the house is locked up tight."

"Your reluctance to remain in Paris wouldn't have anything to do with a certain young footman, would it? Now what was his name again?"

Marie colored deeply. "Pierre, mistress. I mean, your grace. It's Pierre."

The moment Suzanne's lanky son and Marie had set eyes on each other, they were both smitten. Their happiness was only one of the reasons Annique was glad she'd sent for Suzanne and Jacques' lively brood. Maison Corbay had seemed so empty, so quiet after Philippe had left. Suzanne's children had brought life and noise to the place in the month she'd remained there to put things in order before returning to Court.

Annique stepped out of her skirts. "I know his name's Pierre. I was only teasing." She smiled wistfully. "He's a good fellow—a hard worker, and bright—and it's obvious he adores you. You have my blessings." She raised an eyebrow. "And you could certainly do worse for a mother-in-law than Suzanne."

Marie's embarrassment evaporated. She grumbled, "I'm not so sure of that, ma'am. It's been pretty peaceful here in Paris without her around to boss me about."

"Oh, you miss her as much as I do. Don't try to pretend you don't." The cook Annique had hired in Paris lacked Suzanne's irreverent wit and her talent for making the most of simple foods, but Annique didn't regret her decision to leave Suzanne and Jacques in charge of Maison Corbay. She hadn't had the heart to separate the family so soon after they'd been reunited. "It will be good to see them again. And the children." Her voice dropped to a whisper. "It will be good to go home."

Brightening, she laid her skirts across Marie's arms. "Don't worry about Suzanne. She loves you as much as I do. I know she'll approve of the match, no matter what noises she makes at first." The gratitude in Marie's eyes caused Annique's throat to tighten.

"Bless you, ma'am. And thank you."

Annique shooed her toward the door, her own voice husky with emotion. "Now run along and finish my dress. And don't forget to send for the jeweler." As she watched

Marie leave, her smile faded. *Poor girl. She'll find out soon enough what pain love inevitably brings.*

At the ball that evening, the only outward evidence of Philippe's impatience was the fixed smile he maintained as the Duchess of Brecy droned on and on about nothing in particular. They'd been waiting twenty minutes already to be presented, and half a dozen couples remained ahead of them.

Behind his carefully controlled smile, his teeth were clamped together so hard his jaw was beginning to ache. *Blast!* Why in blazes had he ever let Henri badger him into escorting this creature to the ball, even if she *was* Patrice's sister? Philippe had no stomach for these brittle, exhausting entertainments. His eyes settled on the voluptuous blonde chattering away beside him. At least the duchess was attractive, and far more pleasant than her sister, Henri's waspish wife.

And she was willing. He noted the smooth perfection of the forearm that rested in his palm. She had made it known in no uncertain terms that the ball and supper following would just be a prelude to the evening's delights, if he wished. But Philippe did not wish.

Once he would have jumped at the chance, but not anymore. Now such momentary, meaningless seductions seemed empty and degrading. He could blame Anne-Marie for that. Their love—brief and troubled though it had been—had changed him, making mere shadows of anything that had come before or would ever come again.

Philippe frowned. He had reached an uneasy truce with his father, but not with his wife. Even months after she'd rejected his explanations and asked him to leave, he still wasn't free of her. The woman had bewitched him.

The only company he craved tonight was a good bottle of brandy, and he preferred the sanctuary of his study to the boudoirs of Paris. If he was lucky, the Duchess of Brecy would find another more willing companion at the ball. Until then, he would have to pretend to be having a good time.

Philippe was very good at pretending these days. It was what he did best. Pretending not to miss Maison Corbay. Pretending that he wasn't lonely in St. Germain without even Jacques and Suzanne's comforting presence. Pretending that he didn't long for his wife every night, no matter how much he drank, no matter how many women he kissed then discarded.

The Duke of Verigny tightened his grip on Annique's arm as he led her up the grand staircase just inside the royal palace. "Forgive me, my dear. I forget that sometimes these long legs set too quick a pace."

Lacking wind for a reply, Annique could only smile and nod. Saints, but her gown was tight, and her heart was pounding faster than a cobbler's hammer. She probably shouldn't have skipped her midday meal, but she'd been afraid there wasn't room for even a bowl of soup inside her dress, despite Marie's alterations.

She leaned heavily on her escort's arm in an effort to steady herself. A flicker of lust in his eyes told her that he'd mistaken the gesture for encouragement. Annique quailed. She certainly didn't feel up to dodging his advances on the coach ride home. The duke was infamous for his sexual prowess, and he had been one of her most ardent—and challenging—pursuers. On more than one occasion, she had barely escaped his coach with her clothing intact.

Perhaps she should have canceled tonight. She'd thought about it, but hadn't wanted to risk offending the duke. He was an influential man, one who loved to drink and boast. And when he drank and boasted, he gave away many interesting—and useful—tidbits. Annique tried to muster up a convincing smile. "Do forgive my slowness, but I'm saving my energy for our first dance."

On the landing above them, Philippe nodded absently in response to the Duchess of Brecy's whispered comment about the couple ahead of them in line. Under different circumstances, her wit might have amused him, but in his current state, he found her tedious.

Her next observation, however, captured his attention fully. She arched a golden brow and murmured behind her fan, "Ah. Look who's just arrived with the Duke of Verigny. That's your wife, isn't it? I seem to recall seeing the two of them together quite a lot lately."

In spite of himself, Philippe turned and watched their progress across the foyer below. The magnificent Corbay emeralds filled the graceful arc of Anne-Marie's neckline, her coloring a perfect setting for the green fire and surrounding diamonds. As always, she bore herself regally but without arrogance. And as always, Philippe barely noticed the jewels for the wearer.

Gods! Why did he torture himself by looking? She was lovelier than ever, her cheeks flushed, her body voluptuous. Obviously, life without him agreed with her.

His gaze swung to the man beside her. Verigny had no sense of discretion; he was a scoundrel, a loudmouth known for his barracks tales of amorous adventures. Seeing him touch Anne-Marie caused the bile to rise in Philippe's throat. Was she the subject of Verigny's latest boasts? Philippe vowed to find out. He had friends in the guard who would tell him the truth. If Verigny had sullied Anne-Marie's honor, with or without cause, he was a dead man.

Annique trudged resolutely toward the landing, where a glittering line of courtiers waited to be presented. Suddenly the perfumed atmosphere of the foyer became close and cloying, and the steady buzz of conversation seemed to recede, then grow unnaturally loud. By the time she reached the top of the stairs, she was seeing tiny sparks of light at the edges of her vision. She gasped out softly, "Forgive me, sir, but I believe I need to sit down. I feel a bit light-headed."

The Duchess of Brecy laid a perfectly manicured hand on Philippe's arm. "How nice for you both, that your wife's found a friend. And such an *accomplished* friend at that."

The sly remark raised Philippe's temper to a slow boil. Then he remembered Verigny's account of a particularly unorthodox escapade with the duchess, herself. He turned to her and smiled. "Accomplished, indeed. Verigny is famous for his storytelling. I recall a particular anecdote about a certain duchess and a swing." The duchess paled. "He has entertained the entire barracks on many a night with tales of his . . . exploits."

Flushing, she fanned herself in earnest, her eyes darting nervously to the top of the stairs as Verigny and Anne-Marie reached the landing. Then her fan stilled. "Perhaps you'd better turn around, Philippe. Your wife has just pitched headlong into her *accomplished* escort's arms."

He turned to see Verigny lift an unconscious Anne-

Marie into his arms. Philippe bowed briefly to the duchess. "I beg your leave, madame."

She let out a resigned sigh. "Of course. You must go to her." Spotting an unencumbered male nearby, she dismissed Philippe. "I'm sure the Viscount of Nances will be happy to keep me company while you're gone."

The viscount was young, penniless, and ambitious and would doubtless welcome her advances. Philippe strode across the landing. Though the assembled courtiers pretended not to notice his progress, he knew better. His genuine concern for his wife was tempered by resentment that her collapse had made them both the center of attention. The gossips would feast on this for weeks!

Then a twist of fear overrode his annoyance. What if she were, indeed, ill? His steps quickened, taking him past the last curious courtier and within reach of Verigny. Philippe offered the briefest of bows. "Sir, I thank you for attending to my wife, but I shall take care of her now." As Verigny transferred her into his arms, Philippe noted with relief that her color was good. She was breathing easily.

Verigny stepped back and said archly, "I've seen enough artificial swoons to know the real thing. I pray the lady is not ill, Corbay."

The prospect alarmed Philippe more than he cared to admit, but he maintained his decorum. "You need not concern yourself, sir." Anxious to escape public scrutiny, he turned his back and carried her into a nearby salon. Inside, a tall screen blocked the room from prying eyes.

Philippe would have liked to hold her forever, but he laid his wife on a satin-covered chaise and sat beside her, chafing her wrist. It felt so good to be near her, to touch her, to drink in her scent. He only prayed she was not ill. "Anne-Marie? Can you hear me?"

Her lashes fluttered, then opened. For the barest moment, he thought she was glad to see him, but then her features became guarded.

"Philippe? Where did you come from? How—"

He interrupted gently, "You swooned. Are you ill? Does anything hurt?"

Abruptly, she colored and sat up, withdrawing her hand. "Oh, dear. How embarrassing." She turned great, dark eyes toward him. "I didn't mean for you to find out this way. I sent Paoul for you last week, but you were at a house party in the country somewhere—"

Philippe's stomach tightened. "You *are* ill."

Anne-Marie laid a reassuring hand on his. "No." She seemed to be groping for words, her eyes searching his. Then she said, "I'm not ill. I'm expecting our child."

Philippe could no more control the surge of relief that overtook him than he could have snuffed out the sun. He pulled her to him and held her tight. "God, thank God." Then he let the words sink in.

His heart pounding with joy, he murmured against her hair, "Another child. Don't you see? This is another chance for us. We're meant to be together, you and I." But she lay so still against him, her hands unmoving on his back. Philippe drew apart to look at her, and what he saw broke his heart.

There was no anger in her eyes, only sorrow.

Annique looked up at her husband. "Oh, Philippe, I wish it could be that simple, but it isn't." After all the lies, she refused to offer anything but the truth. "I still haven't sorted out what I believe about everything that happened. I'm not even sure, anymore, that it matters." Her voice faltered slightly. "I do love you, but I cannot be a wife to you. Not the way you want, not now. Not . . . yet."

How could she make him understand? Annique no longer needed, or wanted, to hurt him, but she could see the pain her words inflicted. She smoothed the kidskin glove that covered her injured hand. "When I first awoke after I was injured, I thought my hand was ruined forever. I was wrong. The healing process was long and painful, but my hand is useful again. Scarred, but functional." She inhaled deeply, her gaze pinned to his. "Maybe our marriage can be the same. I don't know. All I know is that I'm not ready to be with you, or *anyone,* yet. I need more time to sort things through. That's all I ask of you now."

Philippe had no defense against her quiet, wounded request. He understood why she was pushing him away, but how long would it take for her to realize what he already knew? No matter how much either of them kicked against the traces, destiny had yoked them together. And he could only be patient so long. A surge of frustration and anger rose inside him, but he managed to remain outwardly calm. "Time won't change the fact that I love you, and you love me." Philippe sighed, knowing what he must do. "Still, if it's time you want, time you shall have."

He briefly caressed her upper arms, then rose. "But does that mean you will deny me my child? Doesn't he deserve to have his father with him?"

Annique looked stricken. "Of course, our child deserves a father. And you deserve to know him." Unshed tears glistened in her eyes. "Regardless of our troubles, I will not deny either of you that."

His heart aching, Philippe memorized the sight of her, so near, yet separated by such a gulf he wondered if they would ever breach it. He had reached out as far as he could from his side. The rest was up to her.

He bowed. "Then I shall leave you, madame, not because I want to, but because you ask it. But I'm not giving up." He turned and exited without looking back.

❧ CHAPTER 34 ❧

*A*nnique closed her book and yawned when she heard the hall clock strike twice. She'd marked the chimes since midnight, each time hoping that she'd be asleep before the clock sounded again, but tonight even reading hadn't lulled her. The child within her kicked and moved constantly, keeping her awake.

A particularly vigorous kick prompted her to rub her enormous belly and mutter a scolding whisper. "Just you wait, my little owl. Once you're born, Suzanne will get your days turned right, and I'll get a good night's sleep at last."

Or a last sleep. Many women died in childbirth.

Brushing the thought aside, Annique chided herself for growing morbid so soon after she'd resolved to concentrate only on the most positive possibilities. For now, she needed to concentrate on getting some sleep. Trying to find a comfortable position, she shifted the pillows propped behind her. Dawn was only a few hours away. If she didn't get a nap, at least, she'd be useless tomorrow. Today.

Maybe if she put out the light. She rolled clumsily to reach beyond the open bed curtains and retrieve the snuffer, then swatted at the flame until the candle surrendered and left her in darkness.

Ten minutes later she was still wide-awake and feeling far too warm. Despite the cool May night, her room was stuffy. She threw aside the covers and eased out of bed, puffing breathlessly at even that small effort. Saints! If the baby kept growing like this for the remaining two months of her pregnancy, she'd have no breath left to push it out!

She lumbered slowly through the darkness until she reached the draperies, then pushed aside the heavy curtains and opened the window. There was no moon tonight, but at least she could get some fresh air. A soft breeze blew across the gardens below, bringing with it the distant sounds of frogs and insects and rustling trees. She lifted her face to the wind and inhaled a cool perfume of hyacinths, moist grass, and fresh-turned soil.

Then her ears picked up the muffled crunch of wheels on the graveled driveway. Annique froze. Thank goodness she'd put out the light. Maybe they hadn't seen her at the window.

Retreating into her darkened room, she heard someone stirring downstairs, inside the house. The hairs on the back of her neck rose even as she told herself it was probably just one of the children raiding the larder. Swiftly as she dared, she groped her way back to the end of her bed and donned her dressing gown. No sooner had she tied the ribbons at the neck than she heard footsteps outside her door, followed by insistent knocking.

"Your grace? It's Paoul. Forgive me for disturbing your grace at such an hour, but someone is here."

She overlapped the lightweight silk of her robe across her bulging belly. "Come in."

Mumbling in irritation, a disheveled Paoul shuffled in, his progress lit by a single candle. "It's indecent, that's what it is. No respectable person goes calling at this hour of the night, and I told 'em so, but no. Have to see her grace. Wake no one else, or the guards will put me to the sword." He straightened. "If *she* hadn't come in just then, I'd have raised the household!"

She? Annique's mind raced. Who in heaven's name would seek her out at such an hour, and why? She could think of several possibilities—all of them frightening. "Paoul, what are you talking about? Who is it?"

"Sorry, your grace, but I couldn't see the lady. She's cloaked, her face hidden." His grizzled features crumbled.

"If I hadn't been half asleep, I'd never have opened the door in the first place. Forgive me, your grace. I—"

"Never mind that, now. Where is she? Did you see how many guards there were?"

He waved his candle toward the foyer. "She's waitin' down there now. Sent the guard back to the coach. It was pretty dark, but I think I saw two more guards on the coach, and several mounted beside it."

Annique stroked clammy palms down her cheeks. "Listen carefully and do as I say." There was no time to waste. She tugged open the top drawer of a nearby chest and extracted the loaded dueling pistols she'd kept there since Philippe had left. "Take the back stairs and waken Jacques and Pierre. Quietly! Give Jacques this pistol." She thrust it into his hand. "I'll keep the other one hidden in my robe. Tell Pierre to alert the grooms. Have them stand ready to overtake the coach, but don't let the guards know."

Paoul nodded.

Annique lifted the glass chimney from a nearby lamp and lit it with Paoul's candle. "You and Jacques sneak into the great hall and keep an eye on what's happening inside. If I need help, I'll cry out." She inched open the door and peered into the empty hall beyond. Still barefooted, she stepped into the hallway and motioned Paoul toward the back stairs. Her own progress would cover the sound of his leaving.

She took a deep breath, raised her lamp, and started for the landing. As she neared the railing, the sound of pacing—close-spaced and light of tread—rose from the foyer. A woman's steps, all right. Annique could think of only one woman who would travel at night with a contingent of guards, but that wasn't possible. That woman was under house arrest more than thirty miles away.

Tucking the pistol out of sight in the folds of her robe, she extended her lamp for a look at the figure below.

The midnight caller stopped pacing and looked up, her features concealed in the deep hood of her opulent cape.

Annique didn't have to see her face to know who it was. Suddenly conscious of her bare feet and her clumsy girth, she summoned up her dignity and made her way carefully down the stairs. As she passed the portrait she had rescued from the attic, Annique looked up into the image of her mother's face and said a silent prayer. *Help me, Mother. If you're watching over me from heaven, intercede to protect me—and your unborn grandchild.* She reached the bottom step before she trusted herself to speak without betraying fear. "Good evening, your highness—or should I say good morning? To what do I owe the honor of this . . . most unusual visit?"

Gloved hands drew back the velvet hood, exposing the Great Mademoiselle's golden hair and haughty expression. "I see that you're wearing your insolence more openly these days, Corbay. I find it most unbecoming." Looking her disheveled hostess up and down, the princess daintily extracted her fingers, one at a time, from her leather gloves. "Must I stand here all night? Or have you forgotten your manners entirely?"

Annique colored. The woman had arrived unannounced in the middle of the night with armed guards, and now she expected to be received as if she'd dropped in for a cup of chocolate. Well, Annique was in no mood to play games. She straightened, her posture calling attention to her condition. "It is not *I,* your highness, who seems to have forgotten my manners."

The royal eyes narrowed. "Guard your tongue, Corbay. You should be grateful that I come as I do. And the hour does not excuse your keeping me waiting like a peddler."

Annique stared at her guest. Everyone at Court knew the princess had been banished to her derelict estate at St. Fargeau, barred from returning to Paris by both the king and her own father. Why had she come here? And what was Annique going to do next? She couldn't ask the princess into the salon. Without a servant to open the heavy doors, she'd be forced to do it herself, revealing the fact that she was armed. Annique curtsied deeply to cover her indecision.

They'd have to remain in the foyer; that was all there was to it. Regaining her composure, she rose from her curtsy and crossed to a pair of upholstered chairs that flanked a small table. Annique lifted her lamp above the chair that faced away from the great hall. "I regret that the lateness of the hour prevents me from entertaining you properly, your highness, but please do be seated."

"I shall sit, but only because you are obviously in no condition to remain standing yourself." Glaring at Annique's swollen belly with a curious mixture of pain and contempt, the princess sat and motioned for Annique to join her.

The lamp shook slightly as Annique placed it on the table between them. Careful to keep the pistol out of sight, she lowered herself into the chair.

The Great Mademoiselle leaned back, her features impassive as the silence stretched between them tighter than a drawn bowstring.

Annique spoke first. "Forgive me for repeating myself, but your highness hasn't explained why you've brought armed guards to call upon me in the middle of the night."

To her surprise, the Great Mademoiselle smiled. "You never were afraid to cut straight to the heart of things, Corbay. I have found that characteristic most useful in you. Rude, but useful." Sobering, she arranged her gloves carefully across her lap. Annique had forgotten what dainty hands the princess had. "Strange as it may seem, I've come to speak to you about Philippe."

The sound of her husband's name on this woman's lips sent a surge of anger through Annique. Royal or not, had the princess no shame?

The Great Mademoiselle ignored Annique's look of open hostility. "I think it would be best if we spoke in private. You may dismiss those clumsy servants lurking behind my back. I assure you, Corbay, you won't need rescuing." She nodded toward Annique's concealed hand. "And you won't be needing that pistol, either."

Annique's fingers opened involuntarily, as if the pistol were suddenly red-hot. She regained her grip just in time to prevent the hidden weapon from clattering to the floor.

The princess rose, her action requiring Annique to stand, as well. As she gained her feet, Annique shoved the pistol into the pocket of her robe. Despite the Great Mademoiselle's assurances, she might have need of it, yet.

The princess's voice cut through her unspoken fears. "I've gone to great risk, coming here. If the regent finds out I've come so close to Paris without permission, I may never see French soil again. There's precious little time to waste. We must speak, away from prying ears."

Annique knew better than to trust the princess, yet she had little choice but to oblige her request. She led the way into the library and closed the doors behind them.

The princess sat. "I never forget a debt of honor,

Corbay. You once stepped between me and death, at the dearest cost a woman can pay." Her hard blue eyes softened for a moment, then became bleak. "Perhaps we would both have been better off if you hadn't." She paused, regaining the aloofness that was more impenetrable than any armor. "I've come here tonight to repay that debt. You needn't fear me."

Annique lit the fire with her lamp, then sat down opposite the Great Mademoiselle. "We're alone. No one can hear us here." The flickering firelight accented hollows and wrinkles she had never noticed in the princess's face before.

Her royal guest leaned back and said wearily, "I'm only twenty-five years old, Corbay, and already my sun is set. Even my father has turned against me. But there's still hope for you. That's why I've come—to tell you the truth. I only hope it's not too late."

Annique measured her reply. "I'm still recovering from the last time someone bloodied me with a gift of truth."

The Great Mademoiselle stared into the fire. "Philippe told me what happened at the convent. Most unfortunate."

She said his name so smugly, with such casual familiarity. Smarting, Annique retorted, "I might have known he'd go to you when I threw him out."

The princess's cold blue gaze was as sharp as any dagger. "Only in friendship, after you rejected him repeatedly. And even then, only to ask me to tell you the truth."

What nerve this woman had! Indignation burned away what remained of the hypocrisies Sister Jonah had beaten into Annique. Suddenly she no longer feared the princess, any more than she cared what convoluted indirectness good manners demanded in such a situation. Annique retaliated with brutal frankness. "You came to tell me the truth? How could it possibly help to have you confirm what I know already—that you and my husband made a mockery of his marriage vows . . . *on our wedding night!* Or that he stole my birthright?" Abandoning protocol, she rose and turned away to cover the tears that blurred her vision.

The Great Mademoiselle leapt to her feet. "How dare you turn your back on me? Women of far greater consequence than you have been banished for less."

Annique's tears subsided abruptly. She pivoted to level a

stony accusation at the princess. "How dare *you* come here and tell me my husband has renewed your 'friendship,' as you so euphemistically call it?"

The royal features congealed. No one at Court ever spoke so openly of such delicate matters; it just wasn't done. She shot Corbay a look of withering reproach, but quickly realized that the insolent young duchess was beyond intimidation. Allowances would have to be made. After all, the girl had no rearing. And she *had* saved the princess's life. Honor, above all, must be served, even in the face of such affront.

The Great Mademoiselle flung herself back into the chair, her mouth flattening in frustration. After a moment of silence, she spoke. "Philippe loves you, Corbay, so deeply that he has refused my advances, even at the risk of his own career and reputation. He has never betrayed his marriage vows—not with me." She smiled grimly. "Not that I haven't tried, as recently as last night." She shook her head. "You've rejected him completely, yet still he remains faithful. Who can understand it?"

Annique frowned. "You expect me to believe that? I may be naive, but I'm not a fool."

The princess sat forward, her backbone ramrod straight and her tone once more imperious. "Nor am *I* foolish enough to think you one!" Her small white hands gripped the arms of the chair. "I have gone to great expense and trouble to investigate the allegations about your parents' assassination. I, myself, interviewed one of the men who participated in the raid." She eased back a bit. "Philippe was just a child then. My sources confirm that he rarely saw his father, except to be disciplined. Harcourt would never have taken him into his confidence about such a matter, even years later. There's no love lost between the two of them."

Annique felt her shield of anger wavering. "So Philippe says. But I fail to believe that he married me without knowing who I was."

The princess waved her gloves impatiently. "What does that matter now?" Her nostrils flared in contempt. "What a child you are, Corbay. Most girls outgrow such romantic notions about marriage by the time they're thirteen!"

"Is it childish not to want to be *used*, lied to, and betrayed?"

"Be realistic. Philippe was desperate for money. When the marshal proposed the match, telling him only that you were a distant cousin with a large dowry, he went along despite his reservations. He had no more choice than you did in the matter. You were both pawns. Even so, Philippe ended our friendship long before your marriage. I swear it on my immortal soul."

Annique said nothing. She didn't know *what* to say, what to think.

The Great Mademoiselle cast an anxious glance at the window, then began drawing on her gloves. "It will be light in only a few hours. For your sake, I should be back at St. Fargeau before then." She rose. "None of us can change what's past, Corbay. I have learned only too well that a woman of my station has no right to hope for happiness, but you have a chance at it. Don't throw that away—for the sake of your child, if for nothing else." She murmured bitterly, "At least you can have a child. You should get down on your knees every day to thank God for that."

Annique turned back to the fire. Suddenly she was sick of the sound of the princess's voice, sick of wondering what was real and what was manipulation, sick of dredging up the past. And frightened—frightened to death that what the Great Mademoiselle had said about Philippe might actually be true.

In the past six months, Annique had asked herself a thousand times if there might not be some way her husband could be innocent in all this. Now the princess—with nothing to gain—had sought her out to tell her just that. But if Philippe *were* innocent, how could he ever forgive her? How could they ever regain the closeness they'd shared for those few precious days at the villa?

Annique gripped the mantelpiece and leaned her forehead against its marble edge, a grating whisper all she could manage. "Please, just go away. Leave me alone." She heard the princess step toward the door, then pause.

The Great Mademoiselle's next words rang with challenge, compelling Annique to look up. "Be assured of one thing, Corbay—" Their eyes met. "No matter how much Philippe might love you, no man can remain faithful to a memory." She raised the hood of her cloak. "Should you be foolish enough to reject him again, I will be waiting with open arms. And this time he won't escape me. Think of *that* when you're making up your mind." She turned to the library's double doors and commanded, "Open these doors!"

They swung open, and she swept past a red-faced Jacques and Paoul.

On a cloudy morning three weeks later, Annique paused outside the library. She took a deep breath and tried not to think about the humiliating intimacy of the examination she had just endured. The baby. She'd done it for the baby's sake, and now it was over.

She nodded for Pierre to open the door.

The doctor rose as she entered the room. He was a small man, and like most of the physicians she'd encountered at Court, possessed of a sense of self-importance as overgrown as her enormous belly. She lowered herself into the same chair she'd sat in the night of the Great Mademoiselle's disturbing visit. "Please be seated, sir." Annique had barely slept since then, and had summoned the doctor only at Suzanne's insistence. "What conclusions have you drawn from your examination?"

Clearing his throat, he glanced awkwardly around the room. "Conclusions. Yes. Well . . ."

Annique's eyes narrowed. "Be blunt, if you must. I want the truth, however difficult that might be for either of us."

He folded his hands together, the index fingers extended to tap nervously together. "I'm afraid the news is not good." His expression clouded. "The child is very large, far larger than usual for this stage of development."

A cold spiral of fear coiled through her. "I assure you, sir, I have not miscalculated the time of conception."

He pursed his lips and nodded. "Eight months less a week, then." He hastened to add, "I didn't mean for one moment that I doubted the accuracy of your grace's—"

Why wouldn't he get to the point? Annique interrupted, "So, given that the child is unusually large for this stage of development, what are your conclusions?"

"I think we should postpone this conversation until such time as his grace can be present. I'm sure—"

Again, she cut him off. "I appreciate your concern, sir, but that is neither necessary nor advisable." With effort, she softened her tone. "My husband and I have maintained quite separate lives for the last few months. I have

managed this estate on my own for some time, and I assure
you I am quite capable of dealing with whatever you tell
me."

Obviously unaccustomed to being contradicted by a
mere woman, he glared at her and spoke bluntly, indeed.
"Very well. I advise your grace to make her peace with
God."

"What?"

"Your grace will not be able to deliver the child." He
paused. "In some instances the mother can be saved by
sacrificing the child—surgically removing it from the birth
canal, but in this case, I fear the child is already too large.
In any event, I could never condone such a procedure. The
Church forbids it."

Annique shuddered, repulsed by the thought of butcher-
ing her baby to save her own life. She murmured shakily,
"Who could even *consider* such a thing?" She gripped the
arms of her chair. "Surely there must be some way to save
the baby." She searched for some encouragement in his
eyes, but saw only resignation.

"It is in God's hands, your grace. Medical science does
not possess the means to help you." The doctor bent to
retrieve a knife and blood-encrusted basin from the box
beside him. "I recommend regular bleeding, of course, but
that can only expel the noxious humors from your
grace's—"

"Put those away!" Annique glared at the filthy instruments in his hands. "I have no intention of letting you
bleed me." She rose and paced to the rain-spattered window and stared beyond the droplets to the vibrant green of
early June. Annique knew all too well from her work in the
convent hospital how dangerous childbirth could be. She
had never been allowed to assist with the complicated deliveries, but she had washed many a cold, dead mother and
limp, lifeless baby for burial. And she could still remember
the screams—ear-splitting, hardly human at first, then
weaker and weaker until the only sound was the nuns'
murmured prayers for the dead.

There had to be a way to save the baby. Somewhere in
the recesses of her memory, she remembered something
she had read in her studies . . . What was it? Some famous person . . . She turned to the doctor. "Julius Caesar! That's it!" He looked at her as if she had just lost her

senses. Annique was anything but mad. "I read that Julius Caesar was cut from his mother's womb. That was more than a thousand years go. Surely modern medicine is capable of—"

"Such a notion is impossible, out of the question. No decent Christian would dare interfere with Divine Providence in such a way." As he spoke, he drew a small bottle from his case, poured a few drops into a silver cup, then added a stiff shot of brandy. "It is not uncommon for those facing death to grasp at straws, but I would be doing your grace no service by encouraging such an idea." He extended the potion, his tone softening. "Your grace has had a shock. This will settle her nerves."

"I don't need to settle my nerves. I need a doctor who can save my child." She pleaded, "You're an educated man. You must have read the accounts of Caesar's birth."

He set the potion on the table, then shoved his instruments back into his case. "I *am* educated, your grace—educated enough not to believe such myths just because I find them in the annals of antiquity. The Romans also recorded the exploits of a hundred deities purported to live on the top of Mount Olympus, but I daresay neither of us believes those accounts, which are far more numerous than the myth about Caesar's birth." He tucked the box under his arm and bowed. "Now I must beg your grace's leave. There are patients waiting in Paris who not only treat me with some modicum of respect, but who also follow my advice."

Annique dismissed the insufferable man with a nod. "By all means. You are excused, sir." Let him take his bowls and knives and potions back to Paris. She was glad to be rid of him. Now she could set about finding a *real* healer—one who would try, at least, to save her child.

❈ CHAPTER 35 ❈

*P*hilippe dismounted and strode up to the main entrance of Maison Corbay. Anne-Marie's note had simply asked that he come at his earliest convenience, but Jacques' recent messages about her deteriorating health made her unexpected request cause for concern.

A young footman opened the doors and bowed. "Welcome home, your grace."

There was something vaguely familiar about the lad's voice. When Philippe handed over his hat, he noted that there was also something familiar about the boy's face. "Who are you? I expected Jacques."

The boy grinned. "I'm Pierre, Jacques' eldest. It's an honor to meet you at last, your grace." His expression grew serious. "We children—that is, my brothers and sisters and I—we want to thank your grace for bringin' us here and givin' us work so we can be with our mum and papa. You won't be sorry, sir."

Children? He didn't even know Jacques and Suzanne *had* any! In all the years the couple had served him, they'd never said a word about having any children, so Philippe had never thought to ask. Why on earth would they think he'd sent for them?

Then the truth struck him. Anne-Marie must have found out about Jacques and Suzanne's children and reunited the family. For some strange reason, she'd credited Philippe. He studied the young man who held his hat. "How many of you are there?"

"Seven, master, all of us working our hardest to repay your grace's kindness."

"Seven." Philippe shook his head. "Amazing." He drew off his gloves and handed them to the boy. "The duchess sent word she'd like to speak with me."

Pierre sobered. "Aye, your grace. Her grace hasn't been well, so she asked me to show your grace to her room."

The boy's look of open sympathy caused Philippe's insides to twist. He should have come back sooner, as soon as Jacques had reported that she was ill. He'd stayed away only because he didn't want to risk another rejection.

Now she had sent for him. Had something happened to the baby—*their* baby? Fear tightened his throat as he said, "I know the way to my wife's room. See that we're not disturbed." Philippe took the stairs two at a time. He braced himself for bad news, but was unprepared for what he saw when he entered her bedchamber.

Propped in a chaise by the window, Anne-Marie made no effort to rise when he entered. Philippe wouldn't have wanted her to. He'd never seen a woman so burdened with child. Her face, still lovely despite obvious discomfort, was subtly altered by swelling. Her hands were swollen, too, as were the bare feet that peeked from the hem of her robe. Though the day was quite warm, her skin had a sallow, clammy cast. Philippe tried to conceal his shock, but a flash of recognition in her eyes told him he hadn't succeeded.

"Thank you for coming, Philippe." She motioned for him to sit beside her. "And so quickly. I'm glad you're here." Even her voice was different, strangely husky, and her shallow, labored breathing was like that of a man who'd been shot through the lung.

Philippe lowered himself into the chair. "If I'd known you were so ill, I'd have come sooner."

She smiled without rancor. "You're here now. That's all that matters." Her gaze lingered on his features. "Dear me. I've rehearsed this meeting a thousand times, but still I don't quite know how to begin."

His eyes narrowed. "Is it the child? You look so ill. The child isn't . . ."

Shaking her head in denial, she reached out. "Here. Give me your hand." When he did, she laid it atop her distended belly and pressed until an answering movement pushed back from inside her. "Our child is very much alive."

Philippe's fingers tingled from that first amazing contact with his unborn child. Forgetting himself completely, he slipped to one knee beside his wife and spread both hands across the taut dome of her belly. "There! He kicked me again! By heaven, he's a fighter already."

"Or she. It might be a girl, you know." There was an odd stillness in her voice.

Philippe saw deep sadness beneath his wife's composure. Something was wrong. Before, when she'd regained consciousness at the villa, she had been weak, but not weary. Now it seemed as if the life within her had drained away her own.

Her eyes shifted away from his probing stare.

Suddenly conscious of the intimacy of his touch, he withdrew his hands from her stomach and returned to his chair. "Sorry."

"You needn't apologize. This is your child as much as it is mine." She spoke plainly, reminding him of the woman he'd come to know at the villa. "I *want* you to feel close to our baby. I want you to love it as much as I do."

Philippe's misgivings grew stronger. "What's happened? Why are you saying this now?"

Her eyes sought his. "Because I've wronged you. Because I want you to forgive me. Because this is your child, and a child needs a father's love." She sighed, her hand finding the place where his had been. "I know now that you were telling the truth. About the princess, about your father. It wasn't fair of me to shut you out." Her dark lashes swept down. "I wanted this child so badly. Maybe I hoped to find a love I could trust."

Word by word, she was stripping her emotions bare, exposing her deepest motives almost as a penance. Philippe faltered. He didn't deserve to hear her confession. His own motives in wanting a child had been far more selfish than hers.

As if she had heard his thoughts, she looked up at him and said, "I knew you wanted a child just as badly, for your own reasons, but none of that matters now." Conviction burned in her great, dark eyes. "What matters is that you're here, and I pray you will stay. Please come home, Philippe. Our child needs you. I need you."

He had prayed to hear her say those words, but something about her sent a chill of foreboding through him. "There's more, isn't there?"

"Yes." She shifted clumsily in the chaise, obviously unable to sit comfortably in any position. "I've seen a dozen doctors and as many midwives in the last week. All of them have told me the same thing. They say the baby is so large that neither of us will survive the delivery."

The blood ran from Philippe's face, his heart constricting.

She went on calmly, "I've made my peace with God, but I refuse to give up on our child. I've sent a courier to Lyon. There's a Moorish physician there who practices surgical deliveries. If he can save our child, I shall die content."

"Die?" A surge of anger and denial rose within Philippe. What hope was there in the brutal chance Anne-Marie planned to take? He moved to the foot of the chaise, facing her. "I won't let you sacrifice yourself. There must be another way. Surely we can find—"

Annique shook her head. "No. Every day, I grow weaker. I pray constantly for the strength to survive until the doctor arrives."

As if destiny had been listening, a knock sounded on the door.

Both of them spoke at the same time. "Enter."

Jacques came in, his face brightening at the sight of his master. "Welcome home, your grace." He bowed and proffered a tray bearing a letter. "A courier just arrived from Lyon. Her grace asked me to bring the message right away."

Annique extended her hand for the message. "Thank you, Jacques. That will be all for now." Her finger traced the impression of a crescent moon stamped into the seal. "A Moorish symbol. My messenger must have found the physician." She loosened the seal and unfolded the letter. She scanned the script, murmuring, "His French is abominable, and I can barely read his writing."

Agonizing seconds passed before she let the letter fall to her side, her head rolling back as a single tear escaped the corner of her eye. Philippe held his breath until she whispered, "He's coming."

He snatched the letter from her hand and read the odd, spidery writing. "He says he's saved more than a dozen babies." Hope rose within him. "And mothers. Some of the mothers have lived." He dropped the letter and took Anne-Marie's hands. "He'll be here in just a few more days, and everything will be all right. He's saved other women. You will be the next. You must." He could have sworn that he saw a flicker of the old spark return to her eyes. He declared, "You might have made your peace with God, but I'm not ready to give you up. We've never had a chance at a real marriage. We were both too stubborn, too suspicious, but now I want that chance."

There was so much more he wanted to say, so many things he wanted to ask her to forgive, but words seemed inadequate in this moment. He rose and carefully lifted her into his arms. Her arms circled his neck as he balanced her weight. Despite her heaviness, she still felt right curled against him. He buried his cheek in her hair. "We'll face this together. No matter what happens, I'll never leave you again. I love you."

He could hear the tears in her reply. "And I love you. Even when I thought you had betrayed me, I couldn't stop loving you."

Philippe carried her across the room and sat down on

the bed. They remained there, clinging to each other in silence, her head nestled against his neck.

Why had he ever left her? Even though she'd asked, pleaded, then finally demanded that he go, he should never have done it. Now there was so little time . . .

Her voice interrupted his recriminations. "Promise me something, Philippe."

He smoothed a curl from her shoulder. "What?"

"If I die and the baby lives, promise you'll tell it I didn't want to leave. Swear that you'll tell our child every day how much I loved it."

He rocked her gently. "I won't need to. You'll be there to tell him yourself."

Anne-Marie's hand gripped his forearm. "When I was a little girl, old enough to know that other people had mothers and fathers, I hated my parents for dying and leaving me. The sisters kept saying they were in heaven, and what a wonderful place heaven was. I thought my parents had chosen heaven over me." She shivered. "I was so angry with them, and with God. But I never told anybody, so nobody ever told me that my parents didn't want to leave me." She looked up, pleading, "If our child lives, promise me that you'll tell it every day that I loved it and didn't want to leave it."

"I promise." Philippe held her close, unshed tears stinging his eyes. All these years, she'd borne the secret pain of that childhood rejection, after burying the brutal memory of her parents' murder. Now as she faced her own mortality, her thoughts were for their child, that it might know she loved it more than her own life. His lips touched the sweet, silky waves of her hair. "I promise."

Annique had been up for hours when Suzanne arrived with her breakfast tray. The housekeeper shook her head and frowned. "Your grace shouldn't be out of bed. And where's Marie? I vow, that girl is never where she's supposed to be."

"I sent her to the gatehouse to watch for the doctor."

"Any one of the children could have done that." Suzanne peered at her critically. "Marie shouldn't have let your grace get up, much less remain unattended."

Massaging her lower back, Annique grumbled. "I can barely breathe when I lie down, no matter how many pillows I prop behind me. And my back is bothering me particularly this morning. It feels a little better when I walk around."

Suzanne transferred the tray's contents to a table by the window, then drew up a chair for her mistress. As Annique lowered herself into the chair, the housekeeper offered brightly, "Only three or four more weeks, and your grace'll be able to put that baby *down.*"

Annique sighed. "Three more weeks." She cast a skeptical eye at the soup. Every time she ate or drank anything lately—even water—the baby danced a jig on the bottom of her stomach, leaving her desperately dyspeptic. "Fasting was always so hard for me at the convent. Now I find the prospect appealing."

Suzanne puffed up like a mother hen. "Here now, your grace. You must eat, for the child's sake." She scooped up a spoonful of soup. "It's very light, just a little grated cucumber in some nice, cool broth. No spices to upset the wee one."

Annique took the spoon and obediently swallowed the soup. It *was* refreshing. She mustered up a crooked smile. "Thank you, Suzanne. I can manage the rest by myself."

"Try to finish it. For the baby."

As Suzanne turned to leave, Annique asked, "There's been no word?"

The housekeeper's brows drew together. "Not yet. But don't worry, your grace. The doctor will be here soon, and when he arrives, we'll bring him straight to you."

Annique stroked a figure eight in the soup with her spoon, her face softening. "Has monsieur le duc left for his morning ride?"

"No. His grace told Jacques that he won't be ridin' anymore till the baby comes."

Philippe's voice interrupted. "Why ride, when I'm thinking of you the whole time, wishing I were back here?" Annique looked up to see him standing in the doorway. He smiled broadly. "May I come in?"

Warmth spread through her at the sight of him. "Of course. You know you don't need an invitation."

He crossed the room, turned a chair back against the table opposite her, and straddled it. Philippe tried to appear casual, but she could see that he was worried about her. "How are you feeling today, Annique?"

She loved it when he called her that. Grinning, she replied, "I'm feeling large, as usual." She lifted another bite of soup, but before the spoon touched her lips, a nasty twinge in her lower back caused her to drop it.

Philippe tensed. "What is it?"

"How clumsy of me." Embarrassed, she dabbed at the spattered soup with her napkin. "Now I've ruined my robe. That leaves only one more that's big enough."

"Bother the robe; we can have three more made before the end of the week." His eyes narrowed. "That wasn't clumsiness. I know pain when I see it."

Annique's lips folded inward, tears springing to her eyes. She was so tired, and so uncomfortable. Suddenly the effort of keeping up appearances was too much for her. She closed her eyes and allowed the tears to come. "It's just my back. It's been hurting for weeks, but last night I couldn't sleep a wink." She looked up and smiled in apology, the tears still flowing. "I guess the baby's gotten so big, it's trying to rearrange my bones to make more room."

"Poor Annique." Philippe rose and helped her to her feet. "Don't cry. Come lie on your side, and I'll rub your back."

As she had countless times in the week since their reconciliation, Annique thanked God for the husband who comforted and cared for her. Philippe had read to her for hours at a time, walked with her in the cool of the evening, played chess with her. He'd even taught her an Egyptian board game called "stones," then laughed when she learned it well enough to beat him. As comfortable with silence as with conversation, he always seemed to be there when she needed him.

And she needed him now. Her breath catching spasmodically as her tears subsided, she held tightly to his arm and allowed him to lead her toward the bed. Halfway there, she felt a curious sinking sensation, followed by a warm rush of wetness between her legs.

Horrified, she looked down and saw a dark puddle on the carpet. "Dear heaven. I've shamed myself completely."

Philippe took one look and called, "Suzanne! Come at once."

Annique's tears started afresh. "How humiliating. Now I'm losing control of my bodily functions."

Suzanne bustled into the room, crossed to the spot in

the carpet, stooped, sniffed, and stood. "Calm yourself, your grace. It's not what you think. Your water's broken, that's all."

Philippe's look of relief was quickly replaced by one of concern when he saw Suzanne's somber expression. He knew a great deal about how to see a colt or a lamb well-born, but had no experience with babies. "What does that mean?"

Her reassuring smile didn't fool anybody. "It just means that her grace won't have to wait as long as we'd thought to hold her baby in her arms." After feeling Annique's stomach, she looked at Philippe. "I should have realized what was happening when she complained about her back. She never complains. It's back-labor, I suspect. She may have been having contractions for hours."

Annique gripped Philippe's shirt. "I can't be in labor. Not yet. The doctor's not here."

He pried her fingers from the material, his tone soothing. "Everything will be all right. You'll see. The doctor will be here soon. While Suzanne helps you into a fresh gown, I'll consult the medical books in my library. I remember reading something about a potion for just such a situation as this."

Annique knew he was lying about the potion, but she wanted so much to believe him that she nodded and released his hand. "Yes. Do that. I'll be fine with Suzanne."

As Philippe headed for the door, Suzanne rang the bell on the bedside table, then patted Annique's hand. "I'm just going to stick my head out the door and ask Pierre to fetch Marie. Then I'll bring a fresh gown and some water from the dressing room, and we'll get your grace all cleaned up."

Annique covered her eyes with her forearm, another pain knotting the muscles in her lower back. She said through gritted teeth, "Please hurry."

"I'll be back before you know it." Suzanne scurried into the hallway after Philippe, catching up with him before he reached the landing.

She didn't look him in the eye when she spoke. "Your grace, I'm afraid that potions won't help. There's little good to be gained by delaying labor, now that her grace's water has broken."

"Why?"

"Once the water's broken, the baby must be born soon. If too much time passes, there's a good chance it will be stillborn."

Philippe threaded his fingers into his hair and groaned. "Where is that *doctor?* He should have been here days ago!" He exhaled deeply, then looked up at Suzanne. "There has to be something we can do."

Suzanne shook her head. "We must send for the priest."

His throat tightened. "I won't just sit by and give her over to heaven. I can't. Maybe I can do what the doctor was going to do, myself. I have several medical books from Greece and Arabia—"

Suzanne interrupted him gently. "She's waiting for me. I must go back. Do what you can, your grace. But please, on your way to the library, ask Jacques to send hot water and clean linens and towels—lots of them. And have Pierre fetch Marie from the gatehouse."

Philippe nodded.

She took a step toward the bedroom, then paused. Suzanne spoke only loudly enough for him to hear. "And please, your grace. Send for the priest."

Late that afternoon, Philippe waited impatiently outside his wife's bedchamber for Suzanne to open the door. His apothecary case in one hand and a stack of clean basins in the other, he stood at the head of a caravan of servants. Marie was right behind him, her arms laden with spotless bedlinens and towels. Behind her, three footmen carried the portrait of Annique's mother that, until moments ago, had hung on the grand stairway. Jacques and Pierre brought up the rear, laboring under a stout wooden yoke that supported two large kettles—one bubbling with a noxious-smelling liquid, and the other full of red-hot coals.

The door opened and Suzanne motioned Philippe inside. "You may bring the others in. I've drawn the curtains at the foot of the bed. She's sleepin', poor child, if only for a few moments. The pains are but a few minutes apart, now."

Philippe entered, then spoke softly to the footmen. "Prop the portrait on the large chest, there, opposite the foot of the bed, where she can see it. And be sure you work quietly. I don't want the duchess disturbed."

Turning to Jacques, he motioned toward the hearth.

"Spread the coals, then put the kettle on top of them. Mind you don't knock the stirring staves out." When the two servants obeyed, a cloud of pungent vapor added its odor to the hot, stagnant air.

Last summer Philippe had fought for Anne-Marie's life in another stuffy, curtained room. They'd cheated death then. Could he save her again? Or would destiny demand that the scales be balanced at last?

As he stirred the potion while Pierre fanned the coals, questions overlapped questions in Philippe's burdened mind, a dozen inner voices coaxing, shouting, pleading, reasoning. What if the doctor didn't arrive in time, and Anne-Marie's condition continued to deteriorate? Should he try to save the child, or his wife?

Would he have the courage to lay his surgical knife to her living flesh? What if his efforts succeeded only in killing her, and the baby, too?

Despite the heat, Philippe shivered.

Suzanne's voice roused him back to the matter at hand. She muttered crankily at her son, "Here, now! That's enough. Those coals are plenty hot." She pulled Pierre to his feet, then steered him toward the door. "Run along, and take your father with you. This is no place for menfolk." She glanced apologetically up at her master. "Exceptin' his grace, of course."

Philippe barely heard her. The potion was almost ready. He had searched his medical books for hours to find something—anything—that might help his wife. After locating this formula in an ancient Greek text, he had spent two long hours finding, mixing, and crushing the herbal ingredients in exact proportions. He rolled up his sleeves and said, "This potion will help ward off infection. I've steeped my surgical instruments, some bristle brushes, and some clean cloths in it for an hour, as the instructions required." He poured a pitcherful of the scalding liquid into a basin, then gingerly transferred one of the small wooden brushes from the kettle to the bowl. "As soon as this cools enough to bear touching, I want you to scrub your hands in it. I'll prepare another basin for my own hands." He picked up another clean bowl and filled it, as well, then used one of the stirring sticks to snare a cloth from the kettle's depths. He dropped the steaming cloth into the bowl. "When this has cooled, wash the duchess with it, paying particular attention to her abdomen and the birth area."

Suzanne tucked her ample chin. "I'll do as you ask, sir, of course, but I've never heard of such a thing! Scrubbin' our hands, all in separate bowls! No disrespect intended, but this isn't another of those heathen—"

Philippe interrupted wearily, "Just do it, Suzanne. Marie, too. It doesn't matter whether you understand why. No one must touch the duchess without scrubbing in a fresh basin of the potion. Remember, a fresh basin every time, as hot as you can stand it." He glanced across the room at his pale, fitful wife. "It can't hurt her, and it just might help."

He carried the bowl of steaming potion to the bedside, where a wilted Marie tried to soothe her mistress with cool compresses. He touched the maid's arm. "Please open the bed curtains, then go help Suzanne. I'd like a moment with the duchess."

Marie nodded and obeyed with uncharacteristic silence.

Philippe gently removed the compress and stared at his wife. Beneath the sheet, her knees were raised and spread apart, propped with pillows. All day, her labor had been brutal and unrelenting, yet Suzanne had said there was little progress. Pale and perspiring, Annique's face was more swollen than ever, and her shallow panting was irregular. By all that was holy, did every woman suffer this way to bring life into the world? If so, he marveled that any ever let a man near her again.

Annique opened her eyes. "Philippe?" She struggled to prop herself up on her elbows.

"I'm here." He sat on the edge of the bed and gently coaxed her to lie back. "You must rest while you can."

Easing down into the pillows, she managed a tight, lop-sided smile. "I just had the loveliest dream. My mother was here watching over me." Then she saw the painting beyond him. "So it wasn't a dream."

Philippe turned, following her line of sight to the serene woman depicted on the canvas. "I thought it would make you feel better to be able to look at her." He smoothed a damp curl from his wife's brow. In the dimness, her eyes were almost black. Even between contractions, pain burned dully from their depths.

"Thank you." She clutched his hand to her breast. "That was very sweet."

The concern on Philippe's face made Annique realize how terrible she must look. She glanced down. The sheet covered only her legs, and her thin cotton gown was almost transparent, drenched from hours of fruitless effort, but she didn't care anymore. It had been hours since she'd had the strength for shame. Now she had energy only for survival. And for fear. "I thought I could do this alone, but I can't." She winced, her self-control beginning to slip away at last. Her whole body tightened with the onset of another labor pain. Some of the contractions were bearable, but others were bone-wrenching. The worst ones felt as if they were splitting her pelvis in two. She choked out, "Please stay with me." She squeezed his hand tighter and tighter; the comforting resistance of his grip became her anchor as she rode the swelling wave of pain. A low groan escaped her clenched teeth.

Philippe's words cut through the haze of agony, the sound of his voice as soothing as a forest pool. "Hold onto me until the pain passes. Then you can rest. Listen to my voice. I'm here. I won't leave you. Open your eyes, Annique, and concentrate on your mother's face."

As she obeyed, he kept talking, trying to distract her from the pain. "Look. She's watching over you, just as you said. See how calm she is, how beautiful?"

Annique nodded, focusing with what little clarity she could muster on her mother's face, but the pain continued to grow. Just when she was afraid she would scream aloud, the grinding pressure began to subside.

When her grip eased slightly, he said, "That's it. This one is almost over. Now you can rest, so you'll be strong for the next one. One at a time. That's all you have to worry about. Forget what's come before. Just rest."

Limp with relief, she sagged into the pillows.

Philippe watched her eyes close and her features ease.

Suzanne tiptoed up and offered him a glass of cool, watered wine. "You must be thirsty, your grace. Try some of this."

Without letting go of his wife's hand, he took the goblet and swallowed. "Thanks. That tastes good." He glanced past her. "Where's Marie?"

"I sent her downstairs for some food and a nap. Poor child was worn-out."

"No more so than you, I should imagine."

"I'm fine, but your grace is the one who's holding up the best." Suzanne studied him with quiet approval. "Not many men have the mettle to stay with their womenfolk at times like these." She nodded confidently. "Your grace is very good at this."

Philippe sighed, wishing he knew some way to justify that confidence. As a boy he'd preferred the life and bustle of the stables to the cold emptiness of the manor house, and he'd helped the stableman with dozens of difficult births. But this was different; this was his wife, the woman who had become as much a part of him as the blood that coursed through his veins. Her life, and their child's, hung in the balance. "If only I could help her more." He took a deep draught of wine, then whispered, "Where is that blasted doctor?"

"Now, now, your grace," Suzanne scolded gently. "With or without the doctor, we'll manage somehow." Her brows drew together. "Perhaps I'd better check again to see how things are progressing." She stepped over to the basin on the bedside table and made a great show of washing her hands in the potion, then dried them on a clean towel. "Please turn aside, your grace."

Philippe nodded dumbly and closed his eyes, hearing the rustle of sheets as Suzanne lifted the covers to check on the delivery.

At the sound of Suzanne's groan, he opened his eyes and rose. "What?" When she looked away and hurried to replace the sheet, he grabbed her hand to stop her. Nudging the housekeeper aside, he looked between his wife's propped-up legs. There in the distended, discolored flesh, a single tiny foot protruded from the birth canal. Philippe stared as if he could change what he saw by willing it away, but he could not. He uttered, "A footling breech." The words were a death sentence for both mother and child.

Annique stirred, her brow furrowing in pain.

Silent tears glazed Suzanne's cheeks as she replaced the sheet and whispered, "The priest is downstairs. Please let me bring him up, your grace, to say the rites . . . for the poor babe, at least."

Philippe clamped an iron grip on her forearm. "Not yet.

We've already lost one child. I won't lose this one without at least trying to save it."

"But there's nothing to be done. It's half-born already, trapped in the birth passage."

Annique's eyes fluttered open. She reached frantically for Philippe's hand, almost crushing his fingers as the pain engulfed her again.

Philippe used his free hand to pull Suzanne close. He murmured in her ear, "If she sees the priest, she'll give up. No priest. Not yet."

Her face full of worry and reproach, Suzanne crossed herself, but said nothing.

For the next five minutes, Philippe turned his attention to helping his wife through the wracking contraction, his voice an island of calm in the waves of pain that served now only to further trap their unborn child. When the cycle subsided at last, he sent Marie for fresh towels, then summoned Suzanne to the hearth. "We must do something, or we'll lose them both. During the contractions, her heart beats so rapidly that I'm not sure she'll survive many more." He sank into a nearby chair. "I've got to try the surgery. It's the only chance."

Suzanne's mouth quivered, but her voice was steady. "There's one thing we haven't tried."

He looked up. "What? You said there was nothing . . ."

"Nothing for a human, but I've seen it work with a lamb. We can try to turn the child. Push it back up inside her, then force it 'round right."

Philippe was grim. "*Sometimes* that works with animals, but only rarely. And the duchess is no animal. Such a thing could literally tear her apart, or the baby. The Church would call it murder."

Suzanne folded her hands. "Would you rather cut her open with a knife? What chance would she have then?"

The sound of Annique's voice, weak but determined, reminded them that there was another party to this decision. "Do whatever's safest for the baby, Philippe. I'm not afraid of dying anymore. Save the baby."

He knew she meant what she said, but Philippe hesitated. He was her only hope—and their baby's—yet fear kept him from acting. Philippe looked at the sodden linen bundle waiting on a silver tray beside the kettle. The surgical instruments inside were razor-sharp, the finest in the world. He had watched many field hospital procedures and performed more than a few himself, but this was different. He didn't know where to make the incision, or what he would find once he did. One wrong move, and Annique could bleed to death before his eyes. By *his* hand. By the scalpel *he* chose to use.

He *had* to make a decision, and quickly. Doing nothing would be just as deadly as trying to save her. As he had so many times on the battlefield, he sorted through his options until the consequences became clear, distilling into a manageable landscape of possibilities. And then he chose.

Suzanne was right. What she proposed would be risky, but not as dangerous as the surgery. "All right. We'll try to turn the baby after the next contraction."

Minutes later, Annique panted, "The contraction's over. Turn the baby now."

Philippe watched as Suzanne climbed across the pillows and settled Annique's head into her lap, then firmly grasped her hands. "Ready?"

Annique nodded. She had been so calm, so accepting when he'd explained exactly what he planned to do. Now she begged him to begin just as urgently as she had pleaded with him not to feel guilty if the attempt went badly. "Do it quickly. The next contraction will come in only a minute or two. You must hurry, Philippe. I don't know how much longer I can hold on."

Philippe held his breath and said a silent prayer, then gently grasped his unborn child's foot and shoved upward, invading his wife's body in a way he had never imagined possible.

In spite of herself, Annique cried out. Then she lost consciousness.

Philippe shuddered at the hot, moist resistance he felt as he struggled to force the child back into the womb. His efforts made little progress, but he was afraid to flex his fingers or to apply too much pressure. He closed his eyes and tried again, using touch as his only guide. This time, he felt something give. His hand disappeared inside her, into her womb. "There!" But when he tried to turn the child, he couldn't. Instead, both legs slipped into his palm.

"Blast! This isn't working." He twisted his hand, but there was precious little room, and he had no idea what he was touching. He looked at Suzanne. "I managed to push it back inside, but I can't find the head, and it won't turn. I think I have hold of the other leg, too, now."

Suzanne's eyebrows lifted. "Both legs? Then there's some hope at least, even if you can't turn it."

He pushed his hand further inside, feeling what must be the baby's bottom. He tried again to shift the child, but it wouldn't budge. Then the muscles around his hand began to tighten. "I think another contraction is starting."

Suzanne winced. "You mustn't pull during the contraction, your grace. It might tear the poor thing apart." Her brows knit together, then her face cleared. "Maybe if you can guide both legs out together, the contraction will do the rest. It's all we can hope for, if you can't turn the baby."

Philippe found the baby's thighs, then tightened his fingers around them. He struggled to keep the baby's legs together and guide them out, but gave up when the contraction forced him to withdraw his hand. "I couldn't hold on."

Then, miraculously, two small feet appeared on their own.

"The feet! They're here!" Philippe leaned closer. "And the knees. And the thighs! It's coming."

Annique stirred slightly, pain fluttering across her exhausted features as she regained consciousness. Suzanne held her hands and urged, "Push, your grace! The baby's unstuck. Hold onto me and push."

She whispered, "Push . . ."

Philippe felt the baby's calves. They were warm. "It's alive." But endless seconds later, there had been no further progress. He closed his palm around the small legs and groaned. "Its legs seem to be getting cold. I think we only made things worse. Now I can't operate. The baby is too far into the birth passage."

Annique summoned the last of her strength to lift her head. Hollow-eyed, she rasped, "Pull it out, Philippe. Our baby's dying. You must pull it free." Then she collapsed back into Suzanne's lap.

Suzanne looked at Philippe. "There's no time to waste. As soon as I feel the muscle easing, I'll push from here. You pull." She twisted to snatch the silken cords from the bed curtains. After tying them to the headboard, she deftly looped the ends and slipped one around each of Annique's wrists. "Hold onto these, your grace."

Annique was so weak that she could barely close her fingers around the cords.

Suzanne leaned forward and spread her palms over the top of Annique's belly. She nodded grimly to Philippe. "Wait till I say to pull, but do it gently, lest you hurt the babe."

"Gently doesn't work, Suzanne."

She ignored his comment, closing her eyes to better feel the rhythm of Annique's tortured body. "There. The contraction's easing. I can feel it."

Philippe closed his eyes and murmured, "May God have mercy on us all." Heavy drops of perspiration rolled off his scalp and plopped onto the sheets as he braced himself, closed his palm around the baby's thighs, and pulled. Nothing happened. Dear heaven, would he tear his own child to pieces trying to save it?

Suzanne pushed and kneaded. "Don't give up, your grace. I can feel something shifting inside."

He tried again, using a twisting motion. Philippe felt something give, and he relaxed his grip. A full torso and two little tightly crossed arms spurted into his waiting hands, but the head remained trapped. "It's a girl!" Hope flushed through him. "Push, Annique. Push! Our daughter is almost born."

Annique's hands closed around the silken ropes and she bore down with renewed strength. Veins bulged in her forehead, a primal cry wrenched from her by this last, desperate effort.

Blood and fluid gushed out with the baby's head, and then Philippe was holding a perfectly formed girl-child. She was bald as a goose egg, and small—barely five pounds, from the feel of her in his hands—covered with blood and patches of dark matter and slippery whiteness, but she was very much alive, her tiny fists flailing away. She was so small, despite the dire projections of the doctors. Bursting with pride and gratitude, Philippe choked out, "She's born, Annique! And she's perfect."

The baby sneezed dark matter from her tiny nostrils, then gasped and sputtered, struggling to take her first breath. Philippe looked down at the tiny creature still tethered to her mother. A daughter. They had a daughter.

"Hello, little one," he crooned, wiping her face with a clean cloth.

Suzanne's brusque voice cut into his consciousness. "Turn the baby over, your grace, and give her back a pat." The housekeeper shifted her mistress from her lap and moved to Philippe's side as he carefully obeyed her instructions.

When he did, the baby spit out a mouthful of mucus, then let loose with a thready squall. It was the most beautiful sound Philippe had ever heard.

Dazed, Annique let her hands slip from the silken loops and closed her eyes, silent tears coursing across her temples. She had no strength left for words. At last, she could let go. She had given her child life.

Suzanne took the baby from Philippe, her brisk handling causing the child to howl in earnest. She grinned. "Do you hear that, your graces? She's all right." She laid her on her mother's stomach, looped the umbilical cord and tied it off, then cut it. "There. Now let's get you cleaned up, my little ladyship."

Philippe hovered close by, watching anxiously as Suzanne washed his daughter with the now-tepid potion. Despite the strong herbal scent, the baby seemed to enjoy her first bath. Her cries settled to soft, mewling sounds, and she blinked up at Suzanne with a serious expression. Philippe peered closer while Suzanne swaddled her in soft damask. "What color are her eyes? I can't tell."

"That's hard to say at this point, but I'd guess her ladyship will have her mother's big brown eyes."

Philippe grinned. "I hope so." All these years, he had looked forward to the day when he would have a son, but now, gazing into the face of his daughter, he felt the most blessed of men.

"Time for her ladyship's first meal." The moment Suzanne put the baby to her mother's breast, she began to suckle.

Annique opened her eyes and smiled down at the child tugging greedily at her breast. "Hello, baby." Her free hand crept across the covers to caress the downy little head. Then her lids fluttered shut, and her hand stilled.

Suzanne nodded to Philippe. "Keep an eye on the baby, your grace, while I tend to the mistress."

That was an assignment Philippe was happy to accept.

Suddenly weak in the knees, he pulled up a chair and sat to watch his daughter suckle.

Suzanne spoke softly as she worked. "Here comes the afterbirth. When that's out, the contractions will stop, and you can rest at last."

Philippe kept his eyes on his daughter while Suzanne cleared away the placenta and washed her mistress clean. After gently removing the pillows under Annique's knees and lowering her legs, Suzanne covered her mistress with a freshly ironed sheet. She whispered to Philippe, "Her grace's milk won't come in for a day or so. Would you like to hold the baby for a bit?"

He nodded, then accepted the precious bundle into his arms.

Suzanne smoothed Annique's brow. "You just rest now, your grace. We'll change your gown after you've had a nap."

But instead of a contented nod, Annique's response was a sharp intake of breath. Her eyes flew open and she raised up on her elbows. "It hurts—worse than ever! I thought you said it was over!" Caught off-guard by the vicious contraction, she burst into tears and sobbed. "Dear God, Philippe! Help me! It feels like I'm being torn in two." She curled forward, just as she had in the last stages of labor.

Alarmed by her mother's cries, the baby began to squall. Philippe joggled her in his arms and looked to Suzanne. "What's happening?"

Suzanne shook her head in confusion. "I don't know." She felt Annique's still-distended belly. "Hard as a rock." She jerked back the cover and hastily propped Annique's knees, then stared in amazement at what she saw. "By the Blessed Virgin and every saint of heaven!" She turned to Philippe. "There's another one!"

"Another *what?*"

"Another *baby!* And this one's coming into the world as it ought to—headfirst. It's already crowning."

For a moment, shock erased the suffering from Annique's face. She squeaked, "Twins?" then grabbed the silken ropes and bore down with the contraction.

"Twins!" Philippe paced frantically, unconsciously joggling the baby in his arms so hard her cries sounded like hiccups. He took two steps toward the door and shouted, "Marie! Somebody get Marie!" Then he strode back to the bedside. "Where's the wet nurse? Should I put the baby down and help you? What should we do now?"

Suzanne snatched a clean towel and tucked it under Annique's buttocks. "The first thing *you* should do is stop bouncing her ladyship about like that! You'll scramble her brains. Just hold her. I can manage here by myself." She turned her attention back to her mistress. "There! The head's out!" Beaming, she raised up and addressed Annique. "That's the worst of it, already done, your grace! Just hold on for a bit longer, and it really will be over."

Philippe stepped closer just in time to see the arrival of his second child. Suzanne lifted the baby triumphantly into the air by its ankles. "It's a boy! A boy!" She scooped the baby's mouth clear with her finger, then administered a brisk slap to his little backside. The newest heir to the Corbay line responded with a lusty wail of protest, the sound of which prompted his sister to renew her own.

No sooner had Suzanne laid the newborn on his mother's stomach, then she exclaimed, "Goodness! There's the afterbirth, already. You're making short work of this, your grace, now that you've got the knack." She bundled the placenta into a towel, then covered her mistress's legs before cutting the cord and cleaning the baby.

Philippe watched, fascinated, until concern for his wife drew his attention to her pale face. He laid his daughter into her exhausted mother's arm, then sat beside them. Almost overwhelmed at all she had given him, he whispered to Annique, "A daughter and a son. How can I ever thank you?"

Suzanne settled their son into the crook of Annique's other arm. "Here we are. His lordship's all cleaned up. Now I'll see to her grace." She moved back to the lower edge of the bed to tend her mistress.

Flanked by her children, Annique looked up at Philippe with a faraway sadness in her eyes and murmured, "Remember your promise."

A shadow of foreboding darkened Philippe's euphoria. He took her hand and kissed it. Her fingers lay limply in his, the nails as white as her ivory skin.

Just then, there was a commotion at the door. After a few rapid knocks, Marie burst in without waiting for a response. She blurted out breathlessly, "The doctor! He's here, your grace, on his way up the stairs. Shall I let him in?" The sound of the babies drew her eyes to the bed, and Marie forgot all about her urgent mission. "Sweet saints and all the prophets! Twins!" But a second look at all the blood and her mistress's still form caused her face to fall. "The duchess—she's not . . ."

Suzanne pulled up the sheet as Philippe rose and snatched shut the curtains at the foot of the bed, shielding his wife. He snapped, "The duchess is fine."

Suzanne's voice came from behind him. "I fear she's not, your grace. The bleeding should have stopped by now, but it hasn't. I don't know what else to do."

Philippe stepped past the end of the bed, ordering, "Bring the doctor at once! We need him."

No sooner had Marie opened the door than a slender, olive-skinned man in a silken turban and flowing robes strode past her. The Moorish physician bowed and executed a graceful salaam. "Allow me to present myself, your grace. I am Dr. Haddad." His dark eyes shifted from the blood spattered on Philippe's shirt to the kettle steaming on the hearth. "I humbly beg your graces' pardon for the delay in my arrival. My coach broke an axle, and it took three days to—"

Philippe cut the apology short. "Never mind that, now. My wife is bleeding badly. You must save her." He led the doctor to the bedside.

Haddad scanned the situation with a look of professional assessment. His dark eyes moved rapidly from the babies' ruddy faces to Annique's pale one. He pressed his fingers to her neck to gauge her pulse, then shifted them lower to palpate her still-distended belly. "Please to tell me what happened."

"She's been ill for weeks," Philippe explained. "Weak, with a great deal of swelling. Her labor started more than thirty hours ago. The first child was a footling breech. I pushed its foot back inside her, and both feet came out, but I had to pull the head free. The second baby was born a few minutes later, headfirst."

Haddad extracted a small packet from his leather pouch and handed it to Suzanne. "Mix this with two ounces of wine, then give it to the duchess—one drop at a time, if necessary, lest she choke." Suzanne waited for Philippe to nod his assent before she obeyed. Dr. Haddad bent over and addressed his patient, "It's Dr. Haddad, your grace. Can you hear me?"

When Annique made no response, Philippe realized she had lost consciousness.

The Moor chafed Annique's hand and spoke louder. "Can you hear me, your grace? Lift your finger if you can hear me." Her pale fingers remained motionless.

He turned to Philippe. "How long has she been like this?"

"Only a few minutes. Before that, she was weak, but conscious."

Without a word of warning or explanation, the doctor jerked the sheet off Annique, exposing her damp, soiled gown and bare legs, and beneath her, an alarming stain of bright red blood that seemed to be growing larger by the second.

Philippe recoiled. The scene was just like the one in his nightmares at the villa.

Dr. Haddad shot him a sidelong glance and murmured, "A thousand pardons, your grace, but at this moment madame's life is far more precious to me than her modesty." He unceremoniously raised her gown above her waist, then plunged his hand into the now-pliable skin of her belly. "I can feel that the womb is still large, and far too soft. To stop the bleeding, I must massage it until it hardens." His hand almost disappeared in the soft flesh as he carried out the vigorous treatment. He looked at Suzanne, who had returned with the medicated wine. "Put both the babies to suckle before you give her grace the medicine." He nodded reassuringly to Philippe as she obeyed. "Sometimes that helps slow the bleeding."

Philippe stood rooted, a wave of queasiness rising within him at the sight of his wife's swollen, bleeding body exposed to this stranger. He fought the urge to gather Annique in his arms and cover her, but he knew that Haddad was only doing what he could to save her.

Massaging all the while, the physician checked the bleeding, then turned to Philippe. "The bleeding has slowed, but the duchess will not be out of danger until it has stopped completely for twenty-four hours."

Suzanne's back straightened.

The doctor continued, "There is nothing more you can

do here, your grace. Please, try to get some rest. If Allah is merciful, tomorrow will find her much improved."

Philippe scraped his hand across his jaw, the stubble rasping harshly on his palm. "I could use a shave and a wash, but I won't be gone long. I promised to stay with her." He aimed a piercing gaze at the doctor. "You must summon me at once if anything happens—good *or* bad. Do I have your word on that?"

Haddad nodded. "You have my word."

Philippe took one more reassuring look at his children. They, at least, were out of danger. He touched them both, then turned and plodded wearily toward the corridor that led to his suite.

❀ CHAPTER 36 ❀

*T*wenty hours later, Philippe paced the balcony as the sun descended behind the trees. Sheer frustration had driven him from his wife's bedside. The bleeding had stopped less than an hour after the doctor's intervention, but Annique had yet to regain consciousness.

He paced to the bedchamber's open windows and peered inside. Across the room's dim interior, Annique lay framed by the bed curtains. Haddad had elevated the foot of the mattress slightly, but even that had done little to restore her color. She was still pale as death, and she hadn't moved once all day. From this distance, Philippe couldn't even make out the shallow rise and fall of her breathing.

He turned away, a bitter whisper of despair blowing through him. What if she never woke up? What if he had to go through the rest of his life without her? And the twins. Would they grow up without a mother's love?

He turned and strode to the stone railing, there offering yet another desperate, heartfelt prayer for her life. Then he heard footsteps behind him. Recognizing the soft tread of Haddad's supple boots, Philippe froze, his hands gripping the edge of the railing.

He looked up at the sunset, memorizing what might be his last moment as a whole man, his last moment in a world where Annique still lived.

Dear God, don't let him say the words. Don't let her be dead.

Haddad spoke. "Your grace, please come with me."

Composing himself for the worst, Philippe straightened. "Is she . . . ?"

"Perhaps your grace should see for himself." He led the way into the bedchamber, then discreetly lagged behind.

Philippe kept his gaze downcast until he reached the bedside. As he looked up, he saw that her hand was closed into a fist. When his gaze reached her face, he found himself staring into her deep, luminous eyes. "Annique. You're alive." He turned expectantly to Haddad, who smiled from across the room.

"Her grace has passed the crisis. With rest, she should make a full recovery."

Philippe felt as if he were floating, the weight of his body suspended. It was over, and he hadn't lost her. "You're alive."

"Thanks to you." She paused, her gaze drinking in the sight of him. "I wanted to give up, but you wouldn't let me."

He lifted her fist and kissed the pale knuckles. At the pressure of his lips, her fingers slackened. Annique smiled. "This is for you." She turned her hand in his, and opened her palm to reveal a golden ring burnished by centuries of wear. "I know you will wear it with honor."

"The ducal ring." Philippe had thought his heart could be no fuller, but this gift and all it signified threatened to overwhelm him.

Annique closed her eyes and murmured, "One day, for our son."

Philippe pulled off the replica he had been wearing and replaced it with the ancient original. It fit as if it had been made for him. He kissed her hand again, noting that her nails were tinged with pink. Then he slipped the duplicate ring onto her index finger. "This is for you. I know you will wear it with honor. And after a long and happy life, pass it on to our daughter." Philippe was certain he saw a spark of humor in her eyes when they opened. Her thumb caressed the golden band. He leaned closer. "I need you, and the twins need their mother." They would have a whole lifetime to bring up their children together.

At the mention of the twins, she smiled. "Our babies . . . The doctor said I could see them."

Haddad volunteered, "Suzanne and Marie are bringing them now."

Philippe frowned. "You don't remember them?"

Her features clouded. "I don't remember anything except pain, and fear—" Her fingers tightened in his. "And the strength of your hand as you held onto me."

The bedchamber door opened, and Suzanne and Marie marched in, each bearing her infant charge as importantly as if she were carrying the next ruler of all of France.

Philippe rose and intercepted them. "Here. Let me take them to her."

Marie recoiled, obviously uneasy at the prospect of turning the young lord over to anyone as inexperienced with babies as his father. But Suzanne handed over her charge without hesitation. She couldn't resist a little coaching, though. "Easy, your grace. Remember to keep her little head supported."

"I'll be very careful, Suzanne."

With both maids fluttering about adjusting little blankets and gowns, the babies were transferred to their father's waiting arms. He bore them proudly to his waiting wife.

Philippe sat on the bedside and raised his right elbow to show Annique her daughter's face. "Madame le duchesse, allow me to present your firstborn, a daughter." The tiny girl-child yawned, then worried her fist into her mouth and began sucking. "I think she's hungry." He lifted the other elbow. "And this is our son." Philippe bent to brush his lips across the faint dusting of downy black hair that covered the baby's head. "Mmmm. So soft." The baby didn't stir. Philippe grinned. "He's sleeping. He came into this world just behind his sister, and I imagine he'll spend the rest of his life trying to catch up with her."

A look of joy that would put an angel to shame spread across Annique's face.

Their daughter yawned again, then turned against Philippe's sleeve and began rooting.

Annique opened the neck of her gown. "Here. If she's hungry, let me feed her."

With infinite care, the proud father settled his firstborn to her mother's breast. Then he sat back, his sleeping son still cradled contentedly in his arms. From the corner of his eye, he saw Dr. Haddad shepherd Marie and Suzanne from the room, leaving them in privacy at last.

Annique's breast had grown larger overnight, the nipple ripe and darkened. The baby rooted for only a few seconds before latching on, her tiny fingers spreading across the soft flesh that provided her sustenance.

It was the most intimate moment Philippe had ever known. His voice caught unexpectedly as he asked, "Do you have any ideas about names?"

"We can decide together, later." Annique smiled sleepily down on the tiny bald head. Then she looked up at Philippe. She had made a vow when she was struggling for the lives of her children, and now she meant to keep it. "But I've decided on their godmother."

His brows lifted in surprise. "Godmother?" His forehead smoothed. "Shall it be Mother Bernard, or Sister Thomas?"

"No." Annique inhaled deeply, gathering her strength. She could not rest easy until this matter was settled. She had to make Philippe understand. "I want to ask the Great Mademoiselle."

Philippe stiffened. "But surely, you must be joking."

"I'm serious." Though effort slowed her words, Annique explained, "When I thought I was dying, I made some promises—to God, to myself, and to you. One of those promises was that if I should live, I would try to make peace with the Great Mademoiselle."

Philippe was unconvinced. "She's not—I mean, you don't *know* some of the things she's—"

Annique interrupted, "I know more than you think." For one so weak, her voice was remarkably resolute. "From the beginning, Fate has tangled our lives with hers. We are *still* connected, in a strange sort of way. There are debts of honor on both sides." She paused, groping for the right words. "I have no illusions about the princess. True, she has used us both, but she has also risked much to help us. She is capable of great courage, great sacrifice . . . even great humility."

Philippe exhaled loudly in skepticism. "Humility! When?"

Annique met his gaze levelly. "She risked much to come here in an effort to restore my trust in you. She told me everything, sparing nothing, not even her pride."

He raised an eyebrow. "For that, I am grateful to her, but I hardly think a single gesture—"

Again, she cut him short, her eyes softened with sympathy. "Don't you see? The princess has been even more a victim than we in all of this. Last summer on that parapet, she saved six thousand lives, but sacrificed her own future. Her moment of greatest glory cost her the one thing she wanted more than any other in this life. Now she'll never marry Louis. She'll never be queen."

She stroked her daughter's pink scalp, then looked up at her husband. The lines in his face had deepened, bearing witness to the ordeal of the last two days, but the effect was more rugged and handsome than ever. And when he looked at her or the babies, love and pride glowed openly in his eyes. The two of them had faced betrayal, anger, pain, fear, suffering, and even death, but Annique would live it all over again without changing a thing if that was what it took to bring them to the joy of this moment.

She reached out and took Philippe's hand. "Somehow, we've ended up with everything we've ever wanted. But the Great Mademoiselle has nothing left but her money, and what use is that to her now? She's a virtual prisoner in a drafty old house lacking even the most basic comforts. Paris and the Court were her life's blood, and now she is banished from both, perhaps forever."

Annique sighed, suddenly weary from the exertion of talking, but she forced herself to go on. "She has no crown. No power. No army. No real friends. No influence. No place in society. No husband. No children." She was convinced there would never be any children for the Great Mademoiselle, even if the princess were allowed to marry, but that was a secret Annique would take to her grave.

She hugged the precious, squirming bundle closer to her breast and continued, "Now that old Nourrie is dead, the princess has no one who really loves her. No one." She looked from their daughter to the son sleeping in Philippe's arms. "Our children could love her. We could give her that, at least."

Philippe barely trusted himself to speak. For the first time, he saw the Great Mademoiselle as Annique described her, and with that revelation he felt his soul slipping free of the chains of anger and revenge he had worn since their wedding night. Condemning the princess for her schemes and ambitions was like condemning a hawk for hunting down and killing its prey. Annique was right. From the very beginning, the Great Mademoiselle had been a prisoner of her birth and her own ambitions. She had paid dearly for what she'd done, and would go on paying for the rest of her life.

Perhaps they could afford to share their blessings. There was love enough to spare, even for the Great Mademoiselle.

Philippe cocked his head. "Godmother to our children . . ." Under normal circumstances, such a request would be presumptuous on their part. But with the princess in disgrace, the tables were turned. He nodded. "Perhaps that would balance the scales at last. That is, assuming her highness agrees."

Annique smiled, her face a portrait of that look of complete assurance that has confounded men since the beginning of time. "She'll agree."

His eyes narrowed. Did he detect a hint of smugness behind her angelic expression? Suddenly Philippe realized just how wise his wife's request really was. He chuckled. "And if she agrees, we will have made an ally of a very dangerous enemy."

"An added benefit, to be sure." Annique's words were slow and breathy, her eyes drooping.

Philippe rose, worried that he'd overtaxed her. "Forgive me. I've worn you out with talking." He nodded to their daughter, now curled in contented slumber at her mother's breast. "She's gone to sleep, and so should you." He scooped the baby up and settled her into the crook of his free arm without even waking her. "We'll come back later, after you've had some rest."

Philippe straightened to leave, but his exit was interrupted by Suzanne, who breezed into the room after a perfunctory knock. Marie followed close behind.

Suzanne reached for the babies. "If you please, your grace. Thank you."

In the bob of a curtsy, Philippe was left empty-handed, and the two servants marched away with his children. Suzanne called over her shoulder, "Doctor's orders. We'll bring them back in a few hours, after the mistress has gotten some sleep."

As she closed the door behind her, Philippe muttered,

"This household has become entirely too democratic. Now that I'm back—"

Annique's drowsy voice overtook his own. "Now that you're back, Maison Corbay will be a real home, at last." She yawned. "Our home, yours and mine and the children's, just like I used to dream of when I was a little girl in the convent." Her eyes fluttered shut.

Philippe walked to the window and inhaled deeply, soaking in the sense of tranquillity that filled the house. Annique was right. They had all come home.

Seventeen years ago, bloodline had turned against bloodline, destroying the happy home that Maison Corbay once was. Their marriage had brought those same bloodlines together again—first in struggle, then in sacrifice, and ultimately in love—to be united, heart to heart, forever. The walls of this old house would ring with life and laughter once more—his and Annique's and their children's.

Annique's lids flew open. She lifted her head, searching the room. "Philippe? Where are you? Philippe?"

He hastened back to sit beside her, drawing her scarred hand into his own. "What's wrong, beloved?"

At the word *beloved,* her features eased. "I must have fallen asleep. When I woke up and didn't see you there, I was confused, afraid everything was just a dream, and you were still in St. Germain."

"No dream, my darling. Everything is all right. I'm here, and we have a healthy daughter and a son." He stroked her temple, his words soothing in an effort to banish the last vestiges of fear from her eyes. "Once I promised never to leave you unless you asked me to. Remember? Well, I'm amending that promise. You're stuck with me, no matter what. We're a real family now, Annique, and Maison Corbay is a real home. God willing, we'll spend the rest of our days here, together." Raising her hand to his lips, he kissed the scar that was her emblem of survival. "No shadows will ever come between us again. I swear it on my heart's blood."

Annique pulled his hand to her own lips and murmured, "And I swear it by mine." Secure at last, she closed her eyes and surrendered to her dreams.

Author's Note

With the exceptions of the fictional Corbay and Bourbon-Corbay households, the people and events of this book are taken from the pages of history.

Regarding the Great Mademoiselle, subsequent records indicate that as punishment for her part in the disastrous Fronde of the Princes, she was banished from Paris and the Court for five years. Though her own father had already cheated her out of millions, she still had sufficient wealth to enjoy a comfortable existence. Her days in exile were taken up with riding, lawn sports, entertaining friends, restoring the house and grounds of her estate, and a few charitable projects. During that time, her most notable (and unusual, for that era) act of generosity was the founding and support of a home for orphaned children.

Although Louis XIV allowed the princess to return to Court in 1658, he never forgot the terror and deprivation he had suffered as a result of the Fronde. Nor, apparently, did he forget—or forgive—the Great Mademoiselle's part in that rebellion. Years later, she fell madly in love with the brilliant Duke de Lauzun, a much younger man of greatly inferior status. Since all noble marriages required the king's approval, she petitioned Louis for permission to marry Lauzun. When the king agreed, the Great Mademoiselle set about elevating her lover to sufficient status to become her husband. Only after she had transferred enormous wealth and titles to Lauzun did King Louis XIV revoke his permission and have Lauzun thrown into prison.

Louis XIV then exacted an elegantly cruel and financially practical revenge against the princess. Lauzun would be freed only if he remitted to the crown all the titles and wealth the Great Mademoiselle had given him.

Trapped between her heart and her head, the princess struggled in vain to find some other way to win her lover's release. Finally, after ten long years of imprisonment, Lauzun agreed to the king's terms. His health destroyed, he returned to the Great Mademoiselle a bitter and broken man.

Though some sources indicate that Lauzun and the Great Mademoiselle subsequently married, I was unable to find any documentation of such a union.

The Great Mademoiselle never had any children. Her barrenness was pure conjecture on my part, based on records of a mild case of pox she suffered at nineteen that could have internalized and rendered her sterile.

Although Sister Jonah is based on a historical person, there is no evidence she ever left the convent near Paris that was both her sanctuary and her prison. Since I could not discover her religious name, I called her Sister Jonah after the unwilling servant of God from the Old Testament.

KAT MARTIN

Award-winning author of *Creole Fires*

GYPSY LORD
_____ 92878-5 $5.99 U.S./$6.99 Can.

SWEET VENGEANCE
_____ 95095-0 $4.99 U.S./$5.99 Can.

BOLD ANGEL
_____ 95303-8 $5.99 U.S./$6.99 Can.

DEVIL'S PRIZE
_____ 95478-6 $5.99 U.S./$6.99 Can.

MIDNIGHT RIDER
_____ 95774-2 $5.99 U.S./$6.99 Can.

ANITA MILLS
ARNETTE LAMB
ROSANNE BITTNER

*Join three of your favorite storytellers
on a tender journey of the heart...*

Cherished Moments is an extraordinary collection of
breathtaking novellas woven around the theme of mother-
hood. Before you turn the last page you will have been swept
from the storm-tossed coast of a Scottish isle to the fury of
the American frontier, and you will have lived the lives and
loves of three indomitable women, as they experience their
most passionate moments.

THE NATIONAL BESTSELLER

CHERISHED MOMENTS
Anita Mills, Arnette Lamb, Rosanne Bittner
_____ 95473-5 $4.99 U.S./$5.99 Can.